CW00447376

For
Patrick James "Paddy" Griffin
1977-2016
RIP

CONTENTS

A NOTE ON THE TEXT

Juggernaut is a direct sequel to Robert Louis Stevenson's
[The] Strange Case of Dr Jekyll and Mr Hyde.
Please read them in the order that makes
most sense to you.

ACKNOWLEDGMENTS

Thanks to Kit Foster, Nathan Boon, and Stefan Georgiou
for some visual ideas along the way.
Thanks also to Lisa Fox for support and comments on the
first draft.
Thanks, always, to George Green and to Lee Horsley.
And thanks - and apologies - to RLS, without whom…

The cover's by Kit Foster of Kit Foster Design.

JUGGERNAUT:
THURSDAY 16TH FEBRUARY 1911

'Doctor Latimer.' The words were neither greeting, invitation, nor enquiry. 'You are expected.'

The butler - Hotchkiss, if Latimer remembered right - stepped back, turned, and opened the front door fully in one well-practiced move. 'If you would step inside.'

Tobias Latimer - "Toby" to those few in London with whom he was on familiar terms - was grateful to be out of the street. The walk across February London had begun as invigorating, but had soon turned to uncomfortable, and then to exasperating. The weather was neither one thing nor the other, but seemingly all things at once. Enough wind and drizzle to flick rain into his face and wet his hair where his hat did not offer protection, yet warm enough for the time of year to make the wearing of his best winter coat an awkwardness.

Latimer would have dispensed with the coat and hazarded the elements with an umbrella instead if he had not elected to bring his Gladstone. Toting both bag and umbrella was more inconvenient than walking with bag and heavy coat.

Latimer had learned in a previous life the value of having a hand free wherever possible. The cost of such

1

utility today was clamminess; he felt steamed like a pudding in his outerwear. Perhaps he should have hailed a cab after all.

Walking, though, was how Latimer thought best, and he had much to puzzle over. The time expended in the journey from his consultation rooms had not, however, been productive in offering resolutions to the quandaries battling for his attention.

Latimer removed his hat and coat – he did not wear gloves – and let the man take them. He did not present his case for safe keeping.

'If you would wait in the drawing room,' the butler said, indicating with a nod to a doorway on the right of the hallway. 'You will be joined momentarily.'

'Thank you, Hotchkiss,' Latimer murmured. The butler nodded once more and disappeared down the hall. Latimer entered the drawing room, a room he had once expected never to have seen again.

#

Nothing had changed since Latimer's previous and only visit some six months earlier.

The room was twenty feet long and fifteen wide, with a handsome window offering a view out to the street. This being one of an imposing run of four-storied terraced town houses - five if you considered the basement - there were no other windows. A set of double doors led deeper into the building, and presumably through to a dining room.

The fireplace was a monstrosity of dark mahogany and marble. An insipid fire flickered. Latimer shivered. Already the steam inside his shirt had condensed to cold water down his spine.

Much of the wall space was given over to book cases housing heavy volumes. Legal publications, bound periodicals. There was a larger number of medical texts than might be considered ordinary. There were neither family photographs or portraits, though a run of plain

2

frames held yellowed diplomas. A single armchair was positioned at an angle to the fireplace. The leather was cracked in places. The right armrest was ringed and stained. The seat was sunken; dipping in the centre where it had moulded over time to the favoured position of its habitual user.

A desk stood in the lee of the window to make the best of the available light. There was no chair behind the desk. A pair of dining chairs had been brought in and placed on the opposite side of the desk to the window.

There was a scuttle full of good coal, and a basket of logs. Latimer placed one of the logs on the fire, dislodging the embers so that the glowing undersides would catch the wood all the sooner. He was soon rewarded with an upward drool of smoke.

A clock ticked somewhere. Both loud and distant. The house was otherwise silent. And then Latimer heard a squealing, the sound that reluctant metal makes. The noise edged nearer. Latimer pulled on his cuffs, smoothed his still-damp fringe back out of his eyes.

Two questions were central. What was the meaning of the telegram summons? What did Gabriel Utterson, his most reluctant patient, want?

#

The telegram Latimer had received that morning had been direct, even by the standards of such a blunt method of communication.

Attend Utterson 4pm today. Be discreet.

There was no indication who the message was from. Latimer fancied that it was not Utterson's work, but he could not see how it could be a prank. A telegram was not a cheap way to make mischief, and none of his associates, nor, he fancied, Utterson's, were men to make such sport.

Latimer arranged with Maureen Doyle, who he had inherited along with the practice he'd taken over less than seven months earlier, and who doubled for him as clerk and as nurse, that Doyle should cover the office but not

3

accept any more patients that afternoon. In case of urgency, Doctor Latimer would be available after seven pm and from nine o'clock tomorrow morning. He also left the contact details for Montgomery, who was always complaining about not having enough doctoring work and would be glad of an extra 'emergency' customer or two, should the enquiry need prompt attention.

Latimer's practice had ground floor rooms at the corner of Harley Street and Mansfield Mews. He had latterly been living in Durban, South Africa and had come by his medical qualifications there after military service with His Majesty's forces. He had returned to England the previous summer and had arranged, by correspondence in advance, to take over a bijou but well-heeled business from a retiring quack. He had paid a little over the odds for the premises and the goodwill, but as he could afford both the money and the effort in making the transition back to English life as trouble-free as practicable.

So far, it could not have worked out better. Latimer's intent was maximum comfort with minimum effort, and to those ends he was so far pleased. South Africa had been hard. Latimer wanted to enjoy the early retirement he felt that he was due.

Latimer's clients tended to the upper middle classes; the occasionally impatient, but the unfailingly polite and the always well-paying. Much of the work was social rather than strictly medical: advice on diet or alcohol intake, for example, or on being attentive to those who simply needed someone to listen. Though the week seldom brought anything that would be professionally challenging to any doctor, Latimer thought he balanced that sufficiently by his other work.

He operated a pro bono clinic on Saturday mornings in church premises off Brick Lane in the Whitechapel area of the East End of London. For three hours each weekend Latimer, with Doyle, who was already a willing volunteer and who had made the suggestion to Latimer that perhaps he should volunteer also, did what could be done by way of diagnosis and treatment for the poor of the area. Medicines and other supplies came out of Latimer's pocket, though he was prudent enough to adjust his pricing for his weekday clientele so that the impact on him was one of time only.

When asked by Doyle to volunteer he said that it was the least that he could do. She thanked him. And then she showed in his next patient, Lady Bruntnell, who was rich and lonely and who liked to spend a private hour with a handsome doctor.

Thus began an arrangement of sorts. Latimer now had four such clients; married women with distracted husbands. These arrangements were mutually satisfactory. Each party got, as far as Latimer ascertained, what they wanted from them. There was no mistaking intent on either side, though of late Lady Bruntnell had been somewhat more desperate in her ardour.

Doyle, if she had objections to these appointments, said nothing. She maintained a knowing air about her, though never to the extent where such insight overbalanced into stray remark. She was a model of propriety, discretion and efficiency.

Latimer did not know how he would have got on without her.

#

Latimer had time after receiving the telegram to locate Utterson's paperwork. The file was slim and did not tell him much by itself.

Gabriel Utterson was seventy-five years old. A largely-retired partner in a legal practice, Utterson maintained a handful of clients whom he had dealt with for decades and who were unwilling to trust their affairs to the younger members of his partnership. The clients were, Latimer had ascertained by discreet enquiry shortly after first meeting Utterson, prominent men and business figures of his own generation, though most had withdrawn from public life except when attendance at charitable functions, the House of Lords and suchlike necessitated.

Utterson was not in good health. He had telegrammed Latimer's surgery only days after Latimer had sent a round-robin letter introducing himself as the new physician at the practice. Utterson requested Latimer's attendance in a work capacity at his home the following day.

Latimer asked Doyle if this was usual for the man. No, Doyle had said. To her certain memory Utterson had never troubled the practice in the time she had been in place.

Utterson had appeared pained in a twofold sense, both in physical discomfort apparent when he moved, and – more obviously – a sense of embarrassment, a despondency at having to seek out professional medical opinion.

Men, Latimer had come to understand, and not just men who had been long accustomed to being successful, dominant, or charismatic in their work or domestic arrangements were often reticent to the point of dangerous stupidity when it came to personal health.

Latimer had seen strong men invert themselves, weeping in shame at their body and its deficiencies. He had managed outbursts of defiance, as though angry denial would repel the advance of untreated illness. Utterson had been one such, Latimer reckoned, though he bore more strength of will than many he had encountered. This, Latimer had told Utterson as blandly as he could, would prove to be Utterson's undoing.

On the day in question, Latimer had taken brief details and had made an appointment to call on Utterson. He had been received in the same drawing room he now stood in. Latimer took a fuller case history, asking the usual questions about childhood sicknesses, breaks of bones, adverse reactions to foodstuffs. He alluded to matters of personal endeavour and of recreation. It was not unknown at this point for the new patient to unburden himself, relieved that some secret barrier had been overcome, and now free to refer to some moment of weakness, would reveal that there had been consequences of that indulgence.

Utterson answered the questions with studied patience and exactitude, as though giving evidence against a charge of which he knew he was innocent. There was neither humour nor defeat in him. Stoicism and a certain frostiness was his demeanour throughout.

'Forgive me,' Latimer had said when his notes had been taken. 'But you have given no indication of how I might be of assistance.'

'You should forgive me, I suppose,' Utterson said. 'It is more than twenty years since I either called upon the expertise of a physician or have permitted one across my threshold. That is now, I believe, too long a period. I am sick, Dr Latimer. I am sick and have been for some time. I am, though, neither an uneducated nor an unrealistic man. I ask two things of you. Two things only. You may bill me as you see fit for the services I ask.'

'And those two things are?'

'A confirmation or a rebuttal of my interim diagnosis. If you refute my interpretation of the evidence, then I will listen to you. If you concur, then I ask that you accede to my requests about treatment.'

The butler appeared. He placed two glasses filled with a rich-scented wine on the desk.

'That is kind, Hotchkiss. Thank you.'

'Sir.' A shifting shadow that might have been a man bowing.

Utterson picked up his glass. He sipped. Latimer raised his own. 'Your health, in anticipation.' A dense perfume. The wine was layered with dark fruits, then the alcohol, then a buttery-sweet aftertaste.

Utterson nodded, and swallowed his drink. The swift imbibement invigorated the elderly man. He stood, this time having none of the careful shifting evident the day before. Utterson strode past Latimer to a single armchair by the fireplace. He took his suit jacket off and laid it over the back of the chair.

Latimer brought his glass with him, placing it on the lintel of the fireplace. 'Mister Utterson,' he began, 'what is your diagnosis?'

'I have a cancer of the stomach. It hurts when I eat. It hurts when I drink. It hurts when I pass water. Though it does not hurt me now, I can feel it in me. I know it is there. My appetite is lacking, yet I feel full as though I have gorged. My suits are baggy where they were once close-fitting. I suspect my butler of having my clothes taken in without my instruction to spare me the worst of it. My dreams are of being consumed from within.'

'Go on.'

'More than that, I fear the prospect of pain. The fear of what might come for others is so much worse than the present discomfort for me. I need to live. As long as I may.'

Latimer did not understand Utterson's meaning, though it was not altogether unknown for patients to tend to the dramatic, particularly when concerns for wife and children were invoked. Remain in the present, he told himself. Work the evidence that the symptoms provide.

He would have asked Utterson to strip to the waist, except the lawyer anticipated this instruction.

Latimer opened his bag and withdrew his stethoscope. He checked heart rate and pulse. He pressed Utterson at various points. He pinched the man's skin, felt its greasy paper texture, noted its sallow slackness.

'Doctor?'

'You understand that this is opinion rather than diagnosis. That I would prefer further tests to be done.' There was no point in being anything other than direct.

'Obviously.'

Latimer opened his mouth to disguise the deep intake

of breath he found helpful in delivering bad news. 'I concur with your observations. My recommendation would be -.' The words were cut off.

'Thank you, doctor. This is not news, but confirmation. How long do I have?'

'With a formal diagnosis, an exploratory operatio-'

'There will be no incisions, doctor. I have had my fill of medical men already. Work on the sure determination that I intend to manage my time as best I might without intervention.'

Latimer put his equipment back in his bag. 'You may get dressed,' he said. While Utterson buttoned his shirt, Latimer drank the rest of his wine. Redcurrants and blackberries capered on his tongue.

'So?'

The man's direction was a wonder. 'You have a year at most, nine months at worst. This is a best interpretation you understand. Not a solid timescale.'

'Yes.'

So he wanted the bad news.

'At best, nine months of being functional. Six at worst. You will deteriorate. Your last three months will be difficult. There will be pain. You will not eat. The stairs will become an impossibility. Bodily control will problematic. Sleep disruption is not uncommon, through either the illness or your own concern. Above all, there will be fatigue. You will be tired, but never rest. A state of permanent exhaustion.'

Something approaching relaxation came over Utterson. This was a man used to being right and being proved right, yet there had been concern that he had misjudged the evidence. That he had had rightly anticipated his cancer was, for the moment, more important to him than the consequences that Latimer had sketched. 'Thank you, Doctor.'

'Tobias, please.'

The previous steel returned. 'I would prefer our

9

relationship be kept on a more formal footing, Doctor Latimer.'

'Of course.'

Utterson gave him instructions as to how he would prefer his symptoms managed. He had done his research. Latimer concurred, and promised to provide the requested medications together with instructions for dosage.

#

That had been six months ago. Monthly, Latimer had despatched Utterson the latest batch of the pain-relief medicine along with a similarly-worded note each time to contact him without delay if there was significant worsening in his condition or the presentation of new symptoms. Until today's telegram there had been no response.

The fire in the grate had perked up. Warmth was now penetrating. Latimer glanced in the mirror over the fireplace as he smoothed his drying hair back into style, its shade returning from a dank rat brown to its normal sun-bleached grass tone.

The African tan was faded, though still there. The creases by his eyes betrayed differences in skin coloration. The crows-feet, though an indication that his thirties were almost over, at least served to lessen the nick by his left eye that was his only physical reminder of his military service.

A squeal. And another.

Latimer found himself not breathing. The anticipation seized his lungs at their least inflated.
The squealing grew, reverberating off the walls of the hallway beyond. At last it ceased. Then it began again, a lower pitch this time. Something had changed.

Gabriel Utterson wheeled himself into the drawing room. The chair, noisy at it was, held Latimer's attention for a moment. A new-looking model, as expensive and as well-upholstered as such an item might usefully be.

Utterson was trying not to wince as he pushed the

larger wheels, propelling himself into the drawing room. The squealing was then limited by the rubberised wheels switching surface from the parquet of the floor to the carpeting of the new environs.

Utterson was evidently still a proud man. He had not wanted to have been trundled in like an invalid, insisting at the last to make the entrance under his own motive force.

'Doctor Latimer.'

'Utterson.'

'Please, seat yourself.'

Latimer waited until Utterson had guided the contraption past him and into the space on the far side of the desk. Latimer should have guessed that this was why there was no chair there. The light from the window served to throw Utterson's features into dusk. In the past, it might have been useful in business dealings not to be seen to give too much away. Now, the shade occluded the extent he had been ravaged by the past six months' illness.

The patient breathed quick and fast, drawing only a little air from each intake, trying to accommodate that lack of depth with frequency. Latimer let Utterson compose himself. He resembled nothing so much as an elderly mouse, frail and white, its heart counting down ever-faster towards its demise.

When he was ready, Utterson consulted a pocket-watch from his waistcoat. The movement let some of his face back into light.

Utterson was little more now than an animated skeleton, a bone marionette draped in linen-coloured skin. His clothes were immaculate, but were now several sizes too big. Something had been done about his neck, where the tie served to restrict the amount of gap between collar and flesh, but the contraction the man had suffered over the half year since Latimer had seen him last was all too evident. He was covered rather than clothed. A child playing a dressing-up game.

And then Latimer coughed. The spasm caught him

unawares – he still had the watch in his hand and had not been able to reach for a kerchief – riddling him like a poker through cinders. The cough was arid. Then Utterson coughed again.

Latimer was up to his feet in a second, proffering his own lean handkerchief. Utterson snatched it, the fingers little more than brittle twigs. A closed-lipped grunt that might have been thanks. Utterson swabbed at his mouth, and then coughed again. Eventually, he took the kerchief out of Latimer's line of sight. A fumbling, the return of the pocket-watch to its compartment.

'Late,' Utterson muttered. 'Late.'

'Another is expected?'

Utterson gestured towards the empty chair. 'And the reason for you having been called here. Not my idea. Not my idea at all. I've had my fill of medical men, begging your pardon Latimer, and I've no wish to tarry with your likes any more than necessary.'

The debilitating spread of the cancer had not yet extinguished the old man's temperament.

'The medications provided have been satisfactory and have proved expedient when taken in line with your guidance. The cancer has proceeded very much along the track you were clear in outlining on our last meeting. Your initial diagnosis has been nothing less than accurate.

'I do not doubt that you will be calling on me once more, in a month's time I estimate, to confirm death and to make what notes you might for the purposes of its certification.'

'Then why, might I ask, am I here, if I am not needed?'

'I am still, though you might not credit it from my condition, still working on behalf of clients. I must do my best by them while I may. Naturally I am in the process of passing on what remains of such affairs onto others but there still are elements of these professional relationships that must yet be conducted by myself.

'That said,' Utterson grunted. 'He is late.'

'To whom do you refer?'

'One Jasper Holcombe, of Beech, Everdene and Holcombe.'

'I do not know the name, or the firm.'

'They are solicitors, Doctor Latimer. Both like me and my generation and unlike me and mine in almost every possible respect. Men of the twentieth century, if you will. Heads full of science and technology. Offices replete with machinery and gadgetry. Telephones and typewriters, not clerks and quill. They are the coming mechanised future, Doctor, them and their like and with them some of the instinct of the law will crumble into dust.'

So there it was, or some of it at least. Utterson saw himself as one of the last guardians of a guttering candle-light, an unprotected flame. Something warm and real and lit and guided by hand. Not something dispassionate and electric, its unfeeling light protected under glass.

'And yet he runs late.' Utterson smiled; a mirthless rictus. His lips were dry to the point of cracking.

The point being made, Utterson shuffled back in the wheelchair. His hands gripped the armrests for support throughout.

'And my part in this appointment?'

'There you have me, Doctor. It is at Mister Holcombe's request that you are in attendance. You were asked for by name. I can only surmise that some patient of yours has made a bequest either to you personally or to an organisation, doubtless charitable, to be nominated by you. My attendance may simply be ceremonial, as a witness to the undertaking. I have been party to stranger things before. A man's will is a peculiar document, Doctor, and some take the opportunity to reach out from beyond the grave, as it were, and set all manner of matters aright. Though what this has to do with me and not with whomever you usually factor your dealings through is beyond my ken.'

'I can think of no-one who might be in such a position. No-one who has recently expired and may wish to make any such provision in their will.' Latimer gave it thought even so. No, there was no-one. None of his clients had died since he had taken over the practice.

One other possibility then occurred to Latimer. 'Of course, there may be a bequest for you, and I am the one called to bear witness. If this is indeed some matter concerning a gentleman's estate and the organisation of his terminal affairs.'

Utterson gave what might once have been a harrumph, rendered now as a rattling creaking series of gasps. 'Possibilities all,' he eventually acceded. He dabbed again at his mouth with Latimer's handkerchief. The darker spots on the white linen were unmistakeable.

The doorbell then rang; breaking the stare Latimer had found that he'd had locked onto in wonder at the full advancement of the cancer inside Utterson. The usual sounds of bland greeting in the hallway, the offering of cloak and hat, the ushering in. Latimer stood in welcome as the newcomer was introduced into the room.

'Mister Jasper Holcombe.' Hodgekiss glanced to his employer, took some gestured signal, and then withdrew with a curt nod.

'Jasper Holcombe. Doctor Latimer, I take it?'

'Holcombe, yes. Latimer.'

Holcombe was well over six feet tall, young – certainly no more than thirty – though already balding with tufty outcrops behind the ears. He was clean-shaven, well-attired in a dark three-piece suit of good cut and quality. He held a slim attaché case in his left hand, again indicating both newness and expense. A flash of gold on his proffered right wrist. The expanding band for a wristwatch, doubtless. Holcombe bore the trace of an accent. Canadian rather than American, Latimer fancied, but buried deep in his past as though he had been settled in Great Britain since at least the beginning of his university days.

'Mister Utterson.'

'Holcombe.' Utterson did not stand, though he lifted his hand from the armrest for the new arrival to shake. If Holcombe was in any was perturbed by the way that Utterson presented himself then he did not show it. 'Please be seated, so that we may continue without further delay.'

'Ah, yes, my apologies.' As Holcombe spoke he opened his case, balancing it on one knee. He withdrew a manila folder secured with brads. 'Some traffic disruption I'm afraid. A horse had taken fright and had caused something of a collision en route.'

Latimer offered a hand to shake once Holcombe had settled. The shake was strong. An exchange of business cards. Latimer slipped Holcombe's card away without inspection.

Hodgekiss had already entered the room bearing, as he had on Latimer's first visit to the Utterson household, a tray with sherry glasses filled to the two-thirds mark. He placed them on coasters that he must have brought with him and then vanished himself just as efficiently as he had arrived.

'Most welcome, yes,' Holcombe said, though he did not touch the glass positioned closest to him.

Utterson picked up his and Latimer followed the cue. The wine was the same rich sherry he had tasted on that previous encounter.

'And so to business, if I may,' Holcombe said. 'And this is a day that we at our practice have been anticipating for some years. This,' he said, patting the folder resting on his knee, 'has been quite the subject of much speculation throughout the years.'

Holcombe gave something of a potted history of his company's history. The firm of Beech, Everdene and Holcombe was a relatively recent innovation, being the merger of Beech and some five years earlier. Before that, Everdene & Holcombe had been separate organisations.

The point seemed to be that there had been several changes of ownership and of management over the last fifteen to twenty years and that young Holcombe sat here had a full view of only the last decade's worth.

'As you might credit, it is well within the purview of any longstanding legal firm's responsibilities to continue to exercise its clients' needs and to service their requests as long as may be required. Insofar as the requisite fees are continued to be paid of course.' Holcombe laughed self-consciously here as though aware that his attempt at a legalistic jest might well fall somewhat dejected in the present company.

'The thing is this,' Holcombe continued. 'This letter has been in the safekeeping of several companies for the last twenty or more years. And it is only now, it seems, that the moment is-' he paused, looking across first at Latimer, and then back to Utterson, '-upon us.' He hurriedly opened the folder, barely pausing before continuing to speak. 'These are, of course, my client's express wishes as the following note indicates.'

'Go on,' Utterson said.

Holcombe read from a loose sheet at the top of the pile of papers in the folder. 'This packet is to be opened in the presence of Gabriel John Utterson and also in the presence of his general practitioner or another suitably qualified and experienced medical doctor at that point in the future when it is apparent that Gabriel Utterson's life is drawing to its natural end.'

'That's the most preposterous and tasteless thing I've ever heard of,' Latimer murmured. 'Utterson, what do you make of it?'

Utterson had hunched himself forwards in his chair once more, craning across the desk to see something of the paper. Holcombe passed the sheet across for him to read for himself.

'Typewritten,' Utterson grunted, letting the note fall to the desk.

'As per my client's instruction, sealed within the body of the papers.'

'And how, precisely, were you to ascertain my condition?'

'By no dint of my doing, I assure you,' Latimer interjected.

'I do not doubt that for a second, Doctor. Well, Mister Holcombe?'

Holcombe took a mouthful of the drink sat in front of him. 'My client's instructions were specific and detailed. There were other provisos made for the instance of your sudden death, or of your imprisonment, for example.' Despite their refreshment taken, his voice nevertheless came across as harsh and strained.

'In this case, the client had left ample monies for a range of eventualities to be proceeded upon. You will understand that what I am about to tell you in no way reflects upon the partnership in any way, shape or form. That we are merely the blind arbiters of our instructions, nothing more.'

'I have some experience of the law myself.'

'Your household has been under discreet, occasional and yet thorough surveillance for the last two decades. A watch has been maintained, through various means which I am not at liberty to divulge. This has been purely to remain assured that you were in good health or otherwise and that you had not had any misfortune befallen you. In a way,' Holcombe said, with what sounded to Latimer as much positivity as might be mustered under the circumstances, 'you have been protected.'

'Is that so?'

'Indeed, Doctor Latimer. Our client was of the most ardent wish that this meeting was the eventual outcome. This is, if you will, his preferred option. Today's meeting, I mean.'

'And who is this mysterious client of yours?' Latimer could not hold himself back from enquiring any more.

'Let him speak, Latimer,' Utterson interrupted. His voice indicated tiredness, but not the exhaustion of movement and fatigue. This was more of a resignation, a fated form of relaxation into the arms of the inevitable.

Latimer was struck by a new certainty. Utterson knew the identity of the client.

'Thank you, Mister Utterson. I can only imagine the extent that this is difficult and awkward for you. And you, of course, Doctor Latimer.'

'You are here as you have been the only medical practitioner to have been admitted to the Utterson residence these last few years. Regretfully I must confirm that on that occasion you were followed back to your rooms and afterwards, your identity confirmed and your bona fides checked. We had no doubt that you were the nearest to a medical confidant in Mister Utterson's social circle.'

'You had me followed?'

'And your bona fides checked. I can only apologise. No harm was intended and, I assure you, no slight on your character has been detected. To the contrary, in fact. Your charitable work in the East End is most laudable.'

The notion that his background had been subject to scrutiny did not sit well with Latimer. He breathed through his mouth so that he did not reveal his upset in speaking out of turn.

'To the matter in hand?' Utterson, though still sounding tired, was impatient once more, much in the same manner as he had been during the diagnosis appointment. Once a determination had been made, no matter how injurious the eventuality, he would want to see it through without impediment.

Holcombe broke a wax seal on the sheaf of papers within, and then slid a thin blade through the ribbon binding them together. The cord, a slim velvet strip, would have fallen to the floor had not the lawyer not curled the blade around as the ribbon dropped, catching and winding it up along the blade in one well-practised move.

He cupped the blade as he folded it back in on itself, at the same time letting the coiled ribbon slide off into his palm. He pocketed both. Latimer imagined a collection of velvet ringlets left on a bureau at the end of the working week.

'The first paragraphs are purely preamble. This being the last will and testament and so on and so forth, I the undersigned do hereby...'

'Yes, yes.'

'There is no signature at this point, nor any direct reference to the name. Our instructions are to read the document as given.'

'Then pray do so.'

Holcombe adjusted himself once more, as though ready to recite from the Bible to a new congregation.

#

"'Utterson,'" Holcombe read, "'I greet you from beyond the grave. I may be long dead; I may be recently departed. I believe, though, that I will be remembered to you always.

"'You will forgive the sketchy nature of these quick-written words, but time is not my ally. However, I am fortunate that finances are in my favour and that I have left sufficient funds in trust to see my will be borne out to its fullest extent.

"'It is my dearest wish, Utterson, that you know these things before you die. I am hopeful, by way of extension, that you have had many long years of fearful pondering about the events of a certain year. That your sleep has been troubled. That you wake before sunrise, but dare not open your eyes for what might be leering at you from the darkness.

"'I am your shade, Utterson. The shadow you cast betrays my profile, not yours. But the shadow lengthens. It stretches longer as you move from your own evening to sunset. The shadow straddles the centuries, and long into whatever future follows the end of Widow Victoria's reign.

"'We have battled, Jekyll and I, for so long. But he was always weak. At first, that weakness betrayed itself in his curiosity winning out over his intellect. That he meddled where he ought not to have done. And in doing so with compounds and re-agents he found me.

"'I was seductive. Not quite charming, but assuredly irresistible. And once Jekyll had taken his draughts and so had tasted of the me in him, he was caught. Was not Odysseus wise enough to have himself lashed to the mast of his ship so that he might hear the sirens' call and yet live? Jekyll's precautions were not so sure.

"'For some, Utterson, their addiction is in whisky or opium, and may be delivered to them by the glass or the pipe. For others, in the losing of themselves in the flesh of forbidden others. For a few, in the stimulant of power, of war, of violence against others or against themselves. Jekyll's weakness was always, in a way, for himself.

"'He unlocked me with his potions. At first, as with the woman-beating drunkard or the blood-lusting prison guard, that freedom was a temporary release, and soon bottled back up again, with self-pitying tears or denial as befitted the individual. Henry Jekyll is of the remorseful kind, at least in private. I know, because I was there. Sometimes quiet, but always listening. Once a long-sealed door has been opened, it never closes right again.

"'Some of the rest you can surely guess by now. Whereas the momentary madness of the intoxicated or the infuriated reveals itself in rage and red-puffed cheeks, soon abated, the effect of his elixir was always more pronounced.

"'The greater the torment, the greater the intoxication. And the wilder the violence. There have been some wild old times Utterson, for I have indulged myself on a hundred more occasions and in a thousand-fold more ways than you might understand. Jekyll is drunk on himself to the extent that the self he dares not show in public – a self I daresay many of you harbour within – was made

20

manifest in me.

"'We are one, Henry and I. Name your cliché: sides of the same coin, peas in pod. "Hyde" he named me, as clear a sign as one might wish that he was appalled with himself. And at first I was content to lie within, to relish the opportunities presented to me when the elixir unlocked the gate to Jekyll's dark heart.

"'At first.

'I cannot say with any certainty when the first true loss of control occurred. Not in the loss of control engendered by the tonic began, for in the freedoms the medicine wrought there was licence from the very beginning. The restraint built into the elixir, though; that was something else. Henry Jekyll has wrestled much with this, considering this option and that, wrestling as much at times with his inability to recreate his initial successes as with his developing and consuming addictions.

"'That moment of fracture though – when his body took over from the chemicals - that was such a thing! You will never, not even your vilest imaginings, have encountered such a release as I felt that day. No longer was I an aspect of him, but I was whole in myself. Rather than an occasional visitor, I was an equal tenant in the same premises. To use a factory comparison, if I might, he worked the day shift, and I the night.

"'But Jekyll approached the condition as though it were an intellectual problem. In this he was wrong. He made the assumption that I was only an inchoate being, a furious ball of desire, and though I am certainly that, I am so much more besides.

"'I have been busy while Jekyll is absent. This industry had been in no small part because I can feel that the candle is burning bright and low. This prototype cannot last before some vital part fails. The crash is coming, as inevitable as the night-time train approaching the weakened Tay Bridge in that December storm back in '79.

"'I have been awake. So awake.

"'I have had Henry's papers copied and I have pored over them. I have checked and rechecked his calculations and his presumptions, his dosages and his compounds. I have quizzed his suppliers and I have tested, tested, tested.

"'This vessel will not last. Two spirits wrestle within – one desperate and secretive, one vital and engorged. We will together burst the flask of his mortal body.

"'And so, Utterson, I have made certain arrangements. Plans have been put in place. Plans that will take years to come to bear full fruit.

"'The details are mine, and for the moment, mine alone. But I want you to know, Utterson, while you rest fresh in your coffin, that something of the spirit of Edward Hyde endures. That he remains, that he stalks the streets of London.

"'My children will be born, Utterson. Or rather, I should say, my and Henry Jekyll's children.

"'That is my legacy to you, Gabriel Utterson. My gift from beyond the grave. The knowledge that what Henry Jekyll started I will complete, and that this new beginning may yet be all around even now you though you do not ken it.

"'Check your newspapers. Listen to your servants' chatter. Stay awake at night. Hear the distant cut-off cries. Smell the blood in the runnels.

"'New children for a new century.

"'A scarlet baptism.

"'Die, Utterson. Die knowing this. The red levels will rise.

"'Die.'"

#

Holcombe put the sheaf of papers, secured with a brad and leafed over onto the final sheet, onto the desk, turning it as he did so that Utterson might verify the autograph.

The last page was signed "Edward Hyde". The signature was large and flamboyant, with gobbets of port-red ink dripping from each sweeping curl and point. A final underscore served as both slash and stab, the paper being ripped through and stained on each side of the tear.

Utterson reached for the papers, but as he leaned into the light, he gasped. His outstretched left hand curled, and he brought his right arm up to the shoulder. He grunted.

'Utterson?'

The man was not listening. 'This cannot be,' Utterson said, teeth grinding as he spoke. 'This cannot be.' Spittle flew with the repeated phrase.

'Are you unwell?'

Utterson waved away the enquiry. He snatched the papers from the desk. 'No,' he wheezed, grimacing. 'No!'

Latimer got up. 'Utterson, you're not well.' He got up and moved around the bureau between them. 'Breathe deep. Slow down. Your heart is racing.'

There was spittle at the corners of Utterson's mouth. He tore the pages of the statement from each other, frantic as though some fresh information was to be found within. 'Dead! He was dead! This cannot be!'

Holcombe was also on his feet now. He stood wavering, as though uncertain what to do.

'Get help,' Latimer said. 'Summon the butler. A carriage, a hansom. Utterson needs a hospital.'

Utterson's fingers were wrapped round the sheaf of papers. He began to gouge, a frantic ripping, shearing the words as though their destruction would obliterate them from existence. 'Dead!' There was force behind the word, but little sound. Then a wild intake of breath as though he had taken a fist to his stomach. Shredded paper flew around him.

Latimer pulled hard on Utterson's chair from behind, but the brakes had been applied, locking the wheels in place. The chair rocked on its back wheels. Latimer tugged again, but this time lifting as he did, so he could turn the chair and its occupant around, pivoting the chair on one still-grounded wheel.

The chair reconnected with the floor with a soft thump. Utterson was lost, grimacing and snarling, eyes wild. Drool bubbled over his lips. His teeth were clamped tight. Still he snarled on. 'Dead! Dead!'

Latimer knew what was happening but he knew also that he was all but powerless to stop it. The slavering, the rictus, the pain in the arm. Utterson's heart was giving out on him. He had at best moments left unless something could be done. Latimer had to reduce the strain on this man's heart. He had to do this now.

'You are Gabriel Utterson and you will listen,' Latimer urged, crouching in front of the quivering man.

Nothing. Utterson's eyes were blanks. He was lost to whatever torment the reading of the will had conjured.

'You have to come back.' Latimer slapped Utterson. A harsh backhanded blow, right to left across his face. Utterson whimpered, but he was repeating the same mantra.

A scuffle somewhere near the doorway. 'Sir!' The butler, being held back by Holcombe. At least the young solicitor was doing something useful.

Then Utterson shifted. He rose in his chair. His breathing halted itself. Latimer stepped back to give him some space. Perhaps – just – this was control and calm being reasserted. If only the panic in his brain could be calmed, then there was a chance that the strain on his heart could be eased.

Torn paper fell away from Utterson. He was unsteady on his feet, putting one still-balled fist onto the desk for support. He breathed deep. Two, three breaths. The commotion in the doorway ceased.

'Sir?' The enquiry came from the butler.

A smile. The eyes, though, were as unseeing as any museum marble bust's. 'Hodgekiss. You will forgive the disruption and the mess.'

'Sir-'

'I've taken care of you. Made provision, I mean. You

were always good to me.'

'Sir?'

The hand on the corner of the desktop fell away. At first Utterson thought that Utterson would collapse back into his chair, but the hand travelled only as far as the handle of the topmost of the drawers built into this side of the desk.

'You will forgive me, gentlemen.'

Holcombe uttered an appropriate sentiment – afterwards, Latimer could never remember the exact words used – and Latimer was about to do likewise, before ushering Utterson to first his chair and then, as speedily as he might, into whatever transport the butler had been able to organise, so that Utterson might be taken to St Bartholomew's for treatment and observation. And then he saw what was inside the unlocked drawer.

A revolver. A Mark 1 Webley. Utterson picked up the handgun and put the barrel into his mouth, angling it upwards.

The sound of the shot in the room was nigh deafening. A report, then the noise of glass shattering. Utterson fell back into his chair. The chair toppled over backwards. Latimer found that he'd raised his arms in a defensive manoeuvre between the gun being picked up and the shot being fired.

Oily smoke clung in the wet air. The air was wet because droplets of Utterson's blood and gobbets of brain had been diffused by the bullet. Utterson's body slumped out of the upturned wheelchair onto the floor by the now-broken window. The upper panes, both the broken and unbroken ones, were spattered with gore.

The top of Utterson's head had been taken off by the shot. The recoil had shattered his teeth. The jaw had probably been broken too. Utterson's still-open eyes were haemorrhaging from within. The darkening made him look alive, but this was the sickest of illusions. Gabriel Utterson was dead.

Latimer got up from examining the corpse. His forearms were damp with blood and other matter. A meat and cordite stink. The butler had been stupefied, still as though rendered immobile by some curse. The only movement was that of tears pooling in his already-reddening eyes.

Latimer's ears were still ringing from the blast. A sensation he had not felt since South Africa. He had not missed it, and had never thought he'd have cause to experience the like again. He did not hear Holcombe the first time.

'Latimer. Doctor Latimer. Are you hurt?'

'No. I'm quite fine.'

'Is he-?'

Latimer nodded. 'Someone should call the police.' This roused Hodgekiss into action. He disappeared from the room.

'Tobias Latimer.' There was something flat, something official, in the way he was now being addressed by Holcombe.

'Yes?'

'I'm to give you this.' Holcombe took an envelope from an inside jacket pocket. He proffered it to Latimer.

'What's the meaning of this?'

'Please. Take the envelope. Say nothing of this to anyone. Do not open the envelope until you are quite alone.'

Latimer found he was reaching for the envelope. There was neither name, address, nor other instruction written on it.

'Thank you,' Holcombe said. 'Merely acting in accordance with my client's instructions. Something of this nature was not ... unanticipated. I'm sure you can appreciate my position.'

Dumbfounded, Latimer pocketed the envelope.

Somewhere outside, the shrill note of a policeman's whistle. Then shouting, growing nearer. The heavy beating of fists on a door, and then a rush of dark uniforms into the room.

#

It was late when Latimer got home. There had been rounds of questions. First, by a burly sergeant-type, all practical and deferential. Then a second time, by a slim, dapper, modern-looking individual, all slicked-back hair and careful note-taking in an elegant and minute hand.

The first of these had been conducted at the rear of the study, while the paraphernalia of police work was being deployed around the desk area. Photographs were taken, the weapon removed, and then, much later, Utterson's body was lifted onto a stretcher and covered with an ineffectual white sheet. By the time the orderlies were out of the room, a fatal rose had bloomed where Utterson's head had been.

Both times around, Latimer's answers were the same. His professional relationship with Utterson, any of the same with Holcombe. What did he know of the contents of the will? Nothing. The sergeant had been content with his fact-finding, being concerned chiefly with the who, what, when and where of the incident. The other officer – who at no point either introduced himself or gave his authority or other credentials, Latimer now realised – was more elliptical. His questions weaved and dodged. They backtracked and they manoeuvred. The result was the same, as Latimer had nothing else to offer. He has been summoned to a patient who he had seen once, six months earlier, to confirm a cancer diagnosis. He had no other contact with Utterson, and knew little of his business except in the most general terms.

Holcombe had gone through similar sets of questionings too, as had Hodgekiss the butler. Eventually, on apparently deciding that there was little to be gained by further examination at this juncture, Latimer had been allowed to collect his bag and belongings and take his leave. There had been an exchange of business cards,

Latimer slipping the dapper detective's card into a trouser pocket without reading the inscription. The detective – if that was who he was, Latimer now rued – was more thorough.

'This is your consulting room address, your surgery?'

'It is.'

'No telephone?'

'No. The building management has something of an issue with their installation.' This was true. Latimer had been told that the attaching of wires and the drilling of holes into or inside the property has been expressly forbidden by the owner and that the management company would continue to abide by their standing orders. This caused little enough distress to Latimer, who did not care for the devices himself and who serviced a clientele who preferred to communicate by standing arrangement, by letter, by couriered chit or by telegram. His surgery hours included an open session at the beginning of the day where it was clear that anyone on his books might call without prior appointment and that no record of the ad-hoc consultation would be kept in the diary. This discreet arrangement suited some of his more louche clients well. Nevertheless, Latimer had found himself chided by acquaintances who were at pains to remind him that a telephone number was a business essential in the twentieth century, and one of the outward markers of an outward, forward-minded and prosperous enterprise.

'And you have personal accommodations above? An apartment, perhaps?'

'Latimer shook his head. 'I am resident at the Clayton Hotel.'

This caused the raising of an eyebrow. 'The Clayton? You must be doing well.'

Latimer let the comment go. There was nothing to be gained in antagonising this man. He had his job to do, he supposed.

'Thank you for your time, Doctor Latimer. As you'll

doubtless appreciate and understand there'll be an investigation and the coroner will need to be informed. Between you and me, unless a note making clear Mr Utterson's intentions is found, then an open verdict, or perhaps one of misadventure, may very well be recorded. You will appreciate further that there will remain an ongoing police interest in this occurrence. I hate to sound like a Strand Magazine cliché, but you will do me the courtesy of informing me in advance if you've any inclination to travel outside of London overnight.' He smiled; a bland, pale thing.

'Of course.' Utterson's blood had dried on Latimer's jacket sleeves. The material felt heavy and inflexible.

'Then I'll not detain you further.' With that the detective nodded and withdrew.

Samuel, the evening porter who seemed to take a personal interest in Latimer's wellbeing at the Carlton, had taken the trouble, unbidden, to arrange for a plate of cold meats to be left in the kitchens, evening service having been concluded some time before Latimer had returned to his room.

Latimer sat at the table that served for letter-writing and the taking of occasional meals in his room. A bottle of scotch and a tumbler, half-emptied of its original hefty measure, completed the scene. He picked at the sliced ham but he had little appetite. The drink was doing him no good either.

It was late. There was not much sound from outside apart from drizzle flicking at the windows and the sporadic clatter of hooves and wheels in the street below. Latimer listened for a while. He heard a single motor-car.

What was this all about? Latimer propped up the detective's business card up against the bottle. Spencer Mosley. New Scotland Yard. A telephone number. Nothing else: no rank, no title or other designation.

The suit jacket that Latimer had been wearing that day was on a hanger that he had hooked over the door leading to his private bathroom. He had made an attempt with soap and flannel to remove the worst of the blood. Nevertheless, the grey material was both flecked and smeared with dried-on gore. The shirt that he was still wearing would need professional attention too. Latimer found himself grateful that there was still more than a touch of winter about. That heavy coat had been something of a blessing for the return journey in covering up his garments. A generation may have passed since the days of the so-called Ripper murders, but a toff caked in blood, and with a bag full of medical instruments to boot, would have surely caused a hue and cry that Latimer was in no mood to countenance.

Latimer crossed the room to the jacket and from an inner pocket extracted the letter given to him by Holcombe.

He had said nothing of this to either the sergeant or to Spencer Mosley. Furthermore, he assumed that the solicitor had not seen fit to mention it either. Latimer took his seat again and checked the item over.

A standard diamond-shaped sheet folded so that the front was a blank rectangle and that the back formed the pocket by means of the folded edges being overlapped and gummed into a design approximating the saltire of the Scots flag. The front of the envelope was entirely free from inscription. The back was sealed, encapsulating the message within. The gummed closure had been stuck down and gobbets of sealing-wax had been used to further secure the fastening and, Latimer presumed, to guard against tampering.

The sealing-wax roundels, all three of them, were stamped in their centres with what looked like a design whereby the letters E, H and J ran together. The author's initials, Latimer assumed. The "Edward Hyde" of the letter that had vexed Utterson into death.

What sort of communication could provoke a man, elderly in years and facing a slow death through disease, to take his own life in so abrupt and violent a manner? If suicide was his intention to avoid the agonies of cancer, then why do so in front of witnesses? If Utterson harboured some secret, the revelation of which he could not abide, then why had he not already administered himself a fatal shot? Why had he not sought to cajole narcotics from Latimer? Using the cancer as his excuse, no-one would have ever known. And besides, Latimer thought himself a rational and considerate man, and one open to the will of the determined and justified client. He would not have given a fatal dose to a patient himself. But he might have allowed the patient to discover for themselves certain methods of self-destruction if - as in Utterson's case - the only sure alternative was a lingering and demeaning death. Some of the newer and supposedly non-addictive morphine substitutes such as the Bayer Company's "Heroin" brand would be of use here, and might plausibly be prescribed as a mere cough suppressant to provide symptomatic relief for a cancer patient.

The circles of sealing-wax against the good paper of the envelope resembled nothing so much as bullet holes torn into creamy flesh.

The paper was of the best quality. It was not new, though. Its colour spoke of age rather than of tinting, and there was a vague yet detectable damp scent to it. This note had been kept in safekeeping for some years.

Another conundrum. The letter within it could not have been written with Latimer in mind. None of the relevant dates correlated in any useful way.

Latimer was tempted to take the letter to the grate. Samuel had been good enough to have the fire lit and later banked up with coal earlier in the evening, though there was now little more than a slope of small embers, scarcely aglow. Nevertheless, there was enough life in the fire to keep the evening chill at bay. Enough to burn paper.

The envelope felt as though it held several sheets of paper inside it. Latimer held it to the light. No use. The material was sufficiently opaque to deny any clue escaping from within.

Why not burn it and be done? That way it was finished and over, and even if Holcombe later recanted and confessed to the detective that he had handed something over, without any physical evidence it would be one professional man's word against another. The issue would be cancelled out.

Not that was a likely turn of affairs. Holcombe acted as he should. In accordance with his instructions, as might be expected. If he had been told to pass the letter on in secret, then that was what he would do.

What if there was something within the pages of the correspondence? Something that required divulging to the investigator? On reflection, that would have to be dealt with at the time. There was nothing that Latimer could conceive of that might require such a course of action. Besides, he could always open the damned thing and deal with any consequences afterwards.

There was always the fire, Latimer reminded himself.

It was almost midnight. Latimer picked up the envelope. He put it down. The mantel clock ticked on. He waited, willing the smaller of the clock hands to make its traversal complete between the XI and the hour mark.

And there it was. A new day.

Latimer picked up the whisky glass and sipped. The clean burn of the spirit still coating his tongue, he rang a finger under the enclosure and slit the letter open. He did this careful enough not to rupture the sealing-wax dots.

Latimer took out the folded sheets of paper he found within. There were three, one inside the other, each folded into thirds so that they fit snug inside their encasement. The top and bottom sheets were both blanks. A security precaution, he presumed. A protection.

Only the second, middle sheet of the three had any inscription. The same bold handwriting as had made the signature he'd witnessed on the will.

To my unknown friend, greetings.

If all is right with the world, then Gabriel Utterson is dead at your side and you are a doctor.

Did he suffer? Were there tears? Was it his heart bursting? What did for him? Give me your professional opinion. And spare no exquisite detail!

I have dealt with doctors before and I find them most amusing company. Perhaps you will seek me out. I am in London, notwithstanding that I am quite dead. Catch me if you can! Before I cause more mayhem...

The tide is coming in, dear Doctor.

The red levels are rising.

Your chum,

Edward Hyde.

Latimer read the letter through a second time. There was no mistaking the signature as being identical to the one he'd seen that afternoon.

Latimer went to the wardrobe and from it withdrew a wooden box about two feet by one foot in size, some four inches deep. The top of the box was covered with frayed adhesive labels, bearing evidence of transportation and delivery. The box had travelled thousands of miles.

Latimer slid the box open, the lid slipping out as though it contained an over-large set of dominoes. Inside, the usual paraphernalia of packing a delicate or precious item. Wadded newspaper, brittle clean straw. A second box lay within.

A presentation case. Oak, perhaps. Latimer had never been very good at distinguishing one variety of wood from another. Brass fixings. A catch to open it.

He placed the case on the table, covering the letter, and opened the fastening.

The guns lay inside, two new Colt pistols. A memory of a previous life. The weapons were a gift from a former – 'colleague' was the word, he supposed – now working out of Hartford, Connecticut. They were part of an initial consignment of a new model that was being trialled by the US Army. The Colt Manufacturing Company was apparently very proud of their latest Browning design, and was expecting great things and huge sales across the world. This new model, the 1911, was expected to be the leader in market terms.

That, at least, was if you took the word of a former mercenary who was now a salesman for a gun company.

Latimer picked up one of the two pistols. The weight was both reassurance and concern. It had been a long time since he had wielded such a tool.

There were two clips and a box of ammunition also. A leather pouch containing gun oil, cleaning brush and a cloth.

Latimer placed the weapon back into the velvet-lined case. He finished the glass of scotch.

Decision made. Tomorrow he would search out some answers. If this Mister Hyde wanted to be found, then Latimer would oblige him. For Utterson's sake, yes, but also for the sake of his own curiosity.

JUGGERNAUT: FRIDAY 17TH FEBRUARY 1911

Tobias Latimer took his breakfast at the same time every weekday. Monday to Friday he would present himself at seven fifteen in the hotel dining room. He would select two newspapers from the rack in the reception area, usually The Times and the Daily Mail. If there was a copy of the previous evening's London Evening Standard, there he would take that too. He would do the same at weekends, except he began the day an hour later.

The establishment of such a routine appeared to suit the hotel staff as much as is suited Latimer. In addition, it made certain that his breakfast order, which he scarcely ever varied, was attended to efficiently. Coffee would be provided within moments – Latimer did not care for tea, though if it was all that was on offer somewhere, his experience being that some households did not entertain coffee, he would accept and drink unsweetened and black, like his coffee – and he would drink one cup while grazing over the headlines in The Times. Latimer did not care for sports or gaming. His interests were principally in the politics coverage, in international news, particularly as regarded Africa, and in articles and reportage concerned with exploration, science and in medical advancement.

The newspaper précised, Latimer would order his breakfast – grapefruit, kippers and poached eggs, toast – and spend the interval between ordering and eating indulging himself in the rather more hysterical and sensationalist cheaper press. The Mail he found interesting, not least for its blatant warmongering, rabble-rousing and mouthpiece journalism for its proprietor, and for the advertisements, which were never less than amusing. Nevertheless, he found that the paper reflected to some extent the unspoken views of all too many that he came across. The Standard he treated as a repository of crime stories, almost gleeful, albeit couched in coded language recounting beatings, rapes and murders. Again the advertisements provoked smiles, though there was often value to be found in gossip, snippets about this restaurant or that book, and in some of the background happenings of the city.

Latimer focused on the East End of London here. Part of this was a residual and, he admitted to himself, prurient interest in almost anything that the writers could connect in some way back to the so-called 'Ripper' murders of 1888. Quiet periods when no real news was forthcoming and indeed any connected anniversary would be invoked as reason enough to repeat lurid reminiscences of working girls' bodies found abused and mutilated, of the various suspects, of the haplessness of the police investigations, of the exotic and desperate lives led by all too many of those who lived and worked Whitechapel way on.

There was a professional reason for his attention too. His duties as general practitioner with the clientele he had focused upon were largely one and the same. The well-to-do, the well-nourished, the balanced. Their concerns were of fashion and of business, of social niceties and of custom. Of course, there were always sicknesses, illness and disease, and sometimes physical damage too, but much of Latimer's doctoring was of a social order, the free sessions aside. Part of him was well at ease with this. He had studied, worked, fought and suffered in service of his profession, and in South Africa he had seen injuries and destitution enough to warrant a dozen lifetimes. The recompense was well worth that prior history alone. He liked his present life of evening indolence and he was not so cynical a person as to treat all his clients with disdain, and never to their faces.

Besides, the work presented opportunities, and ethics be damned. Latimer had never figured himself for the marrying type, and his clientele afforded him the ability to visit upon, and be called up on by, usually married women who were both attractive and available to him. A mutually beneficial arrangement, he told himself, and as long as no-one overstepped any unspoken agreement, without any consequence save that of pleasure.

Any residual guilt remaining was assuaged by his charitable work. This led to his interest in the East End. Doyle had approached Latimer concerning a Working Lads' Mission latterly set up in former warehousing premises off Brick Lane. The mission was some offshoot of a nonconformist church. They preached redemption via temperance and physical exercise leading to abstinence. First the bottle, then the body, then the soul was one of Pastor Benedict's private credos. Wean them off the drink then you might get the poor to behave themselves with each other. Stable sober married relationships would lead to contentment, a newfound faith in the Christ who's reached out His arms to them, and ultimately salvation was assured.

Pastor Benedict was enough of a realist to accept that this was very much work in progress for the most part. A deal of his work was in arranging temporary clean accommodations, organising a soup kitchen, and fundraising always. Latimer had little time for the Bible himself, having any youthful faith beaten out of him at boarding school, but what he did have time for was Benedict. The man was something of a warrior. Latimer had once worn a uniform and had served. The dog collar might stand in substitution for officer regalia, but it was rank and order nevertheless. Latimer might have done his soldiering in the deserts and scrub of South Africa, but Benedict's was closer to home. That in itself made the struggle more real, and probably more useful than any with which Latimer had been involved.

To support this, then, Latimer made himself available on Saturdays, between the hours of ten and one. After breakfast and any urgent morning errands, he would cross London and arrive in Whitechapel with a bag full of free – free in the sense that he weighted his fees to his richer clients in advance to take account of this – medicines, bandages and so forth, and did what he could to both patch up the walking wounded, as well as at the same time instruct some of the mission volunteers in the basic principles of field medical operations.

The three hours spent in this manner were enough, Latimer reckoned. There was a difference between being a willing volunteer and being a slave to a calling, and Latimer did not feel summoned by powers either temporal or spiritual. Nevertheless, there was something both charming and pitiful in the way he was received by his Whitechapel patients; a blend of gratitude and forbearance, stoicism and resignation, cheerfulness and resignation, the sum of this undercut with curiosity about the well-groomed doctor who elected to give up a little of his leisure time to administer aid, and who did it with neither a prurient interest in the lower orders and their chaotic and vivid lives, nor with a patronizing zeal.

Latimer found himself looking forwards to his Saturdays, and to the minor rewards – a hot-towel shave at Geo. F Trumper, a late luncheon of potted shrimps then steak and kidney pudding at Simpsons-In-The-Strand, perhaps nothing as ostentatious as a walk along the Embankment – he let himself have afterwards.

Saturdays were good days all around.

He found himself now leafing through a remaindered copy of the previous Wednesday's Penny Illustrated Paper. Presumably one of the staff had neglected to dispose of it when the Thursday papers were replaced with the Friday morning issues. There was little amusing in the barbed comments on society figures that passed for news in the publication, though some of the caricatures in the cartoons were admittedly well-executed of their sort. The chief amusement was to be found in the advertising. Here, an exhortation to send away for Toomey's Costa Rican cheroots, there a lengthy affidavit to the medical benefits to be found in the Pulsocon Vibratory Treatment and associated remedies and regimes provided by one Doctor Macaura. MacNair's Whisky of Glasgow was said to aid digestion. Hill's Nyasa smoking mixture, so the advertisement claimed, complete with crudely-rendered image of an African warrior, to be 'Sweet, Cool and Free Burning'. What that had to do with a Masai escaped Latimer.

The miscellaneous advertising columns provided some diversion too. One could send away for tips on racing certainties, for brochures – lavishly illustrated, Latimer imagined - of corsetry. Pamphlets promised success with finding a marriage partner, or infallible horoscopes.

One section offered readers' – unless they had been written by journalists working on the rag, Latimer rued – suggestions in the form of entries to a previously-run competition to provide an alternative solution to the 'Sidney Street Problem' of the previous month. One correspondent suggested providing coffee impregnated with a sleeping draught, or else have bottles filled with a noxious gas thrown through the windows. The competition first prize went to one who suggested gas again, this time to be introduced by being piped in through the adjoining property and forcing the miscreants out into the waiting arms of the law. The second prize winner, again a gas enthusiast, advocated the fumes being piped in through the chimney. A third entrant, this time playing for a sense of the absurd, suggested disguising a pair of boy scouts as miscreants and, they having inveigled their way into the property, make arrests from within.

The solution the police had arrived at was simple. Acting under information that a gang of anarchists who'd killed police officers in a botched robbery a month earlier were hiding out in a Sidney Street dwelling, the area was corralled off and a siege began. A gun battle had lasted for hours, the Metropolitan Police eventually requesting, and being granted, military ordinance from the Tower of London via Home Secretary Churchill. The Sidney Street house caught light. Churchill, overseeing operations, refused to permit the fire brigade to assist. The criminals did not flee the building. Later, two bodies were found in the burned-out shell, though not of the ringleader, one Peter Piatkow.

The incident had been a public sensation, and purported sightings of Piatkow and reports of possible anarchist elements had been regular features in the popular press for the six weeks since. Doubtless there was concern in government and within the police too at the heavy-handed treatment meted out, though some leader articles had speculated openly that the deliberate robustness of the authorities' response was designed to prove a deterrent against such outrages being committed on these shores again.

Latimer returned to his reading. One article devoted itself to the problem of the wrongful incarceration of people within lunatic asylums, the narrative being laced with scandalous intimations of indignities being perpetrated on these poor wretches. A photograph showed a flotilla of submarines in Portsmouth harbour prior to an exercise in the South China Seas. A short article on temperance, linked to an advertisement for a 'non-alcoholic, non-narcotic elixir, providing stimulation and refreshment to the working man and homemaker alike, and wholly without negative effect'. This miracle juice was supposed to 'prevent the thirst for the demon drink, provide both vigour and stamina, and be altogether a most recommended linctus for the alleviation of both jadedness and for reliance on the crutch of alcohol'. Recommendations followed from several purported medicos. As if to underscore the point, another editorial drew the readers' attention to 'The White Slaves Behind The Bar', an expose of abuses supposedly suffered by barmaids. These included rudeness and general intolerance, the threat of violence and worse. Oblique reference was made to what Latimer could only decode as the so-called Ripper murders of the last century. The paper did not seem to be above mixing advertising with journalistic copy, riddling both with scandal, violence and innuendo presumably to encourage sales of hawked goods and of the journal itself.

Still, the paper was only a penny and furthermore, it was a penny he had not invested himself. Latimer folded the newspaper back, returned it to the rack it had come from, and walked through into the hotel reception area.

'Any messages?' The clerk on the front desk – a whip-thin lad whose name Latimer had never known, checked the cubbyholes behind him. The clerk was about to speak, but his attention was caught by something over Latimer's shoulder.

'Ah, Doctor.'

The detective from the previous day. Hands in the pockets of a light gabardine Chesterfield overcoat, leaning back against a supporting pillar. The man rocked forwards on his heels so he was properly upright. He was smiling. The expression was not altogether a pleasant one.

'I didn't see you there.'

'No. Trick of the trade, you might say. Do you have a moment?'

'Actually, I'm on my way to my offices.'

'Then perhaps I might walk with you. Two birds, one stone and all that?'

'Very well-'

'Oh, introductions. Of course. Mosley. Detective. But as this isn't really a formal visit, then Spencer will do just fine.'

'So what is it that you want, Detective?' Mosley hadn't removed his hands from his pockets and Latimer was damned if he was going to be the man to offer his first.

Mosley ushered Latimer through the revolving front door of the hotel and caught up with him on the other side.

'This whole business with your patient, with Utterson. I must admit that it has me quite foxed. A man takes a pistol to his head while a will's being read? There's no reason to it, no reason at all.'

'And yet it happened, precisely as I described it.'

'Oh, I don't doubt that, not for one instant Doctor. The how and the where and the when of the matter are quite straightforward. It's the why. Why would he do such a thing? An eminent man in his field, well-regarded and successful. No enemies or rivals to speak of. I've made some enquiries as you might imagine and all I find is that he was perhaps not the most gregarious or jovial of men, not a man to suffer fools or fripperies, you might say, but there was neither mystery nor cloud about him. Furthermore, Doctor, he was, as you said, already dying.'

'You've had an autopsy conducted?'

'Oh yes. Utterson was not without prestige, and the matter has attracted some attention. Thus, the mechanics of the investigatory come into operation all the sooner. And the coroner found what you might expect to have found. A tumour in the wall of the stomach of an appreciable size, though I admit that I paid attention to the generalities of the situation and left the Latin terminology and the gory specifics well alone. He would have died nevertheless, and he knew it.'

'And?'

'And if that were the case, which it was, and Utterson was not minded to see affairs through to the bitter end, but rather take matters into his own hands as it were, then why not do it in private? Why burden you and young Mister Holcombe with his self-murder? No, Doctor, it simply won't do.'

'What are you saying?'

Mosley stopped, his arm brushing against Latimer's sleeve as an almost unconscious prompt to have him stood where he was wanted to be placed. 'I am saying, Doctor, that I am presented with a problem. Utterson did not kill himself because of his sickness. He killed himself because of something alluded to in the meeting between him, Holcombe and yourself. My question, Doctor, is simply this. What was it? A previous indiscretion come to light? An allegation from a servant, perhaps. A bastard child hidden in the rookeries come back to claim his right? There are all kinds of melodramatic possibilities.'

The letter he had been given by Holcombe. The letter that Latimer had not mentioned in their previous conversation.

'Holcombe has given me his version of what he said took place. What is yours, Doctor?'

'As I said yesterday. There were introductions; there was a preamble from Mr Holcombe. We did not proceed as far as the actual reading of any will. It was on the mention of the name of the person whose will it was that Utterson became agitated. He then took the revolver from his desk. The rest you know.'

'And the name of the person?'

'Edward Hyde.'

'And does that name mean anything to you.'

'Nothing whatsoever. I had not heard of the man before and wish now that I was still in that happy condition. Furthermore, I had only met Gabriel Utterson on the sole previous occasions as I've already told you. I have had no previous dealings, meetings or correspondences with Holcombe either.'

The detective nodded, ruminating. 'Thank you Doctor. That seems most unambiguous. There's nothing further to add, is there?'

'No,' Latimer lied.

'Very well. It appears as though I have some desk work to do. This Hyde may be dead, he may not. The existence of a will would seem to indicate such, though it would be as well to check.'

'Why the interest, Detective?'

'If Hyde is alive, or if someone else, with knowledge of the effect the mere mention of his name were to have on the unfortunate Utterson, then we would be dealing with a case of murder, Doctor. As simple as that. And if Hyde is dead, and this is some ghost from the past come back to haunt him, then I would rest easier knowing that. In either case, Doctor, I shall not stand by while lives are taken, be it through their own decision or through action at a distance.'

'Well, if I can be of any assistance-' Latimer let the sentence trail.

That knowing smile again. 'Then I'll be sure to call upon your service. Farewell, Doctor.' He was already summoning an approaching hansom. The cab pulled up and Mosley got in. 'Oh, and Doctor, my appreciation.' He spoke through the window.

'For what?'

'Why, your good works in the East End, of course.' The cab pulled off into the street, leaving Latimer stood alone.

He put his hand inside his coat. A firm rectangle in the breast pocket of his suit jacket. The note from Hyde.

The requirement to be at the will reading. The contents of the will, for that matter. Why did Utterson feel he had no alternative but to kill himself there and then? What did it all mean?

Latimer arrived at his consulting rooms none the wiser. What he did have, though, was a plan. Or at least the very beginnings of a way forward.

'Good morning Doctor.'

'Doyle. Good morning. How is the diary?'

Maureen Doyle scanned the ledger open on the desk. 'A quiet day ahead, Doctor. No callers without appointment today. Appointments are at eleven and at noon. Nothing in the diary for later in the afternoon.'

'Good. I'll be taking a long lunch from two and won't return for the rest of the day.'

'Very good.'

'If there's anything urgent, then-'

'-then I'll have a message left at the hotel and you'll call upon the patient this evening. Would seven o'clock be suitable?'

'Very good, Doyle.'

'And if that's not to their liking I'm to refer them on to Doctor Montgomery.'

Latimer nodded approval. 'And tomorrow?'

'Saturday runs as per the norm.'

'So, you'll be joining me at the mission for ten?'

'Yes, Doctor.'

'Very good. And no appointments until eleven, you say?'

'Lady Bruntnell again.'

'Ah. Yes. Lady Bruntnell. I suppose it would do no good to either of us to keep her waiting.'

'No, Doctor.'

'Thank you, Doyle. I've got some papers to catch up on in the meantime.'

'I'll not disturb you then.

'That would be most appreciated, Doyle.'

'Unless you'd like me to bring you through a cup of coffee first.' That slight knowingness about her.

'Thank you, but no. Still full from breakfast.'

'Very good, Doctor.'

Latimer went through to his office. He did not remove his coat. He opened the window and checked up and down the side street. A cyclist, pedalling away. A man and woman, arms linked, crossing Harley Street, their backs also to Latimer. No other traffic.

Nine-oh-five according to the carriage clock on the mantelpiece. This would only take an hour. Latimer ducked out through the window and onto the pavement outside. He turned away from the junction of Harley Street and Mansfield Mews and walked at a brisk pace away from his offices down the side street.

\#

Glaziers were at work at the Utterson household. The front door was open, presumably to allow the workmen access and egress without overburdening the butler.

There was no sign of the detective. Then again, Latimer supposed, if he had placed a man here to keep some kind of watch, then he would not know who to look for. At any rate, there was no suspicious lurker peering over the top of a newspaper or suchlike. And besides, he had a legitimate series of questions to ask and a good reason to be here.

Latimer crossed the threshold, rapping on the knocker as he entered the hallway. 'Is anyone there? Hotchkiss?'

A figure in overalls and neckerchief peered around the study door. 'He's through the back, guv. Want me to fetch him?' The scent of linseed followed his words.

'Thank you, no. I'll not further interrupt your work. I'll find him myself.'

'Right you are. Straight down the hall to the end. Black door, no handle. You can't miss it.'

Latimer was about to press a coin into the man's

hand in appreciation, but he had already gone back to replacing the window-glass.

The door was where the man had said Latimer would find it. At the far end of the corridor, recessed so that it was not readily visible. A brass push-plate, somewhat scuffed, though clean enough and burnished with years of polish, substituted for a handle. A door to open and close, being hinged both ways. Useful when carrying a tray, Latimer supposed.

Latimer knocked again, but the hinge mechanisms were light, and the door pushed open with the first touch. 'Hotchkiss?'

The room beyond was some kind of serving staff ready room. Part cloakroom and storage area, part reception area for deliveries, returned laundry and cooked food. A hatch built into the wall opposite. A dumb waiter leading to the kitchen below. Further doors, one closing off the servants' staircase, the other leading to the tradesman's entrance. And a rough table and two chairs, one of which was occupied by the butler.

A glass and a bottle on the table. A dark liquid, perhaps the same fortified wine served to Latimer the day before. Hotchkiss sat with his head in his hands.

'Hotchkiss?' Latimer spoke soft.

'Doctor Latimer, sir. My apologies.' He made to get up, but Latimer gestured for him to remain seated. Sitting on the other chair, Latimer refilled the glass and slid it towards Hotchkiss.

The butler took the glass, but did not drink. He rotated the glass as he spoke, turning it slow so the wine did not spill. 'I do not know what to do. All my life I have been in service. Now I find myself without a position. Oh, I can make the house clean and so on and so forth, and I can assist with whatever preparations might be required for-,' he hesitated, now not spinning the glass, but instead waiting for the minute waves and ripples on the wine's surface to subside. 'For the funeral. The house sale, one supposes. The packing up of Mister Utterson's papers and his personal items. He has little in the way of family, you know. And I find myself likewise, being wedded to the idea of service and to the orderly administration of the household.' Now he drank.

'I'm sure that provision will have been made for you. Mister Utterson knew what was he was doing. It is surely inconceivable that he would not have thought such matters through.'

'Yes, of course. He mentioned something of the sort before, before...' The butler drank from the glass. The liquid must have revived him somewhat. He sat more upright, finished the glass, and then stood. 'My apologies.'

'Think nothing of it.' From the front of the house, tapping noises, scraping.

'How might I be of assistance?'

Latimer had considered this in the walk across town. 'I thought that it would be a kindness to break the news of your master's death in person to those who were close to him. I understand that he had little in the way of family.'

'That is correct.'

'There would, of course be close companions, colleagues, and the like.'

'There would, though I fear of late Mr Utterson has – had – become somewhat withdrawn into himself. He kept few correspondences that were not business, and he had neither entertained nor been entertained since the onset of his illness.' Hodgekiss took out a key, unlocked and opened a drawer in the table. The drawer contained a cash box and an elastic-bound notebook. He retrieved the notebook and closed the drawer without locking.

'It would, as you say, be a kindness to call upon two people. The first is Guest, Mr Utterson's most trusted clerk, who worked with him for many years. He has entered into a retirement of sorts these last years. He would be grateful of the news being delivered. The second is Richard Enfield. An old friend and a distant cousin.

Once upon a time, they would walk together on Sundays. Mr Enfield may be found at his club I daresay.' There were a few loose leaves of paper folded into the back of the notebook. Hodgekiss pencilled the addresses onto one of the sheets and handed the note over.

'My thanks.'

'No sir. My thanks to you.'

Hodgekiss showed Latimer the door and they parted in the hallway. The glazier and his men were sat on the front steps, drinking what Latimer assumed to be cold tea from flasks. One, an apprentice judging by his age and lopsided young face, swigged from a clear bottle of some cherry-coloured soda water.

"I'll call again if I may.'

'That would be a kindness.'

The exchange encouraged the workmen to cease their snatched labour. The apprentice boy grinned at Latimer, a face full of impudent teeth. 'Guv.' A touch of hand to cap, and then back about his trade. A smirk, then he was gone back into the house. Latimer shrugged the annoyance off.

Bells tolled the hour. Ten, according with the hour asserted by the clock on the neighbouring church.

There was just enough time. Latimer checked the note again to be certain, and then crossed the street. He would be at Guest's soon enough.

#

The windows were dusty. A shop, though one seemingly abandoned, its dejection emphasised by the bustling on both sides. A chop house and a milliner. Nothing expensive in either establishment. Caps and workwear hats. Mash and gammon.

Latimer put his nose to the glass, shielding his eyes so he could peer inside. There were little more than dead flies on display. Shelves and a counter. A single plain chair. Little room to manoeuvre inside.

There was no sign to indicate the trade or business conducted here. Nevertheless, this was the address that the butler had given. This was where Guest now resided.

Latimer knocked. There was no response. He knocked again, this time on the window. The sharpness of the rapping brought stares from the street, then the rattle of a casement above. A head emerged. Balding, bespectacled, elderly. 'Yes?'

'Mr Guest?'

'Yes.'

'I've come from Utterson.'

The window was shut fast. Latimer imagined the movements within. Perhaps braces being pulled over shoulders. The slipping on of a jacket. Then down the stairs. Perhaps an inner door to be unlocked. Then the front door.

The timings worked out about right. Unlocking, then the head again, peering this time around the door.

'Utterson, you say?'

'May I come inside?'

'Please.'

Once indoors, it was clear what this place had been. Spaces for jars on shelves. The scent of tobacco. A taken-down tin advertisement sign, still gaudy with an enamel paint design. A red-cloaked maid. Muratti's "Young Ladies" Gold-Tipped Cigarettes, according to the slogan.

'Come through, come through.' Latimer was led through the opened-up counter into a back room that was little more than a store cupboard. The tobacco smell was stronger here. Other aromas intruded: boiling potatoes, something astringent – a cleaning chemical perhaps – and the workshop smell of metal, grease and oil.

Another door. Latched from the outside. 'He's dead, isn't he? Come up, if you would.' The door revealed a narrow stairwell. Latimer went up first, the door being locked from within behind him.

A bed-sitting room. Clean and well-appointed of its kind, though small. Another room off to the front of the building. Latimer saw the window that Guest had looked down at him from. This room was cluttered with a workbench, a small lathe, racks of tools and shelves of boxes. The engineering works odour was stronger yet.

'I am Guest. Welcome. I'd offer you something under the circumstances, but I don't keep liquor on the premises.'

'That's quite alright. A little early in any case.'

'Just so. How did he die?'

Latimer paused. 'The end was quick.'

Something in his manner must have given the man reason to doubt. 'We were close once, Utterson and I. As close as working colleagues might expect to be. And though I took retirement from lawyering some time ago, I would visit and he would consult, if only to allow a second opinion to reinforce his own.'

'How long has it been since you saw him last?'

'Six months, I should say. He let me know of his illness, which I had suspected, and he said that he would withdraw from life as far as he was able. He wished to spend his remaining months in tidying his affairs and in rekindling his faith which, though strong, had not received as much attention as it perhaps might.'

'He was afraid of dying?'

'No. He was afraid of what might meet him on the other side.' A glimmer from the workshop room. A smile from the other man. 'Come through,' he said, 'and I will show you an old man's folly.'

Latimer took a moment to inspect the new room further. Its walls were shelved out, or else fronted with display cases. Each of the cases showed off pistols. Revolvers. Automatic pistols. Breech-loaders. There were antiquities and there were new models, including a new example of the aptly-named Savage Arms Company of Westfield Massachusetts' own .45 calibre pistol. This had been the handgun that the Colt 1911 had tested against, before losing out in final testing to the Browning design.

A framed poster displayed the text of the 1903 Pistols

Act, an 'An Act to regulate the sale and use of Pistols or other Firearms'. Latimer's own gun licence – a meaningless piece of paper since one could be purchased on request at any post office – was in his wallet.

'Most of my work is repair, though I undertake a few commissions. Not as many as I might, but then this is hobby-work, not labour. I had considered opening premises, which is why I took up here, but I found I had not the stomach for retail. My pleasure is in the craft of manufacture, a whole other set of skills to those of the law.'

'These are beautiful.' They were. Old pieces that had been returned to their original quality. Each was offset by a suitable case, the wood chosen to best match the stock, the inlay of a shade to counterpoint the steel of the weapon.

On the workbench, a small crate, scarcely larger than a cigar box. The case was open, though its contents obscured by packing straw. 'Are you a shooting man?'
'Once, yes.'

'You served, I take it?'

'In the Boer. I was there all the way through. From 99 to 02. Then in the concentration camps. Then I settled, became a doctor, a civilian one. Then I came back.'

'Then you might appreciate this.' Guest took a pistol from one of the cases. He held it out on a bed of chamois leather.

'A Browning Number One. Belgian-made. FN Herstal. I used to have one.' Latimer picked it up, verified that it was not loaded, dry-fired it once. A smooth, crisp action.

'Lovely, isn't it? As a machine, a thing of terrible simplicity. Beautiful, in its way. So much cleaner than the law.'

'Utterson had a revolver.'
'My retirement gift to him.'
'Seeing these I did wonder.'
'You were there?'

Latimer nodded. 'Yesterday. Mid-afternoon.'

'That is strange. I did wonder myself, after him telling me his news, that he might turn the gun on himself one day. He assured me that he would not, though. That he would find some peace with the Almighty and accept his passing with whatever dignity he could muster.'

'That is what I have come to ask you about.'

'About why he would murder himself in public?'

'Yes. There were two of us there. The third was a young solicitor. Holcombe.'

'I don't know the name, though it's been some years since I troubled to keep up with new appointments.'

'Might we sit?'

Guest brought a chair through from the bed-sitting room and offered it to Latimer, who accepted. He sat himself on the stool under the workbench.

'Tell me about yesterday, I beg you. Then I will tell you what I may to assist, though I fear it may not be very much.'

Latimer told Guest everything save the letter from Hyde, which he omitted.

Guest remained still for some moments after the recollection was over. A trill of bells from a carriage clock in the bed-sitting room. That would be the half-hour. Ten thirty.

'Edward Hyde is a fiction. A preposterous invention. Someone, I fear, is about some kind of foul trick. Someone who knows something of Utterson's business of the past certainly, but this cannot be. Edward Hyde does not exist, nor indeed, ever had existed.'

Latimer stayed silent.

Eventually, Guest spoke again. His tone was less strident than before. 'And you say that on hearing the name, poor Gabriel took his own life?'

'Yes.'

'That would do it. You understand that this is the darkest matter, an incident which I dare not relate to you, not least because I swore to Utterson as my employer and as my friend that I would be his confidant.'

'But if someone has assumed the identity of this Hyde or at least invoked it knowing this would cause such a reaction, then this is murder,' Latimer said.

'And yet I will not betray my friend.' Tears were at Guest's eyes. 'I will do this though. Hodgekiss gave you the names and addresses of others too?'

'One other.'

'Enfield?'

'Yes.'

'Then go to him. Listen to what he has to say. If he receives you at all. You will not believe him I am sure. Nevertheless, I will corroborate what I can, though I will not be the man to divulge secrets.'

'For that at least, thank you.'

'My appreciation for telling me this man to man. Go now, please. I would reflect on this. You may call on me again if you have more questions. I can only imagine that you will.'

They shook hands and Latimer departed. Behind him in the street, the front door was locked. Latimer imagined Guest's path back to his workshop. The locking of the internal stairwell door. The relaxing of the braces over the shoulders. The sitting back in the chair, or perhaps reclining on his bed, and thinking about his old friend.

So, who was this Hyde? What was it that caused such secrecy? Why would Utterson have killed himself? Latimer felt that he was only a little further along in finding out. He would have to see Enfield this afternoon.

#

Latimer loped back through the streets, hands in pockets, not quite breaking into a run. As it was he returned to the side street, Mansfield Mews, where his office window opened out into with two minutes to spare. He let himself back into his rooms, removed his coat, let his urgent breathing subside a little, and then walked through to the reception desk.

'All done, Doctor? The paperwork, I mean.' Doyle smiled.

'Quite, yes, thank you.' Damn it, but Doyle was an impudent one at times. Doyle's expression was bland. Any mockery, any complicit knowledge of the doctor's absence from his rooms well-concealed. Nevertheless, Latimer was glad of the booming interruption afforded by Lady Bruntnell, complete with one of her coterie of small savage dogs in attendance.

Doyle took the terrier and an accompanying paper bag of treats for it, and promised to take expert care of the beast. Latimer ushered Lady Bruntnell through into his rooms, let her recline on the couch there, and sat with notebook to hand to record her symptoms. For once, she claimed something of an illness.

'Isn't that so, Doctor?'

Latimer had not been listening. He was still churning the events of the last twenty-four hours over. 'So?' Repeating her last word invariably had the effect of buying some thinking time and also permitting the patient to recommence her interminable monologue.

The gist of it was this. Lady Bruntnell was pained. A gastric pain. Not of the stomach nor of the kidneys, but somewhere in between. The pain was not severe, nor was it anything more than intermittent, but there it was. It was there now. Remedies had been procured. Popular books on the topic of home health had been consulted, and advice from all and sundry in her social circle and beyond solicited. Various brands of liver salts had been taken, with temporary relief of varying durations. Patent medicines had been bought and dismissed, usually on account of their harsh flavours and their overly sticky consistency: 'How will it find its way through, Doctor, if it runs like molasses?' No, lightness of touch was what was required, she was sure.

The self-diagnosis and treatment had extended to

spending two days on a diet of nothing but clear broths, to little good effect, followed by a day eating only dishes containing eggs. 'No, Doctor, the only relief I feel was suggested to me by my maid-of-all-work, if you could believe such a thing. The temerity! Of, to be sure I had words with Cook that she be thoroughly scolded for her boldness, though one admits that her remedy had been at least partially successful.'

The medicine in question was little more than a soda-water preparation infused with a little sweetness and some souring elements.

'Most likely little more than food colouring, honey and a splash of alcohol,' Latimer smiled. 'Nevertheless, I daresay the bubbles will do you no harm whatsoever, and may even ease the passage of gastric gases.'

'No alcohol whatsoever, Doctor. The manufacturers are most adamant on the point. This is a beverage to be recommended for temperance folk of all classes. It says so on the bottle.'

Then if you find the concoction gives you ease, then I have no hesitation in permitting you to carry on this treatment.' Latimer made some notes, more for show than for any real need to keep a history of the appointment. 'And the name of this preparation?'

'Something silly and foreign-sounding. Juggler? Juggernaut? Something of the like I believe.'

Latimer made another note and smiled again. 'I will make a point of looking out for it. Nothing else troubles you, I take it?'

It took a further half hour for Lady Bruntnell to confirm that this was indeed the case. The talk danced around various dinner parties, indiscretions and the like, circling back to how Lady Bruntnell's physicality reacted to each morsel of innuendo on its first hearing.

At the end of the session, they returned to pick up the dog – named George, for the new King – and Lady Bruntnell left, though not before scheduling another visit for two weeks' hence. She promised, on her way out, what a glance to Doyle who appeared to be in on the joke, to be in a much more vigorous frame of mind.

The rest of the working day passed without surprising incident.

'Thank you, Doyle.'

'Doctor.'

'At ten tomorrow?'

'I'll see you there.' Doyle went back to the accounts work that lay between them.

Once outside, Latimer hailed a cab. The walk would usually have been his choice, but the questions inside his head were exerting inward pressure. He needed more information and he needed it now. Even the few minutes saved by taking a hansom across town would help in speeding up that relief.

'Where to, guv?'

'Pall Mall. The Athenaeum.'

'Right you are.'

Latimer needed to get to talk with Holcombe. There had to be something the young lawyer could tell him, and client privilege or whatever they termed it in the law be damned. Something more than the cryptic and threatening-sounding note that he'd been passed. Latimer wanted this whole mess sorted out. He had become too used too soon, he reflected, to his life of easy work and occasional pleasures. He wanted nothing that would cause distress or bring him unwanted attention other than being that efficient, courteous and – though he flattered himself – somewhat handsome doctor who had been recommended by someone whose opinion mattered.

Somewhere he had Holcombe's card. Ah, there it was. Address, telephone number. Good.

The city hummed past outside. The rhythmic clatter of the cab's wheels over cobbles, the counterpoint by the horse's hooves. Rising and lowering tones of automobile engines. The hubbub of passing conversation, of street-noises at corners. Behind it, something electric. Gas was giving way, in much the same way that natural horsepower was being supplanted ever more by that produced by petrol engines. The world was changing all around. London was changing.

'Athenaeum!'

Latimer reached up and paid the driver through the trap door in the vehicle roof. Getting down to street level, he took a moment to regard the building in front of him. The square neoclassical design, the Doric columnar entrance with a portico topped with a statue of the goddess of wisdom, remained as impressive as the first time he'd seen it when walking around the capital on his return last summer. Would Athene see fit to bestow knowledge?

This was not a building Latimer had entered before. He did not consider himself a clubbable man and had politely declined the invitations to membership to other clubs that had come his way through professional acquaintances and through grateful patients. He admitted to himself that his stand might have wavered if he was in need of custom; being a club man might have channelled patients his way, though the closeness of club collegiality and patient-doctor confidence would have felt like a pair of tight hands around his neck. Nor was he sufficiently nostalgic to join an ex-service club, of which there were several. His war days were behind him, and he had listened to quite enough by way of the bluster, self-aggrandizing reminiscences and bullishness of the off-duty officer in his service days. On the whole, clubs were not for him.

A flunkey greeted him at the entrance. A second doorman, evidently of some greater seniority, approached once Latimer was inside. 'Sir?'

'Richard Enfield, if you please.'

'Are you expected?'

Latimer took a business card from the holder he kept in a breast pocket. 'No, though–'

'Mister Enfield does not receive without appointment.' A glance aside; a summons to another out of sight to Latimer. At once there were footsteps approaching across the hallway.

'I bring news of a sudden death. I thought it best that Enfield heard this first-hand, rather than read it in the newspapers in a day or so.'

Another glance. The footsteps stopped. Now a check of the business card. A purse of the lips. 'If you would wait here please, Doctor Latimer.' A squeak of a turn on a heel, then footsteps away.

Latimer was shown to a bench where he could be seated. The doorman left, disappearing into a doorway off the hall. Latimer found himself scare able to breathe. The feeling was like waiting outside the headmaster's office.
He remained standing. The pace here was funereal. Staff moved with a studied grace. Members took their time also. The hall was dominated by a grand staircase to the first floor, though it seemed more for impact than use as there was no traffic up or down it. Every sound felt as though it reverberated in the immensity of the room. This was not a comfortable place, all white marble and a chill from the open front doors.

After five minutes the doorman returned. He was accompanied by another man, tall and slender, dressed in butler's garb. It was the newcomer who now spoke. 'Doctor Latimer. Our apologies for the delay. If you would follow me, Mr Enfield will receive you in the drawing room.'

Latimer was led up the grand staircase. At the top of the stairs he was directed along a corridor. A small group of members came towards him. One or two held ill-folded newspapers. One cradled a brandy balloon and a cigar in the same fat hand. All were grumbling. 'Blast Enfield! Who does he think he is?' 'Nerve of the fellow.' Latimer was glared at by the last speaker as they crossed paths in the corridor.

The doors ahead were shut. The butler opened one, and checked inside. Satisfied at what he saw, he stood back, indicating to Latimer that he should enter.

The drawing room was long and luxuriant. Dark bookcases fitted between the high windows. The curtains spoke of wealth. The furnishings indicated both an area for conviviality – low chairs with lower tables between them, leather and mahogany all – and desk areas for writing letters and for the gentle kind of study best conducted with a warm susurrus of conversation rather than library silence.

The room was empty. Save for one large man, standing at the far end of the room, his back to the entrance.

'Mr Enfield? Doctor Tobias Latimer.'

The door closed behind Latimer. He approached. His footfalls made no sound on the rug.

'Sit, if you will. Stand if you prefer.' Enfield did not turn.

Latimer stayed on his feet.

'Very well,' Enfield said. He clasped his hands behind his back. A ring, almost hidden in fleshy folds. Either Enfield had always been a bulky man, or years of fine living were taking their toll. 'Give me your news.'

'I attended Gabriel Utterson yesterday afternoon. I had been invited to an urgent meeting. The details of the appointment were not given to me in advance. The engagement – at Utterson's home – was the reading of a will.'

'Go on.'

'Utterson has not been well these last six months, and for longer than that if I read his symptoms right. I act as his physician. I had seen him in that capacity once before. At the first meeting I confirmed his suspicions of a cancer in the stomach. He asked nothing more of me and refused other assistance, against my strict advice.'

'Gabriel was always a principled and direct fellow.'

'His condition was not good. His mobility had, by yesterday, been restricted to that permitted by invalid chair. He had, by my reckoning, weeks to live at most.'

Enfield caressed the ring, rotating it around his finger. Latimer was surprised that there was any play in its fit.

Latimer continued. 'We were accompanied by a young solicitor, a Canadian, by name of Holcombe. There was a proviso on the will's reading necessitating my attendance as the last physician to treat Utterson, according to this Holcombe. He began with the preamble to the will. On Utterson's hearing of the name of the man whose will it was, he was seized with a fearful urgency. At first I thought his heart would give in. He opened a drawer in his desk, and withdrew a pistol.'

'Gabriel took his own life?'

'He did.'

Enfield let the ring be. 'Thank you, Doctor. I appreciate the gesture in bringing this to me first-hand.'

Latimer was uncertain if this was meant as dismissal, if this meeting had been adjourned. 'Do you want to know the name? The name that made this man end his life so abruptly and violently?'

'Thank you Doctor, no. There is no need. Only one name could have had such an effect. That of Edward Hyde.'

'That was the name. What does this mean?'

'You are right. I should explain. Please, Doctor, indulge me for a few minutes more. It is a long time since I heard that name spoken, and I had hoped to have been dead before it having to be voiced it out loud ever again. You deserve an explanation.' It was then that Richard Enfield turned to face Latimer.

Enfield was a large man, six feet tall and more. His height helped him in bearing his weight. He gave every impression of a big man gone to seed. His suit was expensive, and generously cut so as to attempt to hide his bulk, but there was no disguising the manifold chins, the raw dough pallor, the leafy pattern of broken veins across his nose. His eyes were dark and wet like a dog's. There might have been some emotion there at the information about his friend, there might not. His mutton chop whiskers were salt-white, as was his hair, though little of it remained except that which clustered around his ears. 'Sit, Doctor, sit. Will you take a drink with me?'

'I will.'

Enfield rang a tiny bell that had been standing on the windowsill. The same butler who had brought Latimer to this room made an appearance from a discreet door. Enfield held up two fingers.

They sat in armchairs, and Latimer attempted some small talk about the club to pass the minutes until the drinks had been delivered. Enfield seemed energised by the opportunity to wax about the place, told him about the Athenaeum's beginnings in the 1820s, about the building itself, about the members past and present ('Elgar, Hardy, Kipling. Barrie, I suppose') and about the long wait on the membership that the club enjoyed, though there were short cuts for those who were favoured friends ('not that Gabriel would entertain the notion, of course') as well as intimating that there were several – each of them current ministers in Prime Minister (and member) Asquith's cabinet who would never rise to the ranks of member no matter what. Enfield then imparted a salacious anecdote about one of that number, allowing himself to indulge at its conclusion in a thick, throaty chuckling which in turn summoned the butler with the refreshment.

'Put them there, put them there.' Two crystal tumblers, a larger crystal container with ice and tongs, a decanter full of a clear brown liquid. 'Bourbon. Like Irish whiskey, but American. You take it with ice, not water.' The butler poured two large measures, added ice to each, and then withdrew.

Once the door was shut, Enfield raised his glass and waited for Latimer to do likewise. 'Gabriel Utterson.'

'Gabriel Utterson.'

'Gin was his drink, you know. In private at least, He had some fool notion that it was less enjoyable than wine, and therefore less of a sin. Never quite understood his reasoning myself, but then again I've never been a man to deny myself a pleasure.'

Latimer had to ask. 'What is your connection to Utterson?'

'We're family, of a sort. Cousins. Distant, and so on and so forth. Nevertheless, we would meet up once a week, him after church and me after Saturday, and we'd take a walk and discuss whatsoever came to our minds. Those were good days. He took some pleasure I believe in both chiding me and experiencing vicariously some of my tales, for I was quite the man about town in my youth and, I suppose, well into my middle years as well, and I in turn, took solace from his forbearance and his counsel. They were, as I said, good days.

'That was how it began, on one of those walks. The whole horrible business. Whatever else comes out of this, of what I am about to tell you, that is one thing that will not be shaken from me. My affection for Gabriel. Utterson was a good sort.' He drank. 'A good sort.'

Latimer let Enfield reflect. He took a sip of his own drink. The bourbon was less refined than much of the malt whisky that he'd sampled, but what it lacked in subtlety, it compensated for in directness. There were clear, simple flavours – wood-smoke, honey, something clean and sweet like melon – and then the rising warmth of the alcohol. A modern taste, he thought. A new drink for the still-new century.

'It was my fault, in a way,' Enfield said. 'It was me that brought Utterson's attention to the matter in the first instance. Tell me, have you ever heard of a medical man like yourself by the name of Henry Jekyll?'

'No.'

Jekyll and I were known to each other, as was

Utterson. Utterson took care of our legal affairs. We dined in the same circles. Jekyll had grown rather distant of late – this would be well into the last century, you understand – and had ostracised himself somewhat. He had an imposing house, a laboratory of his own, and something of a personal fortune. He did not need to work, and indeed spent much of his time in scientific investigation. He'd studied under Hastie Lanyon, you know.'

'Everyone who's ever picked up a scalpel or prescribed a medicine has heard of Lanyon.'

'An eminent man, and not unconnected to these events. Events which, I am telling you must go no further. In any case, I am not sure that you will credit my words.'

Latimer said nothing, and waited for Enfield to resume.

'Jekyll, we thought, had taken up with a new confidant. A younger, queer-looking sort by the name of Edward Hyde. I myself had seen this Hyde brutalise a girl in the street. We gave chase and apprehended the rogue, and pressed him for a sum of one hundred pounds, so that the poor girl, who had been quite crippled, could at least attempt to lead something of a comfortable life. Hyde acquiesced, paying the sum by means of a cheque drawn on Jekyll's account. The paper was good and the girl was paid. I had thought that was an end of it, an odd little tale, except when I told this to Utterson, he took me into his confidence.

'It transpired that Jekyll had bequeathed his estate to this Hyde. We tried to intervene, of course, and Jekyll said eventually that he'd rid himself of Hyde. We were relieved, as you might imagine. Our assumption, unspoken between Utterson and I, but there nevertheless, was that Jekyll, never the marrying kind, had either become infatuated with the man or else was having his good name being threatened. The existence of such a will, as you might imagine, gave us further pause. In my darker imaginings, it might have been the prelude to murder for profit, after all.

'Then Jekyll had a relapse. Worse still, there was murder done. Danvers Carew, a Member of Parliament no less, was struck down fatally one night. The weapon used on him was a cane that Utterson had once given as a gift to Jekyll. So violent was the assault that the cane had been broken in two.

'Matters spiralled from there. Jekyll became a recluse. His staff, becoming afraid of him and of Hyde, and of the noises they heard emanating from his laboratory, went to Utterson for aid. He and others broke into Jekyll's laboratory. Doctor Latimer, you will not believe what they found.'

Enfield refilled his glass, adding more ice to the whiskey. Latimer held his own glass out for a little more. He refused the additional ice.

'Good, isn't it? I have a case or two reserved for me. I have some business interests, inherited mostly, in the Southern states. One of them is a quarter-share in a distillery. There's little profit in it, if truth be told, but their product is remarkable, distinctive, and at times a refreshing and easy-drinking alternative to the Scottish variant.'

'What did Utterson find?'

'He found Hyde. Dead. Dead by his own hand. He'd taken poison. Poison that had been left for him by Jekyll. And with the body, a fresh will and an explanation. First, the matter of the will. The will was Jekyll's but instead of Hyde being named as sole beneficiary, his estate was being left to Utterson. Second, a document of explanation. A confession, if you will.'

The door opened behind Latimer at the far end where he'd entered the room. Enfield leaned forward, scowling. The door was shut fast. Distant hubbub; members waiting to return to their habitual seats, doubtless.

'Ignore them. There are other rooms where they may make their private complaints about my monopoly.' Enfield settled back into his chair. 'I cannot offer anything more than speculation about what I am about to tell you. Jekyll's confession was a simple one, though outlandish, and improbable. Nevertheless, it is one that fits all the facts. Jekyll had been conducting a series of experiments, and there was ample evidence to indicate such, over a series of years. Indeed, he'd had a falling out with his mentor, Lanyon, over the nature of the science he was pursuing.

'Jekyll claimed to be chasing a dream, though it turned into a nightmare, Doctor. In this dream, he wanted to be able to separate the baser instincts of man from his higher intellect. This was to be for no noble reason, no grand explanation of the Godlessness of the world, as adherents of Mr Darwin might have it, but so that he could be free. Jekyll always had a taste for the darker pleasures that life might afford, pleasures which as a man of the world I am sure you will understand if not concord with, might put a respectable man, a learned man with a professional and a social position of some remark, to shame if they were found out.

'Jekyll claimed to have devised a potion to this end, a treatment which, by its very imbibement would foreground these lustful imperatives and push into the background, those aspects of a man's integrity, perspective and, dare I say it, soul, that would inhibit him otherwise.

'He gave a name to this manifestation of his darker self. That name was Hyde. As Hyde, who gave the appearance of comparative youth, smallness, though also of some shifting disfigurement to his appearance, he took to the streets. In Hyde's name, he procured a second home in Soho, even had clothes fitted to the new body he would temporarily inhabit. After the incident with the girl, he also opened an account in the name of Hyde with several thousand deposited there so that future occasions of violence might be bought into silence.

'But, as Jekyll told it, the substances that he'd mixed to make this elixir were wanting. He spoke of some previously-unsuspected impurity in his original batch being the cause of the change. Further batches were ineffective. Worse, he was losing control of himself. Whereas once the potion's effects, in time, would wear off until the elixir were taken, his tolerance was corrupted and now he would merely have to rest his eyes and he would reawaken unbidden in the guise of Hyde.

'With the police in the form of an Inspector Newcomen about to bear down on him, Jekyll made the will alterations and transcribed the affidavit as I have just summarised. As for the body, yes it was that of Hyde, but as Jekyll told it, that was merely Jekyll transmuted. Some last force of will had presumably made Jekyll-as-Hyde choose a private death over a trial and execution, if not a more lingering demise as part of a medical examination of the changes he claimed to have wrought.

'You furrow your brow, Doctor. There is a little more. With the body of Hyde present, he was declared dead. Jekyll's will allowed for disappearance for a three-month period or death before his estate passed over to Utterson. In the event of it all, with Utterson being intimately involved as I have explained, it took something like four years for the matter to be unpicked. In the interim, the Hyde body was buried in a pauper's grave. Jekyll never resurfaced, though I do not understand the science of it, I am convinced that within Hyde's coffin lies Henry Jekyll, or at least what remains of him.

'So when you say that a will exists purporting to be that of Edward Hyde, though no such person ever existed, then that would be the one name certain to drive poor Utterson to a sudden death.'

Little of this made any real sense. Yes, there had been talk in the past of the possibility of a 'transforming draught' but it was a folly, little more than the modern-day equivalent of the medieval alchemists attempting to turn lead into gold.

'At any rate, there we have it. A good man turned

bad, and a better man has taken his own life as a consequence of the matter being dredged back up. I would never hear the name of Hyde spoken again.'

'So, you put this down to mischief-making?'

'I do, though I confess I cannot think of anyone who would wish distress on poor Gabriel.'

'Were there not claimants to the Jekyll inheritance at the time?'

'There was something of the sort. One or two came forwards claiming to be distant relatives, long-lost sons and the like, but their falsehoods were speedily determined.'

'And the monies?'

'They passed to Utterson, who administered them with the utmost probity and diligence. He never took a penny. You may have my oath up on it. With the sale of the house and after settling of some domestic accounts as well as making provision for Poole – that was Henry Jekyll's butler – and generous severance payments to the other staff, there was in the region of a quarter of a million pounds sterling to be dealt with. A sizeable sum now, and a fortune then. After some deliberation, the following solution was seized upon.

'It was apparent, through the testimony that you have now had related and in addition some diligent work through newspapers and police reports and the like, that there were all too many occasions where justice had not been seen to be done in our streets, and in particular in the poorer parishes. Now, I know what you are thinking Doctor, and I wish to halt you right there. This whole incident came to its climax in early 1885, a full three years before the Whitechapel horrors that caused so much scandal in the year of the so-called Jack the Ripper murders. There was no possibility of overlap between them. That being said, by the time the estate had cleared into Utterson's name, those hideous events had indeed taken place. It was clear, both in the generality of London and in the specifics of Brick Lane and its environs, that there was work to do, to whit relief for the poor, aid to the homeless and distressed, soup kitchens and a nurse or so on hand and the like. Basic clean lodgings where the sober unfortunate might lay their head while they gathered themselves anew.

'A charity was thus created, with the Jekyll monies put into trust and administered be a committee. A committee of which, I am proud to say, I sit upon, though I admit these days my input is not of the day to day variety. It was the best remedy we could devise and I think, one which Henry Jekyll might have once approved.

'We have premises in the East End and we ask but one thing. That people help themselves. I am no great Bible-reader, Latimer, but I am a believer in helping oneself. Drink is a luxury the poor can ill-afford. We hold to temperance rather than abstinence. Moderation in all things. That is all we ask, and it is all we might once have expected of poor Henry too.

'So there you have it. The tale of Henry Jekyll and the story of Edward Hyde. Hyde is a fiction, Doctor, a made-up name for a good man's darkest desires, desires so corrupt that they turned his very flesh.'

'It is, as you say, a fiction.'

'It is, though one that happened nevertheless. And we have another shadow of that untruth today. In this will, in Henry Jekyll's estate being put to some good use. The Hawksmoor Charitable Trust - named for the architect, who has some of his most notable work in the area, not far from Spitalfields Market - stands as testament to that.'

'That explains something at least,' Latimer said. 'One of the more minor mysteries.'

'How so?'

'I work in a charitable capacity – a half day a week, no more than that – at one of the Trust's missions. I spend my Saturday mornings there.'

'Do you now?' Enfield sat up, shifting forward so that

his bulk was on the edge of his chair. He offered by way of gesture, some more of the bourbon.

'Thank you, no. It is very good, by the way.'

'I'll have a bottle sent to you.'

'That would be a kindness.'

'It is the very least I can do for one of the Trust's soldiers.'

'I had wondered,' Latimer said, 'why Utterson had selected me to confirm his suspicions about his state of health. Well, I might not quite have the why, but now I know the how.'

'Word had got back to him about your volunteering?'

'That would seem to sit the facts.'

'And Gabriel had but a few weeks to live?'

'Yes.'

'Then perhaps this dreadful business has been of some use, if only in sparing him a drawn out and painful death.'

'I suppose.'

'I cannot pretend that I would have preferred to have met you under more pleasant circumstances, Doctor. But there you have it. The little secret that Utterson and I have held onto this last quarter century. As best you can, Doctor, dismiss this. I doubt we will ever have a satisfactory answer as to who introduced this fake will. Some former client, perhaps. But Gabriel is at last at peace, and that is all that matters. Again, my thanks to you, Doctor.'

Enfield stood, hand out to shake. Latimer rose, and took Enfield's right in his. Again, the little ring, incongruous against the bulky pale skin. Enfield's hand was warm, clammy. The handshake was firm enough though.

'Thank you, Doctor.' Enfield returned to the window and took his position as earlier, hands clasped behind his back, staring out of the first-floor window. Latimer left by the door he had come in by.

A cluster of members was in the corridor beyond the door, though each had assumed the posture of once not expecting the door to be opened at any time soon. Latimer's appearance caused something of a fluster, as the members, each of them not a day under sixty and each dressed in minute variations of the same cut and cloth of suit that Enfield wore, harrumphed their way past to retake their places.

Latimer took the great staircase back downstairs and walked straight out of the open front doors. He nodded at the doorman he'd seen on arrival, and received a careful tip of the hat in return.

The sun was low in the sky, but bright through the clouds. Great orange-yellow patches caught this building and that. The air was clear for once as well, not at all sooty or else filled with the rank clamour of the city. Perhaps a whiff of ozone, nothing more. Then again, he had not eaten since breakfast and the drink in his stomach was nagging at him. Something to settle him sooner rather than later was what was called for.

That said, there were still a couple of hours of business left in the day. Latimer began to walk, taking Pall Mall towards Trafalgar Square. He passed the Crimean War Memorial to his left, the three guardsmen statues below and the figure of Honour, her arms outstretched above them. Her shadow was long. It was unclear of this was meant to indicate to him safety from harm, or approaching darkness.

Latimer cast off the maudlin thought. Dismissing the notion as being provoked by the drink, he walked on, hands thrust in pockets. One minor mystery had been solved – that of Latimer's involvement in the first place. Another had some kind of solution proposed – in the outlandish story about this Hyde and this Jekyll. Latimer was certain that such transformative medicine was little more than poppycock, but he could not fathom why such a story should be created, unless it was to cover an even greater indignity. Abuse of drugs among doctors was not as rare as it ought to have been, and homosexuality was rather more common, and more readily accepted or at least tolerated, than polite society might openly admit. True, there was public humiliation and perhaps ostracisation to be faced. But these men were dead. There could be no shame now, twenty-five years after these supposed events. The crumb of comfort Enfield seemed to take in Utterson's swift despatch was nothing against first the enormity of Utterson's actions, and then the juxtaposition of that against someone else's fallibility, for it was not Utterson who had been brought to shame.

Possibilities entered Latimer's mind. What if there was more to this story? Was Jekyll procuring drugs that were being supplied to others, under the guise of medical treatments? Conceivable, certainly, though many curious preparations had been readily available over the pharmacist's counter in the 1880s, and the law on drugs had not changed substantially since that time. Chemists displayed the statute as it stood, the 1868 Pharmacy Act, which demanded that sales of poisons such as cyanide, prussic acid and arsenic were recorded by the vendor, and could only be sold by licensed druggists. Opium had not even been part of the original list of banned substances, having been added somewhat hastily later. No, this could not be a viable possibility, on reflection.

What if Utterson was merely at the end of his tether, and this was final straw, a little thing that spelled the end for him? That was perhaps more likely.

But even so. Neither of these felt right. A third possibility, however remote, was that Enfield's story was true, or at least enough of it was true for it to stand. Perhaps Jekyll, under the influence of a cocktail of drugs or not, was a violent and brutal creature, and that this whole 'Hyde' nonsense was little more than a cover for his own depravity. That made much more sense. 'Hyde' was a code-word, and not an especially subtle one at that, for activities best kept hidden, such as a prominent doctor's drug addiction and his concurrent propensity to violence. Prolonged abuse of many preparations would have a debilitating effect of one kind or another. Loss of weight, sallowness of skin, aches, fever, loss of teeth, lesions and abscesses. Above all, a hunger, a desperate urgency to have more of the drug that had once brought pleasure or ecstasy, but now which merely stemmed the tide of anguish and hurt.

In any of these instances though, the persona, if that was what the word to use for 'Hyde', would remain a secret, a private joke or a closeted skeleton. Few would know, and even fewer would be alive or be concerned enough to act in the century after these supposed acts had taken place.

And Latimer had been there. Had been called there.

His next step was clear to him. Latimer would call on Jasper Holcombe, and he would hear what the man had to say. Furthermore, he would call upon Holcombe now.

There was a National Telephone Company call box on the Duncannon Street side of Trafalgar Square. There being no directory inside the booth, Latimer rang through to the telephone operator. 'The number for Beech, Everdene and Holcombe, if you would.'

'One moment, caller.'

The telephone box throbbed with traffic noise. Motor cars, omnibuses and hansom cabs, petrol-driven taxi vehicles, a brewery wagon being drawn by a pair of dray horses. The eclectic fizzing of interference on the line. Then the operator's voice, garbled.

'I'm sorry, I didn't catch that.'

The number was repeated.

'And do you have the address there also?'

'Beech House, Chancery Lane.'

'Thank you.' Latimer rung off. He set off towards The Strand. The walk would take no more than twenty minutes. Calling on Holcombe without an appointment might be a little irregular, but regularity could go hang. And besides, Holcombe should be expecting some contact. To do otherwise would be naive.

Beech House was at the southern end of Chancery Lane, not far from the defunct Serjeants' Inn. The brass plate outside the building told him that there were several businesses devoted to the law here. That was only to be expected this close to the Royal Courts of Justice.

No doorman stood outside, but there was a staffed reception desk. The clerk beamed at Latimer as he approached.

'Jasper Holcombe, of Beech, Everdene and Holcombe.' Latimer gave his name.

The clerk used a telephone to enquire. He replaced the earpiece to its cradle and smiled again at Latimer. 'Second floor.' Another broad smile. Latimer took the elevator up.

Holcombe was waiting on the second-floor landing. 'Doctor Latimer, please come through.' He was led past a junior clerk on reception duties down a narrow hallway into a large room intended for meeting purposes rather than into an office. There was a bound folder of papers waiting on the table, together with two drinking glasses paired with glass-stoppered bottles of Malvern Water.

'Please.' Holcombe gestured for Latimer to be seated. The room had windows facing into a courtyard on one side. The other walls held portraits. Judging by the sequence and the shifting fashions and beard styles, they were company chairmen, partners or other directors going back to the foundation of the business, which Latimer estimated to be in the mid-1700s. A dozen baleful faces, each gazing back into the centre of the room.

Latimer took the envelope that Latimer had given him the day before, and he placed it on the table between them. 'Perhaps you can explain this.'

Holcombe busied himself opening the folder. He extracted several papers. 'You will appreciate,' he began, before pouring a glass of water. Did Latimer want a drink too? No, thank you. 'Appreciate, yes, that my role in this is simply in the execution of instructions, and that as such my-' a sip of the water '-my understanding of the client's wishes may be limited, so to speak.'

Holcombe kept his hand on the glass, holding it just off the table. The water inside rippled. As though sensing that he was giving his shaking away, he cupped the glass in his other hand.

'We have both been party to a shock,' Latimer said. He would get nowhere with the man by browbeating him. A softer approach was called for.

'Yes, indeed. Indeed.' A twitchy nodding.

'Perhaps we may conclude the matter, and so have to think no more upon it.'

'I quite agree. Yes.' Holcombe was now able to let go. Condensation mapped out finger marks on the outside of the glass. 'My apologies.'

'There's nothing to apologise for.' The clammy impressions remained.

Something clicked inside Holcombe, a change of gearing into work mode. 'First, the matter of the reading of the will from yesterday. The client instructions were explicit. They were strange, because they were standing instructions that had been left in trust some twenty-five years ago. A cause of some private discussion once upon a time within these walls and, I think it is fair to say, a matter that has provoked some unease in the past. Yet, as time went on, this account simply became another oddity. One of the quirks of the chambers, you might say, and perhaps not the strangest set of instructions we are abided to be mindful of.

'The instructions were as followed. That the will and its associated documents were to be delivered to Gabriel John Utterson of Gaunt Street at a point of our choosing when it was-,' the next word was chosen carefully, '-evident that his health was failing, and that he had but few weeks to live. If Utterson were to die suddenly, in an accident, for example, then there were other provisions made, provisions which need not now be entertained.'

'And you ascertained this "failing" how?'

'Through surveillance. Discreet and at a distance, but surveillance nevertheless. There is no reason now to pretty up the word.'

'Such an endeavour sounds expensive.'

Holcombe shrugged.

'And the will itself?'

'Yes. The will. Our client's instruction is for this to be passed this onto you.' A slim packet of papers, bound, waxed and sealed. Holcombe pushed the bundle forwards. Latimer took out his clasp knife and severed the strings keeping the papers together. There were two envelopes inside, plus a collection of loose clippings taken from newspapers. The newsprint was faded, yellowed. Dates from the mid-1880s. A range of accounts of unsolved murders, brutal night-time beatings, assaults of an unspecified, but evidently sexual nature. The final clipping in the assortment was a death notice. For a Dr Henry Jekyll. The date of death was given, a week before the date of insertion into the periodical. A private funeral had already taken place. There was nothing else.

The slimmer of the two envelopes was next. A knife was run along the top of the uppermost edge of the closure. A single sheet of paper, folded once, lay within. The paper was of good quality. The faintest scent of an astringent. Latimer unfolded the paper. He recognised the handwriting immediately.

My dearest fellow

If I read the future right, then you are a medical man, Utterson is dead, and you are most likely sat in a solicitor's office or meeting room.

Perhaps you have pieced the truth together already. Perhaps you have been told the truth - or an aspect of it -

but you do not credit it.

Hear me then, doctor. Bring your science to bear if you may. The short of it is plainly this; that Harry Jekyll unlocked himself through transformative medicine. I, Edward Hyde, am he, or at least the unbridled aspect of him.

He would murder me by taking his own life or by wrestling with my body with his mind. My time is short I fear. But I have lengthened it beyond the span of science. How did Crookback Richard put it in the Shakespeare? "Plots have I laid, inductions dangerous." My better part does not know the half of it. But you shall, dear doctor. As I taunted him in life shall I taunt you from the grave.

The packet contains a copy of his notes, his experiments, his findings and dosages. The newspaper items are from my own collection, to which should have been added the proof of Jekyll's demise, in whatsoever way it gets reported.

Know this, doctor. The science is right, though Jekyll reckoned on some impurity being the necessary ingredient, further supplies of which have eluded him to date. But such things may recur at any point, as you might appreciate.

As I said, these notes are not the only copy. I have made others. They are, by now, in the unsafest hands.

The red levels are rising, Doctor.

Your chum

Edward Hyde

Latimer read the letter twice, and then turned his attention towards the unopened packet. A glance inside confirmed what Hyde had written. The manila contained notebooks, loose sheets of scrawled annotated mixes and blends, all in Hyde's distinctive hand. The penmanship was rough, indicating that this had been done at speed. Some sections had been completed in pencil rather than in ink, making them faded and somewhat difficult to interpret. There was enough there, in the substances used, in the accuracy of the calculations and in the methodology to show plans that the originals had been the work of a methodical and determined brain.

The evidence of murder. The unsolved nature of the crimes. The ceasing of their reporting with the death of Jekyll. The assertion of the transformative potion. The rigorous experimentation. Latimer poured a glass and took a sip of the water.

He would not have credited it had he not seen the calculations. The mathematics was perfect. This was no elaborate hoax.

The implications were staggering. That Jekyll had found some means of triggering a transformation, unleashing a beast from within him. That he had been unable to control his creation, resulting in bloody murder and his own self-destruction. Worse, that this fell manifestation of his animal urges took control, exhibited agency, was independent and cunning enough to plan ahead, to seek an existence beyond his own destruction.

That was why Utterson had taken a pistol and inhaled a bullet. To have this brought back to him when near his deathbed was a further act of depravity. To live on with two cancers, one of the body and one of impotence, of guilty black knowledge. Oblivion was a rational choice in such a situation.

Hyde was a braggart, a selfish, preening child, even in death. So what had he sought to engineer? What had been done in his name, and by whom?

Nothing in the paperwork was of support here. No clues apart from that odd repeated phrase of Hyde's. *The red levels are rising.* It sounded like a cheapjack mystery phrase, an impressive-sounding bit of bluster. The Shakespeare had told him the same. But Latimer had known the sort in the Army, and more to the point, in the camps after the War. Bullying and cajoling, threats and swagger. They were bedfellows.

'There is one more matter,' Holcombe said. He took a bunch of keys out from a waistcoat pocket. The keys hung on a chain. 'If you would come with me.'

They left the meeting room, Holcombe locking the door behind them. Latimer was led back to the lift, which was summoned. In the elevator, Holcombe slid one of the chained keys into a discreet keyhole below the floor buttons on the control plate.

The wall of the lift opposite slid open, revealing another, shorter, corridor. 'Please follow me.' The air here was heavier, warmer. Latimer guessed he was in the windowless centre of the building. Two rooms off the corridor, one to the left, one to the right. Both were filled with deep shelving containing thick cardboard files of varying sizes. Each room was shelved from floor to ceiling. One worker, sleeves rolled, manoeuvred a trolley stacked with more of the card files. He nodded to Holcombe, who returned the acknowledgement.

At the end of the corridor, a door. An ordinary office-environment door. An entirely mundane door. Except for the twin locks to the centre.

Holcombe twisted a key from the looped metal securing it to the chain. From a pocket, he produced a slim length of steel about the size of a peashooter. He put the key to the steel. The two clicked together with a twist.

His colleague had joined him. His key already assembled, Latimer stood back as they inserted them into their chambers. The dull thudding of gearing mechanisms operating. A sharp snap. The door opened. There must have been some hydraulic or similar principle at work, as the door pivoted open under its own locomotion.

A curtain made of fine-worked steel rings. 'If you would wait a moment,' Lacombe said. Holcombe entered through the curtains, parting them with a hand.

Latimer had seen safety deposit boxes before. In Durban, he had rented one. The mesh made it difficult to see precisely what Holcombe was doing, though the principle was apparent. Someone had a box on deposit here, and something in that box was for Holcombe.

Holcombe returned with another envelope. This trusting to correspondence was beginning to weary Latimer. Why could not men speak plain to each other, and be assured that their word would hold and be accepted without written affidavit?

They returned to the meeting room. The letter was signed on the back of the envelope as being Utterson's handicraft. Another seal, sliced through. Latimer replaced the knife away safe before reading.

Inside was a key on a length of inch-wide red ribbon. It appeared designed to be worn around the neck, presumably under clothing. There was no note, no indication of what the key was to open.

Why would Utterson leave him a key? And a key for what?

Latimer voiced these questions to Holcombe, who could not provide an answer.

Latimer gathered up the sorted papers he'd accumulated.

'I could let you have a bag,' Holcombe said.

'Thank you, yes.'

Holcombe went off to fetch the bag. The key was ordinary enough. The kind one might own to open one's front door. It was new, or at least had been little used from new. Latimer dropped it into the packet of medical notes.

The bag Holcombe returned with was a satchel, the kind you might expect a well-to-do family to pack their son off to a minor public school with. Latimer fancied that this was Holcombe's own, and had seen just such service. The straps were well-worn and there were the colourless indentations indicative of gilt embossed initials long-since faded.

Latimer expressed thanks. They shook hands, a little diffidently. Holcombe gave the distinct impression of being relieved to be rid of the affair. No, there was no rush in returning the bag. Latimer wondered if Holcombe would prefer it if he never heard the words "Utterson" and "Latimer" ever again.

It was dark outside. Traffic was busy, this being, Latimer reckoned, the full of the evening rush hour. It was raining enough to ensure that there were no cabs to be had, and as Latimer was unsure of the omnibus routes hereabouts, he opted to make for the Underground. Temple was the nearest station. He made for the Embankment.

The newspaper sellers outside the station were full of three stories. Some ghoulish murder in the East End, the latest on recent moves to reform the House of Lords and on a forthcoming Official Secrets Act to replace the Act of 1889. Some speculation about the "real reasoning" behind the national census due to be taken in April.

One of the small pleasures, and indeed, one of the minor annoyances of living in a hotel, was that the newspapers were provided. Latimer could not recall the last time he had bought a fresh paper from a street vendor. Besides, if the rain, which was beginning to fall in ever-thicker droplets, was to continue, then he could employ the paper as a makeshift umbrella.

'One, please.'

'Cheers guv.' The seller dropped the coppers into a pouch at his hip. The pocket shuffled with coin. That was when Latimer saw the first one.

He was tall, which did not help him, too tall. And he was holding his own newspaper at an odd angle. For one, the evening rush hour was not a time of day to be loitering outside a tube station. What would there be to kill time waiting for? Either was on one's way home, or one was out for the evening. Second, the angle at which the newspaper was being held was all wrong. He looked, for the entire world, like a man using his Evening Standard as cover.

The second man was felt rather than seen. Whatever primitive instinct that allowed someone to understand that they were being surveilled had been ignited. A cold rush at the back of the neck. Latimer found him by tracking across using Tall Man's line of sight. A glance away from the underground entrance had become a signal, the eyes being reinforced by a flick of the now rolled-up paper. Man Two was in City clerk garb: Bowler hat and pinstripes. Umbrella but no bag. The disguise would have been effective but for the disjunctive between clothes and face. A thin face, smallpox scars. The gauntness under the cheeks Latimer associated with a mouth lacking either teeth or dentures.

Smallpox Man signalled to another. Who? Ah, there he was. Cap, corduroy jacket, a kerchief scarcely containing a neck as thick as a bull's. Bull Neck surged in.

Three men made sense. Two to tail Latimer across London and a series of thirds positioned at all times a couple of streets away. He had not seen that he was being followed earlier, so the initial presumption was that this had only just begun. He had been followed since leaving Holcombe.

The only thing that had changed about Latimer since then had been the acquisition of the documents in the satchel that Holcombe had let him borrow. His trackers were hardly being subtle.

Latimer turned into the tube station and bought a ticket. He went through the gates and began his descent to the trains. Any train would do. For a start, the station was busy enough at this time of day to make following someone difficult. The mere act of taking to the underground might be enough.

The idea was a good one, though he was not sure how effective it would be. The bag was desired - or, more strictly - its presumed contents were. So, Latimer had been under surveillance for some time. Since at least the day before and Utterson's death, he assumed.

Someone knew of the whole affair - of the rumours about Henry Jekyll and his magic potion, about the effect it had had, about Edward Hyde - and had seized the opportunity to learn more. Or else Holcombe's premises had been under watch, the assumption being that at some point there would be an exchange of documents.

The presence of a three-man team indicated organisation and planning. Resources. Intent. The immediate question was whether any of these three had sway over the others. Was one of them in charge? Were they hired hands with no cause or was there motivation here above and beyond their pay?

Latimer took the walkway through to the westbound trains. Footfall here was a little less than in the other direction, though there was still an abundance of commuters. He made his way along the platform to the far end, to where the driver's cab would pull up.

A train must just have left. The empty buffeting of the partial vacuum caused by the train's departure. The refilling platform. Diminishing echoes down the tunnel towards the next station.

Latimer checked the satchel. He swung it around so that it could be seen to be there, then brought it around to his right flank, where it would be obscured from sight down the platform. He felt inside the bag, checking that its contents were still there. He put all the loose papers inside the larger envelope.

A check back down the platform. Tall Man was obvious from the off, his neck craning back and forth. No sight of the others. Latimer had not been seen, not yet. But they would soon have him in their view.

Latimer finished his fiddling with the satchel. He stretched, as one might a tired office worker to do at the end of the day. He put the bag between his feet while he adjusted his posture, while he checked under his coat that his shirt was fully tucked in.

Movement to the left shadows in Latimer's peripheral vision. He turned, affecting disinterest. In the distance, the vibration of approaching rail traffic. Posters along the far side of the tunnel wall. Cigarettes, a new play by Mr Shaw, some patent medicine, a recruitment poster for the Navy.

Tall Man, two thirds of the way back along the platform, was facing clear in Latimer's direction. A ripple in the developing crown of waiting commuters. Bull Neck was pushing his way along the wall, causing first annoyance at the disturbance from other travellers followed by a retraction of their impatience when they saw who it was. Bull Neck was perhaps thirty paces away, moving faster now as the crows were thinned at this end of the platform. No sign of Smallpox Man. No, there he was, another ten yards back, on the open side of the platform, cutting in front of the waiting masses.

The train's rumble was increasing all the while. A shift of light. Perhaps thirty seconds until the train pulled into the platform. Latimer slung the satchel over his neck, and then adjusted the length of the strap. Better.

Bull Neck was in the clear, there being a mere handful of commuters this far down the platform. The train was breaking into the station. A glitter, low and to the left. Bull Neck had slipped something over his fist. A knuckle duster, its thick brass loop now prominent.

Smallpox Man was striding too, his gait keeping him apace with the train now alongside him. The squeal of brakes. Smallpox Man's arm outstretched, and into that extension a wooden handle appeared. A blade sprang out. Smallpox Man was all smiles. Behind him, Tall Man bisecting the crowd.

The train stopped. Doors opened, but at this time of day there was little disembarking to be had. The front carriage was neither full nor empty. Latimer made his decision.

'The bag, if you please.' Smallpox Man lisped when he spoke. *Pleathe.* A sneer in the sound too. He intended the words to menace.

Latimer ignored the demand, and boarded the train. A shout from further along the platform. The Tall Man, cutting across to find a way into a carriage.

Latimer pulled the door to close it behind him, but Smallpox Man had his free hand on the other side. A struggle here would be unproductive. Too many other passengers about. Latimer stepped back into the centre of the carriage. Smallpox Man boarded, followed by Bull Neck.

The train started, the little electric ripple juddering the passengers. Bull Neck stumbled back, his hand pocketed to conceal the brass knuckles. The lack of purchase made him vulnerable. He twisted as he fell, feet tangling over each other. An elderly gent was up in no time to offer assistance. Smallpox Man stepped closer to Latimer. A glimpse of the shielded blade.

The train rattled through the tunnels. In a few seconds' time, they would be at the next station. Latimer positioned himself by the next door along. Bull Neck was still struggling with his hand being wedged in his pocket, with the old toff fussing around him. From the other side, there was no sign of Tall Man. He must have been further down the train somewhere.

They were slowing. Smallpox Man edged in. Bull Neck was upright again and free of the unwanted assistance. Light up ahead, and now to the side. The platform, full of faces. Charing Cross station signage.

Latimer reached out for the nearest exit handle. He gripped the brass as the train ceased its movement.

Smallpox Man realised what Latimer was about to do. He backed up, bundling Bull Neck back into the gent.

'I say!'

Latimer got out fast. He held the door open behind him. Inside the carriage and Smallpox was at the front-most door. He got half out. One foot on the platform edge, one still in the train. Bull Neck was stuck behind him, his way through to Latimer's door blocked by incoming passengers.

If Latimer let go, then he and Smallpox Man would be left alone on the platform. Bull Neck was out of the equation. Tall Man was somewhere lost behind. He could be dismissed too.

A whistle. 'Doors!'

Latimer unloosed the satchel. He stepped back in.

A second whistle. Smallpox Man anticipated the move, and was already inside the carriage.

But Latimer had not shut the door behind. The train shivered, about to move off. Back out onto the platform, the train shifting as the door trailed behind him.

Smallpox moved in response, but stopped as he saw. Holding it high so that he could be seen, Latimer threw the satchel back into the carriage, turned and walked away. He could not resist turning to see. Smallpox Man striding down the train, moving in opposition to the vehicle as though he was treading water. The bag being ripped open. And then the silent howl of rage as he realised that the bag held nothing more than that day's Evening Standard.

The train disappeared into the black beyond. Latimer put his hand to his back, checking that the bundle of papers he'd stuffed into his waistband under his coat at Temple was secure. It was.

He walked on, past a grumbling station attendant. He paid the man no heed. A tumble of fast calculations: the next station was Westminster. A good half mile away. Five, ten minutes to get a train back. Ten to fifteen to retrace their steps at surface level. The chase was over for them.

Latimer took the interchange walkway between the District service and the newer Baker Street and Waterloo service. He would take their new Embankment station exit onto Villiers Street. From there he'd lose himself in central London.

He turned a corner and the Tall Man was there. He was scouting about, evidently unsure if Latimer had stayed on the train or not. Two options presented themselves. One: Latimer could retreat and take another train away from here. The downside of that plan was that it was possible that Bull Neck and the Smallpox Man might return before he was away and luck upon him. Two: that he find a way past.

An alcove up ahead, equidistant between Latimer and the Tall Man. No, another passageway, not in use. It was gated off with concertinaed metal, but the gate was recessed. Not easily seen, perhaps, if one were in a crowd and was looking for a someone, not a somewhere.

Latimer got to the turning and faked hurrying, stumbling into a commuter coming the other way.

'Watch out, oaf!'

The Tall Man swung round. Latimer shifted, slow enough to be seen, into the alcove. He tucked his keys into his fist, turning the flesh into a metal-studded ball.

A dark swish – the Tall Man looping round into the cubbyhole, arm already out – and Latimer stepped into the punch. He drove his fist, keys and all, into the Tall Man's midriff.

The Tall Man buckled. Something dropped from his hand, then hung in mid-air. A cosh, secreted up the sleeve and attached by a leather thong around the wrist. Latimer put his other hand up to steady him. A passer-by might have thought he was holding up a drunk friend.

A second punch. This time, Latimer twisted his wrist on impact. A ripping noise. Jagged metal through cotton. A follow-up was unnecessary. The Tall Man slid down the tiled wall behind him till he was hunched, his gangly legs bent at the knees, on the floor. Latimer blocked this sight from the waves of commuters.

The Tall Man's breath was shallow, rapid. He stared sightlessly ahead. His clothing gaped open. A dark inky splatter where he had been struck.

Latimer hunkered down. He flapped the man's coat over the wound so it would not be seen. 'Who are you working for?'

No response. Latimer pressed down on the wound area. The Tall Man grunted. Latimer repeated the question. Clarity reasserted itself in the hurt man's face. 'Fuck off.'

Latimer selected a key and jabbed it up the Tall Man's left nostril. He clamped his other hand over his mouth. 'Last chance.' He ran the serrated length of the key against the nasal cavity.

'Leave it!' Muscle relaxation followed. 'All right. All right!'

Latimer extracted the key. He wiped blood and mucus from it onto the slumped man's collar.

'So?'

'No idea. Just a hired man. Paid by the day. Good money, no questions.'

'Paid to do what?'

'Just to follow. Observe and report.'

'For how long? How long have you been following me?'

'Just today.'

'Hired by whom?' The Tall Man shook his head. 'By whom?'

The Tall Man shifted as though he was about to stand, but Latimer seized his face and cracked his head into the tiles behind. The muffled thump was followed by a groan.

'Enough. Pocket. Look in the pocket.'

Latimer found a five-pound note. There was some loose change also, but he did not bother with it. Then something else. A lead toy, either crudely cast or worn from age. Perhaps an inch in height. A flat-bed railway cart or similar, on which was perched a domed carriage. He checked the money for writing. There was nothing other than what was printed on the paper.

'Other pocket.' A hip flask. Small enough to only hold about two fluid ounces. It seemed hardly worth bothering with. 'A drink, yes. And then I'll tell you.'

Latimer handed him the flask and let him take his refreshment. The fight had gone out of the man. The shaking of his hands showed as much.

As the Tall Man fumbled with the stopper, Latimer

examined the lead figure some more. 'What's the meaning of this?' The toy had once been finely worked, and though details had been lost through time there was enough to give the figure a feel of the Orient. It spoke of India. Perhaps this man had served there, or had once visited. A childhood gift perhaps, held as a lucky charm or else a love token.

'Oh that,' the man smiled, blood showing between his teeth. He raised the flask to his lips. The closure dandled on a cord at the bottle's neck. 'Why, that's the juggernaut.' He sipped. Then, rethinking his thirst, he drank deeper. Latimer caught a whiff of the liquid. The liquor smelt strange - aromatic, foreign - in the enclosed space.

'That's enough. Tell me who you're working for.'

The Tall Man closed his eyes, letting the drink burn its way down into his belly. He stoppered the flask. His hands were no longer shaking.

Whip-smart, the Tall Man turned to Latimer. When his eyes opened, they were not just clear; they were glittering. They shone red as though the irises had been replaced with rubies. The Tall Man grinned, his teeth now sluiced of the blood from before. He was up onto his haunches, rising over Latimer.

Latimer put a hand out to balance himself as he got up too, but he was too slow. It was as though the draught of drink had invigorated the man. He was up and stretching out. He seemed even taller, as if he were growing in front of Latimer's eyes. A hand to the still-damp tear in his belly. Clotting globules of red on his hand. A taste to the lips. A smile.

This was out of control. Latimer had no leverage here. He bunched the keys around the little lead toy to make a fresh fist, but the Tall Man was fast. Too fast. He snatched Latimer's wrist and pinned it back against the wall. He leaned in close. 'You'll see me again,' he said. His face was twitching as he spoke. 'And then you'll see me again.' Ants under the skin. Worms in the blood. Again, the sweet exotic scent from the liquor. 'And I'll be the man to make one of those occasions our final meeting.'

The Tall Man's eyes widened. Again, the ruby gleam, the tiny pupils accentuating the colour. He gasped, and with a burst of strength Latimer was unprepared for, lifted him up by the wrist and hurled him into the metal grille behind.

Latimer clattered to the floor. A swish of coat and the Tall Man was already gone.

He scrabbled to regain the keys, dropped in his fall. With them was the lead figure, upright on its moulded wheels. Latimer scooped them all up and stood. He did so awkwardly, and then remembered the reason why. The papers he'd taken from the satchel were still stuffed into the waistband of his trousers. They'd given his back a little protection when he'd been thrown.

The commuter traffic was dwindling, but the studied incuriosity of the Underground traveller held fast. No-one paid him any mind as Latimer adjusted his clothing, re-joined the main thoroughfare, and made for the Villiers Street exit.

#

Latimer zigzagged through the city streets until he was certain that he was no longer being followed. He happened upon a chop house and, seeing over the engraved lower portion of its front windows that much of the seating was enclosed in booths, entered.

'What can we get yer?' His waitress was red-faced, round, tired around the eyes. Her hands were as scalded as her cheeks. She held a nub of pencil and a note pad. 'Specials is liver and bacon, fried fish, ham and parsley sauce, beef and ale pie.'

'The pie.'

'Mash?'

'Please.'

'And a drink?'

Tea. Tea was what he wanted, sweet and bland, but

none of the other patrons - all male, each eating alone - was drinking from a cup. 'A bottle of your best.'

The waitress left. Latimer reached behind and took out the papers. He spread them out on the table.

A shadow. The waitress, leaving the drink. She was gone before Latimer could offer any thanks. The place was busy. Men in and out. Eating, swigging the last of their beer, moving on. Condensation on the windows. Cooking smells – gravy, meat being fried – and the clatter of cutlery being used and washed pots being stacked.

Latimer poured from bottle to glass and took a taste of the beer. He found himself thirsty. The beer was good. Notting Hill Brewery Company's "Sparkling Dinner Ale". He turned his attention back to the papers. As he'd previously noticed when back at the solicitors' offices, the work seemed comprehensive and accurate. There was a logic to the process. The method appeared solid. Yet there was also another story; that of diminishing returns over times. Jekyll had battled with the formulae, had increased the doses over time to achieve his intended effects. There was evidence also of an increasingly urgent search for materials, compounds which would replicate the original experiment data.

The outcome, though. That was the nub of this matter. It was evident from the mass of time, effort and monies expended and here documented, that Jekyll had believed in his work. It was clear also that he had become a slave to it. The truth of the serum he concocted or not was not to be found here, but the truth of at least one level of addiction – to the work – was undeniable.

'Here you go.' The waitress placed a full plate onto the table. She took a knife and fork wrapped in a napkin from a pouch in her apron. 'You after a refill?' The pint had been all but finished.

Latimer smiled thanks. 'If you would.'

'Right you are.'

Latimer stacked the papers up at the far end of the

table and drew the meal closer. He tested the mashed potatoes. They were better than he was expecting, being blended with butter and milk, not thinned out with water as he had been anticipating. The pie, hot and rich, was full of chunks of meat and potato with thick gravy. He found himself hungry, the emotion spurred on by the presence of the food.

The second pint bottle arrived, the waitress leaving behind the jotted note from earlier to act as a bill.

Latimer thought as he ate. Discarding for the moment any notion of the truth to Jekyll's work, it was evident that he had believed in it, enough to cause his own self-destruction. His mania had perhaps led to some kind of mental illness, resulting in this Hyde persona. As Hyde he'd either called out for help, or more likely, by blaming the conjured Hyde, he protected his fragile mind from the damage he'd done to himself through his drug experiments.

The damage done – or perhaps the havoc created by Jekyll while in the grip of the drug, or its attendant madness - had long-lasting effects. Utterson's withdrawal from society, perhaps, and almost certainly his reticence to deal with doctors. The whole Jekyll and Hyde affair had affected him deeply; a secret that he had perhaps always dreaded would be rediscovered. Utterson felt guilt for his friend's death. Suicide had been preferable to living, if only for a few months, with that renewed knowledge. Perhaps he had always intended to take his own life, and the mention of Edward Hyde had been the proverbial straw.

The Hyde communications were further evidence of the madness. As Hyde, Jekyll had left all manner of ravings, letters, goadings. The papers that had been left with the solicitors and the notes that had come to Latimer were all elements of this. It was not inconceivable that they were part of an attempt by Jekyll to be noticed, for help to come to him before it was too late. But instead, the legal people had acted will dull efficiency rather than communicating discreetly if improperly with their colleague in law Utterson that Henry Jekyll was not himself.

That seemed to provide an adequate explanation for the matter. Latimer finished the pie and drank some more of the beer. There was too much mash, but that was part of the appeal of these places, he supposed. Decent plain hot food and plenty of it.

He returned attention to the papers. He had been followed from at least Holcombe's office. So, others were aware, or at least suspected, that these papers were in existence and had some potential value.

Holcombe had admitted that his company had been using private detectives to keep an eye on Utterson. But if their own surveillance was in place, then why have Latimer followed? It was known where he lived and worked, and it was known what he had been given by Holcombe. So, would the same people follow him, and to what end?

Options crowded in. One. That Holcombe – alone or with others in the offices – had knowledge of the worth of Jekyll's documents and wanted them for themselves. That did not sound likely. The papers had been in their safe keeping for a quarter of a century. Why not simply have them transcribed at some point in that period? Perhaps the opportunity had not afforded itself, or perhaps this was a recent revelation. Who knew, after all, how many letters with Edward Hyde's signature had come to light with the passing of Utterson?

An alternative idea pressed forward. That this was independent action taken by the people engaged by the solicitors. Between themselves they'd decided that this running about was for some purpose with money behind it, and that they wanted their share. Presumably by seizing and ransoming back the documents, Latimer supposed. That sounded outlandish, but it had to be considered.

A third possibility was that another party already had a copy of Jekyll's notes – hadn't Hyde (not that his word could be relied upon in any way) said so himself? – and that they wished to retain their exclusivity.

A fourth and simpler version muscled through. That someone else indeed wanted Jekyll's notes, had an inkling where they might be (a straightforward assumption might have been that his old friend Utterson had been trusted at some point with them), and was now putting considerable effort into gaining for themselves a copy. Having the notes in the wild, as it were, instead of within the bank-like vaults of Beech, Everdene and Holcombe presented such a chance.

Who could this "someone else" be though? Latimer had no idea. So long had passed since Jekyll's death that it scarcely seemed credible that the opportunity to gain his papers was still sought by someone who was aware of what was supposedly going on at the time.

And to what end?

The first possibility had been that Jekyll has stumbled across – or, Latimer admitted had been successful in his deliberations in – some substance with value. This transformative medicine notion was incredible, so it had to be something else. New drugs were being developed all the time and pharmaceuticals was big business the world over. Maybe there was something else here that a chemist could determine but a relative layman like Latimer did not fathom.

The second option, and a more dangerous one in Latimer's mind, was that this was action without clear understanding of what was being sought. Maybe there had been rumours in the medical and chemical communities of a something that Jekyll had possessed the secret of, but that they had no detail. There was ample paperwork to show that Jekyll had been scouring the wholesalers and importers for a range of materials. Perhaps these others had been trying to reconstruct his work from a distance, working only from perhaps incomplete records of transactions made in his name. That those experiments had yielded nothing of import and thus his notes were the fresh target.

Perhaps. That word over and over.

If only he had got something out of the Tall Man. But he had left Latimer with nothing at all.

No. That wasn't quite true. He retrieved the lead toy, standing it up on top of the sheaf of papers.

The waitress was back once more. 'You after another, then?'

'Thanks, no. I'll be off in a minute.'

'Take your time, love.' She was les flushed than before and Latimer could see beyond her that the place had thinned out. 'Closing in half an hour, mind.'

She picked up the plate with the used cutlery. 'Juggernaut,' she said.

'Excuse me?'

'Juggernaut. Your little boy's, is it?'

'Oh. Yes.' The lie came easy.

'They soon grow up though, don't they?'

'I suppose so.'

'Mind you, they'll soon be everywhere, won't they?'

'I'm sorry?'

'Those little things. All over the place, they'll be.'

'The juggernauts?'

'Oh, yes.' She smiled. 'You look like you haven't heard about them.'

'No.' What was she going on about?

'Give it a couple of days. You'll see. Everywhere. Proper nine days' wonder it'll be, you mark me.'

She was gone with the plate, being called over by one of the few remaining customers. A heavyset man loomed from a rear door. A cold rush of air came with him. The man passed Latimer heading to the front of the premises. Latimer took the moment. He picked up the papers, left money by the bill plus a shilling tip, and headed to the back. He cut through into a kitchen, a second room beyond that stacked high with crates of bottles, bakery trays and sacks of vegetables and out into an alleyway.

Juggernaut. The name stabbed at him again.

Latimer walked on, cutting through side streets and more alleys until he found a landmark. The Lyric on Shaftesbury Avenue. That operetta was still running. *The Chocolate Soldier*. He'd seen the Shaw original *Arms and The Man* years ago, but musical theatre was not to his taste. Then again, what had seemed as light comedy with a good heart when he'd seen the Shaw would have played as hollow farce to him now. War only made amusement for those who'd not experienced it for themselves. Latimer had seen much since those days.

The pavements and the road were equally busy with theatre traffic and diners stepping out. The ordinary reality of the city's bustle brought him out of his thought processes. There would be no thinking here. Latimer elected to continue heading north away from the nightlife. He'd go as far as Oxford Street.

On the way, he found a stationer still open and purchased a document file, some string and brown paper. The papers - the bulk of them, together with a covering note - went inside the file. He borrowed a pen from the proprietor while he made his package up on the counter. Latimer addressed the package to Doyle at his surgery.

'Could you do me a favour?'

'You'd like me to despatch your parcel?'

'If it's no trouble.'

'None at all.' Latimer gave instructions for the package to be held until Monday, and then sent on by hansom. The storekeeper named a reasonable sum, which Latimer paid out, with a small gratuity.

He carried on towards Oxford Street. The securing of the papers felt like a burden released. There was little more he could decipher from Jekyll's records to his experimentations and the safest thing seemed to be as far away from the documents as possible for the time being. The new week would provide its own solutions.

Besides, if he were to be under surveillance, best that he did not have the documents that these people – whoever they were – were after. Irrespective of their motives it was only right to deprive them of their goals. He doubted that searches would be made of either his hotel or the surgery, but one could not be too careful, and there was nowhere or no-one else he could safely have left the papers.

That last point gave Latimer pause. For too long he had made a virtue of being anonymous in the city. He had kept himself to himself perhaps too successfully. Now, at a point in time when someone in his corner might have been advantage, there was no-one he could safely call upon. There was Maureen Doyle, of course, but he would not have Doyle put in any danger. It would have been a mistake and a breach of their mutual trust if he had visited Doyle at her home and pressed the documents into the household's care.

He would carry on as normal. As normal as he could. The weekend would go as planned.

He had work to do though. Latimer had retained the newspaper clippings. He wanted to read more of these events for himself. He would come at these events from another angle and see what arose from that fresh approach.

It occurred to Latimer that he was now not far from his offices. He crossed Oxford Street and headed on north, up Regent Street and left into Cavendish Square. There was a man loitering by the next turning, Chandos Street.

He was too far off for Latimer to make much out about him, but it was evidence enough that he was being watched. Latimer headed back to Oxford Street. There would be someone at the hotel. Then again, it would be more suspicious to not return to the hotel than to do so, and he could legitimately, if pressed, say he did not have the documents.

Not that he would have them over if he had them.

Latimer wanted to know. Who was after this information? What did they expect to find? Was he right in his thinking about a secret so terrible that it would drive a man stoic enough to withstand cancer without complaint to suicide?

He resolved to know. And he would start at the very beginning. With the newspaper reports. With the names of the dead. Under streetlights outside Oxford Circus he rifled through the cuttings, committing names to memory. Not all the crimes had victims identified, and some of the occurrences were coded as to their precise natures, but the meaning was clear. Through the mid-1880s there had been an eruption of violence across London. An eruption that ceased, so the newspaper clippings implied though their juxtaposition with the experimentation data, with the death of Jekyll. One name was key here. One murder stood out among the others. That of the Member of Parliament, Danvers Carew.

Latimer went to find a policeman. He had an idea where to find one.

#

'Any messages for me?'

The reed-thin lad checked over his shoulder, but by the empty cubbyhole, Latimer already knew the answer. 'No sir.'

'Thank you...'

'Albert, sir.'

'Albert, yes. Thanks again.'

'Oh, sir.'

'Yes?'

'There's a gentleman in the lounge. He's been there an hour or more. I did offer him refreshment earlier, sir, but he said no thank you and that he was happy to wait. Never said who for, mind.'

'Oh? Thank you, Albert. I'll look in to see if it's who I think it might be.'

'Very good, Doctor. Will you be dining with us this evening? I can have your usual table reserved or something brought to your room if you'd prefer.'

'That's very kind, but I've already eaten.'

'Very good, Doctor.'

Latimer nodded in passing at one of the duffers who also resided here, then walked into the lounge. As he thought might be the case, there was Spencer Mosley.

The lounge served as library, smoking room and informal meeting area. Mosley was browsing the shelves, his back to the entrance. He reached for a volume and slid it from the bookcase.

'Detective.'

The smile was already in place by the time Mosley turned around. 'Doctor. Evening.' He indicated the book. 'Tennyson. Are you a poetry man?'

'I can't say that I am.'

'Me neither, but as I get older, I find myself nostalgic. My father, rest him, was a one for the poets. That was what we got instead of bedtime stories. Of course, he'd skip bits and jolly things along and half the time me and my brothers didn't know what we were being read, or often as not, recited from memory, but we got it all. The Greeks and the Romans, a Bowdlerised version of Chaucer. Shakespeare, of course. Spenser. Milton, or bits at least. Some of the Romantics. Most of all though, he loved to give us a thick slice of old Alfred here. At the time, I didn't care for the words, but what I loved was the time he took with us. Now, of course, he's long dead and deep gone, and I find it's the poetry I turn back to. Last time I saw him, in the sanatorium, he had some poems to hand. Kipling. *The Seven Seas*. You know it?'

'Kipling's not to my taste.'

'Oh?'

'Simplistic stuff. Naive.'

'A man who's never tasted real war?'

'Something along those lines.'

'At least he's not dull old Alfred Austin.'

'I suppose not.' The current poet laureate was, it seemed, to all too few people's tastes.

'Thank you, Doctor. It perhaps won't surprise you to hear that I don't often get to reminisce about poetry with my colleagues. You're being watched, you know.'

The abrupt shift in the conversation should have been anticipated. Latimer realised this a breath too late. Some tactic they taught when questioning suspects, doubtless. Appear to be open and conversational. Establish trust by giving some little piece of plausible-sounding personal information. Engage the subject in the discussion until their guard is down, and then spring.

There was no avoiding the topic. 'I saw him too. Across the street, not making too much of an effort to remain inconspicuous.' Latimer thought it prudent to reveal that his surgery was also being watched.

'You're a man in demand, it seems. Or at least you're thought to be in possession of something that's wanted.'

'I think I know what is?'

'Care to tell me?'

Latimer nodded. 'I was rather hoping you'd be interested to hear. I might, it appears, need your help.'

'That is, of course, what the police are here for.'

After having removed his coat and requested coffee and a brandy – Mosley accepted a coffee also, though declined the alcohol – Latimer and the detective took seats in the quietest corner of the room. This was furthest from the fire, and there was something of a draught, but there was no chance of their being overheard by the room's other two occupants, both long-term residents, and both the kind of elderly single gentlemen who preferred to dress for dinner, and who liked to take their port and cigar with a newspaper and silence.

The drinks having been delivered, Latimer began. The art in a lie, he knew, was to remain as close to the truth as possible. 'This began with Utterson yesterday. I may not have been wholly straightforward with you then, but as you'll appreciate I had my reasons.'

Mosley said nothing, but sat back with a half-smile that might have been either agreeable and interested, or somehow victorious.

'Utterson, it seems, was the victim of something of a prank. A prank that goes back a quarter of a century. He was, as you must surely know, one a friend of a well-respected doctor-'

'Henry Jekyll.' The smile did not waver.

'-who was implicated in a series of crimes through his association with another,' Latimer paused, expecting the detective to interject again. He did not, though, and so Latimer continued. 'One Edward Hyde. Hyde brought ruin on Jekyll. Hyde died, and Jekyll vanished.' Here the approximation of the truth gave way to fresh fantasy. 'The assumption is that, remorseful of his association with Hyde, he absented himself from London and quite probably England. He had money, quite a substantial sum. Jekyll had left conflicting instructions by way of wills. First, to leave his estate to Hyde, and then to Utterson. Utterson had administered the estate since, directing it towards charitable ends.'

'The Hawksmoor Trust.'

Latimer poured a little brandy into his coffee. He hoped the action would provoke the idea that he was at ease, relaxed, confiding in a new associate. 'Yes.'

'And what of yesterday?'

'This is what I believe, detective.'

'Mosley will do just fine. I rather think that I prefer it to my Christian name.'

'Mosley.' The detective exuded little warmth. 'I work for The Hawksmoor Trust. That is, I volunteer my services for a couple of hours a week in a pro-bono capacity at one of the missions in the East End.'

'Very noble.'

'In truth, Mosley, my work taxes me little and it well –

paid enough for me to live in some comfort. So I offered my service. A couple of hours a week of honest doctoring.'

'It eases the guilt I suppose.'

'I'm not sure that 'guilt' is the word I'd have used, but there is that element. The point is that this is how I came to be involved. I did not know at the time of Utterson's existence and when he originally procured me as his doctor I had assumed it was out of recommendation from a colleague of his. The Jekyll affair had left him, perhaps understandably, reticent to deal with medical men. I was chosen not because I was known to him or because I had a reputation as a good medic, but because I had shown, though my time at the mission, that I was someone who could be trusted, I suppose.'

'And now what do you think?' Mosley asked the question in a manner so languid that there had to be a hidden tension.

'I think that there are others – I don't know who – who believe elements of the Jekyll stories. That there is a fortune being held in trust, for one. A quarter of a million is an immense sum now, but over twenty-five years ago it would have been prodigious. Utterson struck me as someone who was never less than both cautious and diligent. The Trust has not expended its monies on impressive buildings nor on society extravagances being passed off as fundraising galas. I have no doubt whatsoever that the bulk of Jekyll's estate remains unspent, and would imagine that prudent investment and interest accrued has swelled the sum. Doubtless Utterson has suffered false claimants to a supposed inheritance in the past.'

'Doubtless.'

'Rumours have swirled about the precise nature of the relationship between Jekyll and Edward Hyde. Jekyll has not been seen since Hyde's body was found. Innuendo and speculation, even after all these years, is perhaps inevitable.'

'And what do you think, Doctor?'

'Latimer, please. Doctor sounds so formal.'

Mosley nodded at the small familiarity. 'Latimer.'

'I think that,' Latimer pushed himself forwards in his chair, so that he was sitting more upright, 'that this is what has occurred. Holcombe told me that he had arranged for Utterson to be kept under discreet watch, so that the Hyde will could be delivered to him in a manner specified. I was brought along because of the same specification. The will – which was never read – I would imagine was another attempt to inveigle Jekyll's estate from the hands of the Trust and that there were threats contained therein by which to goad poor Utterson with. In the end, what happened was that Utterson's spark, his will, his composure, call it what you will, gave out and he ended his life at the mere mention of Edward Hyde's name.

'I think that, now understanding that there's a chance of a fortune to be had, either the people engaged by Holcombe to watch Utterson are acting under their own initiative rather than under solicitor instruction, or that one of them had let slip what he was tasked to accomplish, and others are acting under the same apprehension.

'Thus, the focus of their observation has been moved, with Utterson's death, from him to me.'

'That is fascinating.'

'I'm thinking out loud now, you understand.'

'Go on.'

'There may even be an idea that I am in some way now charged with administration of the Trust's assets-'

'Which you're not?'

'No. However, until such time as Utterson's own will is read, this might not become clear. I would assume that in whatever articles of incorporation or suchlike that would have been drafted at the time of the inauguration of the Trust, that the terms of reference are clear on who administers what, and what cosignatories are required for the distribution of assets. I can't see how matters would be otherwise. Utterson, I feel certain, would not have had it any other way.'

'That's a very progressive attitude.'

'You never met Gabriel Utterson.'

'Though I've met many a legal man, and many a board member of an educational or other charitable trust, and many a criminal. One wishes it was not always so, but one cannot always judge a man's character by the nature of his calling, nor by the highest good intentions of his profession.'

Latimer thought better than to challenge this last statement. 'So, there we have it. With Utterson's will reading the matter will become clear, and any persons seeking to profit from the proceeds of Henry Jekyll's estate will learn that there is nothing to be gained. The Trust will continue and, I hope, continue to do its good work.'

'Indeed so, though one would hope for a time when the poor did not have to rely on the charity of the wealthy, who often give so little and receive for themselves from the same pot, so much. Perhaps not in terms of gold, but in conscience salved, a pound expended is often returned fivefold to the giver.'

'There I cannot argue, and must admit myself to have at least in part a selfish motivation for the little I do.'

'Though to your credit you do that little, which is more than many.'

Latimer poured another coffee. Mosley declined again. The coffee was cooling in the pot, but it was by no means undrinkable, not least with a splash of brandy, which Latimer now added.

'And there we have it,' Mosley said. 'Though a watch on you remains.'

'I feel not for long. I assume there'll be a will reading soon, and then this will all go away, if those keeping an eye on me don't move on to more readily-profitable pastures by their own accord sooner.'

'Nevertheless, Latimer, you should take care.'

'I shall.'

'There we have it,' Mosley repeated. 'There was something you wished to raise with me, was there not?'

'There was.' Latimer felt relieved that the conversation shifted away from him and onto more neutral territory. He had kept to the truth, or at least a partial facsimile of it, and his suppositions were a plausible reading of the last day. He hoped this was enough to keep the detective mollified, and also to not only keep him away unless needed, but to bring him into Latimer's confidence so that his connections could be used to help Latimer unpuzzle this whole situation alone. Latimer took from his jacket the clippings he'd retained from the package of documents that had been bequeathed to him by Hyde.

'What's this?' Mosley leaned in as Latimer spread the bits of newsprint on the table between them.

'Evidence, of a sort.'

'From?' Mosley did not look up from the articles.

Latimer had already thought about how to bring this up. 'From Holcombe. Intended, I think, to give credence to the notion in the will reading that Hyde's violent predilections were known, or at least suspected, thus stigma attached to Jekyll's friendship.'

There were eight clippings altogether, from the most august to the most scurrilous and sensational newspapers. They were united, though, in their content. Each featured a violent attack, unprovoked, often though not exclusively at night. In each there was no reliable description of the assailant, or any mention of an arrest being made. The impact was of a series of such incidents over time, which the articles later in the time sequence did not hesitate to link together. The most prominent, in terms of coverage and because there was a still-unsolved murder at its heart, was The Times' reportage of the killing of Sir Danvers Carew.

'Murder,' Mosley said, at last. 'Often the simplest crime to solve. Seldom planned, for one. Crimes of passion, of drunkenness, of anger, impulse and stupidity, or of any combination of the above you care to devise. The murderer acts without thought to the consequences, both immediate and subsequent. A murder is reported, then so often we know who the suspect to be apprehended will be even before we reach the scene of the crime. A jealous spouse, a bitter love rival, the colleague or employee who feels slighted or betrayed. Someone who steals or who seeks revenge for being stolen from. Cause and effect, Latimer, the murder being the effect. Thus, if you know the cause, then the arrest will follow.

'But,' he said, pushing the Times article back towards Latimer, 'if the cause is a puzzle, then the murderer may all too easily go free. Take the Ripper murders. No link between the women except they were in reduced circumstances, lived off their wits on and off the streets and were from the same locality. No personal grudge or motive to be ascertained. No chain of evidence except the spilled blood they shared, no matter how the police and the press at the time, and since, plus who knows how many other amateurs, do-goodists, conspiracy seekers and ghouls have tied to make connection between them. To establish links to lead them to the criminal. But links there are none, causes there are none, except that those that might have resided in the mind of the blade-wielder.

'Such thinking does the ordinary man in the street no good. Events must have reasons. Reasons have consequences. Causes intimate that there are solutions. In your own line of work Doctor, do symptoms not indicate illnesses and thus to cures, medicines and other treatments?'

'They do,' Latimer replied.

'They do. But with the likes of Carew here, and these other poor souls, there is little or nothing to provoke such bloody retaliation. Thus, we are clueless, and the criminal absconds.'

'Carew's killer was never caught?'

'Never. He – if the killer be male, as one should never assume too much – was not found, and the witnesses, as the article outlines, were never mush assistance. One might conjecture from the time of death all manner of speculative possibilities, but that do not excuse murder surely. If a man, even such a respectable man as Carew was, is to be abroad in the earliest hours of the morning, what crime is it? His presence on the streets warrants no murder.

'A madman, some said, then and now. A lunatic. But to never be caught. There is reason there. Organisation of thought, Structure. Intent, perhaps, or at least guilty realisation and a sense of self-preservation, else a man would hand himself in to save his mortal soul at the expense of the rope.'

Mosley gathered the clippings into one untidy pile. 'The implication is that Hyde, or Jekyll, were responsible for these, and others unreported perhaps and that one covered for the other. Maybe so. There is nothing that can be done now.

'There can be for others, though,' Mosley continued. 'The newspapers tend not to report so much on the unresolved crime and, since the Ripper days, there having been no sequences to compare, there's little profit in reporting on acts less sensational than Saucy Jack's enterprises. There may be a mention, of course, but without an arrest and a name, there's no trial. Without a trial, no hanging. No end to the story. Better the story not be told at all, because it does not have a happy ending.

'I could tell you, Doctor, of the unsolved murders on file in the Yard. A number greater than you'll credit, I feel sure. Of the clusters of beatings and rapes, of the bloodshed for which there has been neither justice, nor which there may ever be. This is the new century's gift. That crime and punishment are no longer linked. And to that extent, if there's no-one to point and say loud to others that a crime has been committed, then is what's been done truly a crime if it has not been defined as such?'

'I'm no philosopher.'

'Nor I.'

Mosley's smile was more genuine now. 'I think we've come full circle.'

'This is what attracted you to Utterson's case?'

'It's certainly what holds me to it.'

'You're a man who likes reason.'

'I am.'

'So, what of Carew? I wondered, just, if there was a connection here. Something overlooked.'

'That this is done in Carew's name by a vengeful other?'

'A possibility.'

'And one I had not considered, but will do now. Thank you, Latimer.'

'Who will you ask?' Latimer raised a hand for attention and a waiter came over. 'Sure you won't join me in something?'

'Actually, I will. Coffee and a brandy.'

A waiter was summoned. 'For two, please.'

When the drinks had been delivered, Mosley took the lead in pouring them out. 'Mind if I keep these?' he said, indicating the clippings.

'Please.' Part of Latimer was glad to be rid of every scrap of paper to do with the situation. Not every scrap, he remembered. He still had the notes from Hyde. 'Who will you ask?'

'There's only one man for the job. Fred Abberline.'

'Abberline? I'd assumed that he had died.'

'Oh, quite the opposite. Living in Bournemouth these days. Retired, after a fashion. Worked for the Pinkerton people when he left the Yard. Travelled the world. Ended up as European bureau chief. Not bad for a West Country boy. He keeps his hand in, though. Cold cases we call them. Unsolved crimes. They dig at you, Latimer. They get under your skin. We've all got them. People we failed.

Killers who went uncaught. Puzzles still locked. Fred Abberline has two. The Ripper, as you might imagine. And Danvers Carew.'

The potential involvement of someone as pre-eminent as Frederick Abberline was both a blessing and a curse. A curse in that, unless Latimer was to work fast, he could get in the way of what Latimer wanted to do. A blessing in that the death of Utterson would doubtless reignite his interest in the case. Who knew what recollections, notes, eyewitness testimony Abberline might have access to. Then again, he must be an old man by now. Memories fade. The will contracts. Perhaps he would want nothing to do with this. Maybe he would be content to shuffle in his garden and tend his flowers.

'Would he be interested?'

'I can sure of that. I'll telegraph him in the morning. I'm sure of an almost immediate response.'

'Thank you.'

'All part of the great war against disorder, Doctor.' Mosley tasted his brandy for the first time. He looked around the room; the shelved books, the opulent seating, the tall marble fireplace. 'A man could become accustomed to this.'

'I agree.'

'But do you not find that in being sheltered from the world, that you no longer become part of it? That this is at best respite from the rigours of the working week and the still-young century?'

Latimer allowed a smile. 'Sometimes I think so. But other times I feel as though I've seen quite enough of the nineteen hundreds and I should be quite content to reside here.'

A second look around the room from Mosley. 'I should not be so content, I don't think. This is a holiday place, a museum even. Victoria's England, set in aspic. The world has moved on; don't you think? We've had the new Edwardian era, and with him dead and buried-' he raised his glass in a manner not entirely respectful '-and George soon to be crowned. Time marches, Latimer. Like an army. Though when an army marches there are inevitably victims. The war dead, the invalided out, civilians displaced, the domestic mourners.'

'I have done my soldiering.'

'South Africa, wasn't it?'

'How do you know?'

Mosley smiled that smile of his again. 'Nothing sinister, but we keep tabs on comings and goings to some extent. A friend of a friend might have lifted a file and left it where it could have been glanced through.'

Latimer's stomach curled. The brandy and coffee soured inside. 'Oh?'

'And it's all genial enough. As you say, you've done your fair share. And more besides. But can you not feel it, Latimer? The electricity in the air? The distant whiff of something sulphurous, like burning hair? The old certainties are no more, and there will be a reckoning.'

'For a policeman, you speak in riddles sometimes.'

'Forgive me. It's getting late. And I'm not much of a drinker. Put this down to the excellent spirits. And the company and surroundings, of course.' Mosley finished his glass and made to stand. Latimer rose with him.

'Thanks for the assistance, Mosley.'

'You keep a watch out for yourself, Latimer. You may well be right in thinking that your watchers will cause you no harm, but that's no reason to be complacent. As for myself, I'll contact Abberline and take matters from there. I'll be in touch.'

They shook hands and Latimer walked with the detective through into the reception area of the hotel. 'Weekend as usual?' Mosley asked.

'Yes. The mission in the morning and then here in the afternoon I should have thought. Perhaps a walk in Hyde Park on Sunday. Or a museum. This reminds me. There was one more thing, Detective.'

'Oh?'

The woman in the chop house. The lead figurine. The Tall Man's words when he bolted from Latimer in the tube station after taking that drink from his hipflask. 'Juggernaut. Does the word mean anything to you?'

'Juggernaut? Isn't there a Hindu god or suchlike called that? A heavy carriage with a shrine on top that people would either hurl themselves under in devotion or else it would crush the crowds in front of it through its immensity?'

'That was my recollection too.'

'Juggernaut. No, Doctor. But I'll bear the word in mind.' Mosley appeared quizzical; the expression then shifted back to its usual bland scrutiny. 'Good evening.'

'Good evening.'

#

Latimer took the decanter of brandy up to his room. He sat at the small table and stared at the small lead toy until it was past time to go to bed.

JUGGERNAUT: SATURDAY 18TH FEBRUARY 1911

Latimer returned to his room after breakfast. He was still a touch hung over from the previous evening. The kippers and poached eggs had done little to settle his stomach.

He pocketed the lead figure and then went to his wardrobe. He took out the presentation case from the States. Latimer shifted the empty decanter onto the windowsill so he had room on the table to make a fresh inspection. He opened the case. The two new pistols.

Latimer took the box of shells and one of the ammunition clips. He slid the magazine into the handgun. The metal gave a reassuring heavy click as it engaged. The gun went into his left hand outer coat pocket. Latimer poured a thick handful of the shells into his hand. These went into his right pocket. He fought the urge to check through the still-drawn curtains to see if there was anyone loitering outside for him. He would not be caught out again.

Suitably dressed, Latimer made to leave.

The weight of the weapon felt good. It pulled on his shoulder a little, but not much. There was nothing to evidence that he was armed.

Latimer took the stairs rather than wait for the lift. He slid his hand around the firearm's grip. An additional reassurance. Almost a seduction. It had been a long time since he had carried a weapon. It did not matter that this one was not loaded.

There was no-one evident outside. No spies abroad. That did not mean that they were not there though. Latimer crossed the road and made for the underground station.

He resurfaced at Aldgate East, passing under the shell of the burned-out building that had once been Toplis's Tobacco Manufactory. The ruined works glowered down. Latimer turned left into Whitechapel High Street and left again into Osborn Street. Brick Lane started a hundred yards ahead.

Observant Jews clustered around the entrance to the old Methodist church that had been converted into a synagogue. In years past the building had been a Nonconformist mission of some stripe, a holding place for worthies to try to get the growing Jewish population to convert to their form of Christianity. Another sign that London was changing. That the old certainties of the nineteenth century had been replaced by newer truths in the twentieth.

There were other signs too. Poverty was the principle here. There had always been poor people in the East End. A circling of rundown properties, hard but scarce work, desperation and at the same time a sense of community. That these were people, no matter what their backgrounds, creed or outlooks, who were together facing bigger enemies than the comparative window-dressing of sectarian division. Men minded their own, women minded their children, and the children minded for themselves and each other.

Latimer turned right into Chicksand Street. Already there was a queue outside. The mission building, a former brewery warehouse, there being much of a tradition of beer production hereabouts, did its best to stand. There were slates missing on its roof, and panes broken in upper storey windows. Perhaps a dozen young men milling about. Three women with babes over shoulders or strapped to their chests. Two children, each with field dressings of sorts holding arms in manner indicating they were shouldering breaks. Men with no obvious injury or disease.

These walking wounded were typical of Latimer's Saturday clientele.

Maureen Doyle was here already. She was sat at the kerbside in conversation with another woman, the latter with two toddlers in tow. The children were animated creatures, teasing each other with broken-off bits of wood, play-fighting and mock-jousting. 'Mrs Doyle.'

'Doctor. Good morning.'

Latimer tried the door. It stuck for a moment, making him think that it was locked, which would have been unusual. This was a door that was always open. And so it proved.

The ground floor of the old brewery warehouse was now a soup kitchen. There were cots along one wall for the destitute, and a broad wooden staircase to one side. At the far end, there were banners advocating temperance and Christian charity. The barn-like room was never warm, but it was dry and there was the prospect of a hot meal to those who needed it. Yes, there was often a price to pay in terms of having to listen to a little bit of well-meaning gospelling, but the pastor knew well enough not to force religion on people who did not warm to it.

Past the cots there were a series of alcoves. Little more than sheds set up indoors, but nevertheless one that served as an office and the other functioned well enough as a treatment room. It was there that Latimer went.

The treatment room had a desk, two chairs, one more of the cots, and a screen that would be pulled back for modesty's sake when a bodily inspection was warranted. There was also a locked cabinet that held paperwork and some basic medical supplies. Dressings, iodine and the like.

There had been a time when the overwhelming issue had been that of malnutrition and diseases whose root cause could be tracked back to a poor and inconsistent diet. But the soup kitchen's works seemed to be holding that at bay. At least in terms of patients presenting themselves to Latimer, that was. Yes, there were often venereal diseases and physical injuries – most connected to young men brawling or arguments getting out of hand, it appeared – but the Trust had been as good as its word in administering somewhat to the needs of the indigent or desperate of the area.

Latimer wondered what Henry Jekyll would have made of the ways in which his money had been expended. The doctor part of him would doubtless have approved, or at least have seen the sense in it. But the other side to him? What would he have made of that?

The materials checked and found to be to Latimer's satisfaction, he indicated to Doyle that the first of the patients should come forward. This was a girl, probably about twelve years, but sustained lack of reliable nutrition had left her undersized and, Latimer suspected, underdeveloped academically too. She could have passed for a child of eight or nine. Doyle made short notes on forms provided by the Trust. Though the stated aims of the mission were to administer to young men, a blind eye was employed on Saturday mornings and, Latimer supposed, throughout the rest of the week.

The girl was new to Latimer. A full record would need to be taken of her name, address and previous medical history. There being no previous notes to consult, Latimer asked her to tell him of all the times she could remember that she had been ill.

'I don't know that I can, doctor.'

'It's quite all right. Just what you can remember, my

dear.'

The girl glanced at Doyle, wariness evident in her eyes. 'I...'

Doyle stepped in. 'If it pleases you, Doctor, perhaps young Alice here might recount her history to me. Woman to woman, if you take my meaning.'

'Of course, nurse.' Latimer stepped out, leaving the two to it. There was no sense in having the child be embarrassed. Doubtless there were life lessons she had not yet been appraised of.

A delivery at the main doors. Crates of vegetables were being unloaded from a large barrow. Doing the unloading was Bhupinder Singh. Latimer went across.

'Sat Sri Akal.' God is the ultimate truth.

'Sat Sri Akal, Latimer.' Singh's smile split his greying beard. They shook hands and took the last of the boxes from the barrow across to the kitchen area. 'How goes the doctoring?'

'All well, thank you. How goes the building of the gurdwara?'

Singh had been part of a group recently arrived in London who, with support from some rich benefactor back in Punjab, was setting up what would be the first Sikh temple in London. Latimer had met many Sikhs in South Africa after the war. There were more of the turbaned heads distinctive to the Sikh faith evident in London in the last few months. Enough to make the sight something much more commonplace than it had been before Latimer had gone to Africa.

In some parts of London, anyway. Off Brick Lane, where the mix of peoples was as complex as any the capital had to offer, the sight of Bhupinder Singh was still enough to turn heads. Then again, he was an imposing figure, some six foot three, always clad in a good grey woollen suit, often as not with a work apron stretched over his frame.

'The temple goes well, but we are not yet ready to

open our doors. Until then, we must get by as best we can.'

'And I'm sure the Trust thanks you for your charity.'

'This? This is not charity. More of a welcome obligation.' The Sikh custom of *langar*, of providing a meal, had proved popular immediately elsewhere. Any reservations native Londoners might have had of the Sikhs had been swiftly overcome as first the food and then the open and real generosity of those who provided it had made itself apparent. The temple – the gurdwara – was to open in Putney, a part of the city unfamiliar to Latimer. He resolved to visit it once he had a reason to. In the meantime, the developing Sikh community had sought locations from which to provide their *langar* other than in Putney. Brick Lane had been an inevitable and wise choice.

'Nevertheless, it's well received.' The food was basic but filling, and tasty. The lack of meat in the Sikh diet was no issue – in fact, it was an advantage as it invited those who followed faiths with restrictions of one kind or another on the consumption of flesh - and there was both pleasure and novelty to be found in the vegetable curries offered, served with rice in a bowl or folded into a flatbread.

A second Sikh arrived – someone new to Latimer – with another barrow of supplies, but the doctor was called over by Doyle before he could make his acquaintance.

'If you could come and see, Doctor.'

A youth perched on the edge of the cot. He had taken off his shirt already. Doyle was bathing abrasions on his face. He had taken a few good punches and, judging by the way his knuckles were swollen, had given some back as well. A round bruise clouded over the young man's heart.

'This is Thomas, Doctor.'

Latimer nodded.

'Thomas. Let's get you checked out. If you could lift your arms, please. That's it. Thank you. Now I'm going to press slightly across your chest. To check if there are any breaks. If it hurts, you say so.'

Latimer ran fingers over the young man's ribs. The patient balled his hands into fists, and then gasped twice. He swore with the second grunt, and then gabbled an apology.

'I've heard worse,' Doyle said.

'Latimer finished the examination. 'You've cracked ribs down your left-hand side. That's going to hurt for a few weeks, perhaps a couple of months. So, no more scrapping for the foreseeable. Nurse Doyle here will provide a bandage. You keep that on. It'll hold you together. Check back in with us next Saturday and hopefully you'll start to see some signs of improvement by then, when we'll have the dressing changed. Until then, no exertion. Heavy lifting or the like. You'll just make it worse and it'll take all the longer to heal.'

Doyle had by now cleaned the young man's face. An iodine solution was sparingly applied into the abrasions and then the bandage was fixed around his midriff. 'You'll be good as new in no time,' Latimer said.

'You can put your shirt on now, Thomas,' Doyle said. She turned around to make a note on his record sheet. As he shrugged his shirt back on, something clattered to the floor. He made to grab whatever it was as it fell, but the hurt to his chest made Thomas pull up short.

Doyle turned back. 'What is it?'

Latimer crouched and picked up whatever had been dropped out from the under the cot where it had bounced. He thought it was a nail at first, then a cross or other pendant. Some simple token of faith or charm for good luck. No.

A lead figurine. A child's moulded play-piece. A model of a juggernaut.

Latimer held the figure out, and the bandaged man took it. He snatched his waistcoat and jacket and cap and was gone.

'Next.'

'Did you see what he had?'

'The little lead soldier? Yes. What of it?'

'Perhaps it's nothing. But I've seen them everywhere the last day or so.'

'Some new fad or fashion, doubtless.'

'I'm not so sure.'

The next patient was ushered in. He might have been the brother of the previous. Even his injuries were similar: a blackened eye, facial and hand bruising, heavy bruises also to the upper arms. The left hand cradled the right, which was swollen. Very swollen.

'Nurse. What do you detect?'

Doyle lifted the hand for inspection. She laid it gently on her own hand. The patient's pale flesh contrasted with her ruddier complexion. The damaged hand looked waxy and sooty at the same time. 'A simple enough fracture,' she judged. And to him: 'Did you punch a wall?'

The patient laughed. 'It didn't feel like it at the time. But later, God it did.'

'You should be more careful.'

'It was all I could do. Carried away, you see. Taken with the moment. It was either the wall or the face, you know, and part of me could still see that if I connected with the right with the force I was throwing it then I'd have knocked his block off for certain. And if that's been the case then I'd be now sat in the cells awaiting a murder charge than sat here.'

'Then perhaps you did the decent thing.' Doyle washed the hand up to the elbow, and then dried it as careful as could be. Latimer always took satisfaction from watching her at work. The deft handwork, the combination of expertise, authority and care.

'I'm not sure that I could be charged with that ma'am. Decency, I mean.' The young man was blushing.

'Well, you should take care at any rate. And perhaps to watch your drinking if it leads to squabbles.'

'I'm not a drinking man, ma'am. I swear I'm not. This

was just ... horseplay. High spirits. A little out of hand, but that's all it was. I've not touched a drop since I took the pledge. I'm to abstain from all liquor and to build my body up through exercise and good meals.' There was a note of pride in his voice.

Latimer fished his notes from the top of the cabinet. 'Talbot, is it?'

'Joseph Lawrence Talbot, yes sir.'

'And was that your brother we saw not ten minutes ago?'

'It was.'

'I see.'

'Training, we were. Sparring, you might say. Except without the aid of ring or gloves. There's no referee in the street or on the battleground, they say, so what's the point of learning fighting if it'll do you no good in the real world?'

'Perhaps the point is so that you don't hurt yourself to the extent that you can't be useful in the real world.'

Doyle had found some laths of wood to use as splints. She laid one under the young man's forearm, one end of it nestling into the palm of his hand. The other was placed over the arm and bound into place. 'I don't have the materials here to make a more permanent cast, but this strapping will hold you together until Monday. With Doctor Latimer's leave, I'd ask you to attend at his surgery first thing Monday to have this rectified.'

Latimer nodded consent. 'Eight sharp if you can. We'll get you seen to first.'

'You're very kind.'

'Just keep yourself in the one piece until then. So no scrapping, sober or otherwise.'

The lad looked crestfallen. 'Monday's a long time off.'

'A couple of days and that's all.'

'It's just that I'll miss it.' Talbot shut himself up. He reddened again, but this was not caused by social awkwardness in front of a female. This was something more akin to regret.

Latimer took a chance. 'Juggernaut?'

Talbot's eyes bulged in surprise, and then sank back into their rightful place when Latimer let him see what he was holding. The lead model he'd been carrying all day.

'Why sir, yes. Sorry, sir.'

'Whatever for?'

'For this sir. For getting myself all messed up. It was just the high spirits, you know, like I said. I didn't mean nothing by it. And sort of for not knowing you were involved, sir, not in this at any rate.'

Doyle affected disinterest. She was expert at fading to the background, in the way that a butler or head waiter might, when they were present but when it was appropriate to make themselves appear to be absent. The trick was a good one, and one that never failed to impress when it was well-executed. If only Joseph Talbot had learned to be so discreet.

Let's see where this leads, Latimer thought. 'Arm all right now?'

'Thank you, sir, yes. All mended in no time. This won't hold me back will it?'

'Hold you back?'

'From being the first I mean. I've done good, I have. You just ask. Not touched a drop. Done my exercise like I was told to. Kept out of trouble. Fed myself as good as I could. Still growing, I am. Had to get new trousers and everything, so I did.'

'That's good,' Latimer said, using as encouraging a tone as he could. He kept hold of Talbot's records and showed him back out into the main area of the warehouse. Nurse Doyle. Would you be so good to continue while I speak with Mister Talbot here?'

'As you wish, Doctor.' The next patients – a child of perhaps eighteen months, taking toddling steps with a watchful scarfed mother – came forward.

Latimer led Talbot over to a trestle table, one of the

many used for the soup kitchen services. Stacks of enamelled tin plates and mugs occupied one end of the table.

'Sit, Joseph, sit.'

'Thank you, sir.' Eagerness and apprehension in his tone. In the background, Singh and his counterpart were preparing vegetables, boiling water, weighing out and rinsing rice.

'Tell me what you can about Juggernaut.'

'I'm sure I don't know the half of it sir. Not like you gentlemen surely do.'

Nevertheless, it's as well to make periodic checks to understand how well Juggernaut is understood.'

'Yes sir. I see sir.'

'So?'

'So, you're just here on the Saturdays, isn't it, sir?'

'In the mornings, yes.'

'I don't suppose you get much chance to look around the place in the week. When it's all in operation?'

'No.'

'You should come on Monday. Then you'll see a sight.'

'Maybe I will.'

And then it'll all be good, sir, won't it? Because of the free availability. Because of the new start that we're making.'

This was getting out of order. 'Why don't you tell me about Juggernaut from the start?'

'I can't wait for Monday. We'll show them, eh?'

Latimer coaxed what he hoped came out as an easy reassuring laugh. 'We will.'

'So how it started for me was with a job. Jobs for all, the poster said. So me and Tommy –that's Thomas my brother who you were good enough to doctor up just now sir – we came along together because we'd not had much in the way of regular work lately, just day labouring picked up at Smithfield Market, and we wanted something more permanent. Maybe an apprenticeship or suchlike. We've been here since. A month now.'

'Doing what?'

'Tommy works on the machines. He's always been better than me with metal. Greasing up and cleaning down. Spare parts as necessary as it's all old equipment they're working with. Me, I've been on the lines. Women's work, some of them say, but it's just a joke between us lads because there's hardly a girl works in the place. A few in the offices and that, but not on the floor.'

'Factory working?'

'Yes. In the bottling plant. It's been on and off because of what they're doing with the mix, but the work's steady enough and there's a chance you might get selected too.'

'Selected?'

'Yes.' Talbot said the word as though it was obvious what this selection referred to. This was not the moment to pursue that line of information.

'I've never seen the bottling plant,' Latimer ventured.

'It's kept private. As private as a factory can be. They want to keep the surprise.'

'The surprise.' Latimer tried to make the words not sound like a question.

'Monday. That's the day. The day the world starts to hear the Juggernaut approaching.'

'Not long to wait then.'

'And that's why I was afraid of my arm being hurt. That I wouldn't be able to play my part.'

'I'm sure you'll be able to do something.'

Talbot's head dropped. 'I'm not so sure. A one-armed man is little use stacking crates in a factory.'

Frying smells from a huge tureen. Onions and other aromatics. Singh stirring with vigour. Another patient leaving the screened-off cubicle. One more, the last, a heavyset fellow with his cap pulled down over his face, now stood waiting to enter.

'There is something you could so. Something that would carry favour. In return, I would do my utmost to ensure that your injury did not hold you back.'

'I'm not sure.' Talbot's face said different.

'Then I tell you what. A proposition. If I were to meet you here at, say, nine o'clock this evening. Here, outside this very building. If you're there, you're there. If not, not.'

'I don't know what Mister Bradshaw would say.'

'Well, perhaps this should remain an agreement between gentlemen. You and me alone. Not to be spoken of to anyone, least of all your brother.'

'You're nothing to concern yourself about there, sir. Not after this,' Talbot said, indicating the bandaging.

'No, I suppose not.'

Doyle came up to them. She might have been there a moment or two. Latimer did not recall her approach. 'And that's the last of them, Doctor.'

'Is it? Thank you, Nurse. You can get away if you like. I'll tidy up here and I'll see you Monday.'

'Very good, Doctor. You have a good weekend now.'

'And you.'

Doyle left. Talbot watched her go. Latimer was not sure that he appreciated the way Talbot lingered on her departing back.

'So,' Latimer interjected, 'who's this Bradshaw?'

'Mister Bradshaw? He's what you might call the works manager.'

'And you're afraid of him?'

'I don't want to lose the job. And the whole experience. It's been good for me. There are drawbacks, of course sir, but you'd expect that yourself being a medical man.'

'What do you mean?'

A shadow fell over the table. Latimer thought that it was Singh, and almost spoke before turning to address the newcomer as such. But it was Talbot's brother, Thomas, who stood there. 'We should go,' he said.

Talbot stood. 'Begging your leave, sir. Perhaps it's best if I went.'

'Remember what I said.'

The brother butted in. 'And what's that to do?'

'Just to come back next week and have this checked on. And not to injure myself any more in the meantime.'

His brother grunted something. They left together, the brother taking the time to stare back at Latimer as they passed the food station.

It must have been lunch. A queue had formed. Volunteers hustled back and forth, doling out bowls and spoons, pouring mugs of water. Latimer had expected to see some great urn offering fountains of tea, but the only drink on offer was the water.

He went back to the treatment alcove. Doyle had tidied everything away, and had gone so far as to leave a note detailing what needed replacing from the medical supplies. Latimer would authorise the replenishments from his surgery's stock on Monday.

Something didn't sit right. Latimer went to the files and withdrew the paperwork on the Talbot youths. He checked one, then the other. Each file contained two sets of notes. The first held general information: name, address, age and so on. These details were patchy and the clientele of the mission weren't pressed too closely for specifics. It was clear that the Talbot boys had undergone a change of circumstances. At first, they had been underweight, had exhibited symptoms consistent with malnourishment. But they had seemingly caught up on themselves and were both now strapping lads. Instances of disease had given way to instances of injury.

Latimer pulled other files, this time choosing at random, as though he were participating in a conjuring trick, drawing cards from a great fanned pack.

A child. A young widow. A dockworker fallen on hard times. Their records all told similar stories. A shift from illness to wellness. A journey from poverty and malnutrition to fitness and relative prosperity, in body if not wholly in circumstance. The menfolk all shared a common characteristic. Broken fingers. A flattened nose. Internal bleeding in more than one case.

Injuries consistent with violence.

The medical records only went so far. They stretched back only the period that Latimer and Doyle had been offering their services and they were restricted only to those who'd come forward to the free Saturday surgeries.

There was evidence here that the poor of the area were having their health improved. There was a focus on young men. Their ages spanned from fifteen to the early twenties. That much was obvious. And if the food was free and at least plentiful enough to keep hunger at bay then perhaps that charity was having some positive effect in the community.

But what if there was another factor?

Latimer hoped that Talbot would be as good as his word and return at nine that evening. Perhaps an investigation of the bottling plant would answer the questions forming in his mind.

There was one more issue to resolve as well. Bradshaw. The name was familiar to Latimer, but he could not place where from.

#

The answer came that afternoon. Latimer had lunched with Singh at the end of the noontime soup kitchen service. The meal had been a vegetable curry served with both rice and flatbreads. Latimer had eaten a dollop of the rich aromatic sauce parcelled inside a chapatti.

Singh and his compatriot were engaged in washing up the assorted bowls and rinsing through the mugs. Some of the women who had eaten were also lending assistance. Latimer found himself standing back and watching, though every now and then he made some effort by stacking up washed and dried bowls up into stacks.

'Tell me about Bradshaw.'

'Oh, him. You won't see him around today.'

'No, it's the pastor that I normally see.' Pastor Benedict's lack of an appearance hadn't struck Latimer until now. Then again, he often worked through the night tending to those who had nowhere else to stay, and so he wasn't an ever-present on Saturdays.

'He's a good man, the pastor. Takes care of the flock. Even turns the right ones away.' Part of the problem with running a charitable venture like this was the chance of those who fancied a free meal but who didn't need one. Benedict was a useful sort to have around, and both diplomatic and insistent as the occasion demanded. That was how Latimer had found himself talked into volunteering here in the first instance after all.

'So, what's Bradshaw's role in all of this?'

'He's something to do with the charitable Trust. I don't know the specifics as I deal, like you, with the pastor. People like him. He's easy to deal with. And he's a man of faith.'

'You make him sound like a barker.'

'A what?'

Like someone whose job it is to get the curious into the tent at a circus sideshow.'

Singh laughed. 'We have those in Punjab too. Barker. I will remember that. Perhaps so, but he is a good man. Bradshaw I have little to do with. And in any case, he tends to restrict himself to the bottling plant upstairs.'

'What of it?'

'It was left behind when the old brewery closed down. The machinery at least. And an opportunity was seen. To provide work for at least some of the poor of the parish and to provide an alternative through hard work and Christian charity to the vices of the demon drink.'

'So, what is it that they make? What goes in the bottles?'

Singh's smile was as broad as ever. 'That is the secret

of the Juggernaut.'

'What do you mean?'

'I mean that it is a secret. The workers were selected from here. From the itinerant on the streets. Young men, older men too, but mostly the young. All of whom who were undernourished at first. But who showed something. Some spark of vitality. An essence. A violent side. They are being selected for something. Something more than labour. And this has to do with whatever the Juggernaut signifies.' Singh took out a watch on a fob from a pocket in his waistcoat. Threaded into the chain securing the watch was a small lead figurine. It was the same as the others that Latimer had seen.

'The story of the Juggernaut,' Singh continued, 'has many roots. Some say the reference goes back to Moloch. The Old Testament speaks of child sacrifice and other idolatrous practices. Some, as the poppet here infers, refers to supposed Hindu practices of the faithful willingly flinging themselves before a great totem being processed through the streets, and being crushed under its wheels. Milton's *Paradise Lost* has the Juggernaut, as personified by Moloch, as a "horrid king besmeared with blood of human sacrifice, and parents' tears". Bertrand Russell speaks of the cringing submission of the slave before it, cowering in abasement to a terrible power worshipped without thought to questioning the authenticity of that power. Part of the life of a Sikh,' Singh smiled, pocketing the watch, 'is that of the study of comparative religion. That is part of the burden of any new faith.

'Whatever it is, the symbol of the Juggernaut must be seen as fair warning. Someone has chosen this device with thought, with purpose and with perhaps the intent of referencing a multiplicity of meanings. This is dark work, and it shames me that I am not a strong enough man to stand up to it, lest I be crushed beneath its all-devouring wheels.'

Singh fell silent for a moment before continuing.

'Speak to the pastor. He may have more to say. Bradshaw? I would have little to do with him. I have my position to think of. The work involved in establishing the gurdwara. Goodwill goes a long way and I would not lightly jeopardise it.'

'And if there was a greater wrong being perpetrated?'

'There are five evils, we Sikhs are taught. Five sins. You might term them lust, greed, false attachment, rage, and lust. And there are three principles to live by: to be charitable, to work honestly, and to remember God in all things. If such a great wrong were being occasioned, then any good Sikh would find it hard to stand by in idleness.' Singh took out a small white card. 'A telephone number, if it is of use. If I am not here, then I will most likely be there, or it will be known where I am.'

They shook hands. Latimer slipped the business card away. In doing so, he brushed his fingers over the pistol in his coat. 'Thank you.'

The tables were being folded away after the meal. Gymnasium equipment was being set up. Punch bags, medicine balls. A stack of wood, ropes and canvas that could be assembled into a boxing ring.

Latimer left and turned out of the warehouse on Chicksand Street towards Brick Lane. There, the bustle of an ordinary Saturday once more. A gaggle of Jewish boys, all dark ringlets and headgear, kicking a football between them. A dray cart making a beer delivery. Shouts for fresh fish and hot pies. Somewhere, a trumpet and a drum. Calls for recruitment into the King's army. The first fat spots of rain on cobbles.

Latimer turned his collar up and headed back to the tube station. Bradshaw. The name meant something. The foot traffic thickened around the entrance to Aldgate East. Saturday. Half-day closing for some businesses. He had to make haste. He needed to check the documents.

#

It took perhaps forty-five minutes for Latimer to cross

London and to present himself back at the shop where he'd left the packet of papers. If the stationer was surprised to see him, he did not let it register. 'Sir?'

'The package I left here for posting on Monday. Might I see it for a few minutes?'

The stationer retrieved the pack. It was exactly as he'd left it. There had been no tampering. 'If you would like some privacy, then my office is at your disposal.'

'That's very good of you.'

The stationer's office was cramped but clean. Latimer sat at the bureau and opened the files. Latimer scanned the assorted documents, leafing through them at speed. It had to be here somewhere. Think, man, think.

He couldn't see it. The word eluded him. And then, there it was. Not in any of Jekyll's material, not in the other letters, but in annotations in a hand Latimer recognised as Hyde's. The notation was in precise hard pencil, a pale grey single name. Bradshaw.

Now he knew what to look for, the rest came easily. A handful of notes. Instructions to call upon chemists for supplies of reagents and mineral salts. Reference to a small provision to be made out of Jekyll's estate. And though the actual letters were not there, inferences that Bradshaw had been recommended to Jekyll's household by Richard Enfield, and that the then-young man had been useful to Jekyll and Hyde in running errands.

So that was the link.

The same Bradshaw who had been footman to Henry Jekyll now worked for the Hawksmoor Trust.

There were other copies of the experimental notes, if Hyde's letter was to be believed. And Bradshaw was the connection between Jekyll and the charity that his estate had gone on to sponsor.

What had Bradshaw seen in those last days in Jekyll's laboratory? Was there any connection to him and the Hyde persona? A snatch of Hyde's written sign-off came back to Latimer. *The red levels are rising.*

Blood. Splashing up around the wheel arches of a mighty unstoppable icon being drawn through the streets of London. Bones being crushed underneath. The clatter and smash of falling and breaking bottles. Screaming. Latimer gasped.

'Everything all right, sir?' The enquiry was called through from the shop floor.

'Thank you, yes. I'm almost finished here.'

'Very good. There's no rush sir.'

The key that Utterson had left lay there. He had no idea what the key related to, and if there was danger that the documents might be intercepted, then they and the key would be lost together. Latimer having the key served no useful purpose, and it could always be located if a use for it was found. To take it or not? Not, Latimer decided.

He took the pistol from his pocket. From the other side of the coat he extracted the magazine and clipped it into place.

Latimer returned to the shop, the package resealed. 'Again, my thanks.'

'The stationer mouthed some pleasantries, and Latimer bade him a good weekend. He left and headed in the direction of Oxford Street.

It was almost two o'clock. He would return to the warehouse on Chicksand Street for nine. In the meantime, it was important that his movements were a mystery. He was sure that he had not been followed so far today. That surely was both a reassurance and a cause for concern it itself.

Why had he not been followed? The answer surely was that he was being predictable. It was known where he would be. The mission. So, any tail would be placed from the mission onwards. There had been no-one though. Not the Tall Man or any or his cohort. And who were they working for?

Latimer's hand crept for the pistol. There was a secret thrill to be had in walking down one of the capital's busiest thoroughfares with a loaded weapon to hand. The handgun had a power that it exerted. Latimer found that he had missed its call.

The rain that he had felt in the East End was now falling here. Latimer took shelter in the Electric Palace and ordered tea in the Japanese room. The gaudiness of the over-ornate decorations, all red and gold, gold and red was sufficient amusement while his refreshment was being prepared. A maid clad in an awkward costume, halfway between kimono and the attire of a Lyon's Corner House girl, brought his tea through. The drink was pleasant, unremarkable.

The cinema was showing as its main feature a biographical film about Henry VIII starring Herbert Beerbohm as Cardinal Wolsey. The drama held no interest, but among the images he saw in the foyer after finishing his tea, there were photographs of Miss Laura Cowie, the actress playing Anne Boleyn. There was a wistfulness the photographer had caught about her, a pensiveness and a fragility. Her lips were full, her hair tousled and dark against the palest skin. Latimer paid for a ticket.

The film was clownish and crude, none more so when the title character was on the screen. But there was something real about the way he – Arthur Bourchier, according to the foyer notes – communicated real lust and intoxication with Boleyn. As the doomed Anne, Cowie was by turn an ingénue, a flirt, a haughty queen-in-waiting. Her eyes intimated much that no screen would ever dare show.

Too much of the performance focused on the agonies of obligation, trust and faith suffered by Wolsey. The lead actor rolled his eyes and emoted crudely front and centre. Around him, Latimer heard the simpering of many of the mostly female audience as they followed the photo play hero's progress in organising the life of his capricious monarch. The waits between the scenes with Cowie were becoming interminable. Her presence, though, was at once alluring, exotic and charming. And there was an air of knowingness about her that reminded him of someone.

Of Doyle.

He watched the film through to the end of the main feature and left with others, as some remained in their seats to see the whole performance again. Latimer attached himself to the rear of a cluster of perhaps half a dozen women, seemingly a group of friends whose regular Saturday outings consisted of shopping, cinema and then a decent hotel high tea.

Doyle. Where would she be? There was a chance that she had gone back to the surgery. Doyle was diligent and hardworking, and would have attended directly to the reordering and replenishment of supplies used by the morning's surgery.

And Doyle had left before him. Any tail might have taken a chance that she had been taken into Latimer's confidence. That she might be an easier target.

That was why he had not been picked up outside the mission. Because they had already left, and were following Doyle.

Latimer started to run. He burst out of the cinema entrance and made his way south. He cut across the street, dodging behind an omnibus and between motor-cars and hansoms. Shouts from behind him, curses. He kept running, cutting through side-streets, skirting past pedestrians. Where he had to, he ran in the road, paying no heed to horse dung and to the traffic.

Rain was still falling. The streets were slick underfoot. Once, Latimer skidded in some filth thrown into the gutter from a shop. Water flicked into his eyes. He squinted, wiping his sleeve across his face.

A fresh shout from one side. The gun. Latimer had it in his hand, the one he'd cleared his vision with. The weapon was out and was attracting attention.

No time. No time. He was by now only a street away. The roads were quieter here, Latimer slowed to a jog.

Shouts from behind still, though they seemed further away. The pavement was clear. Latimer cocked the pistol, chambering the first round. He passed the consulting room's side window and rounded the corner.

The front door was ajar. Latimer leapt up the steps and burst into the hallway. All seemed as usual. The same polite decoration. The same clean smells of honeyed beeswax, black grate polish and borax. Commercial cleaners were employed. They serviced the surgery on Sundays; a recent innovation in working practices that suited Latimer well.

Then another scent. No.

The waiting room was empty. This led to the office space where Doyle kept front of house and from where she administered the practice. The smell was developing.

Doyle's desk had been swept clean. The floor was covered with its former contents. The in and out tray, the typewriter, inkpad and stamps, loose papers. A potted cyclamen sprawled, its soil dislodged onto the carpet, roots exposed. The chair behind the table had been knocked over.

The filing cabinet had been forced. There were scratches by the lock and the wood had been sheared. The top drawer had been tipped over onto the floor. Other drawers remained inside the carcase of the cabinet, but the paperwork had been rifled through at speed.

That smell. It grew stronger.

Latimer, pistol drawn, went through into the consulting rooms. Silence through the building. No feeling that there was anyone else here.

His office was empty but the same hurried search had been conducted. The private papers he kept in a smaller lockable cabinet here had been removed; again, the lock had proved flimsy against the interrogation of a jemmy or crowbar. Ornaments had been knocked over. A mirror broken. The certificates behind Latimer's desk had been taken from the wall and their frames punched in, the backs removed from the displays.

Now there was sound. A cracking, a rustling. Like paper being rifled through.

The door to the private consultation room was shut. Latimer approached, and the sound grew louder. The door-handle was warm to the touch. Latimer knew what to expect. He knew what to fear.

He opened the door and stood aside in one move. No gunfire barked back at him. That was only a slight possibility, but he had to preserve himself.

The fire was in the middle of the room. A clump of clothing, like an upended basket of washing destined for being dried on the line, was aflame. The fire was not a significant one, more smoke than flame, and it either had not long been started or else was struggling to find purchase after its initial ignition.

Latimer de-cocked the pistol and dropped it onto the couch. He pulled his coat of and smothered the flames with it. The temptation to stamp down on them, to utterly extinguish them with his boot was a strong one, but it would have been no use. And besides, it would have damaged Doyle all the more.

The bundle of clothes was no such thing, but Maureen Doyle's crumpled body.

Smoke was in Latimer's eyes. They burned and ran with water. Latimer dabbed away the last of the fire and turned Doyle over onto her back.

Her jaw was loose, her eye-sockets a pair of slow haemorrhages that gave her the sickest illusion of life. Her nose, likewise bloodied. There was blood, but not much. Some had puddled from her mouth onto the carpet.

Latimer hugged Doyle, clasped her hard to his chest. He knew not how long for. The smell – a mix of burning wool, medical alcohol, blood – faded in time. He crouched there holding Doyle tight. Eventually, he gasped. He had been holding his breath.

In time, he let her go. He laid her body on the chaise

longue and covered her with the white coat he donned for appearances sake during consulting hours with new clients. An emptied bottle of pure alcohol lay on the floor. Latimer picked it up, found the stopper not far off, and put it back in place.

'Mister Latimer.' A voice from behind. Then again, more insistent. 'Mister Latimer.'

It was Spencer Mosley. Latimer had no idea how long the detective had been standing there. 'Come through, Mister Latimer. Come through. There's nothing you can do for her now.' Mosley was not alone. A second man, tall and turned somewhat to stockiness, old but not elderly, mutton-chopped in the late-Victorian manner, stood behind.

'We should talk, should we not, sir,' the second man said.

Latimer, meet Frederick Abberline,' Mosley said. 'Abberline, Latimer.'

'And not a moment too soon,' Abberline said.

#

They sat in the waiting room. Mosley had shut the front door and had placed a constable, who Latimer had not seen arrive, on guard duty outside. Someone – Latimer had not paid attention as to who – had brought through glasses and a jug of water. Mosley arranged chairs into an informal circle and used a fourth chair as an impromptu table. On these he set the jug and glasses.

Abberline produced a decent-sized hip-flask. He poured brandy into each of the glasses. He topped his own with a little of the water. He sipped, as though to judge that the mix was to his satisfaction, and having positively appraised it as such, put the glass back down.

'When Mosley contacted me, I was intrigued. Cases like those of Henry Jekyll's rattle around in the system, and they gnaw at those with old bones like me. And besides, retirement is all well and good, but its best appreciated with intervals of mental exercise and physical labour. I was glad of the communication.

'So, any opportunity to get some of those old ghosts laid to rest was gratefully received. Any chance to finally ascertain what really happened to Danvers Carew could only be welcomed. I was on a train within the hour, had Mosley cabled to have me met, and here I am. A most productive morning.

'Productive, yes,' Abberline continued. 'Mosley suggested that perhaps we should begin as he had ended yesterday, with a visit to your good self. Finding you not at your hotel, and a very pretty place The Clayton appears too, and it being past the time that you would normally finish at your charitable work, and my compliments to you, sir, for that endeavour, we thought that we'd try here before returning to your lodgings.

'Mosley said that I would be involved, I understand. You perhaps won't be altogether surprised to find out that I have certain connections across the globe, both with the police forces and with the Pinkerton Agency. It never ceases to astound me, sir, what might be accomplished with a starting point, with some zeal, with the right contacts and with the trappings of the twentieth century and the industrial age. Give a man a train, a telephone and the means to pay for a telegram, and wonders might be conducted. Even as old a dog as I might grow new teeth.' Abberline sipped a little more of his brandy-and-water.

'And here we find you,' Mosley said. 'To paraphrase Mister Wilde, but to find you with one dead body may be regarded as a misfortune, to find you with a second in two days looks like carelessness.'

Latimer rose, inchoate anger rising with him. Mosley already had a small revolver in his hand. 'Sit down, Latimer, if you'd be so kind. Sit down.'

He did as he was told.

'That's a good fellow.' Now it was Mosley's turn to drink. He kept the glass in his hand after he tasted the beverage. 'So be quiet and consider your next words and actions with care.'

'Look at matters from our perspective. You turn up, twice in twenty-four hours, a corpse in tow. Doubtless you have an internally consistent and to you logical and reasonable explanation for the presence of a body in your offices. We'll come to that. But you must consider us here. We'll be taking you into custody, assuredly. And if you're as innocent as you are just about to say that you are, then you will be found out so sooner rather than later and you will be released. But all in good time. You'll be treated well and fairly, and the law will have its day with you one way or another.

'Some questions first though. We're all gentlemen here and I respect you enough to conduct yourself in an appropriately mature and reasonable manner. Neither histrionics nor outbursts if you would. I'd hate to have to hold a firearm on you all afternoon.'

Latimer breathed deep. He forced himself to give the appearance of relaxing. He dropped his shoulders as far as the tension in him would allow.

'You see,' Mosley continued. 'Already that's better. And it's much more civilised to converse here, with a drink, than to do the same in the altogether less pleasant surroundings of the Yard.'

The veneer of decorum was stripped away now. 'The body. Who?' Abberline had taken out a pencil and notepad and was prepared to take notes. Latimer gave them Doyle's full name. He told them when they had first met. He explained that she worked with him on Saturdays too at the mission. That she had left before he had.

'And there are witnesses to this?'

'Yes.' Which Latimer detailed. He told them where he had gone afterwards, though he omitted the visit to the stationer's office. 'And then I came here.'

'Why?'

Latimer hoped the pause indicated nothing. 'I wanted to make some jottings. To write up what I'd experienced at

Utterson's. Sometimes making a statement to oneself allows you to see matters in a new light. I came here because I wanted it treated like work, and not to spoil the rest of my weekend. And also, when all's said and done, Utterson was a client of mine. A patient. There are formalities to complete when one of yours dies, and I wanted them concluded. A line drawn under him, if you will.'

'I see.'

'The front door was open when I got here. I can only assume that Mrs Doyle was either bundled into the offices by thieves-'

'Burglars,' Abberline interjected. 'Thieves steal from the person. Burglary is committed at a place. Robbery is a little vaguer. Interchangeable, you might say.'

'-either opportunistically or because they fancied that there might have been valuables, cash or drugs one supposes, on the premises, and had been in wait for such an arrival.'

'On a Saturday?' Abberline again.

'Opportunists then,' Latimer said. It sounded weak even to his own ears.

'Happenstance,' Abberline grunted.

'The surgery had been ransacked. I found Mrs Doyle's body. An attempt to burn the place had been made, but it proved unsuccessful. She was alight, but not burning. I put the flames out. She had been battered, assaulted. Her nose broken, her jaw-' emotion had stolen into Latimer's voice. He breathed. He breathed. 'I laid her down and covered her. And there you were.'

Mosley now: 'How long do you think you held her corpse in your embrace?'

'I don't know. Five minutes? Thirty seconds? I don't know.'

Abberline asked Latimer to open his hands and hold them out. He did so. The palms were dark with sooty blackness. The smell of pure alcohol clung to him.

'Forgive the enquiry, Latimer,' Mosley said. 'But I must ask. Mrs Doyle – Maureen – and you. Were you intimate?'

'No.'

'I'm sorry?'

Latimer stared dully at Mosley. There was still smoke and water in his eyes. 'I said that we were not. Not intimate.'

'Thank you.'

Abberline splashed a little more brandy into his glass. He did not offer replenishment to the others.

'I think that'll do for now,' Mosley said.

'Though there is the other matter,' Abberline said. 'The reason why we're here.'

'Yes.' Mosley turned to Latimer. 'When we arrived, I called you by your name, did I not?'

'You did.'

'"Mister Latimer", I said.'

'Yes.'

'Because that's your name, isn't it? Mister, I mean. You're no doctor at all. Never have been. I'll wager that we'll find out that your name isn't even Latimer if we dig deep enough. There was a Doctor Latimer. Once. A medic in the Army, who worked as a sawbones in an internment camp in South Africa. Turns out he's dead, though. Been dead a while.

'And then you land yourself back in London. Let me guess. You've been trading on a doctor's name in Africa. You've got yourself some certificates and very good they look too. I saw then all smashed up in your office back there. You get back to Blighty, and you come across the ideal opportunity. You set yourself up as a doctor. You even read up a little, enough to get through a conversation. And besides, a lot of medicine is simply applied common sense.

'Most sensible of all, you have a nurse. Someone dependable, someone experienced. Someone you maybe pay a bit over the going rate for. Someone who can cover for you, who can actually do the job. While you sit back with your rugged good looks and your war stories and take the credit, the pay, and you lead an easy life. Well-paying patients who need a little conversation and the right kind of advice to cover up any nasty consequences from their social infidelities. Any serious work you can pass on under the guide of referring them to an expert.'

Latimer was about to say something, but Mosley raised a hand. His eyes did not break contact.

'You could have kept this up for years. Might have retired well on the back of your deceit. But something went wrong. Didn't it, Latimer? Did you misdiagnose Utterson and he found you out? There were quite a number of medical textbooks in his library, weren't there? Was there some kind of confrontation with Mrs Doyle? An argument over money? Was she feeling guilty?'

'You don't believe that.'

'It's not what I believe, Mister Latimer, it's what I can get a barrister to infer to a jury. That's what gets a man the rope. Maybe you're just a schemer who's some undone by chance, but maybe you're a killer. Either way, you will see a cell before the day's out, sir. Of that you have my oath.'

'I did not kill Doyle. I had nothing to do with Utterson's death. I think it best if I say nothing more.' Latimer, again controlling every urge in his body, let his head fall.

'And there we have it.' Abberline put his pencil and pad away. He stood. 'Do you have a coat, Latimer?'

'Yes. It's … it's through there.'

Mosley stood. 'I'll fetch it for you.'

'No. I'd like to say goodbye to … to Mrs Doyle.'

'Abberline opened the door. 'We'll come with you, if you'd oblige us.'

'Of course.'

Mosley led the way, Abberline followed up in the rear. On entering the second of the consulting rooms,

Mosley picked up Latimer's coat. The lining was charred in places, but it speared otherwise intact. Mosley ran his hands over the material. 'You put this on,' he said, once he'd checked to his satisfaction, 'there'll be more rain later.'

Latimer took the coat and put it on. Then he knelt by the chaise longue. Doyle's body stretched out in front of him. 'Forgive me, Maureen,' Latimer murmured. He slid a hand under the body. He retrieved the pistol he'd thrown there earlier and cocked it in the same movement. He stood.

'Take the revolver out, Mosley. Do it now.'

Mosley did so.

'Empty the shells.' They dropped silently onto the carpet.

'Now hand me the gun.'

Mosley complied with the instruction. 'You'll hang for this, Latimer.'

'I killed neither of them and I'm going to prove it.' Latimer pocketed the revolver. 'Mister Abberline. Are you armed?'

Abberline acted as though having a firearm pointed at him was a daily occurrence. 'Just a cosh. A memento from my policing days.'

'I'd not deprive a man of that.'

Abberline acknowledged the gesture with a shrug.

Latimer backed further away. 'If I need you, I'll telegram or send a message to the Yard. If not, then this is goodbye.' He undid the latch on the window. 'Gentlemen. Do right by Maureen Doyle. This will all be over soon.'

Latimer stepped out of the window and dropped to the pavement. He turned, pistol out, to ensure no chase was given. He was fifty yards from the house and running at full pelt when he heard the constable's first whistle. And then he was around a corner, crossing into a side-street, and was gone.

#

Latimer shoved Mosley's gun into a pillar box. He had zigzagged across central London until he was no longer sure where he was. The rain had returned, though was falling as a lazy drizzle rather than as anything more demonstrative. The skies above were bullet-grey, smoke-grey. His hair was saturated. Rain ran off him, through his matted eyebrows, into his sight.

He stopped. A fenced–off park within a square. Imposing housing all around. Latimer opened the cast-iron gate and let himself in. The park was empty. He sat on a bench under a yew tree. He did not check if the seating was wet or not beforehand.

Latimer took his handgun out. He examined the piece. He removed the magazine containing the ammunition clip. He thumbed the cartridges into his open hand.

Latimer weighed the metal. He imagined throwing the cartridges, seeing them arcing and scattering in the air. Bouncing and then becoming lost in the grass.

Doyle did not deserve to die. Not like that. Bludgeoned and set on fire in her place of work.

He blinked, and she was there. Her eyes, dark and knowing like a player in the movies. He blinked again and she was gone. Just the park, glittering in the rain.

The police would be after him. Perhaps a sketch artist had already worked up a likeness from Mosley's description. Wanted for murder. The implications were clear. Wanted for Doyle's killing, and probably some charge associated with Utterson as well. He would be captured and he would be tried. Then one day, not long after the guilty verdict was handed down, he would be taken to a courtyard inside a prison and he would hang. The truth be damned.

The information they held about his qualifications would be enough from which to construct motive. That was something he had no defence against. He had taken the opportunity presented to him in South Africa, and had played his hand well for so many years. He had paid for the certificates to be forged, and had presented himself in England with a second-hand set of doctoring paraphernalia. He'd accrued enough money after the War to buy into the practice that the retiring predecessor was happy to let go. Continuing patients with genuine medical issues were either dealt with by Doyle or else were happy, particularly the more elderly ones, to be passed onto another doctor of his predecessor's recommendation.

Latimer worked front of house, essentially being the maître d' in his own restaurant. He had realised when still young that he was charming to women, particularly women of a certain age, and he played upon this.

Water ran off leaves, spattering on the path. Puddles splashed with each little hit. The interval between the tiny explosions increased. Two a second, then one a second. Then one every two seconds. The rain was stopping. Perhaps it had already ceased and this was merely the delay in run-off from the branches.

The cartridges were sweaty in his hand. He flexed. The metal cylinders slipped over each other, loosely rotating in his palm.

Utterson's head, exploded on the floor. Doyle's broken face.

No.

Latimer thumbed the first of the cartridges back into the clip in the magazine. Then the second. The magazine held seven rounds when full. Now refilled, Latimer clipped the magazine into place. He stood.

The rain had stopped. A clock tower somewhere adjacent was chiming the hour. Four bells. He must have been sat here for over an hour. His hair was no longer wet.

He would investigate the warehouse tonight. He would discover its secret. In doing so, he would find out more about Bradshaw and what he had to do with the Jekyll household, with Edward Hyde and with the documents. If he came across the figures he knew only as

The Tall Man, Smallpox Man and Bull Neck, then so be it. There would be a reckoning.

He would tear their worlds open. He would evidence that it was they, not he, who was responsible for Doyle's death. And he would present such evidence to the Yard on Monday.

There would be more than one juggernaut in this world.

#

The first few hours were the worst. Each new street corner contained the possibility of a beat constable equipped with a description. Every turn presented some new danger.

The hotel was off limits. Only a fool would have gone back there. The only item that Latimer would have retrieved would have been the other Browning. A 1911 in each hand would have been a comfort. The ammunition would have been useful too.

Darkness brought with it some semblance of anonymity. The streets became less threatening after dark. Latimer considered taking refuge in a museum, fully inspecting the exhibits until closing time, but counselled himself against it. He could not afford to be hemmed in.

At seven thirty, he headed to the nearest tube station. He crossed London head-down. He felt conspicuous, hatless. Each passenger movement felt as though he was being edged away from, as though death could be smelled on him. Perhaps he looked bedraggled. His coat was damp, his collar stuck to his neck. The carriage was muggy, occluded with tobacco smoke. The train rattled through the tunnels.

Latimer changed, and changed again. At each changing station, he checked for evidence of being followed, or of sentries being posted, but there was none.

The further east he travelled, the sparser the carriages became. He was travelling away from the City and the West End in the dull hours between curtain-up and the final bow. Aldgate East could not come fast enough.

He considered travelling on to Whitechapel and walking back. If there was someone waiting for him at Aldgate, then they'd be avoided. But then again, part of Latimer wanted to be found.

If there was a fight to be had, then he was the man to bring it.

Aldgate East was quiet. There was no-one loitering on either platform. Latimer passed through the ticket barrier and onto Whitechapel High Street. The art gallery had some kind of function ongoing. Top-hatted doormen were welcoming arriving guests. Black tie was the order of the day. From inside, the airy tinkling of glasses, the rise and fall of chatter, stringed instruments bouncing their way through what sounded like one of Mozart's Haydn Quartets.

Latimer stepped into the road to cut around a hansom dropping off guests. A snatch of conversation: two thin-faced gentlemen in evening dress gossiping about "Aitken", whoever he was. One of them glanced at Latimer and immediately turned back to his compatriot. A sneer played about his lips as he went back to denouncing the subject of their discussion and his pedestrian taste in the arts.

A fist in the face would have put paid to his derision.

Latimer kept going. Left into Brick Lane. Raucous piano tumbled out of a pub, The Archers, as did a couple dressed for the art gallery function. A drink was tempting. Valiant outside the pub stood a pair of Salvation Army conscripts. One held a collections tin, the other a sheaf of pamphlets.

'The War Cry, sir?' The tin was shaken at him. 'Christ and temperance be with you!'

Latimer thumbed some coppers into the collection and could not avoid taking one of their newspapers. The pair thanked him twice. Once for buying the paper and once 'For shunning the drink, sir. The way to His love is through sober prayer!'

Half past eight. Latimer was early. With a little time to kill, and with the need to check the surrounding streets for any of the lieutenants who'd tracked him the previous day, he decided to make a recce of at least some of the area. He had not wandered too far off the route from the tube station to the warehouse before.

The first left was Wentworth Street. Latimer cut down here, down a longer-than-expected parade of commercial premises towards another pub at the far end. The Princess Alice. A Truman Brewery house. A burly cove, the landlord, Latimer assumed, was nose-to-nose with another Salvation Army recruit.

'How many more times? You can't come in here and try to tell people not to drink!'

'It will be their ruin!'

'Look. I don't mind you lot, really, I don't. If you want to sell your papers and say your prayers on the cobbles, you go right ahead. But don't muck with the customers. Or I'll cast the first stone all right. At your mutton head.'

Another of the Army faithful came up to Latimer, but he used the War Cry copy to ward her off. 'Apologies, sister.'

'Soldier,' she said.

Latimer left them to it. A right at the junction meant that he was on Commercial Road. A right onto Fashion Street would bring him out almost opposite the Chicksand Street turning, though as it happened, Latimer continued as far as the Ten Bells pub at the corner of Fournier Street.

In doing so, he passed the church on the corner. Christ Church Spitalfields. The baroque hulk loomed out of the dark. The building felt out of place, a great white whale beached on a shoreline. The gates were locked shut against intruders. Out of Fournier Street, two men, in the garb of observant Jews, hurried by. They moved quick to remove themselves from the radius of light and noise spreading out from the Ten Bells. Between Latimer and the pub for a few seconds, they cast shifting shadows, before moving on in the direction Latimer had come.

He could not blame their apprehension. The pub was raucous with song and laughter. Again, twin Salvation Army soldiers trying to gain attention from passers-by and access to the premises. Their way was again barred, not by the licensee but by shrieking women, by pointing, guffawing men, by the hot throb of ale and tobacco smells, the sweat and sawdust.

Latimer did not envy their calling.

Fournier Street was dark. There were lights at upstairs windows, but at the ground floor level there were shutters in place. A doubtless sensible precaution by the Jewish community from unwanted violent attention.

'Do you see? This will not work.' One of the Salvation Army-ers to his companion.

'And I tell you that for some it will. They will see the light of our ministry and be drawn to Christ.'

'They care little but for debauchery and for the forgetting of their ills.'

'And who can blame them? These are harder times than ever before. Uncertain times. A bottle tonight does them more good than the life everlasting in an unknowable future.'

Latimer stepped back into shadow so that he might not interrupt their conversation.'

'Drink is not their friend. It was not mine, nor yours.'

'Indeed brother.'

'There are other ways though.'

'Others than the Army's teaching? You would turn your back on your calling?'

'It was no calling. I was waiting to be asked. That was the difference.'

'And where would you go?'

'There are places. Where once-drinking men who wish to keep their pledge, yet be allowed an evening's simple relaxation might be welcomed.'

'Ha! You'll be off to some Limehouse opium den next.'

'Nothing so debilitating, brother. Something more ... invigorating. That is what's promised. And I intend to know the truth of that promise.'

The conversation was interrupted by a woman staggering out through the pub's double doors. She might have been pushed, or she might have lurched out by her own initiative. Either way; she stepped into the gutter and puked until her lumpy spittle ceased its dribbling.

The Salvation Army men waited until she had finished and then stepped across to attend to her. Latimer took advantage of their distraction to step out of the shadow and carry on his way.

He went down Fournier Street. With the Saturday night shrieks, catcalls and laughter from both ends of the road, and the darkness between, as there was little useful illumination here, one might have felt afraid. Not Latimer. Part of this was the pistol in his hand, already cocked. Part of it was the developing certainty that at last he would get some answers. Some retribution. Some justification.

Part of it was that he no longer had to pretend any more.

He walked down the street. Movement from Brick Lane now some thirty yards ahead. A couple, man and woman, dragging each other drunkenly from the main road into the side street. Laughter and rustling. A gasp and a grunt. The low thump of bodies against a latched gate or a doorway. Low breathing, muttering, as Latimer passed them. He did not look to the side.

Into Brick Lane. Alcohol stink in the air. Part public houses, part a hangover from the Truman Brewery nearby. Toffs and scruffs, working girls and slim, dark-lidded boys. Hansoms dropping off, picking up. A flower-seller, a match-girl.

Chicksand Street was across the way, a little off to one side. There was no evidence of lookouts being posted.

Latimer came out of the Fournier Street turnoff, glad to have left the panting and thrusting behind.

Someone was standing outside the warehouse entrance. A slim grey curl of smouldering tobacco-smoke. One of the Talbot lads. From where he was, Latimer could not make out which of them it was, Thomas or Joseph. Then he saw the sling. The strapped forearm. That made it Joseph.

'Doctor.'

Joseph. How's the wrist?'

'Holding up, thank you sir.'

'Not too painful?'

'Ah, no, it's fine.'

Latimer had not been here at night. That there would be people curled up in the cots inside came as a surprise. The lighting was scarcely adequate to make them out, but there they were. A dozen of the cots were occupied. Any evening meal had long been cleared away, though there was a flame under an urn, promising the availability of tea. A group sat around one of the trestles. Pastor Benedict was among them. A bible was on the table, next to him. On top of the black book was a white enamel mug. The mug was steaming. There was talk about drink, about how though the scriptures mentioned wine often, there was no call from God to over-indulge, and that if one could not moderate one's intake, then it would be best and godliest for a man to abstain, the better to preserve his mortal body and his immortal soul.

'We should walk by quiet, Doctor.'

Latimer nodded. The room was large enough and the light dim enough to make specifics uncertain. A person or two moving about, especially this early in the evening, would cause no commotion. It felt awkward to be creeping like this even so.

He had no reason to feel this way. These people held no sway over him, and the good works he might have pretended to have done in the name of reinforcing his reputation as a medical man no longer needed to be upheld.

Talbot led the way. They went up the staircase at the far end of the warehouse. 'Up here, sir,' Talbot said.

There was no door to bar their way. A simple rope with a tin sign hanging from it. Works persons only beyond this point. The sign was chipped, the painted lettering faded to brown. Talbot unhooked the rope with his good hand and they turned the corner off the landing into a wide-open space.

The room was dark. Black as a coal-hole. 'One second, sir,' Talbot said low. He was fumbling with something, then a match was struck.

The light exposed a table with shelving overhead. On one of the shelves, a rack of battery-powered torches. Latimer tried one, but the power source must have died. The second worked. The match in Talbot's good hand guttered and died.

The electric light was yellow, but strong. Latimer snapped the glove catch into place, keeping the flashlight button pressed into the down position.

The upstairs was divided into two sections. The first, and nearest, was laid out like a small factory. The specifics eluded Latimer, but the principle was clear enough. A section where materials were mixed. Piping conveying the resultant concoction to a second chamber where bottled gas – carbon dioxide, he assumed – was introduced to carbonate the liquid.

Then on to a bottling section. At this end of the section, there were cases of empty bottles. Other cases of metal caps. Additional empty cases for manufactured goods, ready for supply.

The second section was at the far end of the upper floor. Latimer passed the machinery, following the routes taken by the bottles and then the pipes, tracing the process back from completion to its beginning.

An office. Other rooms beyond. The office was

decked out as though for a commercial sales operation. Typewriter and telephone. Filing and paperwork. A cardboard box on the desk. Latimer lifted the lid off the box. He shone the torch in.

A hundred, two hundred tiny elephant faces starred back at him. Lead copies of the same juggernaut toy that he'd seen everywhere over the past day. The box was perhaps half full. Scuffing and dark smudges indicated that this had once been brimming with the figures. Latimer ran his hand through them. The feel of them around his fingers made him feel a child once more.

Posters on the wall. Bottles of the same size as in the bottling area. Though these were full. A red liquid. Capped with a prise-off seal, not a push-off closure. The bottles were unlabelled.

'Here sir,' Talbot said. He pointed to a heavy package on a filing cabinet. There were scissors and glue nearby. Latimer put the torch down to open the envelope. He pulled out a sheet of labels.

Juggernaut. There were other words, too, about the drink being most efficacious, non-alcoholic, a remedy for all manner of ills, a non-habit-forming stimulant and the like. But it was the brand name that caught Latimer. Juggernaut.

A red-and-white variant of the same design used as the basis for the lead models.

Latimer scrabbled in the envelope. Other artwork spilled out. Alternate versions of the labels. Proposed images for posters, advertising hoardings, signage. Each of them proclaiming the same message: that Juggernaut was a health tonic. That Juggernaut was an ideal beverage for those who craved a little stimulation but who did not want to resort to alcohol. That its properties were positive, reviving, invigorating.

Could that really be what this was all about? Some carbonated drink for those who'd taken an oath of sobriety?

It could not be true. People were not killed over recipes for dandelion and burdock. There was little else useful in the office. Another door stood beyond. It was locked.

'Do we have a key for this?'

'Talbot shook his head. 'Mister Bradshaw might. Or ...' His voice trailed away. 'Just Mister Bradshaw. This is his office.'

'And what goes on in here?' Latimer indicated the locked door.

'I'm not certain, sir. Nothing much. I don't think I've seen him use it.'

There was no way to open it except through force. Then Latimer remembered the key left by Utterson. He dug through his clothing until he found it. No good. Utterson's key wouldn't even fit into the hole in the plate.

Smashing the door open would cause an inexplicable fuss. And Latimer was now a wanted man.

He'd have to leave it. For now.

The light form the torch had yellowed and dimmed. The power wouldn't last in the batteries for long. Just enough time for a quick look around before they got out of here.

There were sacks of ingredients stacked by a hopper. Latimer checked inside one. Sugar. Inside another, a white powder with a mildly acidic, lemony taste. Some kind of flavouring, he assumed. Tubing indicated where water was introduced into a mixing tank below the hopper. A second, smaller entry point above the hopper. A range of graduated slim metal poles. A dipstick on an engine. That's what they looked like.

So this was where the batches were mixed up.

The sticks indicated different blends. Different proportions of water, sugar and flavouring. Different strengths of the beverage. And then there others notation. These were not the only ingredients. That wasn't quite correct: in one formulation, these were the only three ingredients. But not in others, according to the measuring devices.

The torchlight was by now orange. It barely cast more than a few feet.

'Wait here,' Talbot said. 'Give me the torch and I'll fetch another.'

Latimer handed the light over. Talbot wound his way past the machinery. Within a few footsteps, the torch was barely aglow.

Latimer found the darkest part of the room. He started into it, willing his eyes to acclimatise to the darkness. With each blink the different greys made themselves more apparent. Pipe work and machinery gained definition. The work became more apparent again.

A scuffing sound from across the room. The snick of a switch being tried. Then a bloom of light on, then off. 'Talbot?'

Footsteps back. 'There in a moment, sir. The switch won't stay locked with this one.' The footsteps grew colder.

Latimer could see Talbot returning, but he didn't see any light. The damned thing must be faulty. 'We can swap the batteries over into the old one.' The switch cover was fine on the first torch.

'Didn't think of that,' Talbot said. His voice was still distant. The footsteps were closer still. Talbot was only a few paces in front of Latimer.

That wasn't right. Talbot's face loomed out of the grey. Torchlight snapped on far behind him, casting the face back into shadow. But it wasn't Joseph Talbot's face. It was that of his brother.

Latimer saw the punch being thrown. A jab to the face. It was going to hurt.

Latimer went down under the force of the blow. He rocked back, and then fell. He didn't black out, but new colours swam before him, and the Talbot brothers' voices sounded as though Latimer was deep underwater.

'He awake?'

'Dunno. Don't think so.'

'As long as he's alive.'

'Didn't hit him that hard.'

Light in the eyes. Latimer retched. His nose felt broken. Blood had collected in his mouth. He coughed. Fluid spattered from him. After-images from the light mixed with the punch-colours. Green-red flecks scattered to the extremities of his vision.

'Pick him up.'

'You do it.'

'You knocked him down. And my arm's still busted, isn't it?'

'That'll get fixed though.'

Latimer was lifted to his feet. Two sets of Talbot eyes stared back at him. The Talbots exchanged glances. Latimer didn't want to reach for the handgun, because he knew he'd never get it out in time to be of any use and he didn't want to draw attention to it being there.

Expecting the second punch didn't make it hurt any less. But blacking out this time did.

#

Water brought him around. A glassful had been thrown in his face. Latimer blinked the wet away. He spat. A gobbet of blood hit the floor.

He had been seated in a swivelling office chair, the kind with a low back that came around on each side to form arm supports. His wrists were tied to the armrests. There were three others in the room. The two Talbots and, in front of them, a dripping tumbler in his hand, a man that Latimer had not seen before.

He was perhaps forty-five. He was tall, balding and gave the impression of a once-slim man who had recently turned to fat. His clothes, though good, were a size too small, as though he'd dressed in another's garb. 'Doctor Latimer,' he said. 'Welcome back.'

'How long?'

'A few minutes only, it seems. I was not far away.'

The door to the windowless room they were in stood ajar. Latimer guessed from the little he could see that they were in the inner office in the back of the bottling plant.

'Bradshaw, I presume.'

The man responded by refilling the glass from a small whisky jug. Latimer winced in anticipation. 'Relax. Take a sip.' He held the water close enough for Latimer to drink. 'So,' he said afterwards, 'we are acquainted.'

Latimer shook his bounds. 'What's the meaning of this?'

'"The meaning of this", he says. You, who betrays the trust the Pastor has put in you. Who betrays, indeed the Trust. You, who sneak abroad after hours. You, who meddle in matters that do not concern you. You, who have developed an uncomfortable knack of being in the wrong place at the wrong time.' He now took a folded piece of paper out and opened it for Latimer to see. 'You, who are wanted.'

A sketch of Latimer's face. A physical description. The sheet was headlined "Murder: Reward £400". Sightings were to be reported to the Director of Criminal Investigations, Scotland Yard.

'You ask what the meaning of this is. Let me show you.' Bradshaw now removed a small vial capped with a rubber-tipped dropper. The vial contained a port-tinted liquid. He dripped two splashes of the red fluid into the remnants of the water in the tumbler. The vial was reclosed and tucked away on Bradshaw's person. 'Good health,' he said, and drank the now-blushed water.

The Talbots took steps back. Bradshaw winced, as though the solution had irritated his throat. He opened his mouth to speak, but only a gasp escaped.

Bradshaw dropped to his knees, clutching his neck. The irritant had become a burn. His hands now came forwards, Bradshaw kneeling before Latimer. His head went down. Bradshaw was coughing, choking, struggling for breath.

The Talbots did nothing to help. They stood back. Watchful, amused.

Bradshaw's bald pate quivered. The skin puckered, contracted. It was tightening. Little follicles became apparent. New hair began to emerge from the formerly-smooth crown.

Latimer pushed himself back in the chair. The castors allowed him a foot or so back before colliding with some obstruction behind. Latimer did not think to check what it might have been. His eyes were on Bradshaw.

Bradshaw was back up on his haunches. His head was still lowered, but his scalp was alive with fresh growth. The same with the backs of his hands. The hands elongated – no, the skin was reforming around them. It was as though an intermediate layer of fat between muscle and skin had been removed.

And now Bradshaw raised his face for Latimer to see. The features were still there, and there the same as before but there was a lightness in the skin, a youth and vitality that had not been there before. New stubble peppered the chin, but this served only to accentuate the sharp definition of the bone structure where there had previously been a more rounding bulk.

Bradshaw stood. As tall as before, but not his clothes no longer strained around him. If anything, they were slack on the body. The new room in the garments reinforced the change. Bradshaw had lost perhaps twenty years. Where a middle-aged gentleman had been, a young man now was.

Bradshaw blinked, and Latimer saw that the red tint in the glass had transferred itself to his irises. The black of each lens was encircled with a sunset.

Red levels had risen.

Bradshaw breathed, open-mouthed. Sweat now pinpricked his brow. The new hair was slick with perspiration, like a baby's when struck with a fever.

But he was alive. So, so alive. He was smiling, now

grinning, exultant. Triumphant.

'Doctor Latimer,' he said, his voice both softer yet raw with exertion. He picked up the tumbler. The glass was thick. It may well have been crystal. Bradshaw cupped the tumbler and squeezed. It crumbled in his hand with a series of sharp cracks. He dropped the shards to the ground. A clear splinter was embedded into the meaty part as the base of his left thumb. Bradshaw slid the piece out, wrapping his hand with a kerchief. He licked the blood from the splinter and dropped the now-clean shard.

Now he opened the hand and dabbed away most of the blood. A new cut, livid and open. It would need stitching.

Bradshaw went back to his haunches so that Latimer could see without any possibility of obstruction. Blood beaded in the cut. Bradshaw licked the wound, drawing his tongue across the flesh in a slow, deliberate manner. Latimer winced at the display, but could not look away.

Saliva glistened over the skin. More blood coloured the pink flesh, oozing from the wound. The blood ran because it was being squeezed out. The cut was closing, as though it was being buttoned up by minuscule invisible fingers.

The fissure sealed itself. The only evidence that it had ever been there: a pale raised welt and a smear of blood. Bradshaw wiped the hand again, and then even that had gone.

'Abracadabra,' Bradshaw said. 'Quite the trick, don't you think?

There was no point in replying. There was little point in goading the man. Latimer waited for Bradshaw to speak again.

'Well, if that doesn't impress you, perhaps this will.' Bradshaw clicked his fingers and Joseph Talbot disappeared into the outer room. He was gone only a handful of seconds, but while he was away, Bradshaw's fingers continued to fidget, as though the muscle memory of the clicking action compelled them to echo the movement and would not be stopped. A twitch now developed in Bradshaw's left eye.

Talbot reappeared with the box of toys, its lid removed. Bradshaw took the once-damaged hand and pulled out a half-dozen or so of the little models. He breathed, open-mouthed. The fist clenched. Bradshaw grunted, soft, just once. The fist reopened. The lead toys were squashed together into a chaotic jumble of trunks and protuberances. Bradshaw tilted his hand, and let the solid lump of fused metal drop to the floorboards. He held his hand open for inspection. A dark flower blossomed, a rose of bruising. But even as Latimer watched, the bruise faded. The palm of Bradshaw's hand returned to its previously uninjured state.

'The qualities of the elixir,' Bradshaw whispered, 'are not easily won. Control is required and there may be ... inconsistencies in the equilibrium between dosage and its effects in any given occasion. Be assured, sir, that the dose that I have taken is not excessive. That this is merely a minor demonstration of the efficacy of the elixir. But bending metal and the repair of minor injury is the work of a magician, one might interject. That these are stage tricks and parlour games best suited for music hall amusement. That this is not the work of serious men.

'Let me assure you, sir, in advance, of the seriousness of our intent. Of the focus of our resolve.' He turned to the Talbots. 'You,' Bradshaw said, indicating Thomas, 'help me carry him down. You-,' he said, now speaking to Joseph, 'find something to keep him quiet.'

Joseph grinned. 'Sorry about this, Doctor.' He started to unravel the binding on his broken wrist. 'Open up, there's a good chap.'

There was no reason to resist. To do so would be to risk another blow. Latimer opened his mouth and Talbot stuffed in some of the bandaging. Latimer made a dam with his tongue to make his mouth seem fuller than it was.

Satisfied that enough was crammed in, Talbot wrapped more of the bandage around Latimer's head, securing the jaw. He tied the cloth off. 'All yours.'

Bradshaw and Thomas lifted Latimer up in the chair and carried his back through the bottling plant. The stairs were wide enough for him to be taken down in with relative ease.

Downstairs, and some of the trestle tables used for the lunchtime soup kitchen had been rearranged to make an impromptu auditorium around the boxing ring. There were perhaps twenty men there. Most of them were dressed in civilian garb indicating status from working man to clerk. Black faces, white faces. There were three in evening dress, lurking at the back of the room. Pastor Benedict was there. He was dressed simply in a black cassock, no dog collar, his sleeves rolled to the elbows.

The warehouse was transformed in atmosphere. There was an ozone charge in the air, the electric expectancy of a lightning storm. The men were hunched forward. Bottles had been distributed from crates. Some smoked pensively. One man removed his cap, turned it round so that the peak pointed back down his neck, and replaced it upon his head.

Latimer's chair was placed into the ground. Bradshaw got up through the ropes and onto the springy boards of the boxing ring. He held a hand up for silence.

'Gentlemen. Gentlemen! My thanks for your attending this evening. A small celebration if you will before the events of the week to come. Our card is short tonight. But two bouts for your delight, your delectation, your amusement. On the undercard, brothers, no less.' The Talbots stepped forwards. 'Joseph and Thomas Talbot. A fight of one round of unlimited duration. No boots, no gloves. No Queensberry rules. A fight to unconsciousness or to the point of interception by our good friend Mister Maynard here.'

Bradshaw indicated a man to the left of the room.

The man had a rifle cradled in his arms. Latimer had seen him before. Smallpox scars pitted his face. Elsewhere in the crowd were the men Latimer had christened Bull Neck and Tall Man. The latter held an arm up in ironic greeting.

The pox-scarred Maynard made a show of chambering a round. The rifle was then returned to its resting place.

'And then, gentlemen, a very special and late addition to the card. Might I present Doctor Latimer, who has lately become privy to aspects of our enterprise? Tonight's presentation will conclude, therefore, with a display of the ancient and noble science of interrogation, conducted by myself.' A susurrus of chatter, quickly faded.

'Gentlemen. Pastor. If we might begin.'

The two Talbots hoisted themselves into the boxing ring, as did Pastor Benedict. A stool was placed on the ring, with two mugs and a jug of water. Bradshaw checked over Joseph Talbot's broken wrist and then told the two young men to strip to the waist and remove their boots. As they undressed he prepared two drinks. One, Latimer noted, contained an additional two drops of the undiluted elixir added to the water.

Ready, and with the excess clothing taken away by an onlooker, the Talbots stood in the centre of the ring. Bradshaw stood between them, Benedict, with the two glasses, to one side. 'Gentlemen,' Bradshaw crowed, 'if you would look upon this young man's arm.' Thomas Talbot held it aloft. 'Note the heavy bruising, the swelling around the wrist area. There is a break here, a fracture. Surely it would be an unfair fight if this could proceed. What say you that we even matters up?'

A cheer from the crowd. The sound was ragged through scarcity of numbers, but it was still fierce.

'What say you we heal this hurt?'

'Another cheer, louder this time, more unified.

'What say you we equip these men to fight?' Some were now on their feet, applauding and shouting.

Benedict held out the drinks. The Talbots toasted the crowd, who lifted their bottles also, and they all drank as one.

Seen second time around the effect was no less astonishing. Latimer fixed on Joseph Talbot throughout. The young man buckled with the first splash of the linctus in him, and dropped, good hand out, to the canvas covering the boxing ring boards. He raised the broken arm.

Some stood on their trestle benches to see better. One or two came forwards. Talbot glowed. His skin pinkened. It shimmered with movement, the skin rippling, pulsing. Sweat pricked the hairs on Talbot's arm. The skin undulations flicked the perspiration off. Water arced through the air. Latimer felt a hundred tiny impacts. Doll's house rain.

He blinked the water away as best he could. Attention was focused around the room onto the Talbot boys. Latimer tried his bounds, but they were tight around his wrists, allowing little play. Even though he still wore his coat, there was no way to reach the pocket. He turned, swivelling the chair by a few degrees. What if the coat was inspected? What if the weapon was guessed through the fabric? What if it tumbled out onto the floor?

Now Talbot was standing up, his brother rising with him. They did not seem younger, not like Bradshaw had done, but they were undeniably more vital. Eyes were clear, skin tight and flawless, musculature lean and supple beneath. They could have been life models for renaissance sculptors. Joseph Talbot punched the air, triumphant. His arm was healed.

The crowd clapped, cheered. Catcalls. Wolf-whistles pierced the applause. Now Bradshaw hushed them, battening them down with his arms. 'Order, gentlemen. Best of order if you will. The rules, by way of recap. One round. No limits. To unconsciousness.' Bradshaw stepped away to allow an unrestricted view. He came to stand behind Latimer. He positioned the chair so that Latimer was forced to gaze at the boxing ring. Bradshaw hunkered down. 'Now, let's see what our men are made of.'

Someone – Benedict? – blew a whistle. The bout began.

Both Talbots dropped into crouching positions, arms hanging loose, fists formed, but lightly, as though the extra energy used in keeping the fingers tight would be accounted for later in a less inefficient punch. Thomas moved first, straightening up and letting loose two rangy jabs. The punches were intended to do little more than keep his brother at bay.

They rotated around each other. Twin planets orbiting an invisible sun. Thomas threw a jab, a left, then immediately followed with a swinging wide right to the head. The fist connected with Joseph's ear. Joseph's head jerked over. A left followed, a jab again, but fairly in the middle of the face. Joseph's nose cracked. Blood flew with the retracting fist.

The impact stunned Joseph, but the combination off blows had left Thomas without any follow-up, so he backed up a step to regroup. The second's pause in the barrage, plus the trickle of blood from the nose over Joseph's top lip was all the persuasion he seemed to need to retaliate.

Face now stained with running blood, Joseph stepped forward and his brother. Left, right. Left. Three snappy blows to the shoulders. These had the effect of further propelling his brother back, plus in addition it put him off recovering his own rhythm. Thomas had no means to counter without regrouping once more. Joseph did not give him the opportunity.

A right to the face snapped Thomas's head back. He was now on the ropes. Joseph's knuckles were smeared red, but it was not his own blood. Nudges with the left kept Thomas upright, while the right repeatedly impacted to the head. Already Thomas's eyes were ballooning. His nose was gone, a mulch of skin and cartilage.

Blood splashed onto the unbleached canvas of the boxing ring. Thomas's mouth hung open as he gasped for air, his nose useless against the torrent of punches. Now a meaty left to the lips forced another cracking. The jaw must have been broken with that last blow.

Latimer winced. There was little way that Thomas could withstand much more. But he refused to drop. The gathering roared its approval, both at the barrage from Joseph and at his brother's fortitude. It was as though there was no pain being inflicted; merely injury.

There were drugs that might induce such imperviousness to pain. And there were drugs that might conceivably induce the capacity to remain single-minded, resolute in either crippling your own kin, or in standing firm against onslaught from one's own.

The Talbots were matted in blood, their hair slick with gore, their bodies streaked with sweat and the bloody evidence of punishment given and received.

Joseph snarled, his teeth masked with ruby liquid. Thomas stood up to his brother to the extent of wrapping his left arm around the top rope to support himself. He would not go down under any circumstances.

Latimer struggled against his bounds, but Bradshaw's hand came down hard on his shoulder, gripping him tight. 'Calm yourself, man. See the levels rise.'

Joseph growled, a guttural animal sound. His teeth still bared, he turned to one side, to fix Bradshaw with a questioning glance. Bradshaw nodded. Joseph's eyes were red. The same red that still pigmented Bradshaw's though this glowed, as though the scarlet light behind them was shining all the stronger.

Bradshaw had given Joseph a greater dose of the elixir. The dosage had healed the break, but it had done more too. Whatever properties it possessed of youthfulness, strength and vitality were accompanied with those of violence, animalistic urges and barely-controlled impulses.

With the nodded command from Bradshaw what little restraint there had been on Joseph Talbot's behaviour was loosed. The dog was allowed to run wild.

Joseph swung again, and this time Thomas's neck broke. An almighty right hand swept his head over almost so that one ear touched the shoulder. Thomas slumped down from the ropes, hanging there by the hand still caught in the rope works. His head lolled uselessly. Blood ran from his ruptured face.

But Joseph was not yet done. The fists barely ceased their destructive motion. Bruising crept visibly across Thomas's chest and along his arms. Another great blow hammered into his exposed ear. With this, a bone sheared through the skin, piercing the neck.

This new corruption cause gasps from the crowd. Latimer tried to back away, but Bradshaw held him in place.

Joseph grabbed his brother's head with both hands and twisted. Muscles and tendons sheared. Bones popped out of true. Skin tore in soft jagged rips. The head did not come off, and with his hands now greasy with gore, Joseph found it hard to maintain a grip. He went to adjust, to finish the job.

An idea must have pierced the drug's control. Unless this new notion was a fresh product of the elixir's operation. Joseph slung his head back, held the head away from the shoulders where it was torn away the most, and sunk his teeth into the ripe red wound.

'Now,' Bradshaw said, the word seemingly too soft to carry far.

A single crack, then the immediate echo of a weapon fired in close proximity in an enclosed space. Joseph Talbot's head was bleeding from a small precise hole at the back, just above the bony lump of the occipital bone. Talbot slumped forwards onto the canvas. This motion dragged his brother's corpse off the ropes. It laid over him.

Maynard, unwrapping the rifle's carrying strap from around his hand. Maynard, expelling a used cartridge. The cartridge clattering daintily on the floor. Then the smell: blood and sweat and smoke and cordite. Then echo, then silence.

And then the applause. As rapturous as might be wrought from the two dozen or so in attendance. Bradshaw now climbed back into the ring, careful to keep to the clean half of the boxing arena.

'Do you see, my brothers? The wonder of the new century.' He held the vial of the elixir aloft. 'A tiny dose brings exhilaration, a freedom from workday cares, a little pep. And alcohol-free, to boot! Enjoyment and relief from dull cares without the misery of intoxication and the privations of abuse and poverty on the working family. There will be no debilitation in the East End, no wasted generation of men, when the Juggernaut is by their side!'

Bottles were raised again, and there was cheering. Glass clinked in toast. Bradshaw continued. 'And we shall build a generation of Londoners, a generation of Englishmen who can withstand any enemy, any threat, no matter how great. And if called upon we shall answer that call, and we shall be victorious!'

The tumult that followed the speech was little short of rapturous. Latimer's bounds remained firm, but he realised that he had been approaching his situation from the wrong angle. He did not have to get his hands loose. He had to get the gun to his hand.

Bradshaw let the excitement subside. He did not force calm upon his followers, though, but eyes bright and beaming, let the atmosphere find a new equilibrium. His attention on the onlookers, and their attention on him, gave Latimer seconds to act.

Latimer trapped a trailing edge of his coat under one of the castors. Satisfied the cloth could be secured, he worked the chair back a touch. The cloth tightened. Now he pushed back, further tautening the material. He shifted to permit the coat to be caught fully in the castor's workings. The lining began to tear along the seam. Latimer felt the stitching pop.

The lining hanging loose, Latimer scrabbled to catch it under a heel. He repeated the stretch and tear manoeuvre. The strain on the pocket was now as much as the material could bear. Again, he felt its resistance give. One more effort and it would shear.

'But do not take my word for it. Listen now to your priest. The man who founded this place as a haven from the outside world and its cruelties and unfairnesses. Who put bread in men's bellies and the fire of Christ in their hearts. Fuel and fire to be driven by the pistons of strong working arms. A man who saw right that Jesus and England best be served not by scrawny wastrels unfit to do a day's honest labour or to wear a uniform in battle, but with soul and body nourished alike, and trained. Trained in Scripture and in the warrior arts. Through fist and with truth!'

Pastor Benedict came forward. He used a stool to help clamber up onto the raised stage of the boxing ring. The pastor was stockily-built, with bushy eyebrows and thinning hair so blonde it appeared almost white. He was clad in his usual cassock-like robe, plain black with a flash of white at the neck. This was no clerical collar, though, but a swatch of loose cloth, almost as though he'd tucked a small napkin in before eating, and had forgotten to remove it after his meal. He unrolled his sleeves as though he'd finished washing his hands.

'Pastor,' Bradshaw said, clasping him close before releasing him. 'What is your role?'

Benedict raised his arms. Latimer knew what was coming. An old invocation. Saint Augustine or some such.

Benedict spoke: 'Disturbers are to be rebuked, the low-spirited to be encouraged, the infirm to be supported, objectors confuted, the treacherous guarded against, the unskilled taught, the lazy aroused, contentious restrained, the haughty repressed, litigants pacified, the poor relieved, the oppressed liberated, the good approved, the evil borne with, and all are to be loved.'

Throughout the recitation, Latimer stretched the coat lining further. It gave, the material giving way fully under the increased tension. It ripped loose as far as his bounds would allow. Far enough.

'All are to be loved,' Benedict said. 'Even those who would stand in our way.'

Latimer dared not move.

At a signal from Bradshaw, Bull Neck and Tall Man left their seats and crossed to Latimer. Bull Neck pulled out a folding blade, a French Opinel, and twisted it open. He ran the sharp edge over Latimer's face. Latimer pulled away. Bull Neck let the blade glide over Latimer's shoulder and down his arm to the cords that restrained him. 'Try anything,' he grunted, 'and you'll get stuck good.' His breath was thick with tobacco.

Bull Neck cut through the binding on Latimer's right hand, and then his left. 'Get up then,' he said.

Latimer stood. He trapped the trailing edge of the lining as he got up.

'You're next,' Tall Man said, shoving Latimer forwards. 'Up you go.'

Latimer made a show of lurching under the blow, keeping the material hard under his shoe. The material sheared across itself rather than along the stitching line. Bull Neck reacted to the sound, turning to suss where it was coming from.

Latimer now staggered, rotating as he went. But he was not out of control. Bull Neck's momentary distraction gave him the time he needed. Latimer, hand in pocket, shot Tall Man. The round caught him full in the gut. Tall Man collapsed back into the chair Latimer had just vacated. The chair careened into Bull Neck, who dropped his knife.

The immediate threat dealt with, Latimer fell to one

knee and fired twice at Maynard. One round hit, not on target, but down and to the left of where he had aimed. A red rosette snapped into existence at the shoulder joint. The rifle, being held at port arms, fell away.

Now Latimer ran. He shifted the pistol to his left hand so it was plainly visible to the crowd as he made for the door. Once there, he fired two more rounds. He shot both times into the air, but the volley did the trick in making men scatter.

The air outside was bracing. Being cloistered inside must have made him foggy. Either that or there was some residual cloudiness from the battering he'd taken.

No time to think on it. Brick Lane was steady with foot traffic; carousers crawling from pub to pub. Latimer ran back the way he'd come. He crossed Brick Lane at a trot, and then sped back up when re-entering Fournier Street. He turned right at the Commercial Street junction and kept zigzagging left then right for six streets or so until he was no longer certain where he was.

He paused to gather breath. He ripped the loose lining away and buttoned the coat to give him some outward semblance of gentility. He checked the ammunition clip. Three rounds left. He knew this, but went through the mechanics of the process anyway.

Three rounds would not be enough.

Latimer started walking again. He found himself not far from Old Street. He could track west across London from here with ease.

So, he had seen the truth of the Juggernaut. Henry Jekyll's potion, or at least variants of it, had been reconstructed, presumably from other scraps of notes found elsewhere. That in itself pointed to a solution of one of the mysteries of the last couple of days. The memos from Hyde had pointed to the existence of copies of Jekyll's work that he'd made. Bradshaw had copies of this work.

The tracing of Latimer, the thugs despatched to lift

the documents from the solicitor's office, the violence that had followed. All this had been to gain exclusivity. They wanted to be absolute that they had the only copies of Jekyll's work.

Or was it?

The effects of the serum were not quite as Hyde's notes suggested. Perhaps they believed that there were some further compound that eluded them, an ingredient that had not been sourced. There was reference in Hyde's notes to Jekyll's belief that there had been some impurity in the original batch, an impurity that had not repeated itself in subsequent supplies of the tincture's raw materials. Perhaps that was the secret that was sought. Not just that they wanted the only copy of the work, but that they felt that they lacked certain vital information. Either a clue as to the nature of the impurity or some other specific.

In any case, what they had done was to manufacture the tincture. More than that, it was evident from the bottling plant, from the mentions of Juggernaut as a quack medicine, as a non-alcoholic tonic, and even from the little lead figures – surely advertising inducements, gewgaws to make the brand that more memorable - that something more was planned.

More notions crowded in. Overlapping ideas. The start point had been the mission. The brand of muscular Christianity that Pastor Benedict had espoused. That the way to redemption lay not just in a saved soul, but in a healthy, active, nourished, and whole body.

And what was so wrong with that? That one might draw a parallel between temporal existence without excess and the reward of life everlasting seemed straightforward enough. That exercise, nutrition, a refusal to indulge in intoxicants and to lead, by extrapolation, a decent Christian life might very well be the foundation of a spiritual reward. Or one might spin the idea around. That in order to try to claim that same reward, one might renounce one's wicked ways, or perhaps be convinced, whether through ministry or circumstance, that the way towards the light was through abstinence and sobriety.

But this was the work of any of several organisations, both religious and secular, who had issues with what that doggerel poet McGonagall had termed "demon Drink" in his terrible poem.

Temperance did not allow for a man to tear another apart.

There were multiple agendas at play. Or were there? Perhaps there was just the one. There was a connection that Latimer was missing. The elements did not combine.

He was now on Old Street proper, not far from the under- and over ground railway stations. He walked west, away from the possibility of trains.

Latimer needed corroboration. There was one man who had said he'd be able to provide some, if it were needed. Guest, the clerk. That would be the next call.

Latimer crossed the road. By now Mosley and Abberline would have retraced his steps as far as they'd been able. The move from Utterson to Guest would have been a straightforward one for them to have judged. This was good in a way, because it led Latimer to reckon that their investigations would have moved on, doubtless with an instruction for Guest to contact Scotland Yard if Latimer were to reappear.

So be it.

He stopped outside a clock shop. The clock-faces in the window display were all halted at the customary ten to two. There was ticking, nevertheless. He checked above, and a timepiece was there, jutting over the shop doorway on a jib like a hanging pub sign. Eleven o'clock. A little past.

Pub noises. Light at upstairs windows. The city had not yet settled down for the night. Latimer resumed, the decision giving his striding fresh purpose.

He would have an answer to his questions before the night was over.

#

It took almost an hour to cover the distance to Guest's street. His premises were shuttered and dark. Latimer drew the gun and used its handle to rap on the door.

Guest could not have been asleep. As he had done the day before, his head soon appeared upstairs. This time Guest said nothing. The head disappeared, and a lamp was lit. The window was closed and locked.

Latimer put the weapon away. He imagined Guest getting hurriedly dressed, coming down the stairs, scurrying through to the front door. He ran a hand through his hair. He unbuttoned and then re-buttoned his coat. He breathed in deep, three, four times. On the last breath, Latimer exhaled slowly. He wanted to appear calm and reasonable. In control.

The door was opened and Guest peered out. He ushered Latimer in.

They went through into the downstairs back room. Without speaking, Guest pulled a chair out for Latimer to sit on and from a cupboard extracted a glass and a bottle of whisky. The scotch was old, judging by the tattered condition of the label. There was perhaps a quarter of the original quantity remaining inside.

'I don't keep strong liquor in the house, I think I mentioned, Latimer.' Guest poured half an inch into the glass. He gestured towards the cupboard as he stoppered the bottle. Patent medicines lined the shelf. A roll of bandages, somewhat yellowed and frayed. The odours of liniment, of kaolin and morphine. 'I don't believe in it.'

'Medicinal purposes?'

'Something like that. Please, drink.'

'Nothing for you?'

'No. Besides, your need is greater than mine, I fancy, and in any case, when this old friend is gone I'll not be replacing it.'

Latimer drank. The scotch had an astringent quality. He wondered if it was a property of the distillation process

172

or of residing for an age next to bottled cough elixirs and muscle rubs.

'Almost midnight. And flustered, too, though you've made efforts to calm yourself down. A story to tell, perhaps, or a story to hear?' Guest pottered while he spoke, lighting a gas ring on the small kitchen stove with a match. He put a kettle – already full judging by the way it was manoeuvred – onto the flames. A teapot and caddy were found, as was a strainer and milk.

Latimer sipped from the glass. Guest kept himself busy with preparing the tea and did not speak until he came back to the small table with the now-filled teapot and two cups. Milk had been poured into a simple small jug. 'There's sugar there, if you take it,' Guest said, indicating a covered earthenware bowl already in the table.

'Just milk, thank you.' Latimer accepted the cup. He poured what remained of the whisky into the cup.

'I thought you may turn up here.' Guest blew across the surface of his tea. Little ripples shimmered on the caramel-coloured brew. 'I've had enquiries.'

'Mosley?'

'And another man. Frederick Abberline himself, no less. Still infamous in these parts as the man who didn't catch the Whitechapel murderer all those years ago. Or the killer of Danvers Carew, come of think of it, though that was overshadowed somewhat by the later events. There was another policeman involved in that investigation. Newcomen, his name was. You're quite the celebrity in the eyes of the law.'

'What did they say?'

'That you were now being considered as a "person of interest" in unspecified but serious crimes. Murder was alluded to, though they did not speak the word. Your reappearance here is to be reported with all speed, no matter what the hour. Little wonder that I was not already asleep when you knocked.'

'What did you say to them?'

'What could I say? I summarised our conversation. I mentioned that I'd suggested that you might seek an audience with Richard Enfield. I recounted my work history with Gabriel Utterson. I offered to show them some of my gun-smithing examples, though they demurred. They were here late afternoon. Four o'clock perhaps. Maybe five. Mosley left me a card with a telephone number.'

'I went to see Enfield.'

'And what did he have to say?'

'He told me exactly what I think you thought he would. Henry Jekyll. Edward Hyde. The whole sorry business and the little good that came of it in the form of the bequest that became the Hawksmoor Trust.'

'Then you have the whole story.' Guest's tea was by now cool enough to drink. Latimer sipped from his own. The liquor made the tea bearable to taste.

'What do you know about the Trust?'

'Not much, really. Soup kitchens and pastoral care in the service of the Lord. Doubtless there's temperance preached and the hope that some of those sheep who are lost or confounded will become soldiers of Christ.'

'And what do you know about Juggernaut?'

'Oh.' Guest added another half a teaspoon of sugar to his cup, and then poured more tea over. He did not introduce more milk to the beverage. He fixed Latimer with a shrewd look. 'What do you know of Richard Enfield?'

'Only what I've gathered these past two days. A man of some means, something of a rogue and a dilettante in his youth. Distant cousin to Utterson, hence his involvement in this sorry affair. I've seen him at his club, where it's clear he holds a position, whether formal or informal, of some seniority and renown. He is on the board that oversees the Trust.'

'Continue.'

'But the Trust, or at least the Chicksand Street refuge,

is a sham. A front for a wider, darker organisation.'

Guest tasted the freshened tea. 'What kind of organisation?'

Latimer organised his thoughts. He poured more tea for himself to buy a moment. 'Chicksand Street operates as a soup kitchen. A refuge for the dispossessed of the area, and particularly for young men. Though ostensibly a Christian organisation, help is taken from all comers, even from Sikhs who are open to offering their custom of hospitality to the poor of the area.

'So, I have this wrong.' The revelation came to Latimer as he was speaking. There was no eureka instance, more of a rereading of words already written while attention had been misplaced elsewhere. 'The pastor, the church trappings, the naming of the trust after a noted church architect. All this is as a shop display. Window-dressing. That the true aims of the organisation are hidden by this placid exterior.'

'And what are those aims?'

Latimer shook his head. 'All I have are the outside signs. Temperance is promoted. There's care and attention paid to the physical wellbeing of the poor of the area. Hence the use of a nurse and latterly a doctor to minister to them. That a muscular form of Christianity is espoused. Exercise, boxing and so on.'

'Discipline,' Guest murmured.

'Yes. And then there is Juggernaut itself. On the surface, it appears innocuous enough. A patent tonic of some sort. A beverage intended as a stimulating alternative to alcohol. The Americans have several of the like, such as Coca-Cola, which started its life as a variant of a French coca wine, a mix of alcohol and cocaine, but has undergone several reformulations. The sales of such a beverage provides employment, generates income, offers an alternative to drink to those incapable otherwise of existence. On the face of it, a valid and indeed progressive enterprise.'

175

'But?'

'But Juggernaut is not the whole truth. Or else this benign version is not. Again, it's part of a deception. Jekyll's work has been continued. No, not continued. Emulated, recreated. They have the research, or at least one copy of it, and they've made multiple variations of his serum. I've seen at least two or three.'

'What do you mean?'

'On Friday. I was accosted, followed into a tube station by three thugs who turned out to be in cahoots with Bradshaw. They wanted papers left for me with Utterson's legal firm. One of them drank from a flask. It was as though that drink gave him an incredible impetus. A sudden burst of energy. And then this evening, on two separate occasions. I saw the potion work up close. One restored a hurt man to full health; one transformed a man - Bradshaw - into a younger version of himself. But the medicine has a darker element to it as well. It induces, at least in certain strengths, not just youth, or a stabilization of one's self at the first flush of full adulthood, since these effects are more pronounced on older men than younger, but something other, something fell, is unlocked. A rage. A compulsion, a capacity for brutality far exceeding the limits of everyday man. An unlocking of the animal within.'

The tea in front of Latimer was drunk. He did not remember having finished the cup, so lost he had been in his narrative. 'So, this is it. Bradshaw and others are using the Hawksmoor Trust to their own ends. The production of Henry Jekyll's elixir.'

Guest stood and prepared to boil another kettle. He sluiced the remnants from the teapot and rinsed the cups out, drying them as Latimer continued. 'And what was my earlier question?' Any answer was not forthcoming, as Latimer had begun again with his own developing thought process.

'It all fits. Bradshaw. He must have seen more than was let on those years ago. He found, or went back to seize from some hidden place, perhaps ransacking Jekyll's property before it was sold, some of the notes. He followed the clues. The early trials were unsuccessful. There were,' he paused, 'miscalculations.'

'So, a more cautious strategy was devised. After all, if a potion promising youth could be grasped, then time itself could be overcome. With the trust in operation there was a cover for the experiments. And so, Juggernaut was begun. He would have used the poor, the unremarked-upon. Fed them up and made them grateful. Would have had careful medical records kept to make assessments to any long-term damage done to individuals after they'd recovered from the immediate effects of the drug. That was why Doyle was there. That was why I was allowed to volunteer. And because of my – my questionable medical qualifications – I was in no position to be any the wiser as to their activities.'

'You believe that Bradshaw intends to market the elixir?'

'In its milder forms, yes. As an alternative to drink to temperance-minded folk, or to those who would be them. This would provide adequate cover for the manufacture of the real product.'

'And in its more…vital doses?'

'As a drug. A vile stimulant in the way that Jekyll used it. So that those who have guineas to spend may despoil themselves. He intends to profit from Henry Jekyll's sin. And that would be the Hyde personality's ultimate revenge. That there would be Hydes – or whatever name these dissolute creatures would be given – across London. That licence would be given to utter violence and depravity.'

'If I were you, I would seek another audience with Richard Enfield.'

'Why Enfield?'

'Enfield has, as you rightly understand, a position of influence and authority. Go to him. His word carries with it the weight of some of the highest authorities in the land, though he might never admit to it. If there is one man who might be listened to with such an outlandish tale as this, it is Enfield. If there is one man with the ability to marshal forces, such as Scotland Yard, both past and present, who are currently opposed against you, it is he. And if there is someone who has a personal investment in this legacy, and so would see the matter through to its zenith, it is he.'

Guest stood. 'Are you armed?'

Latimer withdrew the pistol and held it out, stock outward, for Guest to take.

'The new model? I've heard good things of these.' Guest felt the weight of the handgun, then placed it on the table, incongruous among the tea things. 'If you were unarmed, I might have lent you a piece. You are in an awkward position, and should not be unprotected. Ammunition?'

'Three rounds only. The rest in at my rooms.'

'And it would be unwise to return there. Mosley will certainly have eyes on your residence. One second, if you would.'

Guest disappeared upstairs. He moved with some speed and silence as he was back momentarily. In his hands, a small cardboard box. He lifted the lid off. The box was full of shells. Guest picked up the gun, removed the magazine and thumbed in rounds until the clip was full. He snapped the magazine into the stock. From his pocket, he produced an identical-looking magazine and filled this from the box. 'Preparedness,' he said. He slid the lid back onto the box and placed this out of the way.

'My thanks.'

'There's no need. The least that could be done.'

'I should go.'

'It's early. Stay here. See Enfield in the morning.'

'The only address I have for him is his club.'

'He resides there, as near as makes no difference. His own private pied a terre. By now he will have heard from

Mosley I am sure. He will receive you, or otherwise he will have planned for you to be brought to him, if he is the man I understand him to be. Rest here overnight I've no accommodation to offer you other than the floor, but I have spare blankets. Better that that walking the streets and risking arrest.'

'You're right. Thank you.' Latimer felt weary. Six hours in the last of winter would have been of no use whatsoever to him. He was tired, and the tea and scotch had done nothing to revive him. If anything, the effect had been soporific.

Guest took the box away and returned with an armful of faded but clean blankets. 'Not much, I'm afraid, but there it is.'

'You've been very good.'

Guest laid out two of the blankets, folded over lengthwise, to take the chill out of the flagstones and to provide a little comfort. That left two more. These were placed on the table for Latimer to arrange as he saw fit.

'I'll say goodnight.' Guest went upstairs. Latimer took off his shoes and jacket and laid down. He used one of the spare blankets as a covering, the other being folded over as an impromptu pillow. He rested the pistol within easy reach.

He had not intended to sleep. Just to rest. But he blinked, and blinked again, and when he blinked a third time, six hours had passed.

JUGGERNAUT: SUNDAY 19TH FEBRUARY 1911

It was noise above – Guest getting himself dressed, he supposed – that woke Latimer. He roused himself and put his shoes and jacket back on, and then folded the blanket bedding back up. These were placed with care on one of the kitchen chairs.

Latimer patted some cold water onto his face. He felt unrefreshed, unshaven. He stared out of the rear window over the sink. Neatly-stacked crates, covered with a tarpaulin. Access through to an outside lavatory. A gate in the six-foot high wall that led, presumable, to an alley. There was light, but the sun had not yet risen. A patchwork of blue sky and white clouds, under-lit to the east.

Guest came downstairs. 'Good morning.'

'Morning.'

'Usually I don't take breakfast. Not before chapel. My habit is to take a little something on returning. Porridge usually.'

'Thank you, no. I should go.'

Guest handed Latimer his coat. 'Good luck.'

'Thank you. And for your assistance and the ammunition.'

'None are required.'

'Nevertheless.'

'Just in case,' Guest said. 'Perhaps the back door and the ginnel beyond.' He told Latimer where he'd come out at either end of the passageway. 'Mosley might have posted a constable or at least had the beat-walkers keep their attention focused on the shop doorway.'

Guest unlocked the back door. Latimer and he shook. Guest's hand was soft, warm and dry.

Latimer squeezed out. The tarpaulined crates took up more room than he'd anticipated. There was scarcely any proper access through to the gate. Guest followed out. Latimer unlatched and unbolted the gate and checked left and right. He elected to go right. He did not look back. Behind him, there was the snap of the latch and the grating scrape of a bolt being driven home.

It had rained in the night, but already the dampness was lifting. Latimer started walking.

#

Hoardings clustered by a news seller's pitch outside Leicester Square tube station. A clock chimed eight somewhere. Latimer was unused to central London being so quiet. Early Sunday mornings were usually lost to him, a late-ish breakfast with a fading hangover and a spread of papers being the rule.

He walked across Trafalgar Square. Dark patches on flagstones, the last evidence of rain in the night, criss-crossed his path. Damp granite lions crouched. Nelson stared away, impassive.

A single hansom cut by, the cabbie raising a couple of fingers in acknowledgement as he passed. The unfailing English politeness of the early morning.

It was cold. Not chill enough to have the rain turn to frost, but a smart-enough sensation.

Now church bells. Early communion for the penitent.

Doubtless there'd be something at ten for those more leisurely about their faith. Though, he supposed, that later start would fill something of the dull ache of a listless Sunday.

Was there anyone praying for Doyle? For Utterson? Even for the dead Talbot boys?

And who would cry for Toby Latimer? He ventured that any attendance at his funeral would be sparse. The vicar, a couple of old soldiers, an interested party on behalf of the law, whoever had been rota-ed that week to play the organ. A brace of gravediggers; caps, neckerchiefs and mudded boots, waiting at the cemetery, rolling smokes and blowing into their hands.

Not much to show for almost forty years.

Pall Mall was just as barren. They sky had cleared, the last shreds of cloud being driven off east into the still-rising sun. Latimer walked on until he reached his destination.

He gripped the pistol stock in his pocket. There was the additional reassurance of the spare ammunition clip there also. The plan was simple. A confrontation with Enfield. If Mosley or Abberline stood in his way, then he would use the handgun to get past them. He didn't want to shoot anyone, much less would he aim to maim or kill, but he would not be gainsaid.

The chance that shoot-to-kill orders had been issued against him was there, though he doubted it. Much better to hustle him away, quickly question and arrange for a trial. Or else have him moulder in a cell until any interest in Doyle's death had dissipated. Then a hanging on a busy news day would put paid to any residual questions.

He stood in front of the Athenaeum building. There was no activity outside. Its doors were shut. A single motor-car was parked outside.

Latimer knocked on the imposing door, not bothering to check if there were some more discreet means of summoning the staff. A response came in seconds. The door creaked open, and the same doorman who had greeted Latimer on his first appearance at the club appeared.

'Richard Enfield, if you would.'

The door was opened and the doorman stood aside.

To the right, a member sat snoring in a wing-backed chair. He was white-haired, in full evening dress. There were purple stains around his mouth and on his shirt. A decanter and glass stood on an adjacent table.

'Richard Enfield,' the doorman said.

And there he stood. At the head of the stairs. Enfield was dressed as though for shooting. Tweed trousers and a matching waistcoat. He wore no topcoat. 'Latimer. Do come up. I was rather expecting you.'

Latimer ascended the staircase, leaving the footman and the snoring member behind.

Enfield led Latimer along the same corridor that he had been taken down on Friday and into the same long room. A table for two had been laid in the centre of the room. Enfield strode in. Latimer quickly tucked the pistol into his waistband at the small of his back. The spare clip went into his left front trouser pocket.

'Might I take your coat?' A flunky spoke from over Latimer's shoulder.

'Thank you.' If the tattered garment disappointed the servant, he made no indication.

Enfield gestured to the table. 'Please. Take a seat. You'll pardon me for saying so, but you give the appearance of a man needing a decent meal.'

Latimer said nothing, but took his place.

'As I said,' Enfield continued, floating a linen napkin over his lap, 'your arrival here was not unanticipated. Part of me thought that you'd have made an appearance late last night. I'd even made enquiries about providing a late supper should that have been the case. As it was, I polished off the cold meat platter and the cheese that'd been thoughtfully provided. The Club is remarkably amenable to last-minute requests of all kinds.'

Hot drinks arrived. Latimer had a cup of coffee poured for him. Enfield took tea instead. 'My usual eggs dish for the two of us, I should think. You don't mind me ordering for you?'

'Not at all,' Latimer said evenly. Dark oil swirled on the surface of the coffee. The drink smelled strong and rich.

'Tobias Latimer,' Enfield said. 'Toby to his chums, doubtless. Latterly, it transpires, masquerading as a doctor in general practice. Previous to that, a spotted career. Most of his adulthood spent in South Africa, part of which was in military service, part not. Returned to these shores in the last few months. And now,' he said, 'wanted for murder. The killing of a woman, I understand.'

The same servant who'd taken Latimer's coat returned with two plates. These were positioned in from of Latimer and Enfield. Two split toasted English muffins apiece, topped with thin-sliced boiled ham, poached eggs and a drizzle of Hollandaise sauce. The server returned directly bearing a silver sauce boat with more of the same condiment. Enfield poured more over each of the domes and then applied black pepper from a cruet-stand. He cut into the first of his eggs, releasing a low rumble of what could only be contentment at the rich orange yolk sluicing out and intermingling with the lighter yellow of the Hollandaise.

Latimer tasted the food. It was good, he supposed, but his hunger was at odds with his lack of appetite. He ate mechanically, methodically. Enfield opposite was lost to the indulgence of the rich food.

Finally, Enfield finished. He ran a last regretful finger around the moist spout of the sauce boat and then put the residue to his lips. 'We are all enslaved by our vices,' he said. 'I have long elected not to make any bones about this. Indeed, I have made it something of a credo to find myself freed by indulgence rather than be captured in its grasp. It is,' he concluded, 'simply a matter of perspective.'

Latimer left his knife and fork in the centre of his unfinished plate and pushed the platter forwards enough to indicate that he was sated.

'You don't mind, do you?' Enfield lifted his cutlery out of the way, placed Latimer's plate on top of his own, folded Latimer's used cutlery into a napkin, and set himself to the food that Latimer had left behind. 'My governess was somewhat strict on the matter. Finish up your dinner, she would say, and then you may have your dessert. I so looked forwards to puddings as a boy.'

Enfield ate fast. He cleared the second plate and then dabbed at his lips to remove any trace of yolk. 'Nowadays,' he said, 'my anticipations are somewhat different.'

'Juggernaut,' Latimer said. He took out the handgun and laid it where his plate had been.

Enfield appraised the weapon. 'That's not very sporting.'

Latimer dropped his napkin over the gun. There was no sense in startling the staff.

'What do you want of me, Latimer?'

'A full account. My name cleared. Justice for Maureen Doyle.'

Enfield furrowed his brow at the last comment. 'Anything else?'

'That should suffice.'

'I should think so too.'

Latimer reached out, his hand over the gun.

'You're not really going to shoot me, are you?'

'I'm wanted for murder. My reputation has been shattered, as it's now clear that I was leading a double life as a doctor. I'll never hold down a responsible position in this country again. At best, I'm on the run and discredited under my own name for life. At worst, I'll hang. With a murder charge already tabled against one, where's the deterrent? My choices are twofold: in avoiding capture or in exoneration. I prefer the latter to the former, but if you stand between me in either respect, then I'll have no compunction but to kill you where you sit.'

'More coffee before we begin?'

Latimer waved his hand in assent.

The plates were cleared away. Fresh coffee was brought and Enfield asked that they were not to be further disturbed unless the service bell was rung. They remained at the table, nothing but the napkin-covered pistol between them.

'I was always a greedy lad,' Enfield began. 'At nursery, at school, and then at university. When you're young, you can keep pace with yourself, whether your vices be food, drink, the company of others, or any combination. And I'm not afraid to confess that I have been selfish in my pleasures. Hence the reason why I never married. I wanted to, I suppose, and there was certainly a little pressure from my parents to settle down into genteel respectability – or at least to have the mask of a marriage to give that illusion – but it was ultimately never a priority.

'And I always wanted children. I may even have them. Lord knows there's been ample opportunity for that to have occurred. But, through whatever quirk of circumstance, I've never been saddled with demands for paying out for a bastard. A shame, in some ways. I would have very much enjoyed having a son. Watching him being raised, developing from a child to a man. And seeing what qualities he possesses.'

'And the relevance of this digression?'

'Lest I sound like an old man rambling to you, Latimer, there is a point to all of this. And it's not as though we must rush to get ready for communion, is it?

'It was matters such as this,' Enfield continued, 'which Utterson and I would discuss on our Sunday constitutionals. The conversation on our walks varied from week to week, of course, but there was a general thrust to our deliberations. I would make a confession of sorts and he, in his own way, would live something of a more exhilarating existence, albeit vicariously, than he might have done otherwise.

'That was the beginning of this. For me and for Utterson, when I recounted to him my first meeting with Edward Hyde.'

'The occasion when that young girl was brutally beaten in the street, and when Hyde, under duress from you and others, was forced to make some provision for her future care and did so on a cheque – which proved to be good – in Henry Jekyll's name?'

'The same.'

'You've thought about this for a very long time.'

'Twenty-five years, from then to this. Two monarchs dead and a third yet to be crowned. The calendar turning over from the nineteenth century to the twentieth. Electricity replacing steam. Horses being replaced by motor cars. Nation-states developing into empires. Much is changing and much has changed since the last days of Henry Jekyll.'

'And what of Jekyll's experiments to you?'

'Ah,' Enfield said. 'Do you mind if I smoke? It is a little early in the day for me to take a drink, but I do like a cigar with conversation, and I appear to be in a pleasantly discursive frame of mind.'

'By all means.'

Enfield smiled. 'And could I tempt you with a cigar also?'

'Thank you, no.'

Enfield crossed the room and took a humidor from a drawer in a dresser. He made a little ceremony about the lighting of the tobacco, and returned to the breakfast table directly, having picked up an onyx ashtray on his way.

'I am a rich man by anyone's standards, Latimer. And I have elected not to parlay this advantage in life into overt political or other power, preferring a life of quiet influence in a few well-chosen though particular corners of the world. I am, as I said earlier, selfish. Hence both my apartments here and my authority as regards some elements of the running and organisation of the Club, though I have never held a position. I found out while still a young man that there is both pleasure and profit to be yielded not in control, but in persuasion, and not in logical investment in prudent commodities, but in speculation, in gamble, and in risk.'

Enfield drew on his cigar. Soft folds of smoke exuded. The grip on the 1911 had never looked more inviting to Latimer as it did at that moment. To have the inky grey cloud punctured by a bullet. To have the lead slug tear the air between them apart and drill the life out of Enfield. But he had to know. He had the corners of a jigsaw assembled, but not the whole puzzle.

Latimer had to know everything.

'To that end,' Enfield said, 'I have made a range of investments and speculations over the years of a particularly audacious nature. I have balanced these with some more sober disbursements, but I tell you now that I have learned so much more about the world from a thousand pounds here or five hundred there than on sums fifty, a hundred times those amounts lodged in any bank or traded drearily in precious metals.

'And I was cheeky, too. That impudence extended to forming a company trading on my surname and its similarity to the common name of a certain munitions company. That same spirit was provoked by buying into rail lines and in barbed wire, in new chemicals and in the provision of uniforms to armies. As Europe develops, Latimer, so do the ambitions of its constituent countries. We have scrambled for Africa, grabbing at what we can. And that continent is merely the last of the great territorial acquisitions that we have been at the forefront of over the past two hundred years. First the Indian subcontinent and then islands to the east, such as Australia and New Zealand. At the same time, the Americas, North and South. Then Africa. All that remains are the inhospitable extremities, and they are falling. Peary located the North Pole in '09, and we are even now awaiting news from the South. The nation entire expects, hopes and prays that Captain Scott's Terra Nova expedition has this time claimed the South Pole for Great Britain.

'We have no more worlds to conquer, Latimer.'

'And?'

'And we will, out of necessity, turn upon each other. The martial instinct may be quelled by redirection into paramilitary endeavours such as exploration, but when there is nothing new to be claimed, there can only be conquest of that which was someone else's.'

'And you will be there to profit.'

'I will be there to ensure that Great Britain's interests are upheld. If a little money might be made along the way, then there is no harm in that.' Enfield tapped his cigar. Ash crumpled into the tray beneath.

'You're investing in war.'

'I'm investing in our nation's future. In the twentieth century. And also, in myself.' Enfield balanced the cigar on the ash tray and took out a small glass vial. 'You know what this is.'

The vial was the size of a large chess piece. The glass was smoked, so it was difficult to perceive the contents.

'Henry Jekyll's life's work?'

'And his death's.'

The vial was nothing. It could have passed unnoticed in any chemist's laboratory or in any doctor's surgery. To think that an item so insignificant had caused so much pain.

'Of course, it's not quite as Jekyll had intended.'

'No.' Enfield produced a second item. A lead figurine. It would have also passed, unremarked, a few days earlier. 'And neither was this.'

'Juggernaut.'

'A simple thing, yet so complex. It never fails to entice, an idea. Something so simple, yet strong. Invisible,

189

without mass or substance, yet more driving than any turbine or engine that mankind had yet manufactured. Jekyll had his idea. A means to unlock the baser instincts of man, and yet remain conscious within them, so that he might enjoy as a privileged spectator, the depraved ravages of his creation, Hyde. But he could not control the elixir he'd produced.

'And he could not control the persistence of his vision. I dreamt of his work, I imagined all manner of possibilities.'

A subtle click. Latimer reached for the gun. A second click. The door behind, being opened and closed. Latimer raised the gun, still under the napkin, and pointed it at Enfield.

Enfield opened his hands in a welcoming gesture. His eyes did not waver from the pistol. 'Bradshaw. My good man. Pull up a chair and join us.'

'You'll forgive me if I stand.' Bradshaw was dishevelled, as though he'd been awake all night. Perhaps he had been searching for me, Latimer thought. He was still in the clothes he'd been wearing the night before. His earlier transformation had withdrawn, so he was the older version of the man. If he was armed, he betrayed no evidence of it.

'Where I can see you.' Latimer directed Bradshaw across next to Enfield.

Enfield was all placatory smiles, though the good humour did not extend to his eyes. 'You arrive at a useful juncture. I was just explaining to Latimer here about ideas. About the possibilities of imagination. And I was about to talk on the subject of patience.'

Bradshaw's face was a sold mask of slow-burning hatred. Latimer had seen that face before. In military stockades, on the faces of prisoners. On internees in the concentration camps in South Africa. Bradshaw would like nothing more than to tear his neck from his shoulders.

'It surprises me, in retrospect, how things come

together. The random coalesces into the patterned, almost as though there was some divine ordinance in place, a scheme put in place by the eternals, that this was a destined conclusion. But, as that German philosopher puts is, there is no deity to whom we can call upon. God is dead, and it is us who have killed him. And if we are to free ourselves from the darkness of his shadow, from the blood of his murder, how are we to do this? We become gods ourselves. Or we tell ourselves that we are, for who but a god can kill a god?'

Enfield picked up the vial. 'And here is the key to the new century. A key that might unlock our potential.'

'A key that can make us rich,' Bradshaw said.

'Yes, yes.' Enfield raised his eyebrows to Latimer.

'A key that can make us powerful.'

Latimer thumbed back the hammer on the pistol. 'Get to the point.'

'Bradshaw. Why don't you tell him?'

'Why should I?'

Latimer interrupted. 'How am I supposed to know how clever you've been, if you don't tell me? And besides, I have this pointed at your chest.'

Bradshaw barked in laughter. 'Only the weak hide behind weapons.'

'And the strong?'

'The strong may become Juggernaut.'

'And there we have it,' Enfield said. 'Or an advertising slogan for it at least. That'll do very well on posters on the sides of omnibuses I should think. Why don't you tell him, Mr Bradshaw? Why don't you tell him all?'

'What's in it for me?'

'Gun or no, you can prove the quality of your words. I'll let you kill him. Which is what you want, isn't it?' Enfield turned to Latimer. 'I'd be obliged if you'd lower your firearm, just for a brief while. I'm going to call for a servant to clear away these things so we can talk more comfortably, and we'd hate to alarm the staff, no?'

\#

After the footman had cleared away the table, and fresh coffee and sparkling water had been ordered, the three relocated to the array of sofas and armchairs where Enfield had chatted with Latimer two days earlier. The servant was dispatched once more with strict instructions that the meeting was not to be interrupted.

'I want to know everything,' Latimer said.

'And then what?' Bradshaw's demeanour had not improved.

'And then I may kill you.'

'Indeed.'

'Everything, Bradshaw.'

'Go on, man,' Enfield interjected.

'He was always queer, Henry Jekyll,' Bradshaw said. 'Always. The other staff under stairs had all been with him for a long time, and they felt sorry for him in a way, having never married and not being as famous or as successful as his friend, his mentor I should say, Hastie Lanyon. But he had money and a great house and projects that kept him entertained. And he had his hobbies. Like Mister Enfield here, he had a taste for the gutter. Of course he kept himself to himself in the matter, but it was a secret within the household that he left the house, though a separate exit from his laboratory, and would be gone until the morning.

'And then came Edward Hyde.' Bradshaw took out a small sheaf of folded paper. He opened the sheets, laying them on the table between them. An assortment of newspaper articles: some cut from the page, some torn. A handbill for a play. Printed dust jackets for novels. The covers were garish. They were French.

'What is this?'

'This, Latimer, is Hyde.' Bradshaw spread the pieces of paper so they could be more clearly seen. The newspaper clippings dated back some thirty years at their oldest; some of the newer ones were less than five years old. Some referred to infamous murders, such as those attributed to Jack the Ripper. Others referenced less notorious crimes.

Bradshaw fanned the papers across the table. 'Hyde,' he said. 'In other guises. I was always a reader. I came to my letters later than you fine gentlemen doubtless did, but when I got them I was careful not to let them go. I loved the penny newspapers, the stories of murder and mayhem. And I was taken by reports in solid black ink, like as not with illustrations besides, that gave credence and authority to rumour and tattle, legends and scare-stories.'

He prodded one of the articles. 'Spring Heeled Jack, who shows his face across the city, terrorizing the citizenry, wreaking dark havoc. So, when Hyde came among us, it was as though my darkest childhood fantasies had been given form. Hyde left us, as you well know, but soon enough he was replaced by another Jack, the saucy Whitechapel knifeman. And he was but the first. The greatest by dint of not being caught. Of course, the shadow that he cast put Hyde in the shade and that was just as well, because it made people forget. The murder of Danvers Carew and the strange death of Hastie Lanyon have become little more than footnotes in the history of the Yard.'

'But with the new century, new legends have arisen.' Bradshaw now indicated the dust jackets, stabbing the titles with a finger as he named the pictured monstrous figures on the illustrations. 'Fresh versions of the old tales. See here? And here? Zigomar. Fantomas. Dark angels of the night. Sometimes suave and adventurous, sometimes utterly without moral. On the stage, in print and even in the cinematographic houses. What were once little more than tall tales to frighten children or excuses wrought by the drunk or confused have been made manifest.'

'And Hyde is the source of this?'

'There have always been demons. But what Jekyll did was to breathe life into a creation as none had been done before. Not stories on a page or a stage, but words made flesh. His experiments, his genius, was to loosen the stopper on the bottled genie of our potential as humans.'

'And this is your work, is it?'

'This was always my dream. And when young, the best that I could conceive of was to enter into service, to be near the great and the good and to live a little in the reflection of their glory. How naïve I was, not just in terms of childishness, but of lack of ambition for myself and for others like me.'

He tidied the papers away, folding then with reverence before tucking them back into his jacket. 'But Jekyll was selfish and in his own way stupid. He did not quite know what he was doing. And so, when he made that first successful preparation, he was arrogant enough to think that he had done such by his own science and art alone, not through some impurity in the ingredients he'd combined in his laboratory. Of course, this was not discovered until much later, until after he had died and there had been some sight of his documents.

'There were other copies, fragments at least, material that he – in the guise of Hyde – had salted away from Jekyll as old Henry had lost control of himself. But we thought that there would be more, and the fact that Utterson had been given control over the estate made me suspect that he had access to much more on top of that. What we could not have conceived of was that there was another set of instructions, one that Hyde had set up with Jekyll's money, and had left languishing in some dusty solicitor's vault until Utterson's death.

'This brings us to you, Latimer.'

#

Enfield now spoke. 'You've come here with questions, yes?'

'No,' Latimer said. 'I came here with a gun.'

'Is it answers that you want?'

'No.'

'No? Really?' Enfield shook his head. His chins wobbled as he chuckled. 'Then what is it that you want? It is really something so commonplace as money? If it is, then say so. Money is not a problem, unless it's a problem. And I'm fortunate to be in a position where I'm untroubled by financial woes. You're unfortunate, if indiscreet club gossip from a somewhat senior officer of the Metropolitan Police is to be believed, in that you have some rather pressing legal difficulties. I'm sure that a little travelling fund would not go amiss.'

'You have a proposition?'

'I do. In return for Hyde's documents. For everything that was given to you. Put them in my hands today and I will give you five thousand pounds.'

'That's a lot of money.'

'If you say so.'

'And if I say no?'

'Well, we could simply hand you over to the police, but I don't think that's in our best interests. Lord knows what outlandish things you might say. And besides confession might be good for the soul, but I don't really believe that it would be good for your body. Terrible places, prisons. Full of the most brutal sorts. Anything could happen. Really, anything.

'Thinking about it,' Enfield continued, 'I'm minded to keep matters simple. I'm prepared to bargain because I want the Hyde documents. Five thousand for the papers.'

'And I'd want passage out of the country.'

'I suppose you would. That could be arranged. You'd not be travelling first class on the White Star line, but you could be removed from these fair shores.'

'And the alternative?'

'I'll have Bradshaw here break your neck.'

Bradshaw smiled. His teeth were gapped and yellow. 'Happy to oblige,' he said.

'I do have a gun,' Latimer said.

'Yes, you do. But it's been my experience that the

195

ownership and proximity of a firearm do not necessarily correlate with its successful discharge.'

Bradshaw frowned at this. 'Didn't stop him shooting up the factory last night.'

'Nevertheless,' Enfield said. 'There we have it, Latimer. A deal. If you're agreeable. Or I'll have you killed and we'll retrace your steps. Those papers will be found. And we'll stop at nothing, as I'm sure you'll appreciate, to get them.'

'Five thousand?'

'Sterling. In cash. Today. I can draw on monies held in the Club. My credit will be good until the morning when I can make restitution via my own bank. I feel sure we can even provide you with a case to carry your loot away with.'

'If I agree to this, then I want to know something first.'

Enfield raised his arms, palms open. 'But of course.'

I understand the potion, the history with Jekyll, everything. I can see why and how both Bradshaw and you became involved over the years. I just want to know one thing.'

'Which is?'

'This.' Latimer put the lead figure on the table.

Enfield clapped in glee. 'Oh, the juggernaut!' Even Bradshaw showed a dry mirth play about his eyes.

'The juggernaut. What is it?'

'Oh, it's the alpha and omega. The beginning and the end. You mean you haven't put it all together?'

Latimer raised the handgun. 'Treat me like a fool. Pretend I know nothing.'

'Yes, yes,' Enfield flapped a hand at the gun as though it were no more annoying than a wasp at a summer's picnic. 'But it's all there for you. I think you've been exposed to everything.' Enfield gazed at Latimer. He came to a decision. His eyes hardened. A little moue at the lips.

'The juggernaut is this. Juggernaut. Capital on the first

letter. A brand name. A slogan and a statement of intent all in one. Put it all together man!'

'If he can.'

'You opened temperance missions.'

'We started with one, though there are six across the city. Seven, soon, if you count the one that we're considering helping some Sikh fellows open. Six, though, to be certain.'

'Henry Jekyll's estate was used to bring some aid to poor parishes. Lead the destitute from drink and towards God. Offer sustenance and nourishment where there was deprivation.'

'All of that, yes.'

'And at the same time – no, it was later.' Latimer was assembling the argument as he spoke. 'Later, once you'd secured the first scraps of Jekyll's work, once Bradshaw had approached you, and you'd discovered some commonality of interest, you began to work.'

'We did.'

'You're using the soup kitchens and the charitable work as a front.'

Enfield was enjoying himself 'Not quite.' He corrected himself. 'Yes, I mean, but no at the same time. Pray continue.'

'No,' Latimer found himself agreeing. 'The kitchens are part and parcel of this. The Hawksmoor Trust may do good work, and with Utterson as its unwitting lead, it had more than adequate cover.'

'It's there. Right in front of your face.'

'The Trust nourishes the poor. It provides good food to those who need it. It advocates temperance and exercise.'

'Yes…'

'…because that's what you want.'

Enfield smiled all the wider.

Ideas clustered together, fighting for articulation. 'You want a sober, well-nourished, fit working class.'

'We do.'

'Particularly young men.'

'You want them to work in your factories. To produce your goods. This Juggernaut beverage. Workers who feel obligated to you, who see your company and its product as not merely the provider of their wages but as some kind of badge for life, a way of sobriety and health made manifest in a cordial.'

'Indeed, we do.'

'But that's not it, is it?'

'Go on, Latimer.'

Then it struck Latimer. As surely as a swinging blow to the temple. He had to pace himself, yet speak fast lest he lose some of the torrent of ideas now free-flowing from him. 'Juggernaut is a vehicle.'

Bradshaw leaned over to Enfield. 'Now he understands.'

'A vehicle for so many things, ideas that compete and yet are all of a piece.'

Bradshaw leaned in. 'Now you're getting it.'

'You make the workers the way you want them. Clean and sober, fit and strong. They work for you so there's an obligation. But more than that, there's a kind of calling. A calling which is reinforced by the product itself. A product that is intended as a non-alcoholic substitute. That provides energy, vigour, release.'

'Yes.' Enfield and Bradshaw; together now.

'And Juggernaut exists in many forms. The first is a simple tonic. A patent medicine no different from the hundreds of others promising vitality and long life at little expense. Then a second. A version of the formula that has a touch of Jekyll's preparation, or some reformulation of the same. It's without liquor, so will appeal to the people you want to work with and to others besides, but substitutes the pleasant sensation of intoxication for a glimpse into the release of Edward Hyde's personality.'

'I'm told that the drink is quite stimulating. Most

efficacious. A livener,' Enfield murmured.

'At these doses the drink is probably harmless, but it's addictive. Perhaps nothing in the chemistry is habit-forming, but the effect upon the mind of its imbiber? To taste the vigour of the beverage is to surrender yourself to it. People will drink none other.'

'We have conducted albeit limited trials and can provisionally confirm the same.'

'And then there will be stronger and stronger formulations, available at a price for those with the wherewithal or the thirst.'

'There will.' Enfield's smile was expansive now.

'But that's not all, is it?'

'Whatever do you mean?'

'To go to all this. Setting up a charity. Subverting the good work of others. To play such a long, long game. A generation's wait, and all for a tonic, no matter what its vile properties? There must me more.'

'Keep going, Latimer. You're oh so nearly there.'

Latimer cocked the hammer on the handgun. He de-cocked it. He cocked it again.

'That's a little unnerving. I'd rather you didn't do that.'

Latimer de-cocked the pistol once more. The gun in his hand made him feel secure. The grip was slippery. He was perspiring. The gun? That was it. 'I should have seen it before. You're building an army.'

Enfield's shoulders relaxed to such an extent that Latimer only now realised how tense the other man had been throughout the meeting. 'Yes! An army. Well, perhaps not quite as grand as that just yet, but that's the aim. An army.'

'Bradshaw's not a part of this, is he? Not in quite the same way. Because for him this is all tied up with his stories from childhood, from his desire to climb the social ladder, from his curiosity about the upper classes and their lives, about dreams of power and freedom.'

'You see a lot,' Bradshaw said. 'But to feel it, to experience the release the elixir gives you, that is another reality. You can leave this dull world of class and status and accent and money behind and enter another realm. A nation of the sensory, where only what you will and what you will not are all that matters. Where you are transformed, translated into your ideal youthful self. Imagine it, Latimer. All of your experience and knowledge, your unsated fantasises and unquenched desires. Your frustrations and your ambitions being collided together to produce something new. The sensation is like none other. Imagine driving an all-powerful train along tracks cast from the metal of your imagination, smashing through society's and morality's flimsy barriers. That, for me, is the power of the Juggernaut.'

'As you hear, Bradshaw's quite the philosopher. He's come a fair way since his boot-black days.' Enfield sat up, all business. 'For me it's a little different. First and foremost, this is for me an opportunity. A legacy. Hyde left certain information in his will, and I fully intend to leave something behind. I have no children, Latimer, at least none that I could acknowledge in polite society, so my bequest to the nation will be this work.

'War is coming. With the Germans most likely, though one can never quite tell. Victoria's many offspring being scattered and interbred across Europe, it's nigh certain that when that war comes, when the imperial ambitions of Europe collapse in and their armies fall upon each other, cousin will fight cousin for mastery of the continent.

'We have found to our cost, through mortality rates and through the experience of our own eyes that our many are weak. They lack moral discipline, they lack the basics of a healthy diet, and they lack guidance. For too long we have let them live a farm worker's life of drinking without compunction and working off their beer in the fields. But city life does not allow for this. Our working men cannot doze under hayricks, sleeping off their cider, bread and cheese. We need strong men, fighting men, directed men.

'And more than this, we need men who can be commanded. The coming war will be bloody. We are beyond a gentlemanly, knightly age of chivalrous combat, of redcoats and regulations. The coming war will be muddy, long and fought with a ferocity that will make the likes of Waterloo, Towton, or Crecy seem like a series of croquet games on the vicarage lawn. We need, in short, a set of strong fighting men who are not only prepared to wreak havoc, but who would willingly surrender themselves to the very medicine that would engender that state

'That is Edward Hyde's true legacy. That is my work. This is my gift to the nation. I will give the country such a set of armaments, human torpedoes who will run through machine gunfire, who will rip airplanes from the sky, who would stab every enemy until their bayonet had blunted beyond use and ten they would continue with their fists.

'Juggernaut will beget this.' A fleck of saliva at the corner of Enfield's mouth, flicked away with a darting tongue. 'The greatest weapon of them all.'

A click behind Latimer; the door opening and closing again. Someone had joined them. Latimer dared not take his eyes from Enfield and Bradshaw though. Whoever it was would have to wait.

'And I will make this manifest tomorrow. On the day that Juggernaut begins its journey into the world, in its mildest forms nevertheless, to the grocery stores and general retailers, to the inns and eating houses and pubs of London, I will at the same time meet with the Ministry of War, with Secretary Haldane himself. Now Haldane believes that I will want to sell him some guns, and I do want to make that trade, but I will show him something else. Something mighty. Something irrefutable.' Enfield placed the vial back on the table.

Bradshaw took a step back.

'Don't.' Latimer raised the gun, cocking the hammer.

'Or what? Will you shoot me? Really?' Enfield unstoppered the small bottle. 'Don't be stupid, man. You want to see, don't you? You want to see.' He put the vial to his lips and drank perhaps half of the contents. Shaking, he replaced the bottle on the table and stoppered the bottle once more. 'We need to work on the taste,' he said.

Enfield was a corpulent man. A large man by his nature, his frame was shrouded further in layers of fat. His shooting garb was well-cut to suit his build. His hair was grey, his face at once pale and blotchy, pink smudges on his cheeks for all the world like nappy rash on an infant's behind. Now he shoved his chair back, holding himself up by the lip of the table for support as he rose. The chair toppled over behind.

Enfield coughed; a harsh bark. Then again, and again. With each fresh eruption, his body shuddered. With each shudder, the movement was both less and more. Less in that Enfield was palpably shrinking before Latimer. The jowls rescinded themselves, the heft of his girth melted away. With each convulsion, shocks of ebony-black hair shot through his scalp, supplanting the grey. Skin tightened around the new-forming body. Age fell away from Richard Enfield, and what resulted was both beautiful and obscene.

He had gained something in height, as though the stoop of latter years was corrected, and was thin, thin as you please. Any comedy that might have resulted from his trousers falling away was as nothing to the appalling sight of Enfield before him. The eyes, so dark so alive. The mouth, a ruby snick barely concealing fresh ivory-white teeth and a lithe, alive tongue.

Clothes hanging from him, the new Enfield righted his seat and sat again. 'It hurts to be still,' he said. 'My blood, it sings inside of me. It craves to be pumping through exertion. It wants direction, it wants purpose. Two possibilities: either to surrender to it, and watch from within, exultant as my fresh flesh does what it will, or to take apt instruction. Which will it be, I wonder?' His fingers drummed the table. The little bottle danced to the rhythm. Enfield's nails were long, shaped, and sharp enough to snag the linen cloth covering the table. One caught in such a tear, and Enfield ripped the material in a single, languorous movement. He wrapped the torn length around his right fist with his left. 'Which will it be?'

A voice from behind. From over Latimer's shoulder. 'You need to show a body to the police that they might make a positive identification from. Do it clean. Kill him.' A voice Latimer knew.

That could wait. With the words fresh-spoken, Latimer understood what he had to do. 'Wait,' he said. 'Wait.' He de-cocked the hammer on the pistol. He held the gun up, pointing now at the ceiling. He kept his hands as open as he could. Standing, he reached with index finger and thumb into his pocket and found the spare ammunition. He dropped the clip to the ground and kicked it away.

Enfield quivered with potential energy. It was as though some vital force, some radioactive electricity perhaps, thrummed within, demanding discharge.

Latimer removed the clip from the handle of the gun. He cycled the action to demonstrate that now there was no round chambered in the gun. He swapped the now-empty gun to his other hand, thumbing round after round from the ammunition clip in his hand. Two rounds dropped to the floor. Then three. Then –

'No! Kill him!' The same voice again. Guest.

The fourth round was flicked to the floor. Enfield, distracted by the shout from Guest, reacted to Latimer slamming home the ammunition clip. Too late.

The 1911 took seven rounds. Four – the four that Guest had replaced with rounds that would have turned out have been useless dummies – had been expended in the escape from the Chicksand Street factory. The fifth was fired into Enfield's face.

The shot was not one of Latimer's best. It caught Enfield low in the mouth, shattering his lower jaw. Gore splashed over the white table linen, arcing up as Enfield was lifted into the air, falling as Enfield dropped back and to the left.

Latimer span around, kicking his chair out of the way. Guest had a firearm trained on him. A shotgun. Once a good-looking weapon, it had been adapted by having the barrel shortened and by having the stock removed. Guest had the gun looped to his shoulder on a leather strap.

Bradshaw had backed away further, but had pulled out a folding knife. He locked the blade into place.

'You only have two rounds left, Latimer. I have five.' A Browning Automatic 5. Twelve-bore most likely. Guest was ten paces away. At this range the weapon would blow a hole the diameter of a soup tureen through Latimer.

'One round each. That's all I need. And Bradshaw's blade's no threat.'

A groan from the floor. Enfield, face down, pooling blood granting him a red halo. Still alive, then. Just.

Bradshaw flipped the knife, catching it by the blade. He brought his arm up, holding the knife behind his shoulder in a preparedness-to-throw action.

'He's good with one of those,' Guest noted. 'I've witnessed his work.'

Latimer shifted his aim. Guest, back to Bradshaw, back to Guest. Enfield gurgled on the ground.

A knock on the door Guest had entered by. 'Sirs? Sirs? Is everything well?'

'All is fine,' Bradshaw barked. 'Richard Enfield demands to be left.'

The door was tried. It rattled, locked. Guest must have turned the key when he entered the room.

'So,' Guest said. 'Did poor Richard tell you all?'

'Most of it,' Latimer said. 'I'd wondered about you from the off. I couldn't square the weapons with working for Utterson. Most of all, I couldn't reconcile your giving him the gift of a revolver.'

Guest shrugged. 'A new century demands new weapons.'

'And you must have worked the gun you gave Utterson so that it would have fired on a hair trigger.'

'He was not a strong man, and would have insisted upon certainty, were he to have elected a bullet over a lingering death.'

'So how long have you considered this scheme?'

'Ever since I first heard Henry Jekyll's name. A quarter of a century or more ago.'

'A long time.'

'Not when you consider eternity. Not when you consider the two thousand years since Christ. A lifetime is but a heartbeat in the life of the world, Latimer, and I would have this country preserved until the end of all time.'

'Even if it be at the expense of all of this murder?'

'A man who is truly prepared to die for his ideals is prepared to kill for them. Let Bradshaw have his status. Let Enfield have his indulgences, his pleasures, his military contracts. But give me a forever in the grave in the sure knowledge that I gave the greatest secret the world has ever known its rightful place: in the arms of Britannia. A shield and trident both: Juggernaut.'

The door was rattled again. A commotion from behind the oak. A mass of voices debating what to do. Then silence.

'That is what I have accomplished. What have you done?' Guest asked.

Latimer shot him. The round caught Guest high on the shoulder. Guest stumbled back against the door, the gun dangling uselessly from the shattered arm.

Bradshaw charged at Latimer. Latimer circled to the far side of the table from Bradshaw, gun trained still on Guest.

An appalling roar from the ground. An animal sound,

rather than anything human, wounded but not dying.

Bradshaw got to the table. Guest fought to transfer the shotgun to his left hand. He got the handle into his hand and was trying to level it.

Latimer's second shot did not miss. Guest's right eye detonated, bursting with aqueous humour and blood. He recoiled, his head spinning around. A third shot, and his face sheared off.

Latimer ran to the body. Guest's face was utterly corrupt. Latimer grabbed the shotgun and loosed the strap holding it to Guest's now-limp body.

He turned back, checking the weapon. A shell was chambered. The Browning was one of the newer semi-automatic shotguns: no manual chambering was required between shots, no breaking of the breech to reload, no pump-action needed. An efficient killing machine at close range.

Bradshaw had not been going for Latimer. Instead he had been making for the half-drunk vial of the elixir still on the table.

He had it in his hand.

Latimer stepped forwards, away from the door. He raised the shotgun. There could be no mistake that if he fired now, he would obliterate Bradshaw's head.

A further moan from Enfield. Latimer had heard sounds like it before. Out in the southern African veldt. Great lions, wounded by hunters but not dying. Roaring in impotent pain.

And now Enfield was standing.

The clothes hung from Richard Enfield's frame. But it was not his dress that startled Latimer. His face. Dear God, his face.

The bullet had bisected Enfield's lower jaw. Gore soaked him from the chin down. But, doubtless through some effect of the elixir, the jaw had fused again. The fix had not been a clean one.

Enfield stood, panting as best he might. Sweat ran

from his brow, streaking the blood where the two fluids contacted each other. The elixir was still completing the transformation. Enfield was tautening all over his body. Skin shrank and muscles and sinews bulked in opposition to each other. He was as though a skeleton equipped with an exaggerated musculature, arteries and veins rising proud under the tight translucency of his skin. His hair had grown, his nails lengthened to vicious points.

And now he growled, his lopsided jaw distending as he tried to articulate a human sound through shattered lower teeth.

'Lah – Teh – Muh.' Enfield pointed. And then he grinned.

Bradshaw raised the vial. He was going to open it and then put it to his lips.

Latimer swung the barrel of the shotgun across and down. He fired twice. The first round exploded the table. The second took Bradshaw's knees away from under him.

Bradshaw grunted as flying debris hit him. The shriek he gave as the follow-up blast severed his legs was dreadful.

The door cracked open behind Latimer, splintering and then sundering under what must have been immense force. A shout: 'Down!'

Latimer dropped to his knees and then to the ground. He shot at Enfield as he hit the floor, but Enfield was already moving. Jesus, but he was fast.

From behind, and now above, gunfire. Three separate sources. Two pistols and something larger. Another shotgun, Latimer reckoned. He kept down.

Enfield ran through the remains of the table. The wood was torn apart by Enfield's claw-like hands. Through the obstacle in a single great bound, Enfield picked up Bradshaw's torso, holding it up as a barrier to the onslaught of gunfire.

Bradshaw was still alive. Round after round embedded into him. He convulsed, gouting blood. Smoke

207

was filling the room, as was the conjoined stench of cordite and bloody death.

Enfield had by now crossed the room, his back to the windows looking out over the front aspect of the Athenaeum Club.

He might have snarled something more, but words could not be discerned through the terrible thunder of the gunfire and Bradshaw's dying pleadings.

'Halt! Stop!' Latimer found that it was he that had shouted. He got up, bringing the shotgun up with him. He could not remember if he had shells left inside the weapon or not.

Enfield held Bradshaw's body as though it were a napkin. The weight of the man meant nothing to him. Bradshaw's body had been utterly corrupted. There little to show that the mass of cloth and meat had ever been a man.

Eyes front, not daring to check on who had entered the room, Latimer called out again. 'Do you have your weapons on him?'

'Yes.' Mosley.

'Yes.' Abberline.

'Yes.' A female voice. Latimer did not believe it.

'Doyle?' He had to turn.

Maureen Doyle. Standing, legs apart, two hands holding a revolver trained on Enfield. Her legs were apart because she was poised for balance and because her feet were planted either side of Guest's corpse. 'Latimer,' she said. Throughout, she kept her focus on Enfield.

'Richard Enfield,' Mosley stated. 'You are under arrest. Don't make this any worse for you than it has to be.'

Enfield snarled. Tension gathered in his arms. Latimer thought at first that he was going to hurl the body at the policemen, but instead he sidestepped to the window and threw Bradshaw's body through the glass.

The force of the throw must have been immense, as

the window frame broke away as though it offered no resistance. Cool Sunday morning billowed the curtains, stirring the still-smoky and bloody air.

'No!' Abberline shouted. But Enfield put one hand to the window ledge and vaulted out through the open space. Latimer got to the window first. He kicked something as he raced across the room. Enfield had landed on Bradshaw's collapsed body, and was picking himself up. Another snarl back up to where he had dropped from, and Enfield, all but naked as the baggy, shredded clothing fell around him, loped across Pall Mall in the direction of Waterloo Place.

The cool of the air was a momentary pleasure. Latimer breathed it in, and then faced the incomers.

'Doyle? I held you. You were dead.'

A smile. 'You were never a doctor, Latimer.'

'Forgive us,' Mosley interjected. 'A necessary deception.'

'But why? To what end?' Doyle looked on, amusement playing on her features; along with another emotion that Latimer could not quite place. It was not an impression he'd ever received from Maureen Doyle before. But then, he thought, Maureen Doyle was in no way what she had appeared to be.

'These points must wait. We have more urgent issues with which to deal.' Abberline was still staring out of the window. 'That was Richard Enfield?'

'Yes.'

'And he was transformed by means of this preparation of Henry Jekyll's?'

'Yes, or some variation of it. I think they do not quite have the secret of his work, though they have found other variants of it in the course of their investigations.'

Latimer told them, in brief, of all that he knew. The factory on Chicksand Street, Guest's and Bradshaw's roles as well as Enfield's. The Juggernaut scheme. All of it.

'And you have your papers held safe?'

'Yes.'

'Where will Enfield have gone?'

Latimer could only think of one place. 'Chicksand Street.'

'Why?'

'A property of the elixir. It unleashes the baser instincts, the primal urges. But you can control it, or at least give it direction. Enfield will be willing himself to secure as much of the elixir as he can, for without it he cannot hope to either escape or survive.'

'Can he be stopped when under its influence?' Doyle's question.

'Not easily. Unless…' A possibility came to Latimer.

'Unless what?'

Not a possibility. An inevitability. The item he'd kicked crossing the room. There it was. The dropped half-full vial. Latimer picked it up. He looped the strap attached to the shotgun over his opposite shoulder. 'Do you have shells for this?'

Abberline gave him a handful. Latimer reloaded as he spoke. 'Muster your most trusted men to Brick Lane. Seal Chicksand Street off. Do this now, before Enfield can get there. If anyone leaves that building, destroy him – or it – utterly.'

'What are you going to do?' Doyle asked.

'I'm going to make this better,' Latimer said. And then he drank the potion.

#

The liquid was cold. Not just in terms of its temperature, though it certainly felt as though it had come directly from an ice bucket; but instead of any indication of flavour, it offered an emotion. The cold of grief.

That dark chill extended to the drink's fragrance. Wet stone. Water on metal. Samphire. Oysters. A hint of the iron salt of the sea.

The liquid crept over Latimer's tongue and stole its way down his throat. It felt impossible, as though the fluid had somehow acquired a thousand tiny claws and was creeping, slithering, encroaching into him. It was like swallowing a snake, or like vomiting in exquisite slowness in reverse.

Latimer convulsed. A sweat erupted almost at once with the first contact with his stomach. The invading substance forcing his body's moisture to the surface. No, more than that. This was invasion and retreat.

His body's first buckling was accompanied by a frozen bloom inside. Shards of ice were propelled through his organs, along his arteries. His heart stammered, his kidneys recoiled. And then the potion hit the brain.

Latimer had read scandalised articles purporting to be of true-life accounts of unfortunates who had been paralysed by anaesthetics under operation but who had remained conscious throughout the medical procedure. Poor wretches who had claimed that they had been immobile yet awake while they had been cut up.

This was what it must have been like.

Latimer was in and out of himself at once.

And then the pain subsided. He had lost track of time. How long it had been while he had been wracked by the potion he was unsure. He guessed at a few seconds, but it might have been several minutes. Latimer stood – had he been on the ground all long? – and that was when the wave of exultation struck.

The potion had wrapped itself around his brain. He was alert. So alert.

The breathing of everyone else in the room.

A mouse between the floorboards.

Heavy footfalls, fading. Panicked shouts outside, distant.

Doyle's mouth. Every crease and crenulation of her lips. Her mouth, barely open, moist at the edges where the lips met. White flashes of teeth and behind them, the ridges of her tongue. And now her voice. Vocal cords vibrating.

'Latimer? Latimer!'

'Good God, man. What have you done?'

The second speaker was Mosley.

Latimer blinked. No, not quite. He told himself to blink. The experience was like wearing a suit of armour, or being inside a fancy-dress costume; Latimer was not quite himself. His movements felt alien, as though he was his own puppeteer. More than that, worse than that; the puppet-Latimer was a conscious, motivated creature. The puppeteer-Latimer had to work to keep control. Even standing still was arduous. The creature he inhabited craved its own life.

'A mirror,' Latimer said. The voice was not his. Lighter and huskier at the same time. A youth with a head cold. A whispering child.

Doyle was the one to react. Mosley studied him as she moved. Mosley was curious, observant. Abberline had recoiled. He'd pulled out a nasty-looking cosh. Doubtless some relic of his uniform days. A favourite tool for beating down on suspects.

Not quite a mirror, but it would have to do. A silver salver taken from a dresser. Doyle held it up as though she were Perseus protecting his sight from the gorgon's stare.

Latimer was still there, deep in his own eyes. But beyond that, he was translated. Elements of the beast that stood before him were familiar. The clothes, which hung from him a little, though not overly much. Latimer had retained the slenderness of his youth, had not surrendered to middle-age comfort eating and the accompanying expansion of the belly. The hairline was as it had been before, though a tickle at the back of the neck told him that he had somehow grown more hair up on and down his neck and back.

His hands. His hands! They were longer, slimmer, more monkey-like. His nails were lengthened, sharp. Latimer rubbed the pad of his thumb across them. Such sensitivity! He could feel so much more. Wanted to feel so much more. Doyle's neck was within his grasp. He could just reach out, swipe the platter from her, and be on her in an instant-

No. Keep focus. Control.

His face in the mirror. Shimmering in the silver. Latimer fought to determine his features. They were his, yet not. It was as though the solid metal reflection was distorted No fairground sideshow trick, this, but some property of the elixir. It was impossible to focus on the entire face. The face disputed its own integrity, denied a full identification.

And breathe. Breathing was easy, so much easier that it had ever been. And productive, too. Each fresh intake was like a deep draught of the clearest mountain water. Melted glacial oxygen flowed through him, energising and revitalising. Again, the impulse to move, to act. To be.

'Latimer?' Mosley again. 'Are you with us, man?'

'Yes.' Again, the discordant tone in his own voice. 'Yes.'

'Enfield. You remember?'

He did. Richard Enfield. The man who had done this. The man who had wrought this terrible wrong. Or was it wrong? Really? To be given mastery over one's own desires, one's innate being? To be given keys to the vault of his own being? Was that so wrong?

Enfield. The man who had done murder for gain. Who had plotted and schemed for a generation to steal another man's work and to profit from it. The impudence alone deserved a reckoning.

'I remember.'

Enfield could be heard outside still. He had not gone far. Or, if he had, then Latimer was attuned to him. He knew his prey. His stink was on the city.

'Do what you must. We'll deal with the warehouse. For the love of God, man, go.'

Latimer meant to smile, but it must have come out as a snarl. Oh, what long teeth he had. Abberline had raised his billy club, as if that would have been a preventative against the stomping of his heart. Doyle let the silver plate fall. Such a clatter!

Latimer closed his eyes and let himself go.

#

The drop to the ground from the window was as nothing. As easy as stepping down from a hansom. Latimer landed lightly on the roof of the motor-car, overbalancing a little, but a hand to the roof for a breath and he was back up on two legs, down to street-level and already sprinting.

The air was thick with the sweat of the beast that Enfield had become. Latimer ran free down Pall Mall, past Waterloo Place and towards Haymarket. Traffic was light at this time of day. No omnibuses, nothing in the way of delivery vehicles. A couple of cabs. No motorcars on the road. There were church bells in the distance, and the ticking of a multitude of clocks. Cries of birds on the wing. The Thames, lapping against the embankment. Fires being lit. The susurration of London.

And there, ahead, was Enfield.

Latimer – or the beast in him – roared. No, it was him. The division between the version of Latimer conjured by the potion and the shell it inhabited was dissolving. Now that he had a direction, a mission, there was no need for an artificial divide between the man and his body's actions.

Latimer let himself go. He became one with his new flesh.

Still running, but now checking behind him, Enfield diverted right into Cockspur Street. Latimer charged on, not taking the turn but instead continuing into Pall Mall East. Already he knew what Enfield would do.

Enfield came out of Cockspur Street and dodged left. Rather than continue to Charing Cross and either divert down Whitehall or else go across into the Strand, he began to cross Trafalgar Square.

Latimer ran up to the entrance to the National

Gallery. There he stopped. Trafalgar Square in front of him. Three plinths occupied by great lions, a fourth still and forever empty. The fountains. Somewhere under his feet, Latimer sensed the steam engine driving the pumps for the water. Pigeons. The bird now scattering as Enfield lumbered across the open piazza.

A shriek. A woman – a domestic on her way to her duties or perhaps her place of worship – ran, startled first by the birds' scatter and then by the creature that had caused the disturbance. She dropped something. Latimer sniffed. Stale bread and cake. She had been feeding the birds. The woman carried her own scents: coal tar soap and metal polish, rosewater.

Enfield saw Latimer. He roared. Caught in the centre of the Square, he stood defiant.

Latimer took the steps down from the gallery to the Square three at a time. He swept past the empty plinth and continued downwards, letting his momentum build with each leap down the stone stairs.

Enfield braced himself. There would have been little point in running towards Latimer, or even trying to outrun him such was the velocity that Latimer had developed.

Latimer came in from Enfield's left, throwing a great punch as he got to his prey. Enfield's arms were up, crossed in defence. The blow knocked Enfield back two paces. Latimer roared. His cry came back at him in echo from the four quarters of the square as he pummelled Enfield down.

Enfield dropped to one knee. A blow came up, stroking Latimer between the legs. Latimer retched under the impact, folding forward as he voided from his mouth. A follow-up blow, an uppercut to the chin as Enfield rose, jarred Latimer's jaw. A tooth splintered. His tongue was mashed between molars.

Latimer spat; bile and blood. This caught Enfield, who grinned through the gore. He made to speak, but had to dodge instead as Latimer brought another blow down on him. This snapped Enfield's head across. When he came back to fix his stare on Latimer, there was a new fury evident.

Enfield charged, head down. Latimer sidestepped and Enfield went sprawling. He put his hands out to stop colliding the lip of one of the two fountains in the centre of the Square. He turned, back to the water.

Latimer breathed hard. There was pain from his mouth where he had been hit but it was delicious. His knuckles were already bruising from the impacts on Enfield, but that was simply more evidence of the glorious possibilities of the body.

Enfield glanced left and right. He was looking for a route by which to escape. Latimer took a step forward. There would be no dodging this reckoning.

A sly, lopsided grin then appeared. Enfield began to laugh. His voice was not quite his own. 'Do you feel it? Incredible, is it not? The freedom that the potion gives. The power, the authority. To use it as Harry Jekyll did; that must have been a glorious, triumphant thing. But to channel it? To lay it at the feet of King and Country. You would be remembered.'

'No.' A fat pulse on Enfield's neck. The carotid artery. That would be Latimer's target.

'Yes, you would. As would I. As saviours of our nation. As scientists, eh doctor? As the man who gave the armed forces the equipment they needed for the War yet to come.'

'There'll be no war.'

A croak of laughter. 'You really believe that? Man is a martial beast. Look at yourself, your nature unveiled, awoken from its long slumber under the heavy blanket of civilisation. Expose that and what do we find? A creature that demands to fight, to take, to lustfully indulge in victories over others.'

'I don't want it.'

'I don't believe you. Why else take the potion? Or

perhaps it's something else. You might not want it, but by God, Latimer, you need it.'

Could it be true?

Enfield continued, his breathing now easing. 'You can still have this. Our own private supply. Giving the secret need not mean giving the secret away.' The pulse in his neck slackened as his heartbeat returned to a more normal state.

'No.'

The pulse throbbed a little prouder. At the front of the neck just beneath the jaw. If Enfield had been his old, corpulent self, then it would not have been visible.

'Too many secrets. Too many lies.' Latimer kept his focus on the engorging pulse. 'I have been someone else for far too long.'

Enfield clenched his fists. That was the wrong move for him to be making.

'And besides, your strength now is your weakness.'

'Nonsense. We are indestructible in this form.'

Enfield's knuckles whitened in relief to the blood coursing throughout him as he tensioned for action. The pulse; a fat drumbeat. Marching orders for the body.

Latimer feinted right and Enfield went with it, bringing up his left to parry an expected blow. This left his own right exposed. The neck, arched and proud. The artery, raised under the skin.

The punch was a nothing. A simple jab except with fingers outstretched rather than being balled into any fist. Latimer contacted with Enfield where the neck met the skull under the chin. Impact and then incision. Latimer retracted his arm. The faint release of his nails withdrawing from Enfield's flesh.

Blood spurted from Enfield's neck. The first squirts mixed with fountain water, arcing above in a red-white-blue rainbow. Enfield flailed to get a hand to his neck, but in covering the injury he left the other side of his head exposed.

217

Latimer was inside, looking out. A wave of dissociation flowed in him; a nausea of the soul leaving him powerless.

A blow parallel to the jab he'd punctured Enfield's neck darted in on the other side. The second wound was the twin of the first, though the blood flow was not so spectacular. The red levels rose. Enfield lurched from one side to the other, his attempts to stem the blood loss for all the world making him appear to throttle his own neck. This left both body and head unguarded.

Latimer struck the gut first. A hefty crunch up under the ribcage. Something gave inside Enfield with the impact. Enfield recoiled, lumbering forwards, almost toppling over with the blow.

Latimer met Enfield's advancing head with a swift-raised knee. The jaw buckled, shearing crazily to the right. Bone jutted through skin. Enfield reared back and Latimer steadied him with a rabbit-punch to the ear.

A snick behind him. Distant and distinctive. Metal against metal, well-greased. Perhaps thirty yards back.

Enfield rocked. He stood because he was back against the raised lip of the fountain. It would not let him fall.

They were showered by splashes from the jetting fountain water. Enfield and, he supposed, Latimer were streaked with sweat-streaked blood.

Latimer hit Enfield but he would not fall. Another strike, knocking the broken jaw back across his lower face. Enfield panted. His mouth would not show it, but his eyes betrayed the grin.

This was his final defiance and he knew it. He would not fall under Latimer's onslaught.

Yes, he would.

Latimer drew his right arm back. He would pummel the broken face into oblivion. He would smash this man into blood and dust, here on the stone ground under Nelson's Column. Let all London drink this blood sacrifice.

A murmur and a second metal snick. Enfield heard it too. His focus shifted away.

Latimer's blow never landed.

He felt the bullet rather than saw it. The heightened sensory capability of the elixir granted him that insight.

The air warped. The sky bent around the flying lead. A crack – the sound of the explosion in the barrel – and an impact as one.

Enfield was hit in the morass of cartilage and gore where his nose had been. A hole the size of a sixpence formed. Enfield was caught mid-breath. A fresh sound – dull cracking and splattering. The round took out the back of the man's head.

Splashes. Brain matter and bone slivers leapt into the fountain pool.

Enfield did not drop. He was suspended, half-slumped, half-sat, on the edge of the fountain. The first gunshot still echoed across the Square.

A second bullet must have been fired. Enfield's head dropped, and then perked up as he was hit in the upper chest. Already dead, the body wavered, leaned back and then toppled back over into the water.

Latimer turned around to where the shots had come from.

Three figures. One female, two males. The slimmer male was Mosley. The female had to be Doyle. She leaned over to the third. A man Latimer had never seen before. A man with a rifle.

She said something, nodded. Her words did not carry.

But the bullet did.

Latimer saw it coming. He perceived it cleave the air like a boat through calm water. He opened his arms to receive the benediction. He had been shot before, in a previous life, but never like this.

The impact lifted him a little. Enough. He imagined the point of the lead distending as it met and then broke his skin. As it burrowed, spinning through his flesh.

219

Through meat and bone, through marrow and then back out the other side.

He fell and felt a second impact. His final thoughts were of Nelson. High up, and back turned. Gazing off down Whitehall and out, presumably, to sea.

#

White. Gauze. A blink, and the gauze blistered, like an old cobweb blown by the breeze. A second blink. The gauze was neither material nor spider-silk, but a crackled ceiling.

The place was old. It had not been painted for many a year. Latimer tried to move, but found himself restrained. He pushed back, and was forced down.

The force was nothing. A simple hand, outstretched on his chest. Latimer followed the fingers up to the wrist and along the arm and up. Maureen Doyle's gaze met his.

Her expression was bland, not quite impassive. A mixture of curiosity and amusement. Latimer shuffled to sit up. His left arm was bandaged and in a sling around his neck. There was no pain. This, he assumed, was a temporary state of affairs.

'Welcome back,' Doyle said.

His mouth was sticky. He tried to talk, but nothing came out. Reacting to this, Doyle held a glass of water to his lips. 'Not too much,' she said.

He drank. Feeling returned to his mouth. His head ached and he was parched. He drained the glass and nodded for more.

'Wait. Wait. Don't rush.'

It felt like a whisky hangover. A nasty sensation in the brain and the kidneys, though without the resultant aftertaste of overindulgence.

A shadow at the door. Mosley.

Now perched upright in the bed, Latimer took in his surroundings. A hospital bed and furnishings, though the room felt like a converted office rather than any medical establishment Latimer had seen before. There was none of the scent of astringent cleanser and of distemper he associated with the unwell. 'Where am I?

'New Scotland Yard.' Mosley was speaking as he entered the room He turned a chair around and straddled it. 'Apologies for having you shot, by the way, but we thought it for the best. Doyle here considered that you were out of sorts and might benefit from some time away from things.'

That explained the bandage and the sling, then. 'Enfield?'

Mosley shook his head. 'You put him down, but we stepped in before matters...went too far. You were in a public place, after all.'

'Just as well it was still early on a Sunday morning,' Doyle added.

Latimer raised his eyebrows. 'And I thought you were dead.'

'Apologies for that.'

'And mine too,' Mosley said. 'Let Mrs Doyle explain.'

Doyle kept it brief, but the gist was that she, though trained as a nurse, was an undercover operative within Scotland Yard assigned to monitoring of what she termed 'subversive or problematic groupings'.

'You were undercover as a volunteer at the Hawksmoor Trust?'

'It would be fairer to say that my work at the surgery was the ruse. Utterson has long been on our watch-list because of his many connections to this whole sorry business, and a nursing position at his general practice provided exactly the right cover. When you took over the practice, it was evident from the off that you weren't a doctor, but you were wise enough to cover your tracks and I was there to see that you caused no real harm. And besides, you were easy to control. Having you join me at the Trust's outpost in Chicksand Street only helped me further. Who pays attention to a nurse when there's a doctor in the room?'

'And your "death?"'

'An improvisation. Mosley played his part, but I had to act fast when it became clear that you were becoming implicated via your involvement with Utterson. We had to put you on the run, so to speak, if only to see what would happen when you were followed.'

'I was a hare set off for you to chase the foxes?'

'I'm afraid so.'

'Nevertheless,' Mosley added, 'matters could not have worked out better, if in a somewhat unorthodox fashion. The so-called Battle of Stepney, the Sidney Street siege and the events that led up to it, the details of which need not detain us now, only reemphasised, at the highest levels of government, the need for vigilance against anarchists, Irish dissidents, foreign agitators and the like. Though I work murder cases in the main, it's a regrettable fact of London life that insurrection and homicide overlap.'

'And you'll forgive my discretion concerning details, but it's useful to have women operatives as all too often, male preconceptions lead men to be blind to the potential for surveillance where a woman, and particularly one who does not care to pass herself off as a flighty debutante or similar, is concerned. That is the art of surveillance, Latimer. To watch in plain sight, and to be patient.'

'Doyle was under instructions from the highest authorities to surveil groups of potential interest, and the Chicksand Street charity was making itself noticeable. Cross-referencing violent incidents with the oddly masculine apparatus of what should have been an ordinary decent soup kitchen was cause for place them on the watch list enough. Utterson and Enfield have long had flags on their files, though they were for different reasons. Enfield, as he is known to have odd influence and a somewhat chequered history as a dealer in armaments and the like, and Utterson for both the link through the charity back to Enfield and for his involvement with Henry Jekyll back in the 1880s.'

'And then I stumbled into the middle of it.'

'That you did,' Maureen Doyle said. 'And though matters worked out awkwardly and not without cost, a kind of justice has seen to be done. Utterson can be at rest, knowing that what he must have feared most, a return of Edward Hyde, would not come to pass.' She fixed Latimer with a clear, impassive stare.

Latimer had no choice but to glance away.

'Enfield is disposed of, and the Chicksand Street operation is as we speak being dismantled. Abberline is supervising there. We've avoided a repeat of the Cable Street fiasco, and the week's headlines on the matter will doubtless reinforce both our diligence in the eyes of the public and our need to be watchful. Abberline also hopes to find the secret of the Jekyll solution, though he also wants to know, if truth be told, if there's any clue, no matter how small, that might lead him to conclusively link these occurrences to the murder of Danvers Carew and other,' - a pause, as if not sure how to best phrase what would come next - 'hitherto unsolved murders.'

'There's one connection we haven't made, and with which we'd like some assistance. Think of it as a gesture of your goodwill.'

'And what's that?'

'The other man. Bradshaw we knew about, but the other. Who was he? There was no identification on the body.'

They meant Guest. 'I'm not sure.'

'Really?' Latimer was not sure of the level of faith they had in his answer.

'Yes. But I have something else which may help.'

'Oh?'

'Papers. The documents left in a will purporting to be from Edward Hyde. I have them hidden and can access them again in two days. They're in transit back to me with a Tuesday delivery date.' That would give him enough time, Latimer reckoned, knowing the papers would be with him by Monday latest. 'There may be something in there

223

that would help.'

'And you'd hand those documents over to the Yard?'

'Call at the surgery Tuesday morning, where they'll be delivered to me.'

Mosley brightened up considerably at that. 'Tuesday it is. Say nine sharp?'

'Agreed. Is it still Sunday?'

'It is. You were only out for a couple of hours. I suppose you should rest overnight, but if you discharge yourself then we've no way of detaining you.'

'Technically, that's not true.'

'No, but in light of the service that Latimer here has done his country, albeit unwittingly, we can let matters rest a day or so. Though there'll be no more doctoring for you, I'm afraid, and we'll need to conduct an interview and something of a debrief with you Tuesday. You'll notice on your other arm that there's a small patch of sticking-plaster. We took the liberty of having some blood drawn from you. You were quite the marvel.' He then pursed his lips. 'I'll tell you what. You've got my card still, haven't you?'

'Yes.'

'Make an appointment when your shoulder's healed. After all this business is tidied up. We can always use an extra pair of hands around here, and you're not without resources.'

#

Latimer had one more task to complete. He asked to use a telephone. An orderly came and helped him into a high-backed wheelchair. Latimer was taken to an office. The room was filled with the paraphernalia of a busy doctor. That brought a smile. Latimer rang his hotel.

'Doctor Latimer. Good to have you back. How may I assist?' The voice was that of the whip-thin lad.

'Ah…'

'Neeson, sir. Albert, if you like. Albert Terence to my mother when I'm in her bad books.'

'Albert. Good. Do you have the wherewithal to procure me the services of a delivery vehicle of some kind, and a couple of men to make some moves? I'd also like to rent a second room - on my floor if possible - for a week or so.'

The latter request was no issue whatsoever. Give him half an hour, Albert said, and he would see what he could do about the former. He would call back on this number.

As it was the return call came through within twenty minutes. 'Everything arranged for you, Doctor Latimer.'

It was jarring to be called by that name. 'Plain Mister Latimer will be fine.'

'Of course, Mister Latimer.' There was no inflection indicating surprise or interest in the alteration. 'Where would you like the men to meet you?'

Latimer told them, and then he got out of the chair and walked back down the corridor to find Mosley and ask about the possibility of borrowing some spare clothes from someone.

#

Two hours later and it was done. Latimer had met the men at the end of an unprepossessing rear alley. He led them to a back gate that he had already forced open, and then into the small yard beyond.

A tarpaulin over a stack of crates. The wooden boxes were old stock that had previously belonged to Truman's brewery. Perhaps they had been stolen from there. Each crate held a dozen bottles. The bottles were half-pint size, capped with a simple metal enclosure, and were unlabelled. Clear glass had been used.

The workmen loaded the crates onto their wagon. Latimer rode with them across the city to the delivery entrance of his hotel. He cashed a cheque at the front desk while they took the crates up to the new room that he'd rented. At the desk, he picked up an additional key for the room. When the man came back down he tipped them ten shillings each.

'Sir.' 'Guv.' The money was taken without inspection. Too much for a gratuity, there was little mistaking the desired impression that the note was in exchange for their discretion. They each touched caps in a gesture towards deference, and then went out the way that they'd come.

Latimer took the stairs up to his new, second room. The crates were stacked as neat as you please by the window.

Latimer retrieved a bottle opener and a glass from his own room and then returned. He locked the door behind. He sat on one of the crates and took a bottle in his hand.

There might not have been a label, but there was an indication of the contents. A light white smear of writing in chinagraph pencil told him everything that he had assumed since he had first spied the crates in Guest's back yard. One bottle in each crate bore the same inscription.

But one of the crates contained bottles that were subtly different as to their labelling.

The handwriting, he guessed, was Guest's.

Final trial. Juggernaut Full Strength. Jan 1911.

There were twelve cases. Each with a dozen bottles.

One hundred and forty-four bottles.

A gross.

And twelve of them were special.

Opening a bottle with only one good arm would not be easy. He clasped the drink between his knees. Latimer picked up the bottle opener and toyed with it. He put the opener to the cap of one of the bottles with the written declaration. A tension in the good arm. It would be so easy to pop the cap off. A hiss of release, and then a choice. To pour and savour from the glass, or to guzzle straight from the mouth of the container?

No. He put the opener away.

It must have been getting late. Darkness was encroaching. Streetlights came on outside. A motorcar, its headlights afire.

Latimer left the room empty-handed. He locked the

door and then checked once, twice, that it was secure.

He went down the main staircase to see about something to eat. In the morning, he'd do what he could to close the surgery and remove himself from his previous associations. He was sure that Montgomery would be glad of the extra medical work in the short term. He'd then get hold of the will and its contents, fillet anything he fancied, and then on Tuesday he'd talk to Mosley. After all, he was no longer a physician, and there was much work to do.

He had his own questions, not least concerning Hyde. His references to the "red levels", for example. Was that simply hugger-mugger, scary talk for winter's nights, or was there something else to it over and above a way of describing the sensation felt when under the effect of the elixir?

And then there was the key, a use for which Latimer had not yet found.

So many questions.

And then there was London.

London was a city full of trouble. The war rumours would only continue to circle, and with them suspicion, paranoia and uncertainty. Subversive groups would emerge, and fell strangers would seek to take dark advantage of the insecure times.

The city would need a guardian. Someone unstoppable.

He'd take a month to recuperate. Longer if need be.

And then he'd begin.

After all, as Mosley had said, he was not without resources.

The End

THE STRANGE CASE OF DR JEKYLL AND MR HYDE

ROBERT LOUIS STEVENSON

STORY OF THE DOOR

Mr Utterson the lawyer was a man of a rugged countenance that was never lighted by a smile; cold, scanty and embarrassed in discourse; backward in sentiment; lean, long, dusty, dreary and yet somehow lovable. At friendly meetings, and when the wine was to his taste, something eminently human beaconed from his eye; something indeed which never found its way into his talk, but which spoke not only in these silent symbols of the after-dinner face, but more often and loudly in the acts of his life. He was austere with himself; drank gin when he was alone, to mortify a taste for vintages; and though he enjoyed the theatre, had not crossed the doors of one for twenty years. But he had an approved tolerance for others; sometimes wondering, almost with envy, at the high pressure of spirits involved in their misdeeds; and in any extremity inclined to help rather than to reprove. 'I incline to Cain's heresy,' he used to say quaintly: 'I let my brother go to the devil in his own way.' In this character, it was frequently his fortune to be the last reputable acquaintance and the last good influence in the lives of downgoing men. And to such as these, so long as they came about his chambers, he never marked a shade of change in his demeanour.

No doubt the feat was easy to Mr. Utterson; for he was undemonstrative at the best, and even his friendship seemed to be founded in a similar catholicity of good-nature. It is the mark of a modest man to accept his friendly circle ready-made from the hands of opportunity; and that was the lawyer's way. His friends were those of his own blood or those whom he had known the longest; his affections, like ivy, were the growth of time, they implied no aptness in the object. Hence, no doubt the bond that united him to Mr. Richard Enfield, his distant kinsman, the well-known man about town. It was a nut to crack for many, what these two could see in each other, or what subject they could find in common. It was reported by those who encountered them in their Sunday walks, that they said nothing, looked singularly dull and would hail with obvious relief the appearance of a friend. For all that, the two men put the greatest store by these excursions, counted them the chief jewel of each week, and not only set aside occasions of pleasure, but even resisted the calls of business, that they might enjoy them uninterrupted.

It chanced on one of these rambles that their way led them down a by-street in a busy quarter of London. The street was small and what is called quiet, but it drove a thriving trade on the weekdays. The inhabitants were all doing well, it seemed and all emulously hoping to do better still, and laying out the surplus of their grains in coquetry; so that the shop fronts stood along that thoroughfare with an air of invitation, like rows of smiling saleswomen. Even on Sunday, when it veiled its more florid charms and lay comparatively empty of passage, the street shone out in contrast to its dingy neighbourhood, like a fire in a forest; and with its freshly painted shutters, well-polished brasses, and general cleanliness and gaiety of note, instantly caught and pleased the eye of the passenger.

Two doors from one corner, on the left hand going east the line was broken by the entry of a court; and just at that point a certain sinister block of building thrust forward its gable on the street. It was two storeys high; showed no window, nothing but a door on the lower storey and a blind forehead of discoloured wall on the upper; and bore in every feature, the marks of prolonged and sordid negligence. The door, which was equipped with neither bell nor knocker, was blistered and distained. Tramps slouched into the recess and struck matches on the panels; children kept shop upon the steps; the schoolboy had tried his knife on the mouldings; and for close on a generation, no one had appeared to drive away these random visitors or to repair their ravages.

Mr. Enfield and the lawyer were on the other side of the by-street; but when they came abreast of the entry, the former lifted up his cane and pointed.

'Did you ever remark that door?' he asked; and when his companion had replied in the affirmative. 'It is connected in my mind,' added he, 'with a very odd story.'

'Indeed?' said Mr. Utterson, with a slight change of voice, 'and what was that?'

'Well, it was this way,' returned Mr. Enfield: 'I was coming home from some place at the end of the world, about three o'clock of a black winter morning, and my way lay through a part of town where there was literally nothing to be seen but lamps. Street after street and all the folks asleep - street after street, all lighted up as if for a procession and all as empty as a church - till at last I got into that state of mind when a man listens and listens and begins to long for the sight of a policeman. All at once, I saw two figures: one a little man who was stumping along eastward at a good walk, and the other a girl of maybe eight or ten who was running as hard as she was able down a cross street. Well, sir, the two ran into one another naturally enough at the corner; and then came the horrible part of the thing; for the man trampled calmly over the child's body and left her screaming on the ground. It sounds nothing to hear, but it was hellish to see. It wasn't like a man; it was like some damned Juggernaut. I gave a few halloas, took to my heels, collared my gentleman, and brought him back to where there was already quite a group about the screaming child. He was perfectly cool and made no resistance, but gave me one look, so ugly that it brought out the sweat on me like running. The people who had turned out were the girl's own family; and pretty soon, the doctor, for whom she had been sent put in his appearance. Well, the child was not much the worse, more frightened, according to the Sawbones; and there you might have supposed would be an end to it. But there was one curious circumstance. I had taken a loathing to my gentleman at first sight. So had the child's family, which was only natural. But the doctor's case was what struck me. He was the usual cut and dry apothecary, of no particular age and colour, with a strong Edinburgh accent and about as emotional as a bagpipe. Well, sir, he was like the rest of us; every time he looked at my prisoner, I saw that Sawbones turn sick and white with desire to kill him. I knew what was in his mind, just as he knew what was in mine; and killing being out of the question, we did the next best. We told the man we could and would make such a scandal out of this as should make his name stink from one end of London to the other. If he had any friends or any credit, we undertook that he should lose them. And all the time, as we were pitching it in red hot, we were keeping the women off him as best we could for they were as wild as harpies. I never saw a circle of such hateful faces; and there was the man in the middle, with a kind of black sneering coolness - frightened too, I could see that - but carrying it off, sir, really like Satan.

'If you choose to make capital out of this accident,' said he, 'I am naturally helpless.

No gentleman but wishes to avoid a scene,' says he. 'Name your figure.'

Well, we screwed him up to a hundred pounds for the child's family; he would have clearly liked to stick out; but there was something about the lot of us that meant mischief, and at last he struck. The next thing was to get the money; and where do you think he carried us but to that place with the door? - whipped out a key, went in, and presently came back with the matter of ten pounds in gold and a cheque for the balance on Coutts's, drawn payable to bearer and signed with a name that I can't mention, though it's one of the points of my story, but it was a name at least very well-known and often printed. The figure was stiff; but the signature was good for more than that if it was only genuine. I took the liberty of pointing out to my gentleman that the whole business looked apocryphal, and that a man does not, in real life, walk into a cellar door at four in the morning and come out with another man's cheque for close upon a hundred pounds. But he was quite easy and sneering. 'Set your mind at rest,' says he, 'I will stay with you till the banks open and cash the cheque myself.' So we all set off, the doctor, and the child's father, and our friend and myself, and passed the rest of the night in my chambers; and next day, when we had breakfasted, went in a body to the bank. I gave in the cheque myself, and said I had every reason to believe it was a forgery. Not a bit of it. The cheque was genuine.'

'Tut-tut,' said Mr. Utterson.

'I see you feel as I do,' said Mr. Enfield. 'Yes, it's a bad story. For my man was a fellow that nobody could have to do with, a really damnable man; and the person that drew the cheque is the very pink of the proprieties, celebrated too, and (what makes it worse) one of your fellows who do what they call good. Black mail I suppose; an honest man paying through the nose for some of the capers of his youth. Black Mail House is what I call the place with the door, in consequence. Though even that, you know, is far from explaining all,' he added, and with the words fell into a vein of musing.

From this he was recalled by Mr. Utterson asking rather suddenly: 'And you don't know if the drawer of the cheque lives there?'

'A likely place, isn't it?' returned Mr. Enfield. 'But I happen to have noticed his address; he lives in some square or other.'

'And you never asked about the - place with the door?' said Mr. Utterson.

'No, sir: I had a delicacy,' was the reply. 'I feel very strongly about putting questions; it partakes too much of the style of the day of judgment. You start a question, and it's like starting a stone. You sit quietly on the top of a hill; and away the stone goes, starting others; and presently some bland old bird (the last you would have thought of) is knocked on the head in his own back garden and the family have to change their name. No sir, I make it a rule of mine: the more it looks like Queer Street, the less I ask.'

'A very good rule, too,' said the lawyer.

'But I have studied the place for myself,' continued Mr. Enfield. 'It seems scarcely a house. There is no other door, and nobody goes in or out of that one but, once in a great while, the gentleman of my adventure. There are three windows looking on the court on the first floor; none below; the windows are always shut but they're clean. And then there is a chimney which is generally smoking; so somebody must live there. And yet it's not so sure; for the buildings are so packed together about the court, that it's hard to say where one ends and another begins.'

The pair walked on again for a while in silence; and then 'Enfield,' said Mr. Utterson, 'that's a good rule of yours.'

'Yes, I think it is,' returned Enfield.

'But for all that,' continued the lawyer, 'there's one

point I want to ask: I want to ask the name of that man who walked over the child.'

'Well,' said Mr. Enfield, 'I can't see what harm it would do. It was a man of the name of Hyde.'

'Hm,' said Mr. Utterson. 'What sort of a man is he to see?'

'He is not easy to describe. There is something wrong with his appearance; something displeasing, something down-right detestable. I never saw a man I so disliked, and yet I scarce know why. He must be deformed somewhere; he gives a strong feeling of deformity, although I couldn't specify the point. He's an extraordinary looking man, and yet I really can name nothing out of the way. No, sir; I can make no hand of it; I can't describe him. And it's not want of memory; for I declare I can see him this moment.'

Mr. Utterson again walked some way in silence and obviously under a weight of consideration. 'You are sure he used a key?' he inquired at last.

My dear sir...' began Enfield, surprised out of himself.

'Yes, I know,' said Utterson; 'I know it must seem strange. The fact is, if I do not ask you the name of the other party, it is because I know it already. You see, Richard, your tale has gone home. If you have been inexact in any point you had better correct it.'

'I think you might have warned me,' returned the other with a touch of sullenness. 'But I have been pedantically exact, as you call it. The fellow had a key; and what's more, he has it still. I saw him use it not a week ago.'

Mr. Utterson sighed deeply but said never a word; and the young man presently resumed. 'Here is another lesson to say nothing,' said he. 'I am ashamed of my long tongue. Let us make a bargain never to refer to this again.'
'With all my heart,' said the lawyer. 'I shake hands on that, Richard.'

SEARCH FOR MR. HYDE

That evening Mr. Utterson came home to his bachelor house in sombre spirits and sat down to dinner without relish. It was his custom of a Sunday, when this meal was over, to sit close by the fire, a volume of some dry divinity on his reading desk, until the clock of the neighbouring church rang out the hour of twelve, when he would go soberly and gratefully to bed. On this night however, as soon as the cloth was taken away, he took up a candle and went into his business room.

There he opened his safe, took from the most private part of it a document endorsed on the envelope as Dr. Jekyll's Will and sat down with a clouded brow to study its contents. The will was holograph, for Mr. Utterson though he took charge of it now that it was made, had refused to lend the least assistance in the making of it; it provided not only that, in case of the decease of Henry Jekyll, M.D., D.C.L., L.L.D., F.R.S., etc., all his possessions were to pass into the hands of his "friend and benefactor Edward Hyde," but that in case of Dr. Jekyll's "disappearance or unexplained absence for any period exceeding three calendar months," the said Edward Hyde should step into the said Henry Jekyll's shoes without further delay and free from any burthen or obligation beyond the payment of a few small sums to the members of the doctor's household.

This document had long been the lawyer's eyesore. It offended him both as a lawyer and as a lover of the sane and customary sides of life, to whom the fanciful was the immodest. And hitherto it was his ignorance of Mr. Hyde that had swelled his indignation; now, by a sudden turn, it was his knowledge. It was already bad enough when the name was but a name of which he could learn no more. It was worse when it began to be clothed upon with detestable attributes; and out of the shifting, insubstantial mists that had so long baffled his eye, there leaped up the sudden, definite presentment of a fiend.

'I thought it was madness,' he said, as he replaced the obnoxious paper in the safe, 'and now I begin to fear it is disgrace.'

With that he blew out his candle, put on a greatcoat, and set forth in the direction of Cavendish Square, that citadel of medicine, where his friend, the great Dr. Lanyon, had his house and received his crowding patients. 'If anyone knows, it will be Lanyon,' he had thought.

The solemn butler knew and welcomed him; he was subjected to no stage of delay, but ushered direct from the door to the dining-room where Dr. Lanyon sat alone over his wine. This was a hearty, healthy, dapper, red-faced gentleman, with a shock of hair prematurely white, and a boisterous and decided manner. At sight of Mr. Utterson, he sprang up from his chair and welcomed him with both hands. The geniality, as was the way of the man, was somewhat theatrical to the eye; but it reposed on genuine feeling. For these two were old friends, old mates both at school and college, both thorough respectors of themselves and of each other, and what does not always follow, men who thoroughly enjoyed each other's company.

After a little rambling talk, the lawyer led up to the subject which so disagreeably preoccupied his mind.

'I suppose, Lanyon,' said he, 'you and I must be the two oldest friends that Henry Jekyll has?'

'I wish the friends were younger,' chuckled Dr. Lanyon. 'But I suppose we are. And what of that? I see little of him now.'

'Indeed?' said Utterson. 'I thought you had a bond of common interest.'

'We had,' was the reply. 'But it is more than ten years since Henry Jekyll became too fanciful for me. He began to go wrong, wrong in mind; and though of course I continue to take an interest in him for old sake's sake, as they say, I see and I have seen devilish little of the man.

Such unscientific balderdash,' added the doctor, flushing suddenly purple, 'would have estranged Damon and Pythias.'

This little spirit of temper was somewhat of a relief to Mr. Utterson. 'They have only differed on some point of science,' he thought; and being a man of no scientific passions (except in the matter of conveyancing), he even added: 'It is nothing worse than that!' He gave his friend a few seconds to recover his composure, and then approached the question he had come to put. 'Did you ever come across a protégé of his; one Hyde?' he asked.

'Hyde?' repeated Lanyon. 'No. Never heard of him. Since my time.'

That was the amount of information that the lawyer carried back with him to the great, dark bed on which he tossed to and fro, until the small hours of the morning began to grow large. It was a night of little ease to his toiling mind, toiling in mere darkness and besieged by questions.

Six o'clock struck on the bells of the church that was so conveniently near to Mr. Utterson's dwelling, and still he was digging at the problem. Hitherto it had touched him on the intellectual side alone; but now his imagination also was engaged, or rather enslaved; and as he lay and tossed in the gross darkness of the night and the curtained room, Mr. Enfield's tale went by before his mind in a scroll of lighted pictures. He would be aware of the great field of lamps of a nocturnal city; then of the figure of a man walking swiftly; then of a child running from the doctor's; and then these met, and that human Juggernaut trod the child down and passed on regardless of her screams. Or else he would see a room in a rich house, where his friend lay asleep, dreaming and smiling at his dreams; and then the door of that room would be opened, the curtains of the bed plucked apart, the sleeper recalled, and lo! there would stand by his side a figure to whom power was given, and even at that dead hour, he must rise and do its bidding. The figure in these two phases haunted the lawyer all night; and if at any time he dozed over, it was but to see it glide more stealthily through sleeping houses, or move the more swiftly and still the more swiftly, even to dizziness, through wider labyrinths of lamplighted city, and at every street corner crush a child and leave her screaming. And still the figure had no face by which he might know it; even in his dreams, it had no face, or one that baffled him and melted before his eyes; and thus it was that there sprang up and grew apace in the lawyer's mind a singularly strong, almost an inordinate, curiosity to behold the features of the real Mr. Hyde. If he could but once set eyes on him, he thought the mystery would lighten and perhaps roll altogether away, as was the habit of mysterious things when well examined. He might see a reason for his friend's strange preference or bondage (call it which you please) and even for the startling clause of the will. At least it would be a face worth seeing: the face of a man who was without bowels of mercy: a face which had but to show itself to raise up, in the mind of the unimpressionable Enfield, a spirit of enduring hatred.

From that time forward, Mr. Utterson began to haunt the door in the by-street of shops. In the morning before office hours, at noon when business was plenty, and time scarce, at night under the face of the fogged city moon, by all lights and at all hours of solitude or concourse, the lawyer was to be found on his chosen post.

'If he be Mr. Hyde,' he had thought, 'I shall be Mr. Seek.'

And at last his patience was rewarded. It was a fine dry night; frost in the air; the streets as clean as a ballroom floor; the lamps, unshaken by any wind, drawing a regular pattern of light and shadow. By ten o'clock, when the shops were closed the by-street was very solitary and, in spite of the low growl of London from all round, very silent. Small sounds carried far; domestic sounds out of the houses were clearly audible on either side of the roadway;

and the rumour of the approach of any passenger preceded him by a long time. Mr. Utterson had been some minutes at his post, when he was aware of an odd light footstep drawing near. In the course of his nightly patrols, he had long grown accustomed to the quaint effect with which the footfalls of a single person, while he is still a great way off, suddenly spring out distinct from the vast hum and clatter of the city. Yet his attention had never before been so sharply and decisively arrested; and it was with a strong, superstitious prevision of success that he withdrew into the entry of the court.

The steps drew swiftly nearer, and swelled out suddenly louder as they turned the end of the street. The lawyer, looking forth from the entry, could soon see what manner of man he had to deal with. He was small and very plainly dressed and the look of him, even at that distance, went somehow strongly against the watcher's inclination. But he made straight for the door, crossing the roadway to save time; and as he came, he drew a key from his pocket like one approaching home.

Mr. Utterson stepped out and touched him on the shoulder as he passed. 'Mr. Hyde, I think?'

Mr. Hyde shrank back with a hissing intake of the breath. But his fear was only momentary; and though he did not look the lawyer in the face, he answered coolly enough: 'That is my name. What do you want?'

'I see you are going in,' returned the lawyer. 'I am an old friend of Dr Jekyll's - Mr Utterson of Gaunt Street - you must have heard of my name; and meeting you so conveniently, I thought you might admit me.'

'You will not find Dr Jekyll; he is from home,' replied Mr. Hyde, blowing in the key. And then suddenly, but still without looking up. 'How did you know me?' he asked.

'On your side,' said Mr Utterson, 'will you do me a favour?'

'With pleasure,' replied the other. 'What shall it be?'

'Will you let me see your face?' asked the lawyer.

Mr. Hyde appeared to hesitate, and then, as if upon some sudden reflection, fronted about with an air of defiance; and the pair stared at each other pretty fixedly for a few seconds.

'Now I shall know you again,' said Mr. Utterson. 'It may be useful.'

Yes,' returned Mr. Hyde, 'It is as well we have met; and apropos, you should have my address.' And he gave a number of a street in Soho.

'Good God!' thought Mr. Utterson, 'can he, too, have been thinking of the will?' But he kept his feelings to himself and only grunted in acknowledgment of the address.

'And now,' said the other, 'how did you know me?'

'By description,' was the reply.

'Whose description?'

'We have common friends,' said Mr. Utterson.

'Common friends,' echoed Mr. Hyde, a little hoarsely. 'Who are they?'

'Jekyll, for instance,' said the lawyer.

'He never told you,' cried Mr. Hyde, with a flush of anger. 'I did not think you would have lied.'

'Come,' said Mr. Utterson, 'that is not fitting language.'

The other snarled aloud into a savage laugh; and the next moment, with extraordinary quickness, he had unlocked the door and disappeared into the house.

The lawyer stood awhile when Mr. Hyde had left him, the picture of disquietude. Then he began slowly to mount the street, pausing every step or two and putting his hand to his brow like a man in mental perplexity. The problem he was thus debating as he walked, was one of a class that is rarely solved. Mr. Hyde was pale and dwarfish, he gave an impression of deformity without any nameable malformation, he had a displeasing smile, he had borne himself to the lawyer with a sort of murderous mixture of timidity and boldness, and he spoke with a husky, whispering and somewhat broken voice; all these were points against him, but not all of these together could explain the hitherto unknown disgust, loathing and fear with which Mr. Utterson regarded him.

'There must be something else,' said the perplexed gentleman. 'There is something more, if I could find a name for it. God bless me, the man seems hardly human! Something troglodytic, shall we say? or can it be the old story of Dr. Fell? or is it the mere radiance of a foul soul that thus transpires through, and transfigures, its clay continent? The last, I think; for, O my poor old Harry Jekyll, if ever I read Satan's signature upon a face, it is on that of your new friend.'

Round the corner from the by-street, there was a square of ancient, handsome houses, now for the most part decayed from their high estate and let in flats and chambers to all sorts and conditions of men; map-engravers, architects, shady lawyers and the agents of obscure enterprises. One house, however, second from the corner, was still occupied entire; and at the door of this, which wore a great air of wealth and comfort, though it was now plunged in darkness except for the fanlight, Mr. Utterson stopped and knocked. A well-dressed, elderly servant opened the door.

'Is Dr. Jekyll at home, Poole?' asked the lawyer.

'I will see, Mr. Utterson,' said Poole, admitting the visitor, as he spoke, into a large, low-roofed, comfortable hall paved with flags, warmed (after the fashion of a country house) by a bright, open fire, and furnished with costly cabinets of oak. 'Will you wait here by the fire, sir? or shall I give you a light in the dining-room?'

'Here, thank you,' said the lawyer, and he drew near and leaned on the tall fender. This hall, in which he was now left alone, was a pet fancy of his friend the doctor's; and Utterson himself was wont to speak of it as the pleasantest room in London. But tonight there was a shudder in his blood; the face of Hyde sat heavy on his memory; he felt (what was rare with him) a nausea and distaste of life; and in the gloom of his spirits, he seemed to read a menace in the flickering of the firelight on the polished cabinets and the uneasy starting of the shadow on the roof. He was ashamed of his relief, when Poole presently returned to announce that Dr. Jekyll was gone out.

'I saw Mr. Hyde go in by the old dissecting room, Poole,' he said. 'Is that right, when Dr. Jekyll is from home?'

'Quite right, Mr. Utterson, sir,' replied the servant. 'Mr. Hyde has a key.'

Your master seems to repose a great deal of trust in that young man, Poole,' resumed the other musingly.

'Yes, sir, he does indeed,' said Poole. 'We have all orders to obey him.'

'I do not think I ever met Mr. Hyde?' asked Utterson.

'O, dear no, sir. He never dines here,' replied the butler. 'Indeed we see very little of him on this side of the house; he mostly comes and goes by the laboratory.'

'Well, good-night, Poole.'

'Good-night, Mr. Utterson.'

And the lawyer set out homeward with a very heavy heart. 'Poor Harry Jekyll,' he thought, 'my mind misgives me he is in deep waters! He was wild when he was young; a long while ago to be sure; but in the law of God, there is no statute of limitations. Ay, it must be that; the ghost of some old sin, the cancer of some concealed disgrace: punishment coming, PEDE CLAUDO, years after memory has forgotten and self-love condoned the fault.' And the lawyer, scared by the thought, brooded awhile on his own past, groping in all the corners of memory, least by chance some Jack-in-the-Box of an old iniquity should leap to light there. His past was fairly blameless; few men could read the rolls of their life with less apprehension; yet he was humbled to the dust by the many ill things he had done, and raised up again into a sober and fearful gratitude by the many he had come so near to doing yet avoided.

And then by a return on his former subject, he conceived a spark of hope. 'This Master Hyde, if he were studied,' thought he, 'must have secrets of his own; black secrets, by the look of him; secrets compared to which poor Jekyll's worst would be like sunshine. Things cannot continue as they are. It turns me cold to think of this creature stealing like a thief to Harry's bedside; poor Harry, what a wakening! And the danger of it; for if this Hyde suspects the existence of the will, he may grow impatient to inherit. Ay, I must put my shoulders to the wheel--if Jekyll will but let me,' he added, 'if Jekyll will only let me.' For once more he saw before his mind's eye, as clear as transparency, the strange clauses of the will.

DR. JEKYLL WAS QUITE AT EASE

A fortnight later, by excellent good fortune, the doctor gave one of his pleasant dinners to some five or six old cronies, all intelligent, reputable men and all judges of good wine; and Mr. Utterson so contrived that he remained behind after the others had departed. This was no new arrangement, but a thing that had befallen many scores of times. Where Utterson was liked, he was liked well. Hosts loved to detain the dry lawyer, when the light-hearted and loose-tongued had already their foot on the threshold; they liked to sit a while in his unobtrusive company, practising for solitude, sobering their minds in the man's rich silence after the expense and strain of gaiety. To this rule, Dr. Jekyll was no exception; and as he now sat on the opposite side of the fire - a large, well-made, smooth faced man of fifty, with something of a stylish cast perhaps, but every mark of capacity and kindness - you could see by his looks that he cherished for Mr. Utterson a sincere and warm affection.

I have been wanting to speak to you, Jekyll,' began the latter. 'You know that will of yours?'

A close observer might have gathered that the topic was distasteful; but the doctor carried it off gaily. 'My poor Utterson,' said he, 'you are unfortunate in such a client. I never saw a man so distressed as you were by my will; unless it were that hide-bound pedant, Lanyon, at what he called my scientific heresies. O, I know he's a good fellow - you needn't frown - an excellent fellow, and I always mean to see more of him; but a hide-bound pedant for all that; an ignorant, blatant pedant. I was never more disappointed in any man than Lanyon.'

'You know I never approved of it,' pursued Utterson, ruthlessly disregarding the fresh topic.

'My will? Yes, certainly, I know that,' said the doctor, a trifle sharply. 'You have told me so.'

Well, I tell you so again,' continued the lawyer. 'I have been learning something of young Hyde.'

The large handsome face of Dr. Jekyll grew pale to the very lips, and there came a blackness about his eyes. 'I do not care to hear more,' said he. 'This is a matter I thought we had agreed to drop.'

'What I heard was abominable,' said Utterson.

'It can make no change. You do not understand my position,' returned the doctor, with a certain incoherency of manner. 'I am painfully situated, Utterson; my position is a very strange - a very strange one. It is one of those affairs that cannot be mended by talking.'

'Jekyll,' said Utterson, 'you know me: I am a man to be trusted. Make a clean breast of this in confidence; and I make no doubt I can get you out of it.'

'My good Utterson,' said the doctor, 'this is very good of you, this is downright good of you, and I cannot find words to thank you in. I believe you fully; I would trust you before any man alive, ay, before myself, if I could make the choice; but indeed it isn't what you fancy; it is not as bad as that; and just to put your good heart at rest, I will tell you one thing: the moment I choose, I can be rid of Mr. Hyde. I give you my hand upon that; and I thank you again and again; and I will just add one little word, Utterson, that I'm sure you'll take in good part: this is a private matter, and I beg of you to let it sleep.'

Utterson reflected a little, looking in the fire. 'I have no doubt you are perfectly right,' he said at last, getting to his feet.

'Well, but since we have touched upon this business, and for the last time I hope,' continued the doctor, 'there is one point I should like you to understand. I have really a very great interest in poor Hyde. I know you have seen him; he told me so; and I fear he was rude. But I do sincerely take a great, a very great interest in that young man; and if I am taken away, Utterson, I wish you to promise me that you will bear with him and get his rights for him. I think you would, if you knew all; and it would be a weight off my mind if you would promise.'

'I can't pretend that I shall ever like him,' said the lawyer.

'I don't ask that,' pleaded Jekyll, laying his hand upon the other's arm; 'I only ask for justice; I only ask you to help him for my sake, when I am no longer here.'

Utterson heaved an irrepressible sigh. 'Well,' said he, 'I promise.'

THE CAREW MURDER CASE

Nearly a year later, in the month of October, 18--, London was startled by a crime of singular ferocity and rendered all the more notable by the high position of the victim. The details were few and startling. A maid servant living alone in a house not far from the river, had gone upstairs to bed about eleven. Although a fog rolled over the city in the small hours, the early part of the night was cloudless, and the lane, which the maid's window overlooked, was brilliantly lit by the full moon. It seems she was romantically given, for she sat down upon her box, which stood immediately under the window, and fell into a dream of musing. Never (she used to say, with streaming tears, when she narrated that experience), never had she felt more at peace with all men or thought more kindly of the world. And as she so sat she became aware of an aged beautiful gentleman with white hair, drawing near along the lane; and advancing to meet him, another and very small gentleman, to whom at first she paid less attention. When they had come within speech (which was just under the maid's eyes) the older man bowed and accosted the other with a very pretty manner of politeness. It did not seem as if the subject of his address were of great importance; indeed, from his pointing, it sometimes appeared as if he were only inquiring his way; but the moon shone on his face as he spoke, and the girl was pleased to watch it, it seemed to breathe such an innocent and old-world kindness of disposition, yet with something high too, as of a well-founded self-content. Presently her eye wandered to the other, and she was surprised to recognise in him a certain Mr. Hyde, who had once visited her master and for whom she had conceived a dislike. He had in his hand a heavy cane, with which he was trifling; but he answered never a word, and seemed to listen with an ill-contained impatience. And then all of a sudden he broke out in a great flame of anger, stamping with his foot, brandishing the cane, and carrying on (as the maid described it) like a madman. The old gentleman took a step back, with the air of one very much surprised and a trifle hurt; and at that Mr. Hyde broke out of all bounds and clubbed him to the earth. And next moment, with ape-like fury, he was trampling his victim under foot and hailing down a storm of blows, under which the bones were audibly shattered and the body jumped upon the roadway. At the horror of these sights and sounds, the maid fainted.

It was two o'clock when she came to herself and called for the police. The murderer was gone long ago; but there lay his victim in the middle of the lane, incredibly mangled. The stick with which the deed had been done, although it was of some rare and very tough and heavy wood, had broken in the middle under the stress of this insensate cruelty; and one splintered half had rolled in the neighbouring gutter - the other, without doubt, had been carried away by the murderer. A purse and gold watch were found upon the victim: but no cards or papers, except a sealed and stamped envelope, which he had been probably carrying to the post, and which bore the name and address of Mr. Utterson.

This was brought to the lawyer the next morning, before he was out of bed; and he had no sooner seen it and been told the circumstances, than he shot out a solemn lip. 'I shall say nothing till I have seen the body,' said he; 'this may be very serious. Have the kindness to wait while I dress.' And with the same grave countenance he hurried through his breakfast and drove to the police station, whither the body had been carried. As soon as he came into the cell, he nodded.

'Yes,' said he, 'I recognise him. I am sorry to say that this is Sir Danvers Carew.'

'Good God, sir,' exclaimed the officer, 'is it possible?' And the next moment his eye lighted up with professional ambition. 'This will make a deal of noise,' he said. 'And perhaps you can help us to the man.' And he briefly narrated what the maid had seen, and showed the broken stick.

Mr. Utterson had already quailed at the name of Hyde; but when the stick was laid before him, he could doubt no longer; broken and battered as it was, he recognized it for one that he had himself presented many years before to Henry Jekyll.

'Is this Mr. Hyde a person of small stature?' he inquired.

'Particularly small and particularly wicked-looking, is what the maid calls him,' said the officer.

Mr. Utterson reflected; and then, raising his head, 'If you will come with me in my cab,' he said, 'I think I can take you to his house.'

It was by this time about nine in the morning, and the first fog of the season. A great chocolate-coloured pall lowered over heaven, but the wind was continually charging and routing these embattled vapours; so that as the cab crawled from street to street, Mr. Utterson beheld a marvellous number of degrees and hues of twilight; for here it would be dark like the back-end of evening; and there would be a glow of a rich, lurid brown, like the light of some strange conflagration; and here, for a moment, the fog would be quite broken up, and a haggard shaft of daylight would glance in between the swirling wreaths. The dismal quarter of Soho seen under these changing glimpses, with its muddy ways, and slatternly passengers, and its lamps, which had never been extinguished or had been kindled afresh to combat this mournful reinvasion of darkness, seemed, in the lawyer's eyes, like a district of some city in a nightmare. The thoughts of his mind, besides, were of the gloomiest dye; and when he glanced at the companion of his drive, he was conscious of some touch of that terror of the law and the law's officers, which may at times assail the most honest.

As the cab drew up before the address indicated, the fog lifted a little and showed him a dingy street, a gin palace, a low French eating house, a shop for the retail of penny numbers and twopenny salads, many ragged children huddled in the doorways, and many women of many different nationalities passing out, key in hand, to have a morning glass; and the next moment the fog settled down again upon that part, as brown as umber, and cut him off from his blackguardly surroundings. This was the home of Henry Jekyll's favourite; of a man who was heir to a quarter of a million sterling.

An ivory-faced and silvery-haired old woman opened the door. She had an evil face, smoothed by hypocrisy: but her manners were excellent. Yes, she said, this was Mr. Hyde's, but he was not at home; he had been in that night very late, but he had gone away again in less than an hour; there was nothing strange in that; his habits were very irregular, and he was often absent; for instance, it was nearly two months since she had seen him till yesterday.

'Very well, then, we wish to see his rooms,' said the lawyer; and when the woman began to declare it was impossible, 'I had better tell you who this person is,' he added. 'This is Inspector Newcomen of Scotland Yard.'

A flash of odious joy appeared upon the woman's face. 'Ah!' said she, 'he is in trouble! What has he done?'

Mr. Utterson and the inspector exchanged glances. 'He don't seem a very popular character,' observed the latter. 'And now, my good woman, just let me and this gentleman have a look about us.'

In the whole extent of the house, which but for the old woman remained otherwise empty, Mr. Hyde had only used a couple of rooms; but these were furnished with luxury and good taste. A closet was filled with wine; the plate was of silver, the napery elegant; a good picture hung upon the walls, a gift (as Utterson supposed) from Henry Jekyll, who was much of a connoisseur; and the carpets were of many plies and agreeable in colour. At this moment, however, the rooms bore every mark of having been recently and hurriedly ransacked; clothes lay about the floor, with their pockets inside out; lock-fast drawers stood open; and on the hearth there lay a pile of grey ashes, as though many papers had been burned. From these embers the inspector disinterred the butt end of a green cheque book, which had resisted the action of the fire; the other half of the stick was found behind the door; and as this clinched his suspicions, the officer declared himself delighted. A visit to the bank, where several thousand pounds were found to be lying to the murderer's credit, completed his gratification.

'You may depend upon it, sir,' he told Mr. Utterson: 'I have him in my hand. He must have lost his head, or he never would have left the stick or, above all, burned the cheque book. Why, money's life to the man. We have nothing to do but wait for him at the bank, and get out the handbills.'

This last, however, was not so easy of accomplishment; for Mr. Hyde had numbered few familiars - even the master of the servant maid had only seen him twice; his family could nowhere be traced; he had never been photographed; and the few who could describe him differed widely, as common observers will. Only on one point were they agreed; and that was the haunting sense of unexpressed deformity with which the fugitive impressed his beholders.

INCIDENT OF THE LETTER

It was late in the afternoon, when Mr. Utterson found his way to Dr. Jekyll's door, where he was at once admitted by Poole, and carried down by the kitchen offices and across a yard which had once been a garden, to the building which was indifferently known as the laboratory or dissecting rooms. The doctor had bought the house from the heirs of a celebrated surgeon; and his own tastes being rather chemical than anatomical, had changed the destination of the block at the bottom of the garden. It was the first time that the lawyer had been received in that part of his friend's quarters; and he eyed the dingy, windowless structure with curiosity, and gazed round with a distasteful sense of strangeness as he crossed the theatre, once crowded with eager students and now lying gaunt and silent, the tables laden with chemical apparatus, the floor strewn with crates and littered with packing straw, and the light falling dimly through the foggy cupola. At the further end, a flight of stairs mounted to a door covered with red baize; and through this, Mr. Utterson was at last received into the doctor's cabinet. It was a large room fitted round with glass presses, furnished, among other things, with a cheval-glass and a business table, and looking out upon the court by three dusty windows barred with iron. The fire burned in the grate; a lamp was set lighted on the chimney shelf, for even in the houses the fog began to lie thickly; and there, close up to the warmth, sat Dr. Jekyll, looking deathly sick. He did not rise to meet his visitor, but held out a cold hand and bade him welcome in a changed voice.

'And now,' said Mr. Utterson, as soon as Poole had left them, 'you have heard the news?'

The doctor shuddered. 'They were crying it in the square,' he said. 'I heard them in my dining-room.'

One word,' said the lawyer. 'Carew was my client, but so are you, and I want to know what I am doing. You have not been mad enough to hide this fellow?'

'Utterson, I swear to God,' cried the doctor, 'I swear to God I will never set eyes on him again. I bind my honour to you that I am done with him in this world. It is all at an end. And indeed he does not want my help; you do not know him as I do; he is safe, he is quite safe; mark my words, he will never more be heard of.'

The lawyer listened gloomily; he did not like his friend's feverish manner. 'You seem pretty sure of him,' said he; 'and for your sake, I hope you may be right. If it came to a trial, your name might appear.'

'I am quite sure of him,' replied Jekyll; 'I have grounds for certainty that I cannot share with any one. But there is one thing on which you may advise me. I have - I have received a letter; and I am at a loss whether I should show it to the police. I should like to leave it in your hands, Utterson; you would judge wisely, I am sure; I have so great a trust in you.'

'You fear, I suppose, that it might lead to his detection?' asked the lawyer.

'No,' said the other. 'I cannot say that I care what becomes of Hyde; I am quite done with him. I was thinking of my own character, which this hateful business has rather exposed.'

Utterson ruminated awhile; he was surprised at his

friend's selfishness, and yet relieved by it. 'Well,' said he, at last, 'let me see the letter.'

The letter was written in an odd, upright hand and signed "Edward Hyde": and it signified, briefly enough, that the writer's benefactor, Dr. Jekyll, whom he had long so unworthily repaid for a thousand generosities, need labour under no alarm for his safety, as he had means of escape on which he placed a sure dependence. The lawyer liked this letter well enough; it put a better colour on the intimacy than he had looked for; and he blamed himself for some of his past suspicions.

'Have you the envelope?' he asked.

'I burned it,' replied Jekyll, 'before I thought what I was about. But it bore no postmark. The note was handed in.'

'Shall I keep this and sleep upon it?' asked Utterson.

'I wish you to judge for me entirely,' was the reply. 'I have lost confidence in myself.'

'Well, I shall consider,' returned the lawyer. 'And now one word more: it was Hyde who dictated the terms in your will about that disappearance?'

The doctor seemed seized with a qualm of faintness; he shut his mouth tight and nodded.

'I knew it,' said Utterson. 'He meant to murder you. You had a fine escape.'

'I have had what is far more to the purpose,' returned the doctor solemnly: 'I have had a lesson - O God, Utterson, what a lesson I have had!" And he covered his face for a moment with his hands.

On his way out, the lawyer stopped and had a word or two with Poole. 'By the bye,' said he, 'there was a letter handed in to-day: what was the messenger like?'

But Poole was positive nothing had come except by post; 'and only circulars by that,' he added.

This news sent off the visitor with his fears renewed. Plainly the letter had come by the laboratory door; possibly, indeed, it had been written in the cabinet; and if that were so, it must be differently judged, and handled with the more caution.

The newsboys, as he went, were crying themselves hoarse along the footways: 'Special edition. Shocking murder of an M.P.'

That was the funeral oration of one friend and client; and he could not help a certain apprehension lest the good name of another should be sucked down in the eddy of the scandal. It was, at least, a ticklish decision that he had to make; and self-reliant as he was by habit, he began to cherish a longing for advice. It was not to be had directly; but perhaps, he thought, it might be fished for.

Presently after, he sat on one side of his own hearth, with Mr. Guest, his head clerk, upon the other, and midway between, at a nicely calculated distance from the fire, a bottle of a particular old wine that had long dwelt unsunned in the foundations of his house. The fog still slept on the wing above the drowned city, where the lamps glimmered like carbuncles; and through the muffle and smother of these fallen clouds, the procession of the town's life was still rolling in through the great arteries with a sound as of a mighty wind. But the room was gay with firelight. In the bottle the acids were long ago resolved; the imperial dye had softened with time, as the colour grows richer in stained windows; and the glow of hot autumn afternoons on hillside vineyards, was ready to be set free and to disperse the fogs of London. Insensibly the lawyer melted. There was no man from whom he kept fewer secrets than Mr. Guest; and he was not always sure that he kept as many as he meant. Guest had often been on business to the doctor's; he knew Poole; he could scarce have failed to hear of Mr. Hyde's familiarity about the house; he might draw conclusions: was it not as well, then, that he should see a letter which put that mystery to right? and above all since Guest, being a great student and critic of handwriting, would consider the step natural and obliging? The clerk, besides, was a man of counsel; he

254

could scarce read so strange a document without dropping a remark; and by that remark Mr. Utterson might shape his future course.

'This is a sad business about Sir Danvers,' he said.

'Yes, sir, indeed. It has elicited a great deal of public feeling,' returned Guest. 'The man, of course, was mad.'

'I should like to hear your views on that,' replied Utterson. 'I have a document here in his handwriting; it is between ourselves, for I scarce know what to do about it; it is an ugly business at the best. But there it is; quite in your way: a murderer's autograph.'

Guest's eyes brightened, and he sat down at once and studied it with passion. 'No sir,' he said: 'not mad; but it is an odd hand.'

'And by all accounts a very odd writer,' added the lawyer.

Just then the servant entered with a note.

'Is that from Dr. Jekyll, sir?' inquired the clerk. 'I thought I knew the writing. Anything private, Mr. Utterson?'

'Only an invitation to dinner. Why? Do you want to see it?'

'One moment. I thank you, sir;' and the clerk laid the two sheets of paper alongside and sedulously compared their contents. 'Thank you, sir,' he said at last, returning both; 'it's a very interesting autograph.'

There was a pause, during which Mr. Utterson struggled with himself. 'Why did you compare them, Guest?' he inquired suddenly.

'Well, sir,' returned the clerk, 'there's a rather singular resemblance; the two hands are in many points identical: only differently sloped.'

'Rather quaint,' said Utterson.

'It is, as you say, rather quaint,' returned Guest.

'I wouldn't speak of this note, you know,' said the master.

'No, sir,' said the clerk. 'I understand.'

But no sooner was Mr. Utterson alone that night, than he locked the note into his safe, where it reposed from that time forward. 'What!' he thought. 'Henry Jekyll forge for a murderer!' And his blood ran cold in his veins.

INCIDENT OF DR. LANYON

Time ran on; thousands of pounds were offered in reward, for the death of Sir Danvers was resented as a public injury; but Mr. Hyde had disappeared out of the ken of the police as though he had never existed.

Much of his past was unearthed, indeed, and all disreputable: tales came out of the man's cruelty, at once so callous and violent; of his vile life, of his strange associates, of the hatred that seemed to have surrounded his career; but of his present whereabouts, not a whisper. From the time he had left the house in Soho on the morning of the murder, he was simply blotted out; and gradually, as time drew on, Mr. Utterson began to recover from the hotness of his alarm, and to grow more at quiet with himself. The death of Sir Danvers was, to his way of thinking, more than paid for by the disappearance of Mr. Hyde. Now that that evil influence had been withdrawn, a new life began for Dr. Jekyll. He came out of his seclusion, renewed relations with his friends, became once more their familiar guest and entertainer; and whilst he had always been known for charities, he was now no less distinguished for religion. He was busy, he was much in the open air, he did good; his face seemed to open and brighten, as if with an inward consciousness of service; and for more than two months, the doctor was at peace.

On the 8th of January Utterson had dined at the doctor's with a small party; Lanyon had been there; and the face of the host had looked from one to the other as in the old days when the trio were inseparable friends. On the 12th, and again on the 14th, the door was shut against the lawyer. 'The doctor was confined to the house,' Poole said, 'and saw no one.' On the 15th, he tried again, and was again refused; and having now been used for the last two months to see his friend almost daily, he found this return of solitude to weigh upon his spirits. The fifth night he had in Guest to dine with him; and the sixth he betook himself to Dr. Lanyon's.

There at least he was not denied admittance; but when he came in, he was shocked at the change which had taken place in the doctor's appearance. He had his death-warrant written legibly upon his face. The rosy man had grown pale; his flesh had fallen away; he was visibly balder and older; and yet it was not so much these tokens of a swift physical decay that arrested the lawyer's notice, as a look in the eye and quality of manner that seemed to testify to some deep-seated terror of the mind. It was unlikely that the doctor should fear death; and yet that was what Utterson was tempted to suspect. 'Yes,' he thought; 'he is a doctor, he must know his own state and that his days are counted; and the knowledge is more than he can bear.' And yet when Utterson remarked on his ill-looks, it was with an air of great firmness that Lanyon declared himself a doomed man.

'I have had a shock,' he said, 'and I shall never recover. It is a question of weeks. Well, life has been pleasant; I liked it; yes, sir, I used to like it. I sometimes think if we knew all, we should be more glad to get away.'

'Jekyll is ill, too,' observed Utterson. 'Have you seen him?'

But Lanyon's face changed, and he held up a trembling hand. 'I wish to see or hear no more of Dr. Jekyll,' he said in a loud, unsteady voice. 'I am quite done with that person; and I beg that you will spare me any allusion to one whom I regard as dead.'

'Tut-tut,' said Mr. Utterson; and then after a considerable pause, 'Can't I do anything?' he inquired. 'We are three very old friends, Lanyon; we shall not live to make others.'

'Nothing can be done,' returned Lanyon; 'ask himself.'

'He will not see me,' said the lawyer.

'I am not surprised at that,' was the reply. 'Some day, Utterson, after I am dead, you may perhaps come to learn the right and wrong of this. I cannot tell you. And in the meantime, if you can sit and talk with me of other things, for God's sake, stay and do so; but if you cannot keep clear of this accursed topic, then in God's name, go, for I cannot bear it.'

As soon as he got home, Utterson sat down and wrote to Jekyll, complaining of his exclusion from the house, and asking the cause of this unhappy break with Lanyon; and the next day brought him a long answer, often very pathetically worded, and sometimes darkly mysterious in drift. The quarrel with Lanyon was incurable. 'I do not blame our old friend,' Jekyll wrote, 'but I share his view that we must never meet. I mean from henceforth to lead a life of extreme seclusion; you must not be surprised, nor must you doubt my friendship, if my door is often shut even to you. You must suffer me to go my own dark way. I have brought on myself a punishment and a danger that I cannot name. If I am the chief of sinners, I am the chief of sufferers also. I could not think that this earth contained a place for sufferings and terrors so unmanning; and you can do but one thing, Utterson, to lighten this destiny, and that is to respect my silence.'

Utterson was amazed; the dark influence of Hyde had been withdrawn, the doctor had returned to his old tasks and amities; a week ago, the prospect had smiled with every promise of a cheerful and an honoured age; and now in a moment, friendship, and peace of mind, and the whole tenor of his life were wrecked. So great and unprepared a change pointed to madness; but in view of Lanyon's manner and words, there must lie for it some deeper ground.

A week afterwards Dr. Lanyon took to his bed, and in

something less than a fortnight he was dead. The night after the funeral, at which he had been sadly affected, Utterson locked the door of his business room, and sitting there by the light of a melancholy candle, drew out and set before him an envelope addressed by the hand and sealed with the seal of his dead friend. "PRIVATE: for the hands of G. J. Utterson ALONE, and in case of his predecease to be destroyed unread," so it was emphatically superscribed; and the lawyer dreaded to behold the contents. 'I have buried one friend to-day,' he thought: 'what if this should cost me another?' And then he condemned the fear as a disloyalty, and broke the seal. Within there was another enclosure, likewise sealed, and marked upon the cover as "not to be opened till the death or disappearance of Dr. Henry Jekyll." Utterson could not trust his eyes. Yes, it was disappearance; here again, as in the mad will which he had long ago restored to its author, here again were the idea of a disappearance and the name of Henry Jekyll bracketed. But in the will, that idea had sprung from the sinister suggestion of the man Hyde; it was set there with a purpose all too plain and horrible. Written by the hand of Lanyon, what should it mean? A great curiosity came on the trustee, to disregard the prohibition and dive at once to the bottom of these mysteries; but professional honour and faith to his dead friend were stringent obligations; and the packet slept in the inmost corner of his private safe.

It is one thing to mortify curiosity, another to conquer it; and it may be doubted if, from that day forth, Utterson desired the society of his surviving friend with the same eagerness. He thought of him kindly; but his thoughts were disquieted and fearful. He went to call indeed; but he was perhaps relieved to be denied admittance; perhaps, in his heart, he preferred to speak with Poole upon the doorstep and surrounded by the air and sounds of the open city, rather than to be admitted into that house of voluntary bondage, and to sit and speak with its inscrutable recluse. Poole had, indeed, no very pleasant news to communicate. The doctor, it appeared, now more than ever confined himself to the cabinet over the laboratory, where he would sometimes even sleep; he was out of spirits, he had grown very silent, he did not read; it seemed as if he had something on his mind. Utterson became so used to the unvarying character of these reports, that he fell off little by little in the frequency of his visits.

INCIDENT AT THE WINDOW

It chanced on Sunday, when Mr. Utterson was on his usual walk with Mr. Enfield, that their way lay once again through the by-street; and that when they came in front of the door, both stopped to gaze on it.

'Well,' said Enfield, 'that story's at an end at least. We shall never see more of Mr. Hyde.'

'I hope not,' said Utterson. 'Did I ever tell you that I once saw him, and shared your feeling of repulsion?'

'It was impossible to do the one without the other,' returned Enfield. 'And by the way, what an ass you must have thought me, not to know that this was a back way to Dr. Jekyll's! It was partly your own fault that I found it out, even when I did.'

'So you found it out, did you?' said Utterson. 'But if that be so, we may step into the court and take a look at the windows. To tell you the truth, I am uneasy about poor Jekyll; and even outside, I feel as if the presence of a friend might do him good.'

The court was very cool and a little damp, and full of premature twilight, although the sky, high up overhead, was still bright with sunset. The middle one of the three windows was half-way open; and sitting close beside it, taking the air with an infinite sadness of mien, like some disconsolate prisoner, Utterson saw Dr. Jekyll.

'What! Jekyll!' he cried. 'I trust you are better.'

'I am very low, Utterson,' replied the doctor drearily, 'very low. It will not last long, thank God.'

'You stay too much indoors,' said the lawyer. 'You should be out, whipping up the circulation like Mr. Enfield and me. (This is my cousin - Mr. Enfield - Dr. Jekyll.) Come now; get your hat and take a quick turn with us.'

'You are very good,' sighed the other. 'I should like to very much; but no, no, no, it is quite impossible; I dare not. But indeed, Utterson, I am very glad to see you; this is really a great pleasure; I would ask you and Mr. Enfield up, but the place is really not fit.'

'Why, then,' said the lawyer, good-naturedly, 'the best thing we can do is to stay down here and speak with you from where we are.'

'That is just what I was about to venture to propose,' returned the doctor with a smile. But the words were hardly uttered, before the smile was struck out of his face and succeeded by an expression of such abject terror and despair, as froze the very blood of the two gentlemen below.

They saw it but for a glimpse for the window was instantly thrust down; but that glimpse had been sufficient, and they turned and left the court without a word. In silence, too, they traversed the by-street; and it was not until they had come into a neighbouring thoroughfare, where even upon a Sunday there were still some stirrings of life, that Mr. Utterson at last turned and looked at his companion. They were both pale; and there was an answering horror in their eyes.

'God forgive us, God forgive us,' said Mr. Utterson.

But Mr. Enfield only nodded his head very seriously, and walked on once more in silence.

THE LAST NIGHT

Mr. Utterson was sitting by his fireside one evening after dinner, when he was surprised to receive a visit from

Poole.

'Bless me, Poole, what brings you here?' he cried; and then taking a second look at him, 'What ails you?' he added; 'is the doctor ill?'

'Mr. Utterson,' said the man, 'there is something wrong.'

'Take a seat, and here is a glass of wine for you,' said the lawyer. 'Now, take your time, and tell me plainly what you want.'

'You know the doctor's ways, sir,' replied Poole, 'and how he shuts himself up. Well, he's shut up again in the cabinet; and I don't like it, sir - I wish I may die if I like it. Mr. Utterson, sir, I'm afraid.'

'Now, my good man,' said the lawyer, 'be explicit. What are you afraid of?'

'I've been afraid for about a week,' returned Poole, doggedly disregarding the question, 'and I can bear it no more.'

The man's appearance amply bore out his words; his manner was altered for the worse; and except for the moment when he had first announced his terror, he had not once looked the lawyer in the face. Even now, he sat with the glass of wine untasted on his knee, and his eyes directed to a corner of the floor. 'I can bear it no more,' he repeated.

'Come,' said the lawyer, 'I see you have some good reason, Poole; I see there is something seriously amiss. Try to tell me what it is.'

'I think there's been foul play,' said Poole, hoarsely.

'Foul play!' cried the lawyer, a good deal frightened and rather inclined to be irritated in consequence. 'What foul play! What does the man mean?'

'I daren't say, sir,' was the answer; 'but will you come along with me and see for yourself?'

Mr. Utterson's only answer was to rise and get his hat and greatcoat; but he observed with wonder the greatness of the relief that appeared upon the butler's face, and perhaps with no less, that the wine was still untasted when he set it down to follow.

It was a wild, cold, seasonable night of March, with a pale moon, lying on her back as though the wind had tilted her, and flying wrack of the most diaphanous and lawny texture. The wind made talking difficult, and flecked the blood into the face. It seemed to have swept the streets unusually bare of passengers, besides; for Mr. Utterson thought he had never seen that part of London so deserted. He could have wished it otherwise; never in his life had he been conscious of so sharp a wish to see and touch his fellow-creatures; for struggle as he might, there was borne in upon his mind a crushing anticipation of calamity. The square, when they got there, was full of wind and dust, and the thin trees in the garden were lashing themselves along the railing. Poole, who had kept all the way a pace or two ahead, now pulled up in the middle of the pavement, and in spite of the biting weather, took off his hat and mopped his brow with a red pocket-handkerchief. But for all the hurry of his coming, these were not the dews of exertion that he wiped away, but the moisture of some strangling anguish; for his face was white and his voice, when he spoke, harsh and broken.

'Well, sir,' he said, 'here we are, and God grant there be nothing wrong.'

'Amen, Poole,' said the lawyer.

Thereupon the servant knocked in a very guarded manner; the door was opened on the chain; and a voice asked from within, 'Is that you, Poole?'

'It's all right,' said Poole. 'Open the door.'

The hall, when they entered it, was brightly lighted up; the fire was built high; and about the hearth the whole of the servants, men and women, stood huddled together like a flock of sheep. At the sight of Mr. Utterson, the housemaid broke into hysterical whimpering; and the cook, crying out 'Bless God! it's Mr. Utterson,' ran forward as if to take him in her arms.

'What, what? Are you all here?' said the lawyer peevishly. "Very irregular, very unseemly; your master would be far from pleased."

'They're all afraid,' said Poole.

Blank silence followed, no one protesting; only the maid lifted her voice and now wept loudly.

'Hold your tongue!' Poole said to her, with a ferocity of accent that testified to his own jangled nerves; and indeed, when the girl had so suddenly raised the note of her lamentation, they had all started and turned towards the inner door with faces of dreadful expectation.

'And now,' continued the butler, addressing the knife-boy, 'reach me a candle, and we'll get this through hands at once.' And then he begged Mr. Utterson to follow him, and led the way to the back garden.

'Now, sir,' said he, 'you come as gently as you can. I want you to hear, and I don't want you to be heard. And see here, sir, if by any chance he was to ask you in, don't go.'

Mr. Utterson's nerves, at this unlooked-for termination, gave a jerk that nearly threw him from his balance; but he recollected his courage and followed the butler into the laboratory building through the surgical theatre, with its lumber of crates and bottles, to the foot of the stair. Here Poole motioned him to stand on one side and listen; while he himself, setting down the candle and making a great and obvious call on his resolution, mounted the steps and knocked with a somewhat uncertain hand on the red baize of the cabinet door.

'Mr. Utterson, sir, asking to see you,' he called; and even as he did so, once more violently signed to the lawyer to give ear.

A voice answered from within: 'Tell him I cannot see anyone,' it said complainingly.

'Thank you, sir,' said Poole, with a note of something like triumph in his voice; and taking up his candle, he led Mr. Utterson back across the yard and into the great kitchen, where the fire was out and the beetles were leaping on the floor.

'Sir,' he said, looking Mr. Utterson in the eyes, 'Was that my master's voice?'

'It seems much changed,' replied the lawyer, very pale, but giving look for look.

'Changed? Well, yes, I think so,' said the butler. 'Have I been twenty years in this man's house, to be deceived about his voice? No, sir; master's made away with; he was made away with eight days ago, when we heard him cry out upon the name of God; and who's in there instead of him, and why it stays there, is a thing that cries to Heaven, Mr. Utterson!'

'This is a very strange tale, Poole; this is rather a wild tale my man,' said Mr. Utterson, biting his finger. 'Suppose it were as you suppose, supposing Dr. Jekyll to have been - well, murdered what could induce the murderer to stay? That won't hold water; it doesn't commend itself to reason.'

'Well, Mr. Utterson, you are a hard man to satisfy, but I'll do it yet,' said Poole. 'All this last week (you must know) him, or it, whatever it is that lives in that cabinet, has been crying night and day for some sort of medicine and cannot get it to his mind. It was sometimes his way - the master's, that is - to write his orders on a sheet of paper and throw it on the stair. We've had nothing else this week back; nothing but papers, and a closed door, and the very meals left there to be smuggled in when nobody was looking. Well, sir, every day, ay, and twice and thrice in the same day, there have been orders and complaints, and I have been sent flying to all the wholesale chemists in town. Every time I brought the stuff back, there would be another paper telling me to return it, because it was not pure, and another order to a different firm. This drug is wanted bitter bad, sir, whatever for.'

'Have you any of these papers?' asked Mr. Utterson.

Poole felt in his pocket and handed out a crumpled

note, which the lawyer, bending nearer to the candle, carefully examined. Its contents ran thus: "Dr. Jekyll presents his compliments to Messrs. Maw. He assures them that their last sample is impure and quite useless for his present purpose. In the year 18--, Dr. J. purchased a somewhat large quantity from Messrs. M. He now begs them to search with most sedulous care, and should any of the same quality be left, forward it to him at once. Expense is no consideration. The importance of this to Dr. J. can hardly be exaggerated." So far the letter had run composedly enough, but here with a sudden splutter of the pen, the writer's emotion had broken loose. "For God's sake," he added, "find me some of the old."

'This is a strange note,' said Mr. Utterson; and then sharply, 'How do you come to have it open?'

'The man at Maw's was main angry, sir, and he threw it back to me like so much dirt,' returned Poole.

'This is unquestionably the doctor's hand, do you know?' resumed the lawyer.

'I thought it looked like it,' said the servant rather sulkily; and then, with another voice, 'But what matters hand of write?' he said.

'I've seen him!'

'Seen him?' repeated Mr. Utterson. 'Well?'

'That's it!' said Poole. 'It was this way. I came suddenly into the theatre from the garden. It seems he had slipped out to look for this drug or whatever it is; for the cabinet door was open, and there he was at the far end of the room digging among the crates. He looked up when I came in, gave a kind of cry, and whipped upstairs into the cabinet. It was but for one minute that I saw him, but the hair stood upon my head like quills. Sir, if that was my master, why had he a mask upon his face? If it was my master, why did he cry out like a rat, and run from me? I have served him long enough. And then...' The man paused and passed his hand over his face.

'These are all very strange circumstances,' said Mr.

Utterson, 'but I think I begin to see daylight. Your master, Poole, is plainly seized with one of those maladies that both torture and deform the sufferer; hence, for aught I know, the alteration of his voice; hence the mask and the avoidance of his friends; hence his eagerness to find this drug, by means of which the poor soul retains some hope of ultimate recovery - God grant that he be not deceived! There is my explanation; it is sad enough, Poole, ay, and appalling to consider; but it is plain and natural, hangs well together, and delivers us from all exorbitant alarms.'

'Sir,' said the butler, turning to a sort of mottled pallor, 'that thing was not my master, and there's the truth. My master' - here he looked round him and began to whisper – 'is a tall, fine build of a man, and this was more of a dwarf.' Utterson attempted to protest. 'O, sir,' cried Poole, 'do you think I do not know my master after twenty years?

Do you think I do not know where his head comes to in the cabinet door, where I saw him every morning of my life? No, sir, that thing in the mask was never Dr. Jekyll - God knows what it was, but it was never Dr. Jekyll; and it is the belief of my heart that there was murder done.'

'Poole,' replied the lawyer, 'if you say that, it will become my duty to make certain. Much as I desire to spare your master's feelings, much as I am puzzled by this note which seems to prove him to be still alive, I shall consider it my duty to break in that door.'

'Ah, Mr. Utterson, that's talking!' cried the butler.

'And now comes the second question,' resumed Utterson: 'Who is going to do it?'

'Why, you and me, sir,' was the undaunted reply.

'That's very well said,' returned the lawyer; 'and whatever comes of it, I shall make it my business to see you are no loser.'

'There is an axe in the theatre,' continued Poole; 'and you might take the kitchen poker for yourself.'

The lawyer took that rude but weighty instrument into his hand, and balanced it. 'Do you know, Poole,' he said, looking up, 'that you and I are about to place ourselves in a position of some peril?'

'You may say so, sir, indeed,' returned the butler.

'It is well, then that we should be frank,' said the other. 'We both think more than we have said; let us make a clean breast. This masked figure that you saw, did you recognise it?'

'Well, sir, it went so quick, and the creature was so doubled up, that I could hardly swear to that,' was the answer. 'But if you mean, was it Mr. Hyde? - why, yes, I think it was! You see, it was much of the same bigness; and it had the same quick, light way with it; and then who else could have got in by the laboratory door? You have not forgot, sir, that at the time of the murder he had still the key with him? But that's not all. I don't know, Mr. Utterson, if you ever met this Mr. Hyde?'

'Yes,' said the lawyer, 'I once spoke with him.'

'Then you must know as well as the rest of us that there was something queer about that gentleman - something that gave a man a turn - I don't know rightly how to say it, sir, beyond this: that you felt in your marrow kind of cold and thin.'

'I own I felt something of what you describe,' said Mr. Utterson.

'Quite so, sir,' returned Poole. 'Well, when that masked thing like a monkey jumped from among the chemicals and whipped into the cabinet, it went down my spine like ice. O, I know it's not evidence, Mr. Utterson; I'm book-learned enough for that; but a man has his feelings, and I give you my bible-word it was Mr. Hyde!'

'Ay, ay,' said the lawyer. 'My fears incline to the same point. Evil, I fear, founded - evil was sure to come - of that connection. Ay truly, I believe you; I believe poor Harry is killed; and I believe his murderer (for what purpose, God alone can tell) is still lurking in his victim's room. Well, let our name be vengeance. Call Bradshaw.'

The footman came at the summons, very white and nervous.

'Put yourself together, Bradshaw,' said the lawyer. 'This suspense, I know, is telling upon all of you; but it is now our intention to make an end of it. Poole, here, and I are going to force our way into the cabinet. If all is well, my shoulders are broad enough to bear the blame. Meanwhile, lest anything should really be amiss, or any malefactor seek to escape by the back, you and the boy must go round the corner with a pair of good sticks and take your post at the laboratory door. We give you ten minutes, to get to your stations.'

As Bradshaw left, the lawyer looked at his watch. 'And now, Poole, let us get to ours,' he said; and taking the poker under his arm, led the way into the yard. The scud had banked over the moon, and it was now quite dark. The wind, which only broke in puffs and draughts into that deep well of building, tossed the light of the candle to and fro about their steps, until they came into the shelter of the theatre, where they sat down silently to wait. London hummed solemnly all around; but nearer at hand, the stillness was only broken by the sounds of a footfall moving to and fro along the cabinet floor.

'So it will walk all day, sir,' whispered Poole; 'ay, and the better part of the night. Only when a new sample comes from the chemist, there's a bit of a break. Ah, it's an ill conscience that's such an enemy to rest! Ah, sir, there's blood foully shed in every step of it! But hark again, a little closer - put your heart in your ears, Mr. Utterson, and tell me, is that the doctor's foot?'

The steps fell lightly and oddly, with a certain swing, for all they went so slowly; it was different indeed from the heavy creaking tread of Henry Jekyll. Utterson sighed. 'Is there never anything else?' he asked.

Poole nodded. 'Once,' he said. 'Once I heard it weeping!'

'Weeping? how that?' said the lawyer, conscious of a sudden chill of horror.

'Weeping like a woman or a lost soul,' said the butler. 'I came away with that upon my heart, that I could have wept too.'

But now the ten minutes drew to an end. Poole disinterred the axe from under a stack of packing straw; the candle was set upon the nearest table to light them to the attack; and they drew near with bated breath to where that patient foot was still going up and down, up and down, in the quiet of the night. 'Jekyll,' cried Utterson, with a loud voice, 'I demand to see you.' He paused a moment, but there came no reply. 'I give you fair warning, our suspicions are aroused, and I must and shall see you,' he resumed; 'if not by fair means, then by foul - if not of your consent, then by brute force!'

'Utterson,' said the voice, 'for God's sake, have mercy!'

'Ah, that's not Jekyll's voice - it's Hyde's!' cried Utterson. 'Down with the door, Poole!'

Poole swung the axe over his shoulder; the blow shook the building, and the red baize door leaped against the lock and hinges. A dismal screech, as of mere animal terror, rang from the cabinet. Up went the axe again, and again the panels crashed and the frame bounded; four times the blow fell; but the wood was tough and the fittings were of excellent workmanship; and it was not until the fifth, that the lock burst and the wreck of the door fell inwards on the carpet.

The besiegers, appalled by their own riot and the stillness that had succeeded, stood back a little and peered in. There lay the cabinet before their eyes in the quiet lamplight, a good fire glowing and chattering on the hearth, the kettle singing its thin strain, a drawer or two open, papers neatly set forth on the business table, and nearer the fire, the things laid out for tea; the quietest room, you would have said, and, but for the glazed presses full of chemicals, the most commonplace that night in London.

Right in the middle there lay the body of a man sorely contorted and still twitching. They drew near on tiptoe, turned it on its back and beheld the face of Edward Hyde. He was dressed in clothes far too large for him, clothes of the doctor's bigness; the cords of his face still moved with a semblance of life, but life was quite gone: and by the crushed phial in the hand and the strong smell of kernels that hung upon the air, Utterson knew that he was looking on the body of a self-destroyer.

'We have come too late,' he said sternly, 'whether to save or punish. Hyde is gone to his account; and it only remains for us to find the body of your master.'

The far greater proportion of the building was occupied by the theatre, which filled almost the whole ground storey and was lighted from above, and by the cabinet, which formed an upper story at one end and looked upon the court. A corridor joined the theatre to the door on the by-street; and with this the cabinet communicated separately by a second flight of stairs. There were besides a few dark closets and a spacious cellar. All these they now thoroughly examined. Each closet needed but a glance, for all were empty, and all, by the dust that fell from their doors, had stood long unopened. The cellar, indeed, was filled with crazy lumber, mostly dating from the times of the surgeon who was Jekyll's predecessor; but even as they opened the door they were advertised of the uselessness of further search, by the fall of a perfect mat of cobweb which had for years sealed up the entrance. Nowhere was there any trace of Henry Jekyll dead or alive.

Poole stamped on the flags of the corridor. 'He must be buried here,' he said, hearkening to the sound.

'Or he may have fled,' said Utterson, and he turned to examine the door in the by-street. It was locked; and lying nearby on the flags, they found the key, already stained with rust.

'This does not look like use,' observed the lawyer.

'Use!' echoed Poole. 'Do you not see, sir, it is broken? much as if a man had stamped on it.'

'Ay,' continued Utterson, 'and the fractures, too, are rusty.' The two men looked at each other with a scare. 'This is beyond me, Poole,' said the lawyer. 'Let us go back to the cabinet.'

They mounted the stair in silence, and still with an occasional awestruck glance at the dead body, proceeded more thoroughly to examine the contents of the cabinet. At one table, there were traces of chemical work, various measured heaps of some white salt being laid on glass saucers, as though for an experiment in which the unhappy man had been prevented.

'That is the same drug that I was always bringing him,' said Poole; and even as he spoke, the kettle with a startling noise boiled over.

This brought them to the fireside, where the easy-chair was drawn cosily up, and the tea things stood ready to the sitter's elbow, the very sugar in the cup. There were several books on a shelf; one lay beside the tea things open, and Utterson was amazed to find it a copy of a pious work, for which Jekyll had several times expressed a great esteem, annotated, in his own hand with startling blasphemies.

Next, in the course of their review of the chamber, the searchers came to the cheval-glass, into whose depths they looked with an involuntary horror. But it was so turned as to show them nothing but the rosy glow playing on the roof, the fire sparkling in a hundred repetitions along the glazed front of the presses, and their own pale and fearful countenances stooping to look in.

'This glass has seen some strange things, sir,' whispered Poole.

'And surely none stranger than itself,' echoed the lawyer in the same tones. 'For what did Jekyll' - he caught himself up at the word with a start, and then conquering the weakness – 'what could Jekyll want with it?' he said.

'You may say that!' said Poole.

Next they turned to the business table. On the desk, among the neat array of papers, a large envelope was uppermost, and bore, in the doctor's hand, the name of Mr. Utterson. The lawyer unsealed it, and several enclosures fell to the floor. The first was a will, drawn in the same eccentric terms as the one which he had returned six months before, to serve as a testament in case of death and as a deed of gift in case of disappearance; but in place of the name of Edward Hyde, the lawyer, with indescribable amazement read the name of Gabriel John Utterson. He looked at Poole, and then back at the paper, and last of all at the dead malefactor stretched upon the carpet.

'My head goes round,' he said. 'He has been all these days in possession; he had no cause to like me; he must have raged to see himself displaced; and he has not destroyed this document.'

He caught up the next paper; it was a brief note in the doctor's hand and dated at the top. 'O Poole!' the lawyer cried, 'he was alive and here this day. He cannot have been disposed of in so short a space; he must be still alive, he must have fled! And then, why fled? and how? and in that case, can we venture to declare this suicide? O, we must be careful. I foresee that we may yet involve your master in some dire catastrophe.'

'Why don't you read it, sir?' asked Poole.

'Because I fear,' replied the lawyer solemnly. 'God grant I have no cause for it!' And with that he brought the paper to his eyes and read as follows:

"My dear Utterson - When this shall fall into your hands, I shall have disappeared, under what circumstances I have not the penetration to foresee, but my instinct and all the circumstances of my nameless situation tell me that the

end is sure and must be early. Go then, and first read the narrative which Lanyon warned me he was to place in your hands; and if you care to hear more, turn to the confession of your unworthy and unhappy friend,
HENRY JEKYLL."

'There was a third enclosure?' asked Utterson.

'Here, sir,' said Poole, and gave into his hands a considerable packet sealed in several places.

The lawyer put it in his pocket. 'I would say nothing of this paper. If your master has fled or is dead, we may at least save his credit. It is now ten; I must go home and read these documents in quiet; but I shall be back before midnight, when we shall send for the police.'

They went out, locking the door of the theatre behind them; and Utterson, once more leaving the servants gathered about the fire in the hall, trudged back to his office to read the two narratives in which this mystery was now to be explained.

DR. LANYON'S NARRATIVE

On the ninth of January, now four days ago, I received by the evening delivery a registered envelope, addressed in the hand of my colleague and old school companion, Henry Jekyll. I was a good deal surprised by this; for we were by no means in the habit of correspondence; I had seen the man, dined with him, indeed, the night before; and I could imagine nothing in our intercourse that should justify formality of registration. The contents increased my wonder; for this is how the letter ran:

"10th December, 18--.

"Dear Lanyon, - You are one of my oldest friends; and although we may have differed at times on scientific questions, I cannot remember, at least on my side, any break in our affection. There was never a day when, if you had said to me, 'Jekyll, my life, my honour, my reason, depend upon you,' I would not have sacrificed my left hand to help you. Lanyon my life, my honour, my reason, are all at your mercy; if you fail me to-night, I am lost. You might suppose, after this preface, that I am going to ask you for something dishonourable to grant. Judge for yourself.

"I want you to postpone all other engagements for to-night - ay, even if you were summoned to the bedside of an emperor; to take a cab, unless your carriage should be actually at the door; and with this letter in your hand for consultation, to drive straight to my house. Poole, my butler, has his orders; you will find him waiting your arrival with a locksmith. The door of my cabinet is then to be forced: and you are to go in alone; to open the glazed press (letter E) on the left hand, breaking the lock if it be shut; and to draw out, with all its contents as they stand, the fourth drawer from the top or (which is the same thing) the third from the bottom. In my extreme distress of mind, I have a morbid fear of misdirecting you; but even if I am in error, you may know the right drawer by its contents: some powders, a phial and a paper book. This drawer I beg of you to carry back with you to Cavendish Square exactly as it stands.

"That is the first part of the service: now for the second. You should be back, if you set out at once on the receipt of this, long before midnight; but I will leave you that amount of margin, not only in the fear of one of those obstacles that can neither be prevented nor foreseen, but because an hour when your servants are in bed is to be preferred for what will then remain to do. At midnight, then, I have to ask you to be alone in your consulting room, to admit with your own hand into the house a man who will present himself in my name, and to place in his hands the drawer that you will have brought with you from my cabinet. Then you will have played your part and earned my gratitude completely. Five minutes afterwards, if you insist upon an explanation, you will have understood that these arrangements are of capital importance; and that by the neglect of one of them, fantastic as they must appear, you might have charged your conscience with my death or the shipwreck of my reason.

"Confident as I am that you will not trifle with this appeal, my heart sinks and my hand trembles at the bare thought of such a possibility. Think of me at this hour, in a strange place, labouring under a blackness of distress that no fancy can exaggerate, and yet well aware that, if you will but punctually serve me, my troubles will roll away like a story that is told. Serve me, my dear Lanyon and save

"Your friend,

"H.J.

"P.S. - I had already sealed this up when a fresh terror struck upon my soul. It is possible that the post-office may fail me, and this letter not come into your hands until to-morrow morning. In that case, dear Lanyon, do my errand when it shall be most convenient for you in the course of the day; and once more expect my messenger at midnight. It may then already be too late; and if that night passes without event, you will know that you have seen the last of Henry Jekyll."

Upon the reading of this letter, I made sure my colleague was insane; but till that was proved beyond the possibility of doubt, I felt bound to do as he requested. The less I understood of this farrago, the less I was in a position to judge of its importance; and an appeal so worded could not be set aside without a grave responsibility. I rose accordingly from table, got into a hansom, and drove straight to Jekyll's house. The butler was awaiting my arrival; he had received by the same post as mine a registered letter of instruction, and had sent at once for a locksmith and a carpenter. The tradesmen came while we were yet speaking; and we moved in a body to old Dr.

Denman's surgical theatre, from which (as you are doubtless aware) Jekyll's private cabinet is most conveniently entered. The door was very strong, the lock excellent; the carpenter avowed he would have great trouble and have to do much damage, if force were to be used; and the locksmith was near despair. But this last was a handy fellow, and after two hour's work, the door stood open. The press marked E was unlocked; and I took out the drawer, had it filled up with straw and tied in a sheet, and returned with it to Cavendish Square.

Here I proceeded to examine its contents. The powders were neatly enough made up, but not with the nicety of the dispensing chemist; so that it was plain they were of Jekyll's private manufacture: and when I opened one of the wrappers I found what seemed to me a simple crystalline salt of a white colour. The phial, to which I next turned my attention, might have been about half full of a blood-red liquor, which was highly pungent to the sense of smell and seemed to me to contain phosphorus and some volatile ether. At the other ingredients I could make no guess. The book was an ordinary version book and contained little but a series of dates. These covered a period of many years, but I observed that the entries ceased nearly a year ago and quite abruptly. Here and there a brief remark was appended to a date, usually no more than a single word: "double" occurring perhaps six times in a total of several hundred entries; and once very early in the list and followed by several marks of exclamation: "Total failure!!!" All this, though it whetted my curiosity, told me little that was definite. Here were a phial of some salt, and the record of a series of experiments that had led (like too many of Jekyll's investigations) to no end of practical usefulness.

How could the presence of these articles in my house affect either the honour, the sanity, or the life of my flighty colleague? If his messenger could go to one place, why could he not go to another? And even granting some impediment, why was this gentleman to be received by me in secret? The more I reflected the more convinced I grew that I was dealing with a case of cerebral disease; and though I dismissed my servants to bed, I loaded an old revolver, that I might be found in some posture of self-defence.

Twelve o'clock had scarce rung out over London, ere the knocker sounded very gently on the door. I went myself at the summons, and found a small man crouching against the pillars of the portico.

'Are you come from Dr. Jekyll?' I asked.

He told me "yes" by a constrained gesture; and when I had bidden him enter, he did not obey me without a searching backward glance into the darkness of the square. There was a policeman not far off, advancing with his bull's eye open; and at the sight, I thought my visitor started and made greater haste.

These particulars struck me, I confess, disagreeably; and as I followed him into the bright light of the consulting room, I kept my hand ready on my weapon. Here, at last, I had a chance of clearly seeing him. I had never set eyes on him before, so much was certain. He was small, as I have said; I was struck besides with the shocking expression of his face, with his remarkable combination of great muscular activity and great apparent debility of constitution, and - last but not least - with the odd, subjective disturbance caused by his neighbourhood. This bore some resemblance to incipient rigour, and was accompanied by a marked sinking of the pulse. At the time, I set it down to some idiosyncratic, personal distaste, and merely wondered at the acuteness of the symptoms; but I have since had reason to believe the cause to lie much deeper in the nature of man, and to turn on some nobler hinge than the principle of hatred.

This person (who had thus, from the first moment of his entrance, struck in me what I can only describe as a disgustful curiosity) was dressed in a fashion that would have made an ordinary person laughable; his clothes, that is to say, although they were of rich and sober fabric, were enormously too large for him in every measurement - the trousers hanging on his legs and rolled up to keep them from the ground, the waist of the coat below his haunches, and the collar sprawling wide upon his shoulders. Strange to relate, this ludicrous accoutrement was far from moving me to laughter. Rather, as there was something abnormal and misbegotten in the very essence of the creature that now faced me - something seizing, surprising and revolting - this fresh disparity seemed but to fit in with and to reinforce it; so that to my interest in the man's nature and character, there was added a curiosity as to his origin, his life, his fortune and status in the world.

These observations, though they have taken so great a space to be set down in, were yet the work of a few seconds. My visitor was, indeed, on fire with sombre excitement.

'Have you got it?' he cried. 'Have you got it?' And so lively was his impatience that he even laid his hand upon my arm and sought to shake me.

I put him back, conscious at his touch of a certain icy pang along my blood. 'Come, sir,' said I. 'You forget that I have not yet the pleasure of your acquaintance. Be seated, if you please.' And I showed him an example, and sat down myself in my customary seat and with as fair an imitation of my ordinary manner to a patient, as the lateness of the hour, the nature of my preoccupations, and the horror I had of my visitor, would suffer me to muster.

'I beg your pardon, Dr. Lanyon,' he replied civilly enough. 'What you say is very well founded; and my impatience has shown its heels to my politeness. I come here at the instance of your colleague, Dr. Henry Jekyll, on a piece of business of some moment; and I understood...' He paused and put his hand to his throat, and I could see, in spite of his collected manner, that he was wrestling against the approaches of the hysteria – 'I understood, a drawer...'

But here I took pity on my visitor's suspense, and some perhaps on my own growing curiosity.

'There it is, sir,' said I, pointing to the drawer, where it lay on the floor behind a table and still covered with the sheet.

He sprang to it, and then paused, and laid his hand upon his heart: I could hear his teeth grate with the convulsive action of his jaws; and his face was so ghastly to see that I grew alarmed both for his life and reason.

'Compose yourself,' said I.

He turned a dreadful smile to me, and as if with the decision of despair, plucked away the sheet. At sight of the contents, he uttered one loud sob of such immense relief that I sat petrified. And the next moment, in a voice that was already fairly well under control, 'Have you a graduated glass?' he asked.

I rose from my place with something of an effort and gave him what he asked.

He thanked me with a smiling nod, measured out a few minims of the red tincture and added one of the powders. The mixture, which was at first of a reddish hue, began, in proportion as the crystals melted, to brighten in colour, to effervesce audibly, and to throw off small fumes of vapour. Suddenly and at the same moment, the ebullition ceased and the compound changed to a dark purple, which faded again more slowly to a watery green. My visitor, who had watched these metamorphoses with a keen eye, smiled, set down the glass upon the table, and then turned and looked upon me with an air of scrutiny.

'And now,' said he, 'to settle what remains. Will you be wise? will you be guided? will you suffer me to take this glass in my hand and to go forth from your house without further parley? or has the greed of curiosity too much command of you? Think before you answer, for it shall be done as you decide. As you decide, you shall be left as you were before, and neither richer nor wiser, unless the sense of service rendered to a man in mortal distress may be counted as a kind of riches of the soul. Or, if you shall so prefer to choose, a new province of knowledge and new avenues to fame and power shall be laid open to you, here, in this room, upon the instant; and your sight shall be blasted by a prodigy to stagger the unbelief of Satan.'

'Sir,' said I, affecting a coolness that I was far from truly possessing, 'you speak enigmas, and you will perhaps not wonder that I hear you with no very strong impression of belief. But I have gone too far in the way of inexplicable services to pause before I see the end.'

'It is well,' replied my visitor. 'Lanyon, you remember your vows: what follows is under the seal of our profession. And now, you who have so long been bound to the most narrow and material views, you who have denied the virtue of transcendental medicine, you who have derided your superiors - behold!'

He put the glass to his lips and drank at one gulp. A cry followed; he reeled, staggered, clutched at the table and held on, staring with injected eyes, gasping with open mouth; and as I looked there came, I thought, a change - he seemed to swell - his face became suddenly black and the features seemed to melt and alter - and the next moment, I had sprung to my feet and leaped back against the wall, my arms raised to shield me from that prodigy, my mind submerged in terror.

'O God!' I screamed, and 'O God!' again and again; for there before my eyes - pale and shaken, and half fainting, and groping before him with his hands, like a man restored from death - there stood Henry Jekyll!

What he told me in the next hour, I cannot bring my mind to set on paper. I saw what I saw, I heard what I heard, and my soul sickened at it; and yet now when that sight has faded from my eyes, I ask myself if I believe it, and I cannot answer. My life is shaken to its roots; sleep has left me; the deadliest terror sits by me at all hours of the day and night; and I feel that my days are numbered, and that I must die; and yet I shall die incredulous. As for the moral turpitude that man unveiled to me, even with tears of penitence, I cannot, even in memory, dwell on it without a start of horror. I will say but one thing, Utterson, and that (if you can bring your mind to credit it) will be more than enough. The creature who crept into my house that night was, on Jekyll's own confession, known by the name of Hyde and hunted for in every corner of the land as the murderer of Carew.

Hastie Lanyon

HENRY JEKYLL'S FULL STATEMENT OF THE CASE

I was born in the year 18-- to a large fortune, endowed besides with excellent parts, inclined by nature to industry, fond of the respect of the wise and good among my fellowmen, and thus, as might have been supposed, with every guarantee of an honourable and distinguished future. And indeed the worst of my faults was a certain impatient gaiety of disposition, such as has made the happiness of many, but such as I found it hard to reconcile with my imperious desire to carry my head high, and wear a more than commonly grave countenance before the public.

Hence it came about that I concealed my pleasures; and that when I reached years of reflection, and began to look round me and take stock of my progress and position in the world, I stood already committed to a profound duplicity of me. Many a man would have even blazoned such irregularities as I was guilty of; but from the high views that I had set before me, I regarded and hid them with an almost morbid sense of shame. It was thus rather the exacting nature of my aspirations than any particular degradation in my faults, that made me what I was, and, with even a deeper trench than in the majority of men, severed in me those provinces of good and ill which divide and compound man's dual nature.

In this case, I was driven to reflect deeply and inveterately on that hard law of life, which lies at the root of religion and is one of the most plentiful springs of distress. Though so profound a double-dealer, I was in no sense a hypocrite; both sides of me were in dead earnest; I was no more myself when I laid aside restraint and plunged in shame, than when I laboured, in the eye of day, at the furtherance of knowledge or the relief of sorrow and suffering. And it chanced that the direction of my scientific studies, which led wholly towards the mystic and the transcendental, reacted and shed a strong light on this consciousness of the perennial war among my members. With every day, and from both sides of my intelligence, the moral and the intellectual, I thus drew steadily nearer to that truth, by whose partial discovery I have been doomed to such a dreadful shipwreck: that man is not truly one, but truly two. I say two, because the state of my own knowledge does not pass beyond that point. Others will follow, others will outstrip me on the same lines; and I hazard the guess that man will be ultimately known for a mere polity of multifarious, incongruous and independent denizens. I, for my part, from the nature of my life, advanced infallibly in one direction and in one direction only. It was on the moral side, and in my own person, that I learned to recognise the thorough and primitive duality of man; I saw that, of the two natures that contended in the field of my consciousness, even if I could rightly be said to be either, it was only because I was radically both; and from an early date, even before the course of my scientific discoveries had begun to suggest the most naked possibility of such a miracle, I had learned to dwell with pleasure, as a beloved daydream, on the thought of the separation of these elements.

If each, I told myself, could be housed in separate identities, life would be relieved of all that was unbearable; the unjust might go his way, delivered from the aspirations and remorse of his more upright twin; and the just could walk steadfastly and securely on his upward path, doing the good things in which he found his pleasure, and no longer exposed to disgrace and penitence by the hands of this extraneous evil. It was the curse of mankind that these incongruous faggots were thus bound together--that in the agonised womb of consciousness, these polar twins should be continuously struggling. How, then were they dissociated?

I was so far in my reflections when, as I have said, a side light began to shine upon the subject from the laboratory table. I began to perceive more deeply than it has ever yet been stated, the trembling immateriality, the mist-like transience, of this seemingly so solid body in which we walk attired. Certain agents I found to have the power to shake and pluck back that fleshly vestment, even as a wind might toss the curtains of a pavilion. For two good reasons, I will not enter deeply into this scientific branch of my confession. First, because I have been made to learn that the doom and burthen of our life is bound for ever on man's shoulders, and when the attempt is made to cast it off, it but returns upon us with more unfamiliar and more awful pressure. Second, because, as my narrative will make, alas! too evident, my discoveries were incomplete. Enough then, that I not only recognised my natural body from the mere aura and effulgence of certain of the powers that made up my spirit, but managed to compound a drug by which these powers should be dethroned from their supremacy, and a second form and countenance substituted, none the less natural to me because they were the expression, and bore the stamp of lower elements in my soul.

I hesitated long before I put this theory to the test of practice. I knew well that I risked death; for any drug that so potently controlled and shook the very fortress of identity, might, by the least scruple of an overdose or at the least inopportunity in the moment of exhibition, utterly blot out that immaterial tabernacle which I looked to it to change. But the temptation of a discovery so singular and profound at last overcame the suggestions of alarm. I had long since prepared my tincture; I purchased at once, from a firm of wholesale chemists, a large quantity of a particular salt which I knew, from my experiments, to be the last ingredient required; and late one accursed night, I compounded the elements, watched them boil and smoke together in the glass, and when the ebullition had subsided, with a strong glow of courage, drank off the potion.

The most racking pangs succeeded: a grinding in the bones, deadly nausea, and a horror of the spirit that cannot be exceeded at the hour of birth or death. Then these agonies began swiftly to subside, and I came to myself as if out of a great sickness. There was something strange in my sensations, something indescribably new and, from its very novelty, incredibly sweet. I felt younger, lighter, happier in body; within I was conscious of a heady recklessness, a current of disordered sensual images running like a millrace in my fancy, a solution of the bonds of obligation, an unknown but not an innocent freedom of the soul.

I knew myself, at the first breath of this new life, to be more wicked, tenfold more wicked, sold a slave to my original evil; and the thought, in that moment, braced and delighted me like wine. I stretched out my hands, exulting in the freshness of these sensations; and in the act, I was suddenly aware that I had lost in stature.

There was no mirror, at that date, in my room; that which stands beside me as I write, was brought there later on and for the very purpose of these transformations. The night however, was far gone into the morning - the morning, black as it was, was nearly ripe for the conception of the day - the inmates of my house were locked in the most rigorous hours of slumber; and I determined, flushed as I was with hope and triumph, to venture in my new shape as far as to my bedroom. I crossed the yard, wherein the constellations looked down upon me, I could have thought, with wonder, the first creature of that sort that their unsleeping vigilance had yet disclosed to them; I stole through the corridors, a stranger in my own house; and coming to my room, I saw for the first time the appearance of Edward Hyde.

I must here speak by theory alone, saying not that which I know, but that which I suppose to be most probable. The evil side of my nature, to which I had now transferred the stamping efficacy, was less robust and less developed than the good which I had just deposed. Again, in the course of my life, which had been, after all, nine tenths a life of effort, virtue and control, it had been much less exercised and much less exhausted. And hence, as I think, it came about that Edward Hyde was so much smaller, slighter and younger than Henry Jekyll. Even as good shone upon the countenance of the one, evil was written broadly and plainly on the face of the other. Evil besides (which I must still believe to be the lethal side of man) had left on that body an imprint of deformity and decay. And yet when I looked upon that ugly idol in the glass, I was conscious of no repugnance, rather of a leap of welcome.

This, too, was myself. It seemed natural and human. In my eyes it bore a livelier image of the spirit, it seemed more express and single, than the imperfect and divided countenance I had been hitherto accustomed to call mine. And in so far I was doubtless right. I have observed that when I wore the semblance of Edward Hyde, none could come near to me at first without a visible misgiving of the flesh. This, as I take it, was all human beings, as we meet them, are commingled out of good and evil: and Edward Hyde, alone in the ranks of mankind, was pure evil.

I lingered but a moment at the mirror: the second and conclusive experiment had yet to be attempted; it yet remained to be seen if I had lost my identity beyond redemption and must flee before daylight from a house that was no longer mine; and hurrying back to my cabinet, I once more prepared and drank the cup, once more suffered the pangs of dissolution, and came to myself once more with the character, the stature and the face of Henry Jekyll.

That night I had come to the fatal cross-roads. Had I approached my discovery in a more noble spirit, had I risked the experiment while under the empire of generous or pious aspirations, all must have been otherwise, and from these agonies of death and birth, I had come forth an angel instead of a fiend. The drug had no discriminating action; it was neither diabolical nor divine; it but shook the doors of the prison-house of my disposition; and like the captives of Philippi, that which stood within ran forth. At that time my virtue slumbered; my evil, kept awake by ambition, was alert and swift to seize the occasion; and the thing that was projected was Edward Hyde. Hence, although I had now two characters as well as two appearances, one was wholly evil, and the other was still the old Henry Jekyll, that incongruous compound of whose reformation and improvement I had already learned to despair. The movement was thus wholly toward the worse.

Even at that time, I had not conquered my aversions to the dryness of a life of study. I would still be merrily disposed at times; and as my pleasures were (to say the least) undignified, and I was not only well known and highly considered, but growing towards the elderly man, this incoherency of my life was daily growing more unwelcome. It was on this side that my new power tempted me until I fell in slavery. I had but to drink the cup, to doff at once the body of the noted professor, and to assume, like a thick cloak, that of Edward Hyde. I smiled at the notion; it seemed to me at the time to be humorous; and I made my preparations with the most studious care. I took and furnished that house in Soho, to which Hyde was tracked by the police; and engaged as a housekeeper a creature whom I knew well to be silent and unscrupulous. On the other side, I announced to my servants that a Mr. Hyde (whom I described) was to have full liberty and power about my house in the square; and to parry mishaps, I even called and made myself a familiar object, in my second character. I next drew up that will to which you so much objected; so that if anything befell me in the person of Dr. Jekyll, I could enter on that of Edward Hyde without pecuniary loss. And thus fortified, as I supposed, on every side, I began to profit by the strange immunities of my position.

Men have before hired bravos to transact their crimes, while their own person and reputation sat under shelter. I was the first that ever did so for his pleasures. I was the first that could plod in the public eye with a load of genial respectability, and in a moment, like a schoolboy, strip off these lendings and spring headlong into the sea of liberty.

But for me, in my impenetrable mantle, the safety was complete. Think of it - I did not even exist! Let me but escape into my laboratory door, give me but a second or two to mix and swallow the draught that I had always standing ready; and whatever he had done, Edward Hyde would pass away like the stain of breath upon a mirror; and there in his stead, quietly at home, trimming the midnight lamp in his study, a man who could afford to laugh at suspicion, would be Henry Jekyll.

The pleasures which I made haste to seek in my disguise were, as I have said, undignified; I would scarce use a harder term. But in the hands of Edward Hyde, they soon began to turn toward the monstrous. When I would come back from these excursions, I was often plunged into a kind of wonder at my vicarious depravity. This familiar that I called out of my own soul, and sent forth alone to do his good pleasure, was a being inherently malign and villainous; his every act and thought centred on self; drinking pleasure with bestial avidity from any degree of torture to another; relentless like a man of stone. Henry Jekyll stood at times aghast before the acts of Edward Hyde; but the situation was apart from ordinary laws, and insidiously relaxed the grasp of conscience. It was Hyde, after all, and Hyde alone, that was guilty. Jekyll was no worse; he woke again to his good qualities seemingly unimpaired; he would even make haste, where it was possible, to undo the evil done by Hyde. And thus his conscience slumbered.

Into the details of the infamy at which I thus connived (for even now I can scarce grant that I committed it) I have no design of entering; I mean but to point out the warnings and the successive steps with which my chastisement approached. I met with one accident which, as it brought on no consequence, I shall no more than mention. An act of cruelty to a child aroused against me the anger of a passer-by, whom I recognised the other day in the person of your kinsman; the doctor and the child's family joined him; there were moments when I feared for my life; and at last, in order to pacify their too just resentment, Edward Hyde had to bring them to the door, and pay them in a cheque drawn in the name of Henry Jekyll. But this danger was easily eliminated from the future, by opening an account at another bank in the name of Edward Hyde himself; and when, by sloping my own hand backward, I had supplied my double with a signature, I thought I sat beyond the reach of fate.

Some two months before the murder of Sir Danvers, I had been out for one of my adventures, had returned at a late hour, and woke the next day in bed with somewhat odd sensations. It was in vain I looked about me; in vain I saw the decent furniture and tall proportions of my room in the square; in vain that I recognised the pattern of the bed curtains and the design of the mahogany frame; something still kept insisting that I was not where I was, that I had not wakened where I seemed to be, but in the little room in Soho where I was accustomed to sleep in the body of Edward Hyde. I smiled to myself, and in my psychological way, began lazily to inquire into the elements of this illusion, occasionally, even as I did so, dropping back into a comfortable morning doze. I was still so engaged when, in one of my more wakeful moments, my eyes fell upon my hand. Now the hand of Henry Jekyll (as you have often remarked) was professional in shape and size: it was large, firm, white and comely. But the hand which I now saw, clearly enough, in the yellow light of a mid-London morning, lying half shut on the bedclothes, was lean, corder, knuckly, of a dusky pallor and thickly shaded with a swart growth of hair. It was the hand of Edward Hyde.

I must have stared upon it for near half a minute, sunk as I was in the mere stupidity of wonder, before terror woke up in my breast as sudden and startling as the crash of cymbals; and bounding from my bed I rushed to the mirror. At the sight that met my eyes, my blood was changed into something exquisitely thin and icy. Yes, I had gone to bed Henry Jekyll, I had awakened Edward Hyde. How was this to be explained? I asked myself; and then, with another bound of terror - how was it to be remedied? It was well on in the morning; the servants were up; all my drugs were in the cabinet - a long journey down two pairs of stairs, through the back passage, across the open court and through the anatomical theatre, from where I was then standing horror-struck. It might indeed be possible to cover my face; but of what use was that, when I was unable to conceal the alteration in my stature? And then with an overpowering sweetness of relief, it came back upon my mind that the servants were already used to the coming and going of my second self. I had soon dressed, as well as I was able, in clothes of my own size: had soon passed through the house, where Bradshaw stared and drew back at seeing Mr. Hyde at such an hour and in such a strange array; and ten minutes later, Dr. Jekyll had returned to his own shape and was sitting down, with a darkened brow, to make a feint of breakfasting.

Small indeed was my appetite. This inexplicable incident, this reversal of my previous experience, seemed, like the Babylonian finger on the wall, to be spelling out the letters of my judgment; and I began to reflect more seriously than ever before on the issues and possibilities of my double existence. That part of me which I had the power of projecting, had lately been much exercised and nourished; it had seemed to me of late as though the body of Edward Hyde had grown in stature, as though (when I wore that form) I were conscious of a more generous tide of blood; and I began to spy a danger that, if this were much prolonged, the balance of my nature might be permanently overthrown, the power of voluntary change be forfeited, and the character of Edward Hyde become irrevocably mine. The power of the drug had not been always equally displayed. Once, very early in my career, it had totally failed me; since then I had been obliged on more than one occasion to double, and once, with infinite risk of death, to treble the amount; and these rare uncertainties had cast hitherto the sole shadow on my contentment. Now, however, and in the light of that morning's accident, I was led to remark that whereas, in the beginning, the difficulty had been to throw off the body of Jekyll, it had of late gradually but decidedly transferred itself to the other side. All things therefore seemed to point to this; that I was slowly losing hold of my original and better self, and becoming slowly incorporated with my second and worse.

Between these two, I now felt I had to choose. My two natures had memory in common, but all other faculties were most unequally shared between them. Jekyll (who was composite) now with the most sensitive apprehensions, now with a greedy gusto, projected and shared in the pleasures and adventures of Hyde; but Hyde was indifferent to Jekyll, or but remembered him as the mountain bandit remembers the cavern in which he conceals himself from pursuit. Jekyll had more than a father's interest; Hyde had more than a son's indifference. To cast in my lot with Jekyll, was to die to those appetites which I had long secretly indulged and had of late begun to pamper. To cast it in with Hyde, was to die to a thousand interests and aspirations, and to become, at a blow and forever, despised and friendless. The bargain might appear unequal; but there was still another consideration in the scales; for while Jekyll would suffer smartingly in the fires of abstinence, Hyde would be not even conscious of all that he had lost. Strange as my circumstances were, the terms of this debate are as old and commonplace as man; much the same inducements and alarms cast the die for any tempted and trembling sinner; and it fell out with me, as it falls with so vast a majority of my fellows, that I chose the better part and was found wanting in the strength to keep to it.

Yes, I preferred the elderly and discontented doctor, surrounded by friends and cherishing honest hopes; and bade a resolute farewell to the liberty, the comparative youth, the light step, leaping impulses and secret pleasures, that I had enjoyed in the disguise of Hyde. I made this choice perhaps with some unconscious reservation, for I neither gave up the house in Soho, nor destroyed the clothes of Edward Hyde, which still lay ready in my cabinet. For two months, however, I was true to my determination; for two months, I led a life of such severity as I had never before attained to, and enjoyed the compensations of an approving conscience. But time began at last to obliterate the freshness of my alarm; the praises of conscience began to grow into a thing of course; I began to be tortured with throes and longings, as of Hyde struggling after freedom; and at last, in an hour of moral weakness, I once again compounded and swallowed the transforming draught.

I do not suppose that, when a drunkard reasons with himself upon his vice, he is once out of five hundred times affected by the dangers that he runs through his brutish, physical insensibility; neither had I, long as I had considered my position, made enough allowance for the complete moral insensibility and insensate readiness to evil, which were the leading characters of Edward Hyde. Yet it was by these that I was punished. My devil had been long caged, he came out roaring. I was conscious, even when I took the draught, of a more unbridled, a more furious propensity to ill. It must have been this, I suppose, that stirred in my soul that tempest of impatience with which I listened to the civilities of my unhappy victim; I declare, at least, before God, no man morally sane could have been guilty of that crime upon so pitiful a provocation; and that I struck in no more reasonable spirit than that in which a sick child may break a plaything. But I had voluntarily stripped myself of all those balancing instincts by which even the worst of us continues to walk with some degree of steadiness among temptations; and in my case, to be tempted, however slightly, was to fall.

Instantly the spirit of hell awoke in me and raged. With a transport of glee, I mauled the unresisting body, tasting delight from every blow; and it was not till weariness had begun to succeed, that I was suddenly, in the top fit of my delirium, struck through the heart by a cold thrill of terror. A mist dispersed; I saw my life to be forfeit; and fled from the scene of these excesses, at once glorying and trembling, my lust of evil gratified and stimulated, my love of life screwed to the topmost peg. I ran to the house in Soho, and (to make assurance doubly sure) destroyed my papers; thence I set out through the lamplit streets, in the same divided ecstasy of mind, gloating on my crime, light-headedly devising others in the future, and yet still hastening and still hearkening in my wake for the steps of the avenger. Hyde had a song upon his lips as he compounded the draught, and as he drank it, pledged the dead man. The pangs of transformation had not done tearing him, before Henry Jekyll, with streaming tears of gratitude and remorse, had fallen upon his knees and lifted his clasped hands to God. The veil of self-indulgence was rent from head to foot. I saw my life as a whole: I followed it up from the days of childhood, when I had walked with my father's hand, and through the self-denying toils of my professional life, to arrive again and again, with the same sense of unreality, at the damned horrors of the evening. I could have screamed aloud; I sought with tears and prayers to smother down the crowd of hideous images and sounds with which my memory swarmed against me; and still, between the petitions, the ugly face of my iniquity stared into my soul. As the acuteness of this remorse began to die away, it was succeeded by a sense of joy. The problem of my conduct was solved. Hyde was thenceforth impossible; whether I would or not, I was now confined to the better part of my existence; and O, how I rejoiced to think of it! with what willing humility I embraced anew the restrictions of natural life! With what sincere renunciation I locked the door by which I had so often gone and come, and ground the key under my heel!

The next day, came the news that the murder had not been overlooked, that the guilt of Hyde was patent to the world, and that the victim was a man high in public estimation. It was not only a crime, it had been a tragic folly. I think I was glad to know it; I think I was glad to have my better impulses thus buttressed and guarded by the terrors of the scaffold. Jekyll was now my city of refuge; let but Hyde peep out an instant, and the hands of all men would be raised to take and slay him.

I resolved in my future conduct to redeem the past; and I can say with honesty that my resolve was fruitful of some good. You know yourself how earnestly, in the last months of the last year, I laboured to relieve suffering; you know that much was done for others, and that the days passed quietly, almost happily for myself. Nor can I truly say that I wearied of this beneficent and innocent life; I think instead that I daily enjoyed it more completely; but I was still cursed with my duality of purpose; and as the first edge of my penitence wore off, the lower side of me, so long indulged, so recently chained down, began to growl for licence. Not that I dreamed of resuscitating Hyde; the bare idea of that would startle me to frenzy: no, it was in my own person that I was once more tempted to trifle with my conscience; and it was as an ordinary secret sinner that I at last fell before the assaults of temptation.

There comes an end to all things; the most capacious measure is filled at last; and this brief condescension to my evil finally destroyed the balance of my soul. And yet I was not alarmed; the fall seemed natural, like a return to the old days before I had made my discovery. It was a fine, clear, January day, wet under foot where the frost had melted, but cloudless overhead; and the Regent's Park was full of winter chirrupings and sweet with spring odours. I sat in the sun on a bench; the animal within me licking the chops of memory; the spiritual side a little drowsed, promising subsequent penitence, but not yet moved to begin.

After all, I reflected, I was like my neighbours; and then I smiled, comparing myself with other men, comparing my active good-will with the lazy cruelty of their neglect. And at the very moment of that vainglorious thought, a qualm came over me, a horrid nausea and the most deadly shuddering. These passed away, and left me faint; and then as in its turn faintness subsided, I began to be aware of a change in the temper of my thoughts, a greater boldness, a contempt of danger, a solution of the bonds of obligation. I looked down; my clothes hung formlessly on my shrunken limbs; the hand that lay on my knee was corded and hairy. I was once more Edward Hyde. A moment before I had been safe of all men's respect, wealthy, beloved - the cloth laying for me in the dining-room at home; and now I was the common quarry of mankind, hunted, a known murderer, thrall to the gallows.

My reason wavered, but it did not fail me utterly. I have more than once observed that in my second character, my faculties seemed sharpened to a point and my spirits more tensely elastic; thus it came about that, where Jekyll perhaps might have succumbed, Hyde rose to the importance of the moment. My drugs were in one of the presses of my cabinet; how was I to reach them? That was the problem that (crushing my temples in my hands) I set myself to solve. The laboratory door I had closed. If I sought to enter by the house, my own servants would consign me to the gallows. I saw I must employ another hand, and thought of Lanyon. How was he to be reached? how persuaded? Supposing that I escaped capture in the streets, how was I to make my way into his presence? and how should I, an unknown and displeasing visitor, prevail on the famous physician to rifle the study of his colleague, Dr. Jekyll? Then I remembered that of my original character, one part remained to me: I could write my own hand; and once I had conceived that kindling spark, the way that I must follow became lighted up from end to end. Thereupon, I arranged my clothes as best I could, and summoning a passing hansom, drove to an hotel in Portland Street, the name of which I chanced to remember. At my appearance (which was indeed comical enough, however tragic a fate these garments covered) the driver could not conceal his mirth. I gnashed my teeth upon him with a gust of devilish fury; and the smile withered from his face - happily for him - yet more happily for myself, for in another instant I had certainly dragged him from his perch. At the inn, as I entered, I looked about me with so black a countenance as made the attendants tremble; not a look did they exchange in my presence; but obsequiously took my orders, led me to a private room, and brought me wherewithal to write. Hyde in danger of his life was a creature new to me; shaken with inordinate anger, strung to the pitch of murder, lusting to inflict pain. Yet the creature was astute; mastered his fury with a great effort of the will; composed his two important letters, one to Lanyon and one to Poole; and that he might receive actual evidence of their being posted, sent them out with directions that they should be registered. Thenceforward, he sat all day over the fire in the private room, gnawing his nails; there he dined, sitting alone with his fears, the waiter visibly quailing before his eye; and thence, when the night was fully come, he set forth in the corner of a closed cab, and was driven to and fro about the streets of the city. He, I say - I cannot say, I. That child of Hell had nothing human; nothing lived in him but fear and hatred. And when at last, thinking the driver had begun to grow suspicious, he discharged the cab and ventured on foot, attired in his misfitting clothes, an object marked out for observation, into the midst of the nocturnal passengers, these two base passions raged within him like a tempest.

He walked fast, hunted by his fears, chattering to himself, skulking through the less frequented thoroughfares, counting the minutes that still divided him from midnight. Once a woman spoke to him, offering, I think, a box of lights. He smote her in the face, and she fled.

When I came to myself at Lanyon's, the horror of my old friend perhaps affected me somewhat: I do not know; it was at least but a drop in the sea to the abhorrence with which I looked back upon these hours. A change had come over me. It was no longer the fear of the gallows, it was the horror of being Hyde that racked me. I received Lanyon's condemnation partly in a dream; it was partly in a dream that I came home to my own house and got into bed. I slept after the prostration of the day, with a stringent and profound slumber which not even the nightmares that wrung me could avail to break. I awoke in the morning shaken, weakened, but refreshed. I still hated and feared the thought of the brute that slept within me, and I had not of course forgotten the appalling dangers of the day before; but I was once more at home, in my own house and close to my drugs; and gratitude for my escape shone so strong in my soul that it almost rivalled the brightness of hope.

I was stepping leisurely across the court after breakfast, drinking the chill of the air with pleasure, when I was seized again with those indescribable sensations that heralded the change; and I had but the time to gain the shelter of my cabinet, before I was once again raging and freezing with the passions of Hyde. It took on this occasion a double dose to recall me to myself; and alas! six hours after, as I sat looking sadly in the fire, the pangs returned, and the drug had to be re-administered. In short, from that day forth it seemed only by a great effort as of gymnastics, and only under the immediate stimulation of the drug, that I was able to wear the countenance of Jekyll. At all hours of the day and night, I would be taken with the premonitory shudder; above all, if I slept, or even dozed for a moment in my chair, it was always as Hyde that I awakened. Under the strain of this continually impending doom and by the sleeplessness to which I now condemned myself, ay, even beyond what I had thought possible to man, I became, in my own person, a creature eaten up and emptied by fever, languidly weak both in body and mind, and solely occupied by one thought: the horror of my other self. But when I slept, or when the virtue of the medicine wore off, I would leap almost without transition (for the pangs of transformation grew daily less marked) into the possession of a fancy brimming with images of terror, a soul boiling with causeless hatreds, and a body that seemed not strong enough to contain the raging energies of life. The powers of Hyde seemed to have grown with the sickliness of Jekyll. And certainly the hate that now divided them was equal on each side. With Jekyll, it was a thing of vital instinct. He had now seen the full deformity of that creature that shared with him some of the phenomena of consciousness, and was co-heir with him to death: and beyond these links of community, which in themselves made the most poignant part of his distress, he thought of Hyde, for all his energy of life, as of something not only hellish but inorganic. This was the shocking thing; that the slime of the pit seemed to utter cries and voices; that the amorphous dust gesticulated and sinned; that what was dead, and had no shape, should usurp the offices of life. And this again, that that insurgent horror was knit to him closer than a wife, closer than an eye; lay caged in his flesh, where he heard it mutter and felt it struggle to be born; and at every hour of weakness, and in the confidence of slumber, prevailed against him, and deposed him out of life. The hatred of Hyde for Jekyll was of a different order. His terror of the gallows drove him continually to commit temporary suicide, and return to his subordinate station of a part instead of a person; but he loathed the necessity, he loathed the despondency into which Jekyll was now fallen, and he resented the dislike with which he was himself regarded. Hence the ape-like tricks that he would play me, scrawling in my own hand blasphemies on the pages of my books, burning the letters and destroying the portrait of my father; and indeed, had it not been for his fear of death, he would long ago have ruined himself in order to involve me in the ruin. But his love of me is wonderful; I go further: I, who sicken and freeze at the mere thought of him, when I recall the abjection and passion of this attachment, and when I know how he fears my power to cut him off by suicide, I find it in my heart to pity him.

It is useless, and the time awfully fails me, to prolong this description; no one has ever suffered such torments, let that suffice; and yet even to these, habit brought - no, not alleviation - but a certain callousness of soul, a certain acquiescence of despair; and my punishment might have gone on for years, but for the last calamity which has now fallen, and which has finally severed me from my own face and nature. My provision of the salt, which had never been renewed since the date of the first experiment, began to run low. I sent out for a fresh supply and mixed the draught; the ebullition followed, and the first change of colour, not the second; I drank it and it was without efficiency. You will learn from Poole how I have had London ransacked; it was in vain; and I am now persuaded that my first supply was impure, and that it was that unknown impurity which lent efficacy to the draught.

About a week has passed, and I am now finishing this statement under the influence of the last of the old powders. This, then, is the last time, short of a miracle, that Henry Jekyll can think his own thoughts or see his own face (now how sadly altered!) in the glass. Nor must I delay too long to bring my writing to an end; for if my narrative has hitherto escaped destruction, it has been by a combination of great prudence and great good luck. Should the throes of change take me in the act of writing it, Hyde will tear it in pieces; but if some time shall have elapsed after I have laid it by, his wonderful selfishness and circumscription to the moment will probably save it once again from the action of his ape-like spite. And indeed the doom that is closing on us both has already changed and crushed him. Half an hour from now, when I shall again and forever re-induce that hated personality, I know how I shall sit shuddering and weeping in my chair, or continue, with the most strained and fearstruck ecstasy of listening, to pace up and down this room (my last earthly refuge) and give ear to every sound of menace.

Will Hyde die upon the scaffold? or will he find courage to release himself at the last moment? God knows; I am careless; this is my true hour of death, and what is to follow concerns another than myself. Here then, as I lay down the pen and proceed to seal up my confession, I bring the life of that unhappy Henry Jekyll to an end.

ABOUT THE AUTHORS

Eamonn Martin Griffin is also the author of *The Prospect of This City* (2015) and *Torc* (2016).
He's online at www.eamonngriffinwriting.com
and on Twitter at @eamonngriffin

Robert Louis Stevenson (1850-1894) is the author of *Treasure Island* and *Kidnapped* among many fine novels and other writings.
You can find out more about RLS here:
http://robert-louis-stevenson.org/

20953840R00181

Printed in Great Britain
by Amazon